Praise for

LUCY

"Gonzales poses some big questions that readers will think about long after turning the last page. *Lucy* is a great read—and not just for adults." —*Chicago Sun-Times*

"Gonzales's Lucy is an improbably delightful young lady. . . . *Lucy* pulls the reader in because of the sweet girl at its center, but the novel also makes one think about what it means to be human, and how love can be a bridge to understanding and acceptance." —*BookPage*

"Timely and provocative. . . . Gonzales injects [his dialogue] with doses of frivolity, wit, and a youthful insight at once frightfully innocent and calculatingly wise to the power of media and technology." —*The Boston Globe*

"[A] coming-of-age-except-I'm-also-part-bonobo biotech thriller. . . . This is an enjoyable ride that makes you think about what it means to be human." —*Outside*

"The clever ending Mr. Gonzales has come up with for *Lucy* marks a complete departure from the *Frankenstein* template, and it's oddly satisfying on an emotional level." —*The New York Times*

"*Lucy* is more than a high-school drama, a fish-out-of-water novel about how a hybrid girl tries to fit in at a suburban Chicago high school. . . . This *Lucy* is an action-packed politically charged thriller that puts evolution forth as an unassailable fact, and raises ethical and moral questions about biotechnical science, government power and the morality of leadership." —*Chicago Tribune*

"Laurence Gonzales presents us with a captivating lead character. . . . Part science thriller, part tender novel, *Lucy* is written with a full awareness of the evil people are capable of. Gonzales, like Mary Shelley before him, shows us on the brink of a terrible knowledge." — *The Free Lance-Star* (Fredericksburg, VA)

"Harks back to the science fiction of the mid-twentieth century. . . . Lucy [is] a likeable and thoroughly intriguing character with a unique perspective. . . . Reveals a generous spirit and a flair for suspense." — *The Columbus Dispatch*

"Love and loss are at the core of this unusual story that analyzes life, relationships and issues of evolution." — *Woman's Day*

"Gonzales excels at creating universal moments." — *The News & Observer* (Raleigh)

"Shrewd social critique. . . . Gonzales raises profound questions about identity, family, animal and human rights, and genetic engineering without compromising the ever-escalating suspense. Lucy is irresistible, her predicament wrenching, and Gonzales's imaginative, sweet-natured, hard-charging, and deeply inquisitive thriller will be a catalyst for serious thought and debate." — *Booklist*

"A riveting, moving and informative survival story." — *San Antonio Express-News*

"Lucy is much more than an 'ape' and this novel is much more than just a summer beach book." — *Curled Up With A Good Book*

"Gonzales does a great job of keeping the action moving at a fast pace. . . . Gonzales comes back to the question of what it means to be human again and again. . . . Reading *Lucy* is an interesting way to confront this question and find your own answer." — *The Advocate*

Laurence Gonzales

LUCY

Laurence Gonzales is the author of three novels and five books of nonfiction. His bestselling book *Deep Survival* has been published in six languages.

www.laurencegonzales.com

LUCY

LUCY

A Novel

Laurence Gonzales

Vintage Books
A Division of Random House, Inc.
New York

FIRST VINTAGE BOOKS EDITION, JULY 2011

The Library of Congress has cataloged the Knopf edition as follows:
Gonzales, Laurence.
Lucy : a novel / by Laurence Gonzales. — 1st ed.
p. cm.
I. Genetic engineering—Fiction. 2. Primatologists—Fiction.
3. Congolese (Democratic Republic)—United States—Fiction.
4. Biotechnology—Fiction. 5. Humanity—Fiction. I. Title.
PS3557.O467L83 2010
813'.54—dc22 2010003898

Vintage ISBN: 978-0-307-47390-5

Book design by Soonyoung Kwon

www.vintagebooks.com

Printed in the United States of America
10 9 8 7 6 5 4 3 2

*This book is dedicated to my children
Elena, Amelia, and Jonas*

"... beauty remains, even in misfortune."

—ANNE FRANK, age fourteen

LUCY

JENNY WOKE TO THUNDER. There was no light yet. She reached into the darkness and found a tin of wooden matches on the ammunition case beside her bed. She selected one and struck it on the case. The flame flared red then yellow and sulfurous smoke rose. Newborn shadows danced on the walls of the hut. She touched the match to the wick of a candle and a light grew up from it like a yellow flower tinged with blue. Smoke hung in the still wet air. The interior of the hut seemed at once bare and cluttered. The walls were unpainted board, the floor was buckled plywood. Against one wall was a crude desk made out of a door, a few photographs tacked to the wall above it: Her mother at home near Chicago. Snapshots of the bonobos. Her friend Donna with the bonobos at the zoo.

Jenny swung her feet to the floor and listened. She'd heard the hissing of the rain all night. But now another sound had crept in. She pulled on her boots and stood, tall and tan and rangy in the yellow light. She ran her hand through her sandy hair and secured it carelessly behind her head.

She heard the sound again: Thunder. But now she heard the metallic overtones as the report echoed up into the hills, then returned. As she grew more awake Jenny realized that she was hearing guns. Big guns. The Congolese insurgents were firing rocket-propelled grenades. It had been a calculated risk for her to be here. But she had found the beautiful great apes known as bonobos irresistible. Year after year she had returned despite the danger. The fighting had flared and died down and flared up again for more than a decade and a half. Now the civil war had begun in earnest and she had to leave immediately. Her old friend David Meece at the British embassy in Kinshasa had warned her in no uncertain terms: You have no value and so they will kill you. When the shooting starts, go to the river as quickly as you can.

A whistling overhead. Another charge of metallic thunder. The concussion shook the pots above the camp stove. She heard answering fire from another direction.

She had expected to have more warning, an hour, half an hour. But they were upon her. She grabbed a flashlight, the machete, and the backpack that she kept ready for travel. She picked up a bottle that was half full of water and drank it in one long bubbling draught. Gasping for air she picked up a full bottle and clipped it to her belt.

She stepped out the door and into the clearing. She knew that entering the forest at night was a risk, but staying would be worse. She looked back at her hut and felt a rush of sadness, even as her pulse pounded in her neck. Then she turned and ran toward the forest, feeling the water sway uncomfortably in her gut.

The rain had stopped. The jungle before her was black and glistening in the flashlight beam. She had promised herself that she would make an effort to reach the British researcher, Donald Stone, whose observation post was on the way to the river. He had been courteous enough the few times she'd seen him. But their camps were far enough away that it had made dropping in for a casual visit impractical. All she knew was that he was studying bonobos, too, but didn't seem to want to collaborate. Nevertheless, Jenny had decided to do her best to help him if it ever came to that. She'd heard that he had a daughter and if so . . . Well, this was no place for a child.

As she loped through the forest along familiar paths, she heard the low thump of a mortar, the whistling of the shell, then the steely shock of another explosion to the east. She smelled smoke. Then came the sporadic firing of automatic weapons.

As she hurried on, the first light of day began to penetrate the forest canopy. She switched off her flashlight and let her eyes adjust. Another shell went off and she ran ahead. Think, think: What was next? Check on Donald Stone. Then get to the river. If she could find someone with a radio, David would help. If he was still there. If the embassy was still standing. If, if, if.

She ran on through the day, following the one broad path that she knew led in the direction of Stone's camp. She was concerned for the bonobos. They were amazingly strong yet paradoxically delicate creatures. The shock of loud noises could kill them. On the other hand, they were smart. They'd be miles away by now in the tops of the trees. Sometimes it seemed to Jenny that they were almost human. In graduate school in 1987 she had gone to work with the largest population of bonobos in captivity at the Milwaukee Zoo. They were among the last of the great apes. The first time Jenny had locked eyes with the dominant female at the zoo, she knew that she was looking at a creature who was far more like her than unlike her. Whenever she wasn't working, she'd spend hours watching the bonobos. But once she'd gone to Congo to see them in the wild she knew where she belonged.

At a bend in the trail, she stopped to listen. The shelling seemed to have moved off to the east. She swatted at the flies and mosquitoes around her face. Sweat had soaked her shirt and was dripping from her scalp into her eyes. She wrapped a bandanna around her head and pressed on. Then a brief but intense rainstorm drenched her and she resigned herself to being wet. At least it had knocked the insects down.

She desperately wanted to rest, but as night fell she took a headlamp from her pack and kept on going. All night long she heard the fighting fade, then move closer, then fade again. Twice in the night she smelled the smoke.

Morning came slowly. A mist began to rise. The path narrowed, and she knew that soon she would see Stone's camp. She'd been there only twice before. On both occasions she'd suggested that they work together, but Stone had politely pointed out that he had a feeding station for the bonobos while Jenny did not. The two approaches to research were incompatible. She had let it go. She was too busy with her own work to worry about his.

Jenny stopped running so abruptly that she tottered back and forth like a weighted doll. At first she thought she was looking at a twisted branch. Only now—now that her body had stopped without her consent—did she realize that it was a dark brown forest cobra perhaps a meter in length. It was coiled loosely along a branch holding its head high. She remembered what the toxicologist at the university had told her the first time she came to Congo: If you encounter one of these in the wild, don't breathe. They read your carbon dioxide signature. If you're bitten by one a kilometer from home don't bother running: You will die. And you'll be conscious the whole time while the venom gradually paralyzes you until your diaphragm stops working.

Jenny began a Tai Chi move, shifting her weight as slowly as she could. She moved back by centimeters. A minute passed. Two minutes. She had moved back only a foot or so when a shell landed. The cobra seemed to startle at the noise. It dropped to the ground and shot off into the undergrowth like a stroke of dark lightning flowing to the earth.

Jenny let out her breath and took off again. Damn him, she thought. Damn Donald Stone for not having a radio. They'd been in radio contact for the first few years. Although she rarely saw him, he was cordial enough during their occasional chats, always ending by saying that yes, he would most definitely come for tea just as soon as he could. He never came. Then he had stopped answering the radio calls.

Another shell whistled and landed and this time she heard the fragments rattling through the leaves and branches overhead. Now she ran flat out.

Half an hour later she emerged, panting, into the clearing. She froze. She heard no sound but the buzzing of the flies. The evidence was all around: The revolutionaries had been there. The fuel tank on its metal stilts had been shot up, rank kerosene spilled on the ground. Stone's things were strewn around. Books splayed open. Shakespeare. Blake. Milton. Mary Shelley. Melville. College math and science texts. Jenny thought that odd. Then she remembered the girl. Was there a girl? That was just a rumor. She'd never seen a child.

She approached the cabin cautiously. The door was broken on

its hinges. She pushed it back, scraping the earth, and peered into the darkness. She could smell the residue of smokeless powder and the sharp reek of a latrine. She reached her flashlight, switched it on, and moved the beam around.

They'd shot him in the doorway and he'd fallen back inside. She did not have to touch him to know that he was dead. The blood from his shattered head had pooled around him. The few supplies they hadn't taken were scattered and trod on by sandals, boots, bare feet. Small orange notebooks pulled down from shelves. His desk, a folding table, overturned. A boot kicked through its top.

Now, she thought, run. Go now, go to the river. There's nothing you can do for him. But she stood staring at the dead British researcher, thinking: It could as easily have been me.

As she stepped over the debris she saw a curtain that divided the room. She pushed it aside. There on the floor she saw two more bodies, that of a teenage girl, naked, and a dead bonobo. The girl's head was resting on the bonobo's chest as if she had died trying to protect the animal. It struck Jenny that the rebels must have raped the girl before killing her. They always did.

"Oh, no."

At the sound of Jenny's voice the girl lifted her head and looked up. Jenny startled so badly that she screamed, clutching her chest and gulping air. The girl was small, with long dark hair standing out in a wild profusion of curls. Her smooth tan skin was slick with blood and covered with scratches. Her fine-featured face was smeared with mud. She was odd-looking, Jenny thought, exotic in some way that she couldn't put her finger on. She looked out at Jenny with haunting dark green eyes.

At last Jenny said, "Are you hurt? Did they hurt you?"

The girl put her head back down on the chest of the dead bonobo and began wailing in high keening notes.

"Are you Dr. Stone's daughter? Where's your mother?"

The girl continued to cry, both hands covering her open mouth. Jenny crossed to her and knelt and put her arm around the girl.

"I'm sorry. I'm so sorry. We have to go. It's not safe." Jenny stood and made another examination of the hut to see if the mother's body was concealed somehow. But she found no sign of her. She began gathering the orange notebooks and stuffing them into Stone's backpack. It was all that was left of the man. "Get your clothes. Take what you need. Hurry. We won't be coming back." She found two passports among the debris and took them. "Come on. Please. I can't leave you."

The girl stood reluctantly and pulled on jeans and a shirt, still sobbing in ragged gulps, her chin trembling. Jenny picked up a framed photograph, its glass cracked, and put it in her own pack. Another shell whistled and burst nearby. The girl went back to the dead bonobo and fell on it, weeping.

Jenny took the girl's limp hand. She pulled the girl away and helped her to her feet. "I'm sorry. We have to go to the river and find help." She put her arm around the girl and drew her toward the door. "Can you speak?" The girl said nothing.

They went out of the hut and across the clearing. Then they were hurrying through the rain forest, which was interrupted here and there by great fields of flowers, bird of paradise, orchids, lobelias. They fled along worn paths beneath tunnels of red cedar, mahogany, and oak. The mist hung in the air like strips torn from bolts of cloth. As the fighting grew louder they broke into a run. Jenny could hear gunfire, explosions, and now screams. She caught occasional glimpses of a clearing sky, and as the sun drew high, the whole forest exhaled its steamy breath. When the noises of war grew faint once more they slowed to a walk. They walked all day, until the sun began to sink. They emerged into a grassy clearing, yellow in the late light. There they ate a cold meal of fruit and nuts. Though she could no longer hear the fighting Jenny dared not make a fire. They squatted on the ground, eating.

"I'm Jenny. Jenny Lowe. What's your name?"

The girl just looked at her with those sad otherworldly eyes. Then Jenny felt her heart ache as tears ran down the girl's cheeks. She put her arm around her and the girl leaned against her and wept.

"It's okay. You don't have to talk now. Let's get some sleep."

Jenny waited until the girl's sobs subsided and her breathing became regular. Then she gently lay her head down in the grass and covered her with a shirt and mosquito netting from her pack. She sat back against a tree and watched the girl sleep. She's probably in shock, Jenny thought. She can't even talk. She wondered if the girl had grown up in the forest and what life was going to be like for her now.

She thought back to her longest visit with Donald Stone. It must have been fifteen years ago now. He had served her tea and tinned biscuits with marmalade that had been sent from England. He had a generator and a record player on which he played old vinyl albums of opera. They'd had a spirited discussion about which of the ancient ancestors of humans had had language. *"Erectus,"* he had said, "surely *Homo erectus* had language. I mean, look at the evidence of those elephant hunts in Spain. It might have been just sign language, but I doubt it. After all, the forest is alive with language. Listen to it now." And he had paused dramatically, sweeping his arm all around the camp, which was walled in by the impenetrable gloom of the forest. Jenny had listened to all the jungle sounds echoing back and forth through the trees. "You see," Stone said. "A positive flood of information, an eternal stream. It's The Stream. The Stream, don't you see? Everything speaks, even the trees." She had liked him, liked his sharp mind and quick wit. But she was still mystified by how little he had wished to interact with her, the only other scientist for a thousand kilometers.

As Jenny lay musing in the darkness, she fell asleep. When she woke, the girl was gone.

JENNY STARTLED AND LEAPT to her feet. She turned in a circle, peering into the dark jungle. She thought of calling out, then remembered the soldiers. How could the girl have simply disappeared? Could she have been kidnapped? No, they would have killed them both. Then Jenny heard a rustling and spun around to see the girl emerging from the forest carrying a mound of fruits and berries in a sling improvised from her shirt. She moved into the clearing as if Jenny weren't there and set the fruit down. She sat on the ground and picked up an avocado. She split the skin with her fingernail and twisted the fruit in half. Then she began scooping out the green meat with two fingers and eating it. In between bites, she smeared some of the meat on her bare arms like body lotion. Jenny watched her, fascinated. Then the girl seemed to notice Jenny for the first time. She stopped chewing and stared at her. Then she picked up a handful of brown figs and held them out to her. Jenny crossed the clearing and took them. The girl watched her intently, waiting. Jenny took a bite. The brown-skinned fig had a pink center.

"Mmm. It's good."

The girl smiled at her and continued eating.

"Can you talk?"

"Of course I can talk."

Jenny breathed a sigh of relief. She felt silly now for asking. "Of course. It's just that yesterday . . ."

"Yesterday is gone. Today everything is different."

Jenny sat across from her and they ate in silence for a time. "I'm Jenny. What's your name?"

"Lucy."

"Lucy. That's a nice name. How old are you?"

"Fourteen."

"Did you grow up here?"

"Yes."

"How did you survive the attack?"

"I hid in the trees."

"You are Dr. Stone's daughter, aren't you?"

"Yes."

"I'm so sorry about your father."

"Death is natural, but theirs was not. Humans bring grief wherever they go."

"Did your father teach you these ideas?"

"He taught me everything."

"What about your mother? Where is she?"

"She died."

Jenny was about to question her further when Lucy paused in her eating and lifted her nose. "The wind has changed," she said. "I can smell the river. It won't be long now. Let's go."

As they set off through the forest, Jenny took heart in the girl's confidence. Lucy fairly flew across the ground now. Jenny had to run to keep up. As they hurried along, they frightened a pair of pheasants, which went cackling and complaining into the woods. Lucy held up her hand. At first Jenny saw no reason to stop. Then a snake as thick as her leg flowed out of the forest and across the trail. When it had passed, Jenny was about to ask Lucy how she had known to stop before the snake appeared. But the girl was already far down the trail.

As they drew closer Jenny began to smell the river, and the flies and mosquitoes grew more persistent. The river had a scent that was unmistakable, a mixture of perfume and sewage, of life and death. The trees grew closer together and were lashed up with vines and creepers. Giant white flowers exploded out of the darkness, gathering what little light there was and broadcasting it about them like skirts of lace.

At last they caught sight of the metallic surface of the water, a substance at once bright and black. The air was suffocating with heat and moisture. They quickened their steps down the last reach. Then Lucy held up her hand and they stopped to take in the full view of the Congo. Hippos wallowed in the shallows, and crocodiles sunned themselves on the silver sand. The water beyond was sluggish and mobbed with small islands of ravening vegetation. A flock of cormorants appeared from the right, flew low along the span of the river, and settled onto the surface, each leaving a silver wake that vanished into the oily blackness.

"We won't stay here," Lucy said. "We'll go downriver. There's a landing this side of Lisala." She began walking west along the river at a respectful distance from the crocodiles. Jenny followed her into the shimmering afternoon.

They reached the landing in an angled light. A wooden pier stretched from the forest out into the slow current. As Lucy and Jenny sat on the landing, eating and watching the river, Lucy seemed to stiffen. She raised her chin.

"Let's go into the forest."

"Why?" Jenny asked.

"There's someone coming."

Jenny had heard nothing, but they gathered their fruit and retreated into the darkness. They sat in hiding with a view of the river. Half an hour passed before Jenny asked, "How do you know someone's coming?"

Before Lucy could respond Jenny heard the engine. Then a gray steel cutter swung into view with 40 mm cannons mounted on its deck. Riding low in the water, the boat was crowded with men bearing Kalashnikov rifles and rocket-propelled grenades. Lucy and Jenny watched, barely breathing, as the craft hammered past. Diesel smoke hung in its wake above the gleaming black water.

They slept in the forest again and woke in the night to fight off a swarm of ants. The next day they watched the river. At midday they saw two black and bloated bodies float past facedown, one with a shiny raven on its back. That night they slept once more. On the following morning they were picked up by a family in a wooden boat, a man, two women, and a small child. Lucy knew them and spoke to them in Lingala.

As soon as they had boarded the boat, Jenny fell asleep against a cargo of aromatic grain in burlap sacks. When she woke it was late afternoon and she came to consciousness with the realization of how rigid she'd been holding herself for days.

They reached a small village at dusk. It was a squalid littoral of huts and trash with pigs and chickens wandering to and fro and naked children who hid behind their mothers when Jenny and Lucy appeared. Swarms of black flies hung in the shifting smoke of cook fires. Lucy spoke to a man in Lingala, and he led them to a hut at the forest's edge. A cable ran out of the hut and up to the top of a crude wooden tower where a metal antenna pointed a crooked finger at the sky.

Jenny followed Lucy and the man into the darkness and let her eyes adjust. She listened to them chatter, catching only a few phrases. The man who owned the radio was old and withered and as black as a nut. He wore a Rolling Stones T-shirt and surfer shorts. The floor of the hut was littered with beer cans and the place smelled of urine and stale cigarette smoke. The old man, whose name was Denis, smiled with but a few teeth left in his mouth. The people of the village began crowding into the hut to see what was going on.

Lucy spoke to Denis in French, gesturing at Jenny. "He speaks French," Lucy said.

"How many languages do you speak?" Jenny asked.

"Oh, not many. French and Lingala. English, of course. Italian and Spanish. A little German. Dutch." Lucy laughed. "Well, Dutch is easy." Then she seemed embarrassed and stopped talking.

Speaking French, Jenny told Denis that she needed to talk to David Meece, the British ambassador at the embassy in Kinshasa.

Denis sat and worked the radio, speaking first in Lingala, then to someone else in French. As he did so he sipped from a can of Bud Lite and smoked a Marlboro. Denis wheezed heavily as he waited for someone to get David Meece on the line. He finished his beer and sent the can clattering to the floor. At length a man's voice came on the radio speaking in French. Denis stood and motioned graciously for Jenny to sit. She picked up the microphone.

"David? Is that David Meece? It's Jenny, over."

"My God, Jenny. Yes, it's David. Are you all right, over?"

David Meece was from a family of diplomats, old money from London. He wore bow ties even in the African heat. Jenny's oldest friend, Harry Prendeville, was a doctor who came to Africa once a year to volunteer for Doctors Without Borders. He had introduced Jenny to Meece the first time she came to Congo. They'd become fast friends, and David had helped Jenny out on more than one occasion.

"They've killed Stone. Things are very confused. I have his daughter with me. We came downriver with some locals and are now in a village hoping that you can get us out of here, over."

"Damn straight I can."

"Thank God."

"Can you give me your position, over?"

"Stand by, David."

Jenny spoke to the old man in French, asking if he knew the coordinates of the village. He rummaged in a desk drawer and brought out a Garmin GPS. Jenny rolled her eyes. She clicked the mike and said, "Hang on, David, they have a GPS here, if you can believe that, over."

She heard him laugh. "Not bloody surprised, over," he said.

The next morning they heard the helicopter long before they saw it. It came thundering in and circled a few times before landing in a clearing a short distance away. The entire village turned out to examine the machine. Four hours later they were touching down at the Kinshasa airport. In another hour they were in an office at the embassy watching David Meece hurriedly pack his things.

"The rebels are just a few miles outside the city, I'm told. We have a plane going to London. I can get you on, of course. But what about the girl?"

"I found these." Jenny fished the passports out of her filthy pack and handed them to David. He opened one and set it aside with a sad shake of his head. He opened the other and studied it with a frown. Jenny looked over his shoulder and understood David's expression: The passport had been issued when Lucy was four months old. David tapped it in the palm of his hand, muttering, "Spot of bother about that photograph . . . No visa. She's been in-country illegally for fourteen years?"

"I don't know. Lucy?"

"I don't understand," Lucy said.

"Do you have any family in England who can vouch for you, dear?" David asked.

"No, sir."

"No one? Really?"

"I grew up in the jungle. I was in London only once. I was a baby."

"How irregular." David thought for a while, then said, "Well, right now, we have to get out of here."

Jenny looked at the girl, so exotic and smart. She seemed pure even in her filth. Jenny wondered what would become of her. She looked as if she were still in shock.

"I hear the guns."

"She has incredibly keen hearing," Jenny said. "If she says they're coming then they're coming."

"Come along, then. Spit-spot. We'll talk about this on the plane. I've had my whack of this place."

The military plane waited on the ramp with its engines running. Dozens of diplomats and businessmen were hurrying up the cargo ramp. As Jenny and David walked on either side of Lucy, the young girl stopped. Jenny said, "Come on, Lucy. Let's hurry now." But Lucy went rigid, her eyes wide. "What's the matter, Lucy?"

"I've never been on an airplane. Except when I was a baby."

"I assure you it's perfectly safe," David said. "Safer than here by a long shot."

Jenny took Lucy's hand but Lucy pulled back and began weeping. David dug in his briefcase and came up with a bottle of pills. He shook one into his hand and offered it to Jenny. "Give her this. It'll make her sleep."

"What is it?"

"It's just Valium. Five milligrams. She'll be fine." He handed Jenny the bottle. "Here, take the lot. I can get more."

Jenny coaxed Lucy into taking the pill, explaining that she would feel better in a little while and that they had to go now. When a shell landed near the perimeter of the airfield, Lucy at last moved up the ramp and into the dark interior of the plane. She and Jenny and David took the last three seats. They were designed for carrying troops, small and uncomfortable, with tubular frames and canvas backs. The plane was taxiing before the ramp was all the way up. Everyone cheered when the wheels lifted off the runway.

Lucy closed her eyes and put her hands over her ears, but half an hour into the flight she was fast asleep. Jenny watched her sleep for a time, then asked David, "What do you think we should do with her?"

"I'm sure I don't know."

"We can't simply throw her into an orphanage."

"What choice do we have?"

"I don't know. I brought her out. I feel somehow responsible. I could try to find her family."

"She says she has no family."

"She said her mother's dead, but there must be someone. People don't come out of nowhere."

"Well, Stone had no living relatives. He was the last in his line. Old money, gone to seed. But if the girl has relatives on her mother's side, do you think they'd take her in?"

"I don't know," Jenny said. "I want to go home."

"Well, you can't take her with you."

"I can if you fix her passport."

"You'd do that? You'd take her home?"

"Well, just for a couple of weeks. Until I find her relatives."

"You don't even know her, Jenny. And in any event, I don't know that I can fix her passport. The British authorities have gotten awfully sticky."

Jenny stared at her hands in her lap. "I can't think straight. I have to get some sleep." She covered her eyes with her bandanna and slept fitfully. Two hours later both Jenny and Lucy woke up, looking bleary-eyed. Jenny yawned and patted Lucy's hand. "You see? We're all just fine."

Lucy craned her neck this way and that to see the faces of the other passengers. Then she whispered to Jenny, "Are we flying?" As if it were a secret.

"Yes." Jenny pointed out the tiny window. "Look."

"Oh. Oh, my. I'm afraid."

"Don't be, dear. We're perfectly safe. Honey, you're shaking."

"Please may I tell you a story? It always calms me down. Papa used to have me tell stories when the big cats came and I was afraid."

"Really? Yes, of course you may. David. Lucy's going to tell us a story."

"Splendid. The movie on this flight sucks."

"Pardon?"

"He's joking, dear. Go ahead. Tell us a story."

"Hmm," she said, tilting her head and thinking. Then she began:

In the sea, once upon a time, O my Best Beloved, there was a Whale, and he ate fishes. He ate the starfish and the garfish, and the crab and the dab, and the plaice and the dace, and the skate and his mate, and the mackerel and the pickereel, and the really truly twirly-whirly eel. All the fishes he could find in all the sea he ate with his mouth—so! Till at last there was only one small fish left in all the sea, and he was a small 'Stute Fish, and he swam a little behind the Whale's right ear, so as to be out of harm's way. Then the Whale stood up on his tail and said, "I'm hungry." And the small 'Stute Fish said in a small 'stute voice, "Noble and generous Cetacean, have you ever tasted Man?"

For the next hour Lucy recited stories and poetry from memory, and gradually other passengers crowded around to listen. For her finale, Lucy recited "Jabberwocky," by Lewis Carroll. Then she announced that she was tired and promptly fell asleep again.

Jenny watched Lucy sleeping in her filthy clothes. David asked, "Are you quite sure about this, then? Taking her home with you?"

"No. Far from it. But when I found her in the jungle, afraid, alone . . . her father shot . . . I don't know. It was just horrible, David. And now this: Reciting Shakespeare and Kipling? What am I supposed to do? Abandon her?"

"Most people would."

"I don't think I can. She reminds me of the girls at the shelter where I volunteer at home. I'd always be wondering, you know."

David seemed to fall into deep thought for a moment. "Come to think of it," he said, "there are a couple of chaps who might help us out with that passport."

"Who's that?"

"Two SAS types who owe me a rather large favor. I helped to get them out of a Congolese prison. I take it you've never seen the inside of a Congolese prison."

"I think I'd remember."

"Well, they were thorough thugs and frankly belonged in a jail of some sort if you ask me. But when we'd sprung them, they made a point of telling me that if I ever needed anything—the more irregular, the better—I was to look them up. I quite think they meant it, too."

Heathrow was swarming with African refugees, many in native dress, along with throngs of escaping businessmen clamoring for preferential treatment. David took advantage of the confusion to press Jenny and Lucy to the head of the line. He flashed his diplomatic passport at a functionary, who gave no more than a cursory glance at Jenny and Lucy before waving them on.

Once they were safely through customs David made a phone call and a car came to take them to an accommodation address in a London slum called Heygate Estate. The car stopped before a towering concrete apartment building with torn curtains billowing out of broken windows. The apartment was even more foul than Jenny had guessed it would be.

"I'm sorry about this," David said. "But it's where these people work, for the sake of security. I promise we'll get you out of here as soon as possible."

Jenny examined the small apartment and found that the bath and shower were unusable. Fortunately, the toilet worked.

A man arrived a few hours later, a large stooped figure who might have been some sort of city inspector in his cheap suit and threadbare trench coat. "Give us the old passport," he told David. The man studied it for a moment and then looked at Lucy, who was squatting against the wall, her arms wrapped around her muddied knees. He crossed the room and knelt before her.

"There, then," he said. "You've been through a lot, eh?" Lucy said nothing. "Cat got your tongue, eh? Well, all right." He reached into his pocket, brought out a small colorful plastic bag, and offered it to Lucy. She merely stared at it. "Go on then. It's gummy bears. Big fan of gummy bears, I am." At last Lucy took the bag and held it in her hand.

The man stood up, chuckling to himself. He pulled a wooden chair up against a wall, scraping it across the floor. "Sit there, please." Jenny rushed over and wiped the dirt off of Lucy's face with a wet cloth. She straightened her hair as best she could. Then the man took Lucy's photograph with a digital camera and went away.

David went out and came back with takeout Chinese food. Jenny ate voraciously, but Lucy just looked at her plate. When Jenny encouraged her to eat, all Lucy said was, "Am I going to be all right?"

"Yes, dear, you will. You're coming home with me, and then we'll find your family." Jenny glanced up to see David's skeptical frown. She shrugged at him and shook her head.

David left them alone for the night. Jenny thought she heard Lucy cry out in her sleep but was too tired to verify it.

The next day David returned and another man arrived a short time later. He looked like a truck driver in jeans and a flannel shirt. He handed David a brand-new British passport wrapped in tissue paper. "You never saw this," he said. "And you never met me. I think we're even now, mate."

"Absolutely. Super. Thanks." But the man had already turned on his heel to leave.

David helped Jenny to get money wired from the States for plane tickets. Then he drove Jenny and Lucy to the airport and stood with them at the curb amid the roaring buses and taxicabs.

"David. Please promise me that you'll help find Lucy's family."

"Of course."

"She must have someone. You'll do that, won't you?"

"Absolutely." He turned to Lucy and said, "You're a very lucky young lady." Then he hugged Jenny and got back in the car. Fifteen hours later, Jenny and Lucy were in Harry's car, arriving in front of Jenny's ivy-covered house in a quiet suburban community north of Chicago.

3

LUCY STARED UP at the moon and thought: It looks so pale and weak here. Flat, not round. The stars and planets looked as if they were being smothered in the fog that rose from the new place in which she found herself. She watched the fog rise all night long and then before morning saw the moon dissolve and heard the dogs begin to bark. The dogs frightened her.

When Jenny had gone to sleep, Lucy had opened the window to let the air in. She removed her clothes and lay out on the bed and gazed at the sky through the trees. When the moon swung into view she felt a sadness in her stomach, an aching for home. She mused on her home, thinking that she'd likely never see it again. She felt a longing to drink in the aroma, the million scents of flower and dung, of water and life, of the exploding growth, the eternal rot. She wanted to hear the wild braying of the forest song as she went to sleep.

Jenny was kind, and Lucy knew that she wanted only to protect her. But she felt that she might never fathom this place. She felt that she ought to be grateful for all she had, thankful to be alive. Lucy understood that Jenny could have left her for dead in the jungle. As she lay there, she tried to feel grateful, but all she could feel was loneliness, sadness, even anger.

She had cried in bed those first few nights, watching the lonely moon. There was too much light. The forest had been dark, but here the night glowed like a phosphorescent fungus. Even after the moon went down there would be a dull glow. Lucy was aware that she could not have stayed in the forest. The soldiers would have come back. Jenny had told her that she'd get used to this place, but Lucy felt hopeless. The food was strange. The water tasted bad. She hated clothes.

Clouds moved across the moon. She smelled the air and knew that it wouldn't rain that night. She feared another thunderstorm. In the forest she had loved the thunderstorms. When they came, everyone danced on the top of the ridge in the flashing light and the pouring rain. She recalled Grandpa Dondi tearing branches and dragging them around and Faith and Viaje hiding in the trees, afraid. But in this place the other people lived so close. Lucy wondered what would happen if they saw her dancing.

She put her feet over the side of the bed and stood shivering in the cold night air. Summer was almost over. Jenny said that it would grow cold, cold such as she had never known. She said that Lucy would have to return to England and go to school. Lucy crossed the room and closed the window and slipped back into bed beneath the sheets. She tried to imagine what snow was like. She had seen it in pictures. Solid water. Such an odd concept. She wondered what it felt like.

She tried to drift off to sleep but the machines kept growling on the road beyond the end of the street. Cars. Trucks. A train crying plaintively in the distance. She heard night sounds, too, but they didn't tell her anything that she could understand. In the forest Lucy would know if a sound was from a monkey or a bird, a cat or pig. When she heard a sound or a voice, she could tell if it was good or bad or nothing that concerned her. Jenny had told her that the far-off wail of a siren meant that something bad was happening. But what sort of bad? And who might be in trouble? Jenny said to ignore the sounds, you couldn't tell what they meant. Lucy thought that learning such a thing in the forest might be fatal.

The night was half over before the road quieted down. The mechanical noises faded away and Lucy drifted into sleep. In her dreams she was back in the forest and Papa was listening to her read in French from the book by Montaigne: "A mere bookish sufficiency is unpleasant." The day was over and she felt safe in her home, but she worried because her father was weak from a bout of malaria. He'd contracted the disease long ago, before the good medicine. He'd been in bed for days.

Then the explosions began in the distance. Her father stopped reading and held the book loosely on his lap. Lucy had never seen him so concerned. He turned to her. Like cool water in mountain terrain, his blue eyes, bloodshot from illness, looked upon her from out of his chiseled features. His shock of gray hair was in disarray, his skin pale. They listened to the advancing guns and began to smell their sharp smoke. At last her father said, "Go with Viaje and the others and hide. I can't run. I'm too weak. You must hide in the trees." He kissed her and said, "I love you, Lucy. Always remember that." Lucy followed the others into the trees. As she slept, she was vaguely aware that she was in a dream, struggling to get out. She wanted to say something to her father but couldn't speak.

She scrambled into the trees with Toby and Viaje and Faith and watched as the soldiers moved in disorderly columns, swinging their eerie lights through the darkness while the bombs fell ahead of them. She saw her father slouch into the hut, and then Leda came running out of the forest screaming and trying to reach the hut to protect him. A soldier raised his rifle and fired. A loud crack split the air. Leda jerked and staggered into the hut. Lucy's father appeared at the door and several soldiers fired at once. He fell back into the darkness. Toby and Viaje and Faith cried out and the soldiers shot them, too. Lucy watched in horror as the bodies fell. The soldiers ransacked the camp and left.

Lucy woke with a start. On several nights she had tried to stay awake to avoid that dream. But even when she was able to stay awake it made no difference. She'd remember and couldn't keep herself from going over and over the attack in her mind.

She had come out of the forest as soon as the soldiers left, but the others were frightened and stayed away. Lucy ran into the hut and saw her father lying on the floor. She fell on him and wept. Then she found Leda behind the curtain and held her and cried.

She couldn't remember how long she lay like that. Her mouth grew dry from crying. Her eyes hurt. Then Jenny came.

· · ·

Lucy had dozed off. She woke to find that the moon had gone. The light was coming. She had loved the first moments of morning in the jungle, the crescendo of voices in the trees; the rising smells of life around her; the big cats flowing through the forest in the dim light; and then the drama of the sun pushing thin cylinders of light through the murk as if searching for something. As she watched the light swell behind the window, she felt sad for the sun. It had grown so weak. She feared that its fire might go out and then everything would freeze. She was aware that it was a childish thought. Her father had taught her all about the cosmos. But she was unable to control her thoughts at times.

She lay in bed trying not to think at all. But a word rose to the surface: School. Her father, who had been her only teacher, had told her about school, but she still had no idea what it might be like. She worried that there would be too many people. It would be loud. Everything in this new place was loud. Already she could hear the roaring of the road. Sometimes men came in the day with frightful machines to cut the grass up and down the street and blow everything around with a terrible noise. Lucy hid in her room and trembled when they came.

Now she could smell Jenny's coffee. She had heard her rise a while ago. Jenny had tried to tiptoe to the bathroom. But Lucy could hear her. Lucy thought it no wonder that Jenny didn't know how to be quiet. How could she when she lived in such a loud place? Lucy knew quiet. Termites, she thought. Termites are quiet even when they're making their sounds. Quiet sounds.

When Jenny and Lucy had arrived after their long journey, Jenny had showed her this room. By that time they had been on the move for many days. Lucy had worn clothes the entire time, but the moment she was left alone, she took them off and reveled in the feeling of freedom once more. She had stood looking around at the strange room, which was populated with things that she'd seen only in books: The framed prints of Monet's water lilies on the wall, the vase with dried weeds in it, a decorative rug, a writing desk, lamps, the big bed with the flowered bedspread, a box of tissues, and an electric radio that told the time in lighted red digits.

That first day, she had crossed the room naked and approached the floor lamp. She turned it on. Then she turned it off. She switched it on and off and on and off over and over, marveling at the light, feeling its heat. So much light, she thought. The street was brightly lit all night like a stage set for a play. But no one ever came. Her father had rationed the light. They often didn't have enough fuel for the generator. But when they did, he would make light in the evening and play music on an old machine and teach Lucy to sing arias.

That first day in her new home, Lucy had heard a sound as she switched the lamp on and off. She stopped to listen. It was faint, coming from the floor. She moved toward it, listening: It was termites. Quiet but not silent. A pleasant and familiar sound. Something was living after all, eating the house. Lucy took a straw from the vase of dead weeds and went to the wall, smiling to herself, thinking about what her father had always said: Life will find a way. She worked the straw into a small gap where the wall met the floor. She'd had to eat such strange foods since leaving the forest. She thought that termites might be a welcome treat.

As she squatted on the floor, listening and fishing with the straw, Jenny came to the door. "Good morning, Lucy. What are you doing?"

"Looking for termites."

"Termites? Really? Termites?"

"They're in the floor. They're good to eat. Do you want some?"

"Well, are they the same as the ones we had in Congo? Those were good when I tried them once. But who knows what sort of chemicals our local termites might have. I'd be afraid to eat them here."

Lucy stopped. She withdrew the straw, looking disappointed.

"I didn't know the house had termites."

"I suppose you're right," Lucy said. "I just felt happy when I realized that there were termites. The food here is so strange."

"I know. Speaking of chemicals. Who knows what's in our food for that matter? But we'll have to make do. So about your clothes . . ." Jenny gathered them up and put them on the bed. "I know you don't like clothes. Actually, I don't either. I often went without in the forest. It's okay with me if you want to go around the house naked. But I'm afraid you're going to have to get used to clothes. Come on. I'll find something that you'll like to eat. I promise."

Lucy admired Jenny, such a good and caring person. She allowed herself a momentary vision of the two of them racing through the forest together enjoying the bounty and the beauty. Then Lucy realized that Jenny would never be able to keep up. And that made her think: I have no one else in the world now. Lucy wanted Jenny to know her but she didn't know how.

But now it was a new day. She could hear Jenny clanking dishes in the kitchen. I'm here, Lucy thought, and I'll just have to make the best of it. She sighed and rose and began to dress, thinking, I guess I'd better get used to clothes, as Jenny says.

She went down the hall to the bathroom and turned on the water in the sink. She let it run over her hands. She splashed it on her face. She bent down to drink from the spigot. Such a miracle, she thought. Water is life, as her father used to say. And here it just gushed endlessly out of a silver spout as if all the rivers of all the world had magically flowed to this one spot for no purpose other than to please Lucy.

She dried her hands and face and descended the stairs to find Jenny standing at the counter reading a newspaper. Lucy watched as Jenny calmly pored over the endless tales of catastrophe and meanness while sipping coffee from a mug decorated with paintings of yellow pears tinged with pink. Jenny was pretty in a sturdy sinewy way, tall and thin with sandy-red hair curling past her shoulders. She had long delicate fingers, but her hands were calloused from working in the forest, the fingernails battered. Her hands looked as if they had an intelligence all their own.

On the table where Jenny rested a hand, Lucy saw a shiny silver toaster, a pepper mill, coarse salt in a small ceramic bowl, a wicker basket of paper napkins, all these things that she'd seen only in photographs from the books and catalogs and encyclopedias that her father had sent upriver. Those books were tiny windows that connected the dark jungle to a bright and alien world, and Lucy had spent hours on end just peering through, trying to imagine what it might be like to be there in the flesh. Now here she was, and she saw that it was real, so real and bright that it almost hurt her eyes to look. She watched as the light fell through the window and crept over those magical objects, illuminating them as if each one had a living heart within it.

Jenny sighed, wearied by something she'd read. Then she put on a bright smile and turned to Lucy. "Well, Lucy, what would you like for breakfast? I can make you just about anything you want."

"Thank you."

"How about fruit and yogurt?"

"That would be fine."

Jenny busied herself slicing peaches and laying out bowls of berries and nuts and yogurt. She poured orange juice into a ceramic pitcher that matched the coffee mug. Lucy admired the kitchen. It was all very pretty. But somehow it struck her as almost too pretty. She tried to reconcile the bright prettiness with the ominous sounds of the place. She felt as if all the prettiness concealed some truer, deeper, and more menacing world that lay just beneath the surface.

Jenny spooned Greek yogurt into bowls, and they sat together at the small table. Lucy regarded the fruit with curiosity. It seemed not quite real. She tasted a strawberry. It tasted only faintly like fruit. She missed the fruit of the forest, dark and sweet and musky. And she told herself, Stop your whining. You're homesick. Snap out of it.

To distract herself, she asked, "What will we do today?"

Jenny bit her lip and thought for a moment, scooping berries into her bowl. "Well, what would you like to do? There are so many things to do in the city."

"May I please watch your television? I caught only glimpses of it at the airports. I've not really tried to watch."

Jenny shrugged. "Sure. Okay. But daytime television is pretty stupid. Come to think of it, nighttime television is, too."

"Yes, I know. Papa told me. But I'm curious to see what it is." To Lucy the idea of television sounded very powerful. If she could learn television, then she might understand this culture better.

After breakfast Jenny led Lucy to the den and showed her how the remote control worked. Lucy pushed the button to turn it on. But when the image came to life and the sound began to blare, she dropped the remote and put her hands over her ears, a look of pain creasing her face. Jenny couldn't help but laugh. She picked up the remote and pressed the mute button.

"Sorry. I don't know why it's turned up so loud. Oh, Nydia. The house sitter. She likes to watch." She handed Lucy the remote. "Play with it. You'll get the idea." Then Jenny retired to her study to work. Lucy pushed a button. The screen showed an advertisement for something called Scalpicin. It showed a woman scratching her head with a worried expression on her face. A disembodied voice said, "The clear solution to a healthier scalp." Lucy thought that odd. Scratching? She thought scratching was good.

She pushed a button and some sort of drama began. People were arguing. Lucy recognized one of them as an old dominant female, but something had been done to her to make her face look younger. Lucy was puzzled that someone would wish to look younger and give up the status that age conferred. She found the story hard to follow. It seemed that a baby had been born and someone had stolen it and there was a murder plot like in a play by Shakespeare and someone's wife was mating with someone else's husband. Someone was in the hospital, though it wasn't clear why. Everyone seemed mean and angry. It was very confusing. Then it switched to an urgent-sounding message about a new kind of sponge on a stick to mop the floor with, and then a doctor was telling Lucy that her joints hurt. A big boat appeared and someone who Lucy couldn't see was shouting about it, telling her that the boat was going to take her to the Caribbean. But she didn't want to go to the Caribbean. She wanted to be with Jenny. She worried that all of these invisible people might kidnap her and take her away. They all talked so loud and fast. Lucy had never met anyone who shouted in that rapid-fire way. She wondered, Who are these people? Where are these people? Do they really exist?

Lucy began to feel dizzy and had to stop. She couldn't keep up. She pressed a button and the screen went blank. As she put down the remote control and crossed the room to look at the books on a bookshelf, she felt somehow deficient for being unable to understand television. She ran her finger across the spines of the books and stopped at a familiar one: *The Old Curiosity Shop*. She read, "Night is generally my time for walking," and felt her shoulders drop, her mind clear. Books are so much simpler than television, she thought. A book goes logically from one thing to the next.

Lucy lay on the rug reading and feeling a sense of relief that she didn't have to go anywhere. When they'd first arrived, Jenny had taken her to buy clothes, and the experience had been terrifying. The speed of driving had been disorienting and nearly made Lucy ill. She felt that her eyes couldn't focus on anything for more than a second. Lucy considered it a very bad sign that they had to be strapped into the car before they could begin. It had been one of the things that had frightened her about airplanes: She'd never been tied up before.

When they arrived in the town, the buildings had seemed to reach to the heavens. It was both frightening and oddly beautiful, little villages in the clouds. She had read about all of those things in books, of course, but seeing them was a shock nevertheless.

The noise inside the mall was deafening. Loud music played everywhere. Lucy couldn't seem to get away from it. She couldn't avoid the television screens with people screaming incessantly. When she had read Orwell's novel *1984*, Lucy couldn't imagine a place such as the one he described. She thought it a mere fantasy. Now she saw that he'd been right: His Telescreen was everywhere, and you couldn't turn it off.

The mall smelled like flowers and sugar. People were swarming everywhere, but Lucy could detect no signals from them, no light of recognition. The older ones seemed as if they were walking in a trance and the younger ones had plugs in their ears. Lucy asked Jenny about them.

"Those? They're headphones. For music."

"Music on top of music! How can they stand it?" But Jenny just laughed good-naturedly and squeezed her hand.

The colors were so bright and dazzling. Lucy couldn't decide where to look or what each thing meant. And the lights overhead hummed and hissed like snakes, keeping her constantly on edge. Lucy gripped Jenny's arm tighter, and Jenny said, "Lucy, you're hurting me. Don't worry. I won't let you go."

Jenny had led her across the store, through the cosmetics department, where Lucy covered her nose and mouth with her hand against the smells. They approached an escalator and Lucy stopped walking and went rigid. She had read about such things but had never seen a real escalator before. She stood before it attempting to comprehend the mystery of this vanishing staircase, which seemed to embody some deep magical property like the

Möbius strip that her father had once made for her from a piece of paper.

"Step onto it now." Lucy remained planted, her eyes wide. She began making high-pitched barking noises at the escalator, and Jenny said, "Lucy, please. Shh. It's not like in the forest. We have to be quiet." Then people were staring at them, passing by with odd expressions of alarm. "I'll help you. Come on. It's perfectly safe."

Lucy held tight to Jenny's arm and closed her eyes as Jenny dragged her onto the escalator. Lucy's eyes remained shut, and she trembled with fear. Then she stumbled over something and almost fell, but Jenny kept her upright. Lucy found herself on solid ground once more and opened her eyes to look around. Then for the first time, she laughed.

"There. That's it. See? It's easy."

Jenny led Lucy to the Junior Miss department and told her she could pick out anything she wanted. But as Lucy appeared incapable of choosing, Jenny selected clothes for her to try on. They stood in the dressing room together, and Lucy writhed and squirmed as if the clothes had insects in them, until Jenny was stifling her laughter and apologizing. "You look adorable. Don't worry, they'll feel better after I've washed them."

Walking between stores they witnessed a scene that carried Lucy back to the forest. They were trying to get through a crush of people who were milling and moving in every direction by a central fountain. The crowd parted and two small children, one little girl in pink and one small boy in tiny blue jeans, rushed across the open space shrieking with joy, expressions of ecstasy on their faces. They ran straight toward each other without restraint and flew into an embrace, dancing and hugging and twirling around. Soon two parents, a big man and a petite woman, came rushing up and tried to separate them. But the blue boy and the pink girl were in transports of joy that could not be extinguished. Lucy recalled a time when she was very little and had met a family of bonobos moving through the forest. All at once she had caught sight of a beautiful little bonobo boy. The two had rushed at each other with cries of delight and they hugged and rolled on the ground together, as the adults greeted one another and slapped backs and cried out. As Lucy now watched the two little children experience the miracle of discovering another, she saw Mariposa and Chantel and little Faith, all equally capable of the joy that Robinson Crusoe must have felt when he found a footprint on the beach. It told him, Yes, yes, you are not alone. But Lucy felt sad, because she saw that in Jenny's culture one could not display joy openly except when very young. Those children were like little bonobos. Soon they would grow up to be like everyone else in the mall. That world of joy would be forever closed to them. And at that moment Lucy vowed that no matter how accustomed she became to this place, she would not let go of her joy.

Seeing something familiar had relaxed her somewhat, but it also made her feel a terrible pang of nostalgia for her beautiful protective home in the forest. She felt a longing for the rich pastel colors and the sudden blaze of blue as clouds parted after a hissing rain to let golden shafts of light slant through the trees at the end of the day. Here all of the bounty and beauty had been swept away. And she wondered why people would want to do that to their home.

When they had finished shopping, Jenny had taken Lucy to a place with restaurants of all sorts. They discussed what they might eat. On the long way home from the jungle they had already discussed food a great deal. "Everyone wants to kill something," Lucy had said. "But Papa and I didn't eat meat in the forest. We'd eat grubs and earthworms and insects of all sorts. The caterpillars that fell from the botuna trees were best. Occasionally someone would catch a small monkey but most of the time they'd only play with it and groom it. I ate the little fish and shrimp that we'd find in the shallow streams. I ate bird's eggs. But none of us really ate meat. What shall we eat, Jenny?"

Lucy's father had told her that killing was wrong. The bonobos didn't know any better, he said. They couldn't think things through the way people could. He told her that once you start killing one kind of animal, then pretty soon you're killing everything. He said that to be human was to have a mission in life beyond eating and making babies, something larger than yourself.

"How about falafel? It's chickpeas."

A man in a little stall made falafel and fresh carrot juice and Lucy liked it.

"I hadn't known that you could squeeze a carrot," she said, and Jenny laughed. Lucy thought that Jenny laughed an awful lot.

But by the time they reached home, Lucy was already feeling ill. She told herself that it was the stress of shopping and all the new things. Her father had warned her about how delicate her constitution was. Stress could make her sick. When the Germans bombed London during World War II, her father had said, the bombs didn't hit the zoo. But all the bonobos had died from the noise.

4

COMING HOME FROM LONDON, Jenny thought: I ought to have my head examined. I don't even know this person. But another part of her kept up a rational counterargument: She would take care of the girl until they could locate her family. Lucy would be there for a few weeks, perhaps a month. David was searching for her mother's relatives now. Surely he'd find someone who would want to care for such a bright, engaging, pretty girl. But Lucy was strange, too, there was no doubt about that. Who wouldn't seem strange, raised in the jungle like that?

Jenny recalled the episode of the shower when they'd arrived home that first day. The first thing that Jenny always wanted when she returned from Congo was a shower. All they'd had in London was a sponge bath in that horrid apartment. As desperate as Jenny had been for a shower, she had let Lucy go first. She took her hand and led her up the stairs. At the top was a guest room. At the other end of the hall was the master suite with its own bath, Jenny's bedroom. In between the two was the guest bathroom, exactly as it had been when Jenny's parents built the house in 1955, with yellow tile halfway up the walls and an unglazed mosaic floor in three shades of yellow. A print of Sargent's *Egyptian Girl* was on one wall, and Jenny had hung a basket of dried flowers on another.

Jenny showed Lucy how to adjust the temperature, saying,

"Careful. Not too hot or it may burn you." She had started the spray of warm water, and Lucy stood staring at it for a long time. "Have you seen a shower before?"

"I read about this. But I didn't know that it would be like making it rain indoors."

"Well, yes, a little I guess. So you just get under the spray and wash yourself." And before Jenny could stop her, Lucy had jumped in and was dancing under the spray.

"Lucy, Lucy, please." But Lucy wouldn't stop until Jenny turned the water off.

"Oh, I'm sorry," Lucy said, wiping the water from her face. "It feels so good. Can I please do more?"

"Yes, but take your clothes off first. I'll get you some fresh ones. Just call if you need me." Jenny left the bathroom shaking her head.

She sat in her favorite chair and looked around the living room. She sighed. It was good to be home. She loved the forest, but that little hut got old. When she was in Congo, she missed her "stuff," as Harry called it. She'd done her best with the 1950s styling of the house. The walls were painted soft green, and she had put wicker baskets around and African masks and pottery to give the place a more natural feel.

Jenny began to go through the piles of mail, but when an hour had passed and Lucy hadn't come down, she went up and peeked into the bathroom to see if she was all right. She found Lucy still dancing and turning under the water. But her teeth were chattering and her lips were tinged with blue.

"My God, Lucy, look at you." Jenny turned off the water and wrapped the girl in a big bath sheet. But Lucy was smiling even as she shivered.

"No more shower?"

"My turn." Jenny had had to wait another hour before there was enough hot water.

Nydia, the house sitter, had left little in the way of food, so after they had cleaned up, Jenny took Lucy to the grocery store to stock up. Lucy stood staring as they entered. She couldn't seem to move at first. She looked all around her, eyes wide, mouth agape, sniffing the air, her fingers clenching and unclenching as she tried to process the scene.

"It doesn't smell like there's anything to eat here."

"Welcome to America. It's all about packaging."

"Don't they ever turn the music off?"

"No. Never."

"Wait, I see fruit." Lucy pounced on a big bin of grapes. She took a whole bunch and bit into it, the juice dripping down her chin. "Mmm. These are good." She took another bite.

"We should probably weigh that first." But Lucy couldn't seem to stop herself and took another bite. "Oh, well. A little shoplifting never hurt anyone." Jenny pushed the cart down the aisle and Lucy followed, leaving a trail of juice.

As they moved along among the shelves, Lucy kept asking, "What's this? Oh, my, what do you call these? What's in this box?" One question after another. After they'd been shopping for a while, Lucy seemed to go a little crazy. She went running up and down the aisles, grabbing cans and jars and packages off the shelves seemingly at random and throwing them into the cart, saying, "Oh, let's have this. And this. Can we take some of these? Oh, look at this!" People turned to stare.

"Lucy, Lucy, Lucy." Jenny put her arms around the girl and held her close. "Lucy, stop. Stop!"

Lucy went limp in Jenny's arms. People turned away in embarrassment. Jenny imagined that they must think that Lucy was mentally impaired in some way. And then the thought occurred to her: The girl has Tourette's syndrome. As Jenny was holding her, inhaling her curious scent, she felt Lucy's compact and powerful body press against hers and was struck by how solid she was despite her delicate appearance.

Lucy looked up forlornly. "Jenny. What are Fruity Cheerios? Do people really eat them?"

Jenny couldn't help but laugh. And as she held Lucy, she remarked to herself what a beautiful child she was. Maybe she was a blessing in disguise. Jenny had always wanted children. At least temporary children. That was one reason that she volunteered at the shelter. Maybe she could try to exercise her maternal instincts with Lucy for a few weeks.

On the way home in the car Jenny said, "Lucy, dear, it's not like the forest here, where you can just express yourself any way you want."

"I'm sorry. I didn't do it on purpose. It just happened."

"I understand. Just try to exert a little more . . . control."

"I will. I'm sorry."

"It's not for my sake, honey. I don't care what people think. But when you're reunited with your family it might make it easier on them. And then when you go to school you'll get along better if you fit in."

Lucy gave Jenny a pained look. Jenny wondered if her odd behavior was the result of post-traumatic stress disorder and made a mental note to get her to a therapist as soon as they were settled.

When they arrived home from shopping, Lucy had helped to carry in the groceries. Jenny noticed that she seemed flushed. As Jenny unpacked the food, Lucy drifted over to the back door and wandered out into the garden. It was a warm and sunny day, and Jenny thought nothing of it. She spent the next hour preparing a roasted red pepper lasagna. When it was ready to bake, she went outside to check on Lucy.

The sun cast slanting bars of yellow light across the stone patio overlooking the garden, which was crowded with prairie plants. Jenny kept thinking that in a moment Lucy would pop up from behind the tall grasses that concealed stone walkways. Jenny gradually began to wonder what would happen if the girl wandered off and was lost. "Lucy," she called. Then louder: "Lucy!" She felt her heart beating in her temples. She thought, Good Lord, I got her out of the jungle only to lose her in the suburbs.

Jenny stepped around the barbecue grill and went part of the way down one of the stone paths. She called again. Nothing. She turned back, then ran down another walkway. Lucy was nowhere to be seen. As Jenny returned to the patio, she felt the beginning notes of panic flutter in her chest. Then she heard a rustling sound and looked up into the maple tree that overhung the patio. There in a high branch she saw what appeared to be a great green nest of broken and interwoven branches. She couldn't imagine what could have made a nest that size at this northern latitude.

She was just beginning to reach for a familiar image in her mind when she heard a moaning sound. "Lucy? Are you up there?"

Again she heard the soft cry. "What are you doing in a tree?" No answer.

Jenny hurried to the garage and brought out a ladder. She propped it against the tree and climbed it to reach the lowest branch. Cautiously, she negotiated the rest of the climb to find Lucy curled up in the nest of branches. Jenny looked at the thickness of the broken branches and wondered, Had the girl done this? Was she that strong? Lucy was flushed and shivering. Jenny touched her forehead.

"My God, you're burning up."

"I'm cold."

"Come on, let's get you to bed."

"I am in bed." And Jenny went still with some emotion that she could not quite place. It sounded so odd to hear the girl say that. But why? There was no time to think it over. She had to get her down.

"Can you climb down? I have to take your temperature." Lucy didn't move. "Come on, honey, climb onto my back. I'll take you down."

Jenny managed to get Lucy draped across her shoulder. "That's it. Hold my neck." She felt Lucy's arm come to life and grip her neck. Jenny gingerly picked her way from branch to branch. At the bottom she held Lucy's arm and led her inside. She urged her up the stairs and into the bed, then pulled the covers up without bothering to undress her.

By the time Jenny had found the thermometer, Lucy's temperature was 103 degrees and her teeth were chattering.

"Am I going to die now?"

"No, no, of course not. You just picked up a bug."

"Bug?"

"I mean, you must have the flu or something. You're sick. You'll get well." Lucy's hair was matted with sweat. Her green eyes glistened as she glanced around in fear, fixing on the tree outside the window where birds were calling. "Harry is a doctor. Remember Harry? I'll call him."

"But what about the London Zoo?"

Jenny assumed that she was delirious. "I'll be right back. I'll get ibuprofen. Don't worry. Try to sleep."

Jenny went down the hall to her bedroom to phone the hospital. "Could you page Dr. Prendeville, please?" she asked the nurse. Jenny thought, It was those long airplane rides with all those people breathing one another's air. But she still felt personally responsible. Harry came on the line at last, and Jenny explained the situation.

"Over in a flash," he said, and hung up.

Jenny waited forty-five minutes for the ibuprofen to take effect, but when she checked Lucy's temperature again it had gone up to 104. Jenny undressed the girl as gently as she could. Lucy's body was almost like that of a boy. Fourteen years old, on the cusp of womanhood. Her breasts were small, her belly concave. But her pubic hair, though wispy, was such a dark brown that it appeared almost black. Her limbs were faintly furred with dark hairs and cabled with muscles and veins that contrasted with the soft feminine appearance she had in clothes.

Jenny wet a washcloth and sponged her all over. Lucy whimpered at the touch of the cold water and shivered violently. But half an hour later her temperature had fallen to 102. Her muscles seemed to convulse now and then as if from a startling dream. Twice she gave a weak cry.

The doorbell rang, and Jenny hurried to let Harry in. He stood in the doorway for a moment, holding a red motorcycle helmet in his arms with the bearing of a knight. Jenny's hair was awry, her face flushed and seamed with worry. She wore a sweatshirt that said, "Point Beer: Not Just for Breakfast Anymore," along with battered old jeans and filthy jogging shoes.

Harry cracked a smile and observed, "Basic black and a string of pearls. Very elegant. I'd reconsider the shoes, though." Jenny pulled a face and turned toward the kitchen with a squeak of her heel. Harry put his helmet on the oak island in the middle of the room and sat on one of the stools. He was a tall man in his fifties with salt-and-pepper hair and a sad smile. He looked as if he'd slept in his clothes. A stethoscope dangled out of his jacket pocket. He'd probably forgotten that it was there. But he was the best diagnostician that Jenny had ever met and a kind and thoughtful soul. It was Harry who had helped her to get to Congo in the first place.

Ever since Jenny was in grade school, she had intended to

become a registered nurse. She met Harry while doing an internship after graduating from college. She was twenty-two, and Harry was a passionate doctor in his mid-thirties. He swept her off her feet. He had the most piercing hazel-colored eyes. Sometimes he'd just train his eyes on Jenny and she could feel her knees begin to buckle. And for a rumpled intellectual he cut a very romantic figure. He owned a small airplane and on weekends in the fall, he'd perform operations all day, then hop in his plane, fly to New York, and attend the opera. He took Jenny with him once and she felt like the queen of Manhattan.

Then she discovered the bonobos in the Milwaukee Zoo and changed course. She entered graduate school in biological anthropology. At the time, Harry was going to central Africa once a year to perform surgery on children for Doctors Without Borders. He'd sometimes be on his feet eighteen hours a day. Jenny thought he was a god and was relieved that he didn't take himself too seriously. He referred to the odd multinational collection of physicians as "Doctors Without Licenses." He took Jenny to Sudan as his assistant one summer. When they were finished, he introduced her to David Meece and she made her way down to Congo to see bonobos in the wild for the first time. By then Harry and Jenny had bonded permanently. They had tried but could never quite kindle a romance, especially with both of their busy schedules. But she could always count on him. It was Harry who had wired the money to get Jenny and Lucy out of England. As they stood in the kitchen now, Jenny told herself, You were a fool not to marry him. You could have had children. But that was long ago.

"We couldn't really talk when I was driving you home from the airport," Harry said. "I mean, she was right there in the car. But what on earth were you thinking, bringing her here? Have you lost your mind?"

"I couldn't throw her in an orphanage, Harry. I rescued her. I brought her out of the jungle. And then it was like with those girls at the shelter. I had to help."

Harry let his shoulders drop. "Well, you're right, of course. You have a good heart, Jenny. Maybe too good for your own good." He took her in his arms and rubbed her shoulder. He found a spot and scratched. "You still itch there in the mornings?"

"Yes." She felt like a little girl in his arms.

"I'm just glad you're safe. I hope you'll stick around a while. Not planning on going back there, I hope."

"Take a look at her, will you? Go make yourself useful and be a doctor."

"Yes, of course. I'll run some tests. Make sure she doesn't have Ebola or something lovely like that."

"Hey. You're the one who took me to Africa."

"Not Congo. Congo is different. Dart of Harkness, it is." And he vaulted up the stairs two at a time.

Lucy seemed to be sleeping more peacefully. Harry rummaged in his pockets for a flashlight, then pulled back her eyelids and shined the LED into her pupils. He looked in her throat and ears, listened to her lungs and heart with his stethoscope. "Clear lungs," he said. "Strong heart." Then he drew two vials of blood. Lucy didn't flinch.

When they had returned to the kitchen Harry said, "There's something very peculiar about that girl."

"Like what?"

"I can't say. Just a sense I get. Her eyes are strange. Her skin is different. Her hair. She smells funny, too. Has she bathed?"

"Yes, of course." Jenny had noticed it, too.

"Well, I'm going to run these over to the lab."

"You're a saint."

"I'm a doctor. Don't fret. Her vital signs are good. She probably just has the flu."

Yes, Jenny thought, as she watched Harry go: It's probably just the flu.

5

JENNY SLEPT ON A PAD at the foot of Lucy's bed. She took her temperature twice in the night, and the second time it was normal. Relieved, she slept soundly after that. Now she thought she was dreaming. She heard a beautiful voice singing in Italian. She luxuriated in the sound, the sleep, and then with a start, she was awake. The lilies were in bloom, and their aroma reached her on the breeze. She sat up and saw that Lucy's bed was empty.

> Quando me'n vo' soletta per la via,
> La gente sosta e mira
> E la bellezza mia tutta ricerca . . .
> ricerca in me,
> Da capo a pie' . . .

Jenny rose and followed the voice down the hall and into her own bedroom. She went to the open window and looked out into the garden. Lucy sang sadly while picking strawberries from the bushes that grew against the fence. She wore not a stitch of clothes. With a gasp, Jenny grabbed her robe and ran downstairs. She hurried out and down the stone path, calling out in a cheerful voice, "Good morning, Lucy!"

"Good morning." Jenny wrapped the robe around Lucy's shoulders. "Do I have to wear clothes even in the garden?"

"Yes, dear, you do. Sorry. I know it's silly. I wish it weren't so. But we're not in the rain forest anymore. The neighbors wouldn't understand."

"Why do people live so close together?"

"I think greed is the answer. People bought the land, divided it up, and sold it."

"Wouldn't you rather live in the forest?"

"Yes, I guess I would. But I teach at the university, and it would take too long to get there. And then my mother gave me this house. She got old and couldn't handle it anymore. So here I am."

Lucy gazed at the sky. "Those are airplanes? Like the ones we were in?"

Jenny followed her gaze and saw the tic-tac-toe of contrails from the airliners passing overhead. "Yes. Exactly."

"They've put the sky in a cage."

"You're right. They have put the sky in a cage." Jenny tied the sash on the orange robe. "I'm so happy to see you up and about. Come on, Lucy. Let's go in and get something to eat."

Lucy sighed, "Oh, all right." So like a normal teenager: Exasperated.

They went back up the stone walkway among the prairie grasses and toward the kitchen. A few minutes later, Jenny was making oatmeal.

"Lucy. What were you doing in that tree? Did you make that nest?"

"Yes. I made it."

"Why? How?" Jenny recalled the moment when she'd first seen it. She had been reaching for an image in her mind, but the urgency of the situation had prevented her from completing the thought. What was it?

"I slept like that sometimes. In the forest. I was afraid of the cats, and it was safer up there. I learned a lot of things like that from the bonobos."

The bonobos, Jenny thought. Of course. They made nests like that each night and slept in the trees. It would make sense that Lucy had learned to do the same, growing up in the jungle. With Dr. Stone's feeding station, the bonobos were always nearby.

"Want to eat outside?" Jenny asked.

"That sounds delightful. I'll take things out."

They sat at a wrought iron table under the maple. Lucy drenched her oatmeal in honey from a pot that Jenny's mother had given her. It had a picture of Winnie-the-Pooh on it.

"May I please have one of your bananas?"

"Certainly, Lucy. I want you to feel at home. Take whatever you like."

Lucy went back into the kitchen and returned with a banana. She sat and bit the end off without peeling it.

"Lucy, what are you doing?" Lucy looked up, puzzled, her mouth full. "Don't you peel them?"

Chewing self-consciously now, Lucy shook her head, uncertain. She swallowed. "Sorry. That's how we all did it at home."

"No, it's quite all right. I was just thinking . . . Maybe wash it first . . . Never mind."

But Lucy was no longer paying attention to Jenny. She was staring intently at a squirrel that was sitting on a branch, screeching. "There's a big hawk up there."

"Really?"

"I don't see it yet. But listen."

Jenny shrugged it off, thinking only that Lucy had learned to be especially alert in the jungle. She watched Lucy as she listened and ate with such intensity. At the shelter, Jenny had seen a few teenage girls with such an air of fierce concentration. But Lucy was so gentle and kind and innocent seeming, unlike some of the girls at the shelter, who could turn violent in a heartbeat.

Jenny heard the squirrel crying, "Caw! Caw! Caw!" And as she watched, Lucy turned her gaze on Jenny. Those eyes. It wasn't quite like the feeling she had when Harry looked at her, into her, but it was equally powerful.

"What?"

"I hope we don't have to go to any stores today."

She said it with such earnestness that Jenny turned away, her lips pursed over a smile. "No. No, we don't. We'll just take it easy today. But I have some work to do, so you'll have to entertain yourself."

"I saw that vampire series, *Twilight*, on the shelf in your living room. May I please read those? Papa said that was trash. He always wanted me to read intellectual things. But I want to read trash, too."

"Of course. You should consider this your home until we find your family." And Lucy gave Jenny that pained look again. As Jenny was trying to read into it, the phone rang.

"Listen, doll," Harry began, "the girl is clear of any infections that we could find with lab tests."

"Yeah, she seems a hundred percent this morning. Thanks for being such a champ and getting that done. I owe you one."

"You'll have to let me think about how to collect on that."

"You do that."

"Gotta run. Illness beckons."

"Goodbye, Harry." Jenny turned to Lucy. "Harry says you're okay."

"I feel better. A little tired."

"So I'm going to clean up these dishes and then do some paperwork."

"I'll clean up. You can go work."

"That would be great. Just ask if there's anything you want. I'll be in my study."

Jenny had turned a sunroom into an office. She loved the bright light, the lush green of the garden, bursting now with pink and yellow hollyhocks. She had planted local vegetation and let it grow naturally after her mother had moved to an apartment. Great heavy tree limbs plunged down to the earth, and a flowering hedge towered ten feet tall. A high cedar fence to the east added privacy. Her mother had been horrified at what Jenny had done with the garden.

"You've turned my nice backyard into your own private jungle," she had said more than once. "Don't you get enough of that in Africa? Well, it's your house now."

Jenny smiled, musing about her mother and turned to her desk. She found her backpack where she'd dropped it by the window that first day. Even after they were safely home, Jenny had felt shaky from the experience. She had been through two wars in Congo, the first in 1996, then again in 1998. She had missed several years of research because the Hutus and Tutsis were busy killing what would eventually amount to five million people. But most of the fighting was to the north and west of where Jenny worked. It wasn't until the last outbreak that she'd actually come under fire.

She lifted her bag and sat at her desk. Her father's big antique Shelbyville. She'd always thought of the desk as a part of her father. He had died when she was ten, and afterward, she would sit in his chair with her head on his desk and smell the oiled wood. She still used the same oil.

She opened her pack with a heavy heart. She knew that in all likelihood she wouldn't be going back to Congo again, and she already missed the rolling green hills, so green that the color seemed impossible beneath an exploding cobalt sky with clouds scudding along like great white schooners.

The first thing she saw when she opened her pack was the photograph that she'd salvaged from Stone's hut. Even in her panic, she had thought that the girl might want the photograph. It showed Stone down on one knee with his arm around Lucy, who was about ten years old. They were both smiling. He had a rugged face, craggy but kind. He had bright eyes, a nice smile, a mischievous look. Lucy's great mane of curly hair engulfed her small face. But she had the same intense smile that Jenny had come to know. She set the frame on the desk.

She pulled her chair closer to the desk and felt her foot touch something. She looked down. When she saw Stone's backpack, she had a thought and bent to unfasten the top. The pack contained the notebooks she'd collected. She had no idea what he'd been doing all those years while he was studying bonobos. He hadn't published in twenty-five years. He didn't even have a university affiliation any longer. He was quirky and shy, polite to a fault, yet difficult to get to know. The last of his family had left him money, and Stone had given up writing grant proposals. Maybe his notes would hold some clue that could lead them to a relative of Lucy's mother.

They were small orange sketchbooks, about four by six inches, numbered and dated. She removed a few from the backpack. They smelled of the naphthalene that he'd used to prevent them from rotting in the jungle. She flipped through a couple of them. The text was densely lettered in pencil in a small but neat hand. She laid them out on the big wooden desk and arranged them in chronological order. Then she went to refill her coffee cup.

Jenny tiptoed through the kitchen, noticing that Lucy had done a good job of cleaning up. She went to the front hall and peeked into the living room. Lucy was lying on her stomach on the floor in a shaft of sunlight, still wearing the orange robe. Her bare feet were in the air and she was twiddling her toes as she read one of the popular books about vampires. She glanced up and smiled at Jenny, then went back to her reading. Jenny thought, She's perfect in every way. Nothing strange about her at all. And she does chores. Jenny knew already that she would miss Lucy when she returned to England.

She went back to her study and sat in her favorite chair in a sunny corner. She opened the first notebook, begun more than a quarter century before, and read, "I will not attempt here to give a reason for undertaking this project. That is more of a philosophical task and one more appropriate to another time and place, if not perhaps another author. For now I will only recount what I do and how well or badly it goes. In any event, if all goes well, my children will speak for me, as I will instruct them in who they are and why they are here."

She paused, curious about the tone and vagueness of Stone's notes. What did he mean, "this project"? What project? This certainly didn't seem like the conventional field notes of a scientist. But she recognized in it the polite and cordial tone he'd always adopted when speaking with her on the radio: Yes, I must have you over for tea very soon . . .

She read on: "Having thoroughly investigated interspecific hybrids, I have no doubt that what I plan to undertake is physiologically possible even without the extraordinary preparations I have made. There is now convincing evidence that even after chimpanzees and humans diverged from each other genetically some six million years ago, they continued to breed and produce hybrids (see Prager and Wilson, 1975). With modern biogenetic techniques, there seemed no theoretical barrier to returning to a condition in which interspecific breeding would be possible."

She felt a morbid thrill at the thought: I hope he's not talking about what it sounds like he's talking about. She turned back to the notebook, alert and slightly alarmed as well.

"Indeed," Stone wrote, "the genetic structures of human and bonobo are more alike than those of horse and donkey, which can breed to produce a mule. And healthy hybrid individuals have been born through a cross between bonobos and chimpanzees as well.

The many similarities are well detailed elsewhere. The key, in my view, was to first create a hybrid karyotype by inserting fragments of human chromosome material into the genome of the bonobo. This would ensure, for example, that the CMP-sialic acid hydroxylase gene was deactivated and that the retrotransposon subfamilies of LINE-1 nuclear elements known as L1Hs were present. It would also overcome any potential incompatibility between mother and fetus due to antigenic sugars on the surface of the cells.

"Therefore, employing conventional gene-splicing techniques, I managed to produce a live female bonobo, Leda, whose genetic profile was even closer to that of a human being than naturally born bonobos."

Jenny felt a chill run over her. "No," she said aloud. She must be misunderstanding what he was talking about. She read on, her heart racing with excitement.

"Leda is in every way morphologically indistinguishable from an ordinary bonobo, including her body hair, genitals, lack of speech, dark-hued sclera, and so on. And yet I have brought her just slightly closer to the human genotype so that, in my view, she should be more likely to produce a 'virtually human' child, that is, one who looks and thinks and talks like a human but who has certain of the advantageous features conferred by the bonobo genome."

"Oh, man, this is nuts," Jenny heard herself say. She felt the hair stand up on her arms and neck as she wondered, Could this be a hoax? A scientist who'd fallen into obscurity, out to grab the spotlight for himself? Was he planning to publish this and create a sensation? Of course. That must be it. Or was this perhaps the ranting of some heart-of-darkness lunatic who'd gone mad out there in the bush? Jenny knew that anything was possible in Congo. But Stone certainly hadn't looked or acted mad when she'd met him.

Then again, others who were presumably not insane had actually attempted it. Jenny vaguely knew the details from a class about AIDS that she'd taken as a graduate student. A biologist named Ilya Ivanovich Ivanov was sent by the Russian Academy of Sciences to Africa in 1926. The purpose of his trip was to inseminate female chimpanzees with human sperm. The effort had been supported by the Institut Pasteur in Paris, which kept captive chimpanzees at Kindia in what was then French Guinea. Ivanov, who pioneered the techniques of artificial insemination, had already done extensive work creating hybrid animals when he introduced the idea of a human hybrid at the International Zoology Congress that was being held at Graz in 1910. In fact, Ivanov ultimately did inseminate three chimpanzees, but none of them became pregnant. It was an ugly time, in which local hunters killed chimpanzee parents and brought the children to the scientists at Kindia. The researchers were unaware that it took chimpanzees eight or ten years to reach puberty. Once Ivanov had realized his mistake and obtained mature females, the brutal procedures he used to inseminate them were likened to rape by later researchers. His failure to impregnate any of the female chimpanzees led him to ask for permission to inseminate human women with chimpanzee sperm in a hospital in Congo—without informing them of what was being done. Although there's no evidence in the literature that the women were actually inseminated with sperm from an ape, the AIDS pandemic was genetically traced to west equatorial Africa and first appeared in humans around 1931. Before that, the HIV virus was found exclusively in apes. The grad school professor who taught the course that Jenny took believed there was a connection.

In the period from the early 1900s through the 1920s, several European scientists attempted to create a human-ape hybrid. In Russia, biologists even organized the Commission on Interspecific Hybridization of Primates to oversee the job of making a human-ape baby. Indeed, among scientists on both sides of the Atlantic, there seemed to be no strong objection to the idea at that time. More recently, in the 1970s, J. Michael Bedford had shown that a human sperm could penetrate a female ape's ovum under laboratory conditions. Jenny thought it was an interesting concept. But the more rational part of her, the scientist, said, No. No one would do that today, because of all the ethical issues involved. Besides, no one would have a scientific reason to do it. What could be gained? There must be another explanation.

Jenny dove back into the text with her mind racing. She skimmed until she found what she was looking for: "In light of that, I raised up Leda, the genetically modified bonobo, to the age of maturity and began my first experiment March 3 three years ago, inseminating her with my own materials using a mild sedative to keep her calm and employing the conventional method of artificial insemination that has been proven effective in captive populations." Jenny heard herself groan out loud. The words swam on the page. For at the same time that she was fascinated with the concept, she felt her whole body revolt at the idea. And she was acutely aware of Lucy as the living, breathing child with whom she had just had breakfast. She wiped her eyes to clear them and read, "The process failed again and again, producing no results at all until the summer before last, when I inseminated her for the ninth time on June sixteenth and succeeded in producing a zygote. The child, a male, came nearly to full term but was badly deformed and had to be destroyed."

Oh, no, Jenny thought: He killed a deformed baby. Could this be real? It must be a hoax. Or else he must have been mad. Jenny was standing now, pacing her study, her heart pounding. She felt queasy as she read, "After another four failed attempts, the following insemination produced a pregnancy beginning in August of last year. Lucy was born without incident April fifth of this year, weighing 2.7 kilograms."

"Oh, God," Jenny said. "Oh, no."

It all made sense now. All the odd behavior, the nest in the tree, the girl's superior strength. The crazy outbursts. Her keen senses . . . All at once, Jenny's scientific curiosity fell away and her heart went out to the girl. Jenny felt herself flooded with emotions. She was angry at Stone, his megalomania, his lack of empathy. She was fearful for Lucy and what would come. She was fascinated as a scientist at the prospect of learning about someone who was half bonobo. And at the same time she was trying to figure out all the implications of the situation that she and Lucy were now in. For all at once Jenny recognized that she was deep in, too. Perhaps well over her head.

She read on, her stomach churning. "I examined the child thoroughly at birth and found her to be normal in every way and completely human in appearance. This proved one of the main points of my experiment, to wit, that humans can be moved into a more favorable spot in the evolutionary matrix, a position in which we may enjoy some of the superior qualities of our bonobo cousins. That gives me hope that by this means, a new race of people, more like the bonobo but with human intelligence and language—therefore better suited to living in harmony with nature—can gradually evolve, beginning with this lineage, which I hereby bequeath to the future."

"He went mad," Jenny said. That was the only explanation. Whether he was telling the truth or not, he clearly went stark raving mad. Maybe there's a real human mother somewhere and Stone himself was simply schizophrenic. Lucy seemed like such a normal girl in most ways. Maybe this was Stone's psychotic fantasy world.

But at the same time, Jenny knew that modern genetic engineering could indeed make it possible. Stone really might have created a human-bonobo hybrid. And if he did, then the result of his experiment was in the living room reading *Twilight* by Stephenie Meyer.

With hands shaking and her mouth dry, Jenny skimmed quickly through the sections concerning Lucy's early childhood, nursing, and then the rapid, vaulting progress of a living child. When Lucy was four months old, Stone flew with her to London to obtain a passport: the one that Jenny had taken from Stone's cabin.

A year later Stone noted, "Lucy is definitely a bipedal creature and shows every sign of normal language development in so far as is appropriate to her age."

Flipping through the pages, Jenny read lists of the words that Lucy was saying, such as Leda, Papa, book and ball, and "nana" for banana. There was a discourse on Stone's attempts to balance his human upbringing of Lucy with allowing Leda to take her into the forest and teach her the ways of her cousins, half siblings (for Leda subsequently gave birth to babies by bonobo fathers), and other relations there. Year by year, he laid out Lucy's progress.

Around the time that she was four years old, Stone apparently began to have a crisis of conscience. "Lucy has become a whole and genuine person," he wrote. "I now recognize that what I did with all good intentions may turn out to be the most monstrous folly. What I conceived of in the passion of my youth as the salvation of the bonobos—and perhaps of mankind—may simply be the worst sort of punishment for this lovely child, who has come into this cruel world through no fault of her own." So, Jenny thought, he could at least feel remorse. Perhaps he wasn't a monster.

Stone went on, as if explaining to himself how he could have come to do such a thing. It had all begun with his passion for the bonobos and his certainty that people were going to drive those marvelous creatures to extinction. The only way to save them, he believed, or some of their best qualities, was to selectively breed them with humans. Although he saw their extinction as inevitable, at least part of their unique and brilliant character might be preserved if he could safely lock the bonobo genes inside humans. "Their extraordinary sweetness and perceptiveness had stolen my heart from the beginning," he wrote. And Jenny began to see it another way: Perhaps he had not been such a madman. Perhaps Stone was a brilliant primatologist faced with the impending extinction of a beautiful creature to whom he had devoted his life. Jenny had had similar feelings about bonobos. It was what had drawn her back to the jungle year after year despite the dangers. Of course, it had never occurred to her to do what Stone did. She had never even thought through the details as he had. It was just too far-fetched.

Over the years Stone seemed to vacillate between breast beating and trying to justify himself: "I understand that what I have done will seem beyond the pale to some. But to that charge—and to history—I have this to say: Humankind has destroyed most species with which it has come into contact and is rapidly destroying itself. Something must change in human nature. And I offer Lucy as proof to the world that, even though the ethics of what I've done may be questioned, the results are unequivocal. Anyone who meets this fascinating, intelligent, and beautiful girl will have to marvel at her, no matter the means of her creation. Lucy, in short, is the best argument in my defense. The way she has blended human intelligence with a bonobo's ability to process the richness of sensory signals from The Stream, along with her gentle and loving social instincts, prove that I was right: Lucy is love made manifest. And as her offspring and their offspring continue to reproduce, a new kind of human—more human than human—will evolve."

Jenny felt a bizarre blend of admiration and revulsion as she realized that Donald Stone had deliberately brought this sweet, intelligent girl into the world for the purpose, in effect, of breeding. Much as he seemed to love the bonobos and her, there was something twisted and indecent in what he had done, even if, as he said, the result was unequivocally noble and beautiful. And then this thought entered Jenny's mind: They're going to kill her if they find out. The right-wing religious nuts. The media. The government busybodies. The crackpots and cranks and white-power mobs. How would she ever manage to protect Lucy if word got out?

There were many other notebooks, but Jenny was too over-wrought to read them. She flipped through the last one and saw this scrawled in a shaky hand on a single sheet in the middle of an otherwise blank book: "Lucy, forgive me."

Jenny paced her study, trying to think through all the implications. What had Stone done? What had Jenny herself done by bringing Lucy here? She turned to find the girl staring at her from the doorway.

"I sensed a disturbance in The Stream. I thought I'd see if you were all right. I hope you didn't catch my flu."

And in that moment, Jenny felt that she had all the proof she needed. What she'd just read was real. The Stream. Of course. Stone himself had talked of it. It's the way that all animals communicate. Jenny had sometimes felt it herself in the jungle. But as a product of American culture, she was inclined to dismiss it.

Her swirling emotions overtook her now, and Jenny felt a wave of love for this girl, a powerful urge to protect her from what was coming. But could she do it? Could Lucy be protected in this world? Unable to control herself at the sight of Lucy, Jenny burst into tears.

Lucy crossed the distance between them and pressed Jenny into her arms, patting her gently on the back as one might do with a child who has fallen. Lucy's head barely came up to Jenny's breasts. So small. So vulnerable. Yet so powerful. Jenny felt Lucy's energy surging through her. She now believed what Stone had written. Lucy was real. And she knew that she mustn't let anyone find out. She must protect the girl at all costs.

"What's wrong? What's wrong?" But Jenny couldn't speak and simply let her tears flow. The room was suffused with sunlight. The squirrel was still in the tree, screeching about the hawk.

6

LUCY'S FIRST THOUGHT WAS that she had made Jenny sick. But then her eyes fell on her father's notebooks scattered around the chair, and she understood. Lucy had completely forgotten that Jenny had taken the notebooks from the camp. Now Jenny stood on the brink with Lucy, and all the evidence that she'd been ignoring flooded in on her in one great wave. Lucy held Jenny in her arms as she wept briefly. Then Jenny gathered herself and held Lucy at arm's length to study her.

"Why didn't you tell me?"

"I'm sorry. I didn't know how."

"Of course. Of course." Jenny let go of Lucy and turned, taking a few steps toward the window. She turned back and said, "With the attack, the murders—it was too crazy for me to think clearly. Not that I would have believed you anyway. Oh, wow, I just don't know what this means yet. I'm afraid for you, Lucy."

"Papa warned me that people wouldn't believe. Or that if they did they'd want to destroy me. He also said that there would be good ones. Good humans. I sensed that you wouldn't care that I'm not human."

"You are human. You're as human as I am. You're no different than if you had . . . I don't know. Some other genetic difference. An albino is different. There are all kinds of people. You're human," Jenny repeated, as if trying to convince herself. "You're human."

"It's okay, Jenny. I know what I am. I'm something completely new. Papa made sure that I had no illusions about how people might react."

"This is real, right? It's not some sort of hoax?"

"It's real."

"Then that was your mother? The dead bonobo in the hut?"

"Yes. Leda."

"I'm sorry."

"I know."

"What was the plan? I mean, I'm trying to get my mind around this. What was your father's ultimate plan for you? What on earth was he thinking? He talked about breeding, like you were some sort of prize animal. How could he do this to you?" Jenny looked as if she might begin to weep again, but she held back her tears. "Why would someone do this to a child?"

"We were supposed to move to London next year. He'd been grooming me for this my whole life. I was to go to college in England. People would be told that Papa had lost his wife to a disease in Congo. Papa's idea was that I would be the universal Eve for a new race of people."

"So you were supposed to have children?"

"Yes. Assuming that I could get pregnant. That was always a question. It still is. But if I could, then I'd raise my children to be leaders, teachers, thinkers. They would have children . . . and so on."

"Breeding . . . He created you to breed. Oh, God."

"Yes, that. But also because Papa loved bonobos. They would be spared extinction, at least in part. Papa envisioned a new race coming into its own in perhaps as little as a thousand years, because they would have the advantage of a material culture that had already been invented. And language."

Jenny sat heavily in her chair and looked down into her lap, breathing in and out. She gave a shuddering sigh. Then she looked up and stared at Lucy. "Do you understand how crazy this is?"

"No, not really. It's all I've ever known. It was always the plan. I knew that he felt a lot of guilt in the end. I wasn't sure exactly why."

"Lucy. I'm sorry. But to take another human being and—" Jenny stopped herself and gestured. "We'll talk about this more as time goes on. But that plan, his plan . . ." She took a deep breath. "Just let's wait until you've become a bit more used to things outside the jungle."

"What will we do now? Are you going to send me away?"

"No, no, of course not. I can't. I mean, I brought you here." Jenny thought for a moment and then fixed her eyes on the girl. "Then you really don't have any family in England, right?"

"No. My family's in the jungle. I'm a humanzee."

"Where did you hear that word?"

"It was in one of Papa's books. Half human, half pygmy chimpanzee."

"Don't ever call yourself that. You're a person." Jenny hugged herself as if she were cold. Bands of yellow sunlight lay hot across her knees. "I just have to think and plan. You can't go to England. You obviously can't go back to Congo."

Lucy took a step and stood before her chair. Jenny raised her head and they looked at each other for a long time. "I'm afraid, Jenny. I'm afraid of what you'll do now that you know. You're a scientist. What if you think and plan and then you decide that the best place for me is in somebody's laboratory?"

Jenny took Lucy's hands and firmly pulled her down until she was kneeling. Jenny's sandy-red hair hung around her face in great cascades of curls. "I would never do that. I would never do anything to harm you. I'm in a bit of shock, that's all. Lucy, I promise you this: I won't abandon you. I'll take care of you. But we have to think ahead in case the truth comes out."

"All right. I trust you, Jenny."

Jenny stood with a sigh. Lucy sat back on her heels on the African carpet and watched as Jenny went to the window to look out into the garden. Lucy could feel Jenny's sadness pouring through her.

"Obviously, you'll have to stay here."

"I'm sorry that makes you sad."

Jenny turned to face her. "That doesn't make me sad. You're charming and lovely and I've already grown very fond of you. What makes me sad is thinking about the future and what might happen to you—to us—because I brought you here."

"What will I do here?"

"You'll go to school just like any other teenager. You'll live with me. That's all there is to it." And then brightly: "I could adopt you. You'll be an adult in less than four years. I could adopt you in the meantime."

Lucy felt a thrill at the thought. "You'd do that?"

Jenny thought for a moment and then laughed carelessly, almost crazily. "I can't believe this is happening. Yes, I suppose I would do that. I don't see any other way. You have to stay here now. That will make it official."

Lucy desperately wanted to have a place in the world once more. But she didn't want to ruin Jenny's life. "There will be trouble," she said. "I'm afraid I'll bring you grief somehow."

"How? No one will know."

But Lucy had a sinking feeling. She heard the squirrel calling. The hawk. The hawk is always out there, circling. "Maybe. But then what if someone does find out?"

"That's what we have to plan for." Jenny seemed to be gathering her inner strength. "I have to think. Think this through. But for now we'll just live." She took a deep breath and Lucy could see Jenny trying to think things through logically. "There's no reason that you can't have a normal life. You'll go to school and make friends. I will adopt you. You'll become an American citizen. We'll go to the beach and have parties and take trips and see new places." And then more enthusiastically: "Let's take a trip before the school year begins. That'll give us time to think. We'll go up to the Boundary Waters. It's old forest. Not like Congo, but I think you'll like it."

"I'm certain I will if you say so, Jenny."

Jenny took Lucy's hands and gave her a hard look. Then a look of surprise crossed her face. "Oh, no. I just had a thought."

"What?"

"Harry has your blood. He's got your DNA."

"What will he do with it?"

"Nothing, I would think. He has no reason to. Anyway, he's a dear friend. But it's over there in the hospital. I'd better get it back just in case."

Jenny picked up the phone and paged Harry. Outside the window silence had fallen. The hawk had taken the squirrel. The only sound was the ticking of the clock on Jenny's desk. Then the phone rang, and Jenny asked Harry to bring the blood samples to her, saying, "No, no. She's fine," and, "I'll explain later." Lucy noticed the photograph on the desk and picked it up. She remembered the day it was taken. One of the men who brought supplies upriver took it with a new digital camera. He had brought them the print on his next trip. Lucy felt a wave of love for Jenny for having the presence of mind, the heart, to salvage it for her.

That evening the doorbell rang. Lucy watched from the stairs as Jenny opened the front door. Harry came in carrying a red motorcycle helmet and a plastic bag.

"So what's this all about?" He seemed too large for the entryway, a broad handsome man in disheveled clothes.

"I'll explain later."

"Is she okay?"

"She's fine, Harry. Let's talk later."

"Jenny, come on, it's me, Harry. What's going on?"

"Harry, love, be a dear and let me tell you about this later, okay?"

"What-ever," he said in an odd, high voice as he turned to leave.

"Hey." Jenny grabbed his coat sleeve. Harry turned back, stared down at her, and then they embraced. "Thanks," she said.

When he left at last, Jenny leaned against the door, threw her head back, and rolled her eyes at the ceiling as if shutting out a storm. Then she climbed the stairs past Lucy and went into the bathroom. Lucy followed her and came to the door just in time to see Jenny washing her blood down the sink with trembling hands.

7

ONE MORNING, they were eating breakfast at the wrought iron table on the patio, beneath a green umbrella in the shade of the maple. The sun was high, and a contrail was growing longer in the eastern sky. Another squirrel was screaming in the trees.

"You talked about The Stream and the squirrel warning you about the hawk," Jenny said. "Tell me about that."

"It's just our language. How we communicate. All the animals. We're all in The Stream."

Lucy recognized that in some ways she was a scientist's dream come true. Her father had told her that this might put her in grave danger if she fell into the wrong hands. Lucy didn't mind the questions. Indeed, she had as many questions for Jenny as Jenny had for her.

"Why do the people have grass around their houses?" Lucy asked. "You can't eat it. And those men come and cut it down so that it never grows long enough to be useful."

"I don't grow grass."

"No, but everyone else does." They had finished eating and were bringing their dishes inside. Lucy held the door for Jenny. "And another thing. Every few days a big roaring truck comes to take our things away, things that might be useful."

"What things?" Jenny crossed to the sink, and Lucy followed.

"All that stuff you buy at the grocery store. You put it all in that container by the alley."

Jenny laughed, running water over the bowls in the sink. "That's garbage."

"But it's all perfectly good stuff. All the boxes that the cereal comes in. Those beautiful plastic containers for the blueberries. It seems so sad to throw it all away. Won't the person who made it be sad?"

Jenny turned to look at Lucy and felt a rush of emotion for the girl. "You're right. It's a deep mystery how we came to live this way."

One night Jenny packed clothes and supplies in duffel bags and stowed them in the back of her beat-up Toyota station wagon. The next morning before dawn they began the drive north. Lucy could hardly believe how vast the city was. It seemed to go on forever. So many people, Lucy thought. Who would have guessed there were so many? All along the highway great signs with photographs on them seemed to scream out at them and the message was always the same: To crave more, to buy more, to have more.

When at last the city ended north of Milwaukee, Jenny drove on through fields of crops. Lucy watched a flock of red-winged blackbirds rise from the fields and grow to such a size that it nearly darkened the sun. It wheeled about in a great vortex and then vanished once again like smoke flowing inexplicably into the green and yellow fire of tasseled corn.

Jenny left the highway and took the back roads. She told Lucy that she preferred them, and Lucy was relieved. The small roads were more human in their scale, and the car traveled more slowly. She saw little towns and trees and real people. They stopped outside of a small town at a dairy farm that made cheese. Lucy thought that the people seemed friendly, a fat woman in a stained and threadbare flowered dress, and a thin gray-haired man in overalls. They had a daughter about Lucy's age who sat fixedly watching a small television set. She didn't even look up to see who had arrived. She was one of the first human teenagers that Lucy had ever observed closely. Lucy wanted to touch her and talk to her but the girl seemed so absorbed that Lucy was afraid to disturb her. Lucy wondered what it felt like to be inside her brain.

Jenny bought cheese and bread and they sat out in a meadow

of clover to eat. The cheese was sweet and sharp with crystals of sugar in it. Lucy lay in the cool grass, which was alive with bees. When they'd finished the cheese and bread, Jenny watched as Lucy dug in the moist earth with her fingers and brought a fresh grub to her lips.

Lucy caught her looking and gave a guilty smile. "Sorry."

"It's okay." Jenny looked away discreetly and Lucy popped it in her mouth.

That afternoon they passed through Duluth. An hour later the old green car plunged into the woods and up a road called the Gunflint Trail. As different as it was from the Congolese jungle, the shaggy old forest made Lucy feel at home. It was dense and cool and hung with moss. The smells and creatures were all very different from what she had known.

They reached the cabin on the edge of a lake at dusk. Inside it was all knotty pine and flowered curtains and a wood-burning stove in the common room. Lucy and Jenny worked side by side in the kitchen, cutting vegetables for soup. That night Lucy slept well for the first time since leaving the jungle. It seemed so long ago now. From her bed she could see the moonlight coming through the shaggy trees and hear the sounds of the forest. There was no unnatural glow, no fog, no sound of machinery.

The cabin was secluded in the woods and the weather was warm. Lucy slept without clothes and didn't bother to dress in the morning. Jenny didn't mind. They both came alive in the woods. They had been missing the forest. Jenny taught Lucy how to paddle the canoe, and together they crossed the lake. A raven came low overhead, cutting the still air with a sound like ripping canvas. In the afternoons Jenny chopped wood or sat in the sun on the deck and drank iced tea and watched Lucy play in the water. In the evenings they read or recited stories and poetry from memory.

Lucy spent long hours exploring. Out in the forest, Lucy returned to The Stream and learned new signals of deer and moose and red fox and timber wolf. Mouse. Rabbit. Eagle. Beaver. She saw few people out there. She had plenty of warning the few times that she did see people, because they made so much noise. Lucy could easily slip up a tree and then continue her explorations when they'd passed. Lucy thought: They would make easy prey.

But without realizing it, Lucy was lulled into complacency.

Not all people were alike. She was taken by surprise by a quiet one. By the time she realized it, a boy of perhaps twelve had sneaked up to within sight of her. She caught only a glimpse of him. He had a camera around his neck. Lucy bolted and was gone in a second but the incident worried her. She was more cautious for the rest of the trip and was not caught out again.

One night the weather turned cool, and Jenny and Lucy put on sweaters and built a fire on the shore and sat eating grapes and watching the constellations rise and the satellites arc overhead toward the north. Lucy listened to the crickets talking about what had happened that day and the day before and during their long history on earth. They had very high voices but Lucy could slow them down and understand. They sounded like a choir singing Gregorian chants. Her father had taught her: The crickets collect their memories and sing about them. They talk so much because they have so much to say. Some birds do that, too, and Lucy liked to sit out in the morning and listen to them reminisce about the days of the dinosaurs.

One night when they were sitting on the shore after dinner, Lucy asked Jenny where she was from. "You now know much more about me than I know about you."

"Oh, it's pretty boring. I grew up in the house where we live. My mother's house. Of course, it was once my father's house, but he died when I was still in grade school so I always thought of it as my mother's."

"So we both lost a father at an early age. I'm sorry. How did he die?"

"He had a heart attack. As I grew up I realized that I hadn't really gotten to know him very well. He was a lawyer. He and my mother had me late in life. He was very successful but that meant that he was also gone a lot. Trial lawyer. Then he was gone altogether."

"What do you think is going to happen to us?"

"I'll teach at the university, I guess. Write some more papers. Volunteer at the shelter."

"Shelter?"

"Yeah. It's a place for girls who've been abused and have nowhere to go."

"What do you mean abused?"

"Beaten. Raped. Or just girls who happen to be homeless, because their parents aren't around."

"Like me."

Jenny looked at Lucy, and her lips tightened into a sad smile. "No. That place isn't for you. I want you to grow up with me. Go to college. Find something in life that you really want to do."

They sat with their heads angled toward each other, near the fire. Jenny's face was regal in the sharp shadows. Lucy's face was vulpine, her eyes gleaming out of the cave made by her hair.

"You know what I think?" Lucy asked.

"What?"

"That someone's going to take me away to a laboratory and do experiments on me."

"I won't let that happen. I will never let them take you. Never." She sat for a time letting that sink in. "Besides, no one will ever know. As far as anyone will know, you're just an American girl."

A few days later they were on their way home. They stopped at the grocery store in Duluth to buy snacks for the road. They were coming out of the store eating Cheetos, and Jenny was reading the ingredients on the bag. "I should be arrested for letting you eat this junk."

"Why? They're good."

"Oh, well, I guess it's in the orange food group."

As they passed a coin box that sold newspapers, they both stopped to stare. "Local Teen Reignites Big Foot Debate," the headline read. They studied the blurry image of a creature in the forest running away from the camera. It was taken from the back, but both Jenny and Lucy recognized it for what it was.

"I'm sorry. He sneaked up on me."

Jenny put her arm around Lucy and directed her back toward the car, glancing around as if everyone must already know. As they drove away, Jenny said softly, "We have to be very careful now, Lucy. We can't let things like this happen anymore."

8

EVEN AFTER THEY RETURNED from the north woods, Jenny was still trying to get her mind around who Lucy was. She kept going over and over their time together, all the clues that she had ignored or had written off as the oddities of a girl who had been raised in the jungle. Of course, anyone would have done the same simply because the truth was so unthinkable. But by the time they were home, Jenny had begun to recognize a few undeniable truths about their situation. Jenny understood that her own inability to see what Lucy was, despite the clues, would work in their favor. Even the story in the Duluth newspaper told her something about the way people think. When people encountered Lucy, so bright, so pretty, and in some ways such a normal teenager, the truth would be the farthest thing from their minds.

So it was that Jenny began the process of getting Lucy settled in her new life. They went to the high school and explained Lucy's situation, an orphaned child from Africa, whom Jenny planned to adopt. The people at the school welcomed them generously. There would be tests, they said, since she had been schooled at home. Jenny began to think that things were going to work out. Lying in bed late at night, she'd tell herself over and over: Lucy's a teenager, Lucy's a regular teenager. Jenny would fall asleep repeating that mantra and wake from a dream of Lucy barking at an escalator in a mall while shoppers pointed and screamed like something out of *Invasion of the Body Snatchers.*

At the same time, Jenny wracked her brain for some sort of strategy they might adopt if they were ever found out. Should they run? Harry had a farm in the Wisconsin woods. Should she tell him the truth so that they could plan to go there?

She recognized that her true situation was so complicated that it was virtually unknown legal territory. She could assert her rights as a parent, but that might be legally invalid if the authorities found out that Lucy was only half human. And what rights would Lucy have? Could Jenny be liable under the laws against importing great apes? Did the Convention on International Trade in Endangered Species mean that it had been a crime to bring Lucy out of Africa? Could they then take Lucy away? Those were the thoughts that preoccupied her during those first weeks.

Jenny was going to file the adoption papers the next day and begin the process of Lucy's naturalization. That night Jenny and Lucy sat in the living room reading. Lucy sat on the couch with her legs crossed beneath her and thumbed through a big book of art.

"Oh, look at this," Lucy said.

Lucy brought the book to Jenny and showed her a print of ballet dancers by Degas. "Isn't it beautiful?"

"I love that painting."

"Don't you wish you could actually see the real painting someday?"

"I can. I have. We'll be downtown tomorrow. We can have lunch there."

"Where?"

"The Art Institute. That's where all those paintings are. Look." Jenny closed the book and showed Lucy the cover. It was a book of paintings from the collection at the Art Institute of Chicago.

Lucy's eyes grew wide. "Oh, my, oh, my. You mean we can really see the real paintings?"

Jenny laughed. "Yes, dear, we can. We will. Tomorrow. I'm going to bed now." Jenny considered telling her that American teenagers don't say, "Oh, my, oh, my," but thought better of it. The kids in school would be teaching her how to talk soon enough.

. . .

There was a place where the elevated commuter train plunged into the earth and then accelerated forcefully through a dark tunnel that was illuminated only by faint yellow lights that went flickering past. Then the train hit a broad curve and the metal wheels began to howl against the rails, and Lucy began howling along with the wheels and everyone in the el car turned to stare and then looked away and pretended not to notice.

Jenny wasn't sure at first if Lucy was in distress or having fun. Then the track straightened out, the howling stopped, and Lucy turned the most beatific smile on Jenny. What a glorious child she was. They sat grinning at each other, unable to speak, and Jenny saw love in Lucy's eyes, too. For a moment Jenny felt that they were communicating through what Lucy called The Stream. She asked herself how anyone, seeing Lucy, could possibly care what was in her genetic profile. But when Lucy turned to look out the window again, Jenny saw her face in the glass. The distorted reflection rearranged her features slightly, and Jenny was able to see her animal nature more clearly than ever before. She felt a chill of foreboding wash over her.

When they had reached the station and climbed the stairs from underground, Lucy was breathless at the sight of downtown Chicago. The buildings tilting to the sky made her dizzy, and she held on to Jenny, her head thrown back, turning around to see them all. They were like two dancers spinning and laughing in a musical, and people turned to stare.

After filing papers in a drab office, they crossed Michigan Avenue to the Art Institute. Jenny watched as Lucy approached it, eyes wide, mouth open, as someone might approach a great and holy cathedral. As they ascended the stone stairs, Jenny took her arm. "Honey. Now, no loud noises, okay?"

"Okay. I'll try."

When they entered the great hall of Impressionist paintings, Lucy grew very still. She turned slowly around, her eyes alighting on each canvas. Jenny stood beside her waiting. Then Lucy whispered, "These are real, aren't they?"

"Yes. They're real."

Lucy stepped gracefully around the room, her body tensing

and relaxing as she moved and paused. It was as if she were anticipating and then receiving an urgent message from each work of art. Cézanne, Pissarro, Monet, Renoir, Degas, Gauguin . . . She circled the room once, then began again more slowly. Jenny sat on a black bench in the middle of the room and watched. Lucy had none of the giddy distractibility that Jenny had seen in teenagers visiting the museum with school groups. She seemed in full communion with the works of art. After she had circled the room a second time, Lucy came straight across to Jenny almost on tiptoe. She bent down and cupped her hands to whisper, glancing around self-consciously.

"These, these, these . . ."

"What, honey? What is it?"

"These paintings. It's like they're talking to me."

Then she flew across the room and stopped before Degas's *Frieze of Dancers*. She looked at it, into it, for a long time, and then squared up her stance, put her hands to her face, and began to weep softly. Jenny stood and went to put her arm around Lucy's shoulder. She saw that Lucy was peering through her fingers even as she cried.

"Are you okay?"

"Yes, yes. Oh, yes. It's all so beautiful. It's a bit overwhelming, that's all. I think I need to take this a little at a time. Thank you for this wonderful gift you've given me. But can we come back again? Can we please, Jenny?"

"Of course we can."

9

SCHOOL BEGAN ON A COLD and drizzly day. Lucy had tested out of every class. Her father had expected her to go straight to college in London, but the high school suggested that she enter her senior year because of her unusual circumstances. It would give her time to adjust.

She had been apprehensive about the crowds and the noise, but was surprised to find that sitting in the big classrooms surrounded by humans was exhilarating and endlessly fascinating. She had never been in such close quarters with so many people before. She found it strange and initially delightful to be among those frail and delicate creatures, packed into a classroom so tightly that it seemed as if they might reach critical mass and turn to pure energy.

The tile halls of the building echoed with cries and shouts, and as Lucy wove her way through the crowd between classes, she couldn't help thinking how like the forest it was in some ways, the screeching and calling and swinging to and fro. The way the students jockeyed for position and competed for status was no different at all. She watched the top females hold court by the entrance to the cafeteria, grooming one another with light touches and small gestures. They were catered to by a group of favored boys, tan and muscular, who puffed themselves up to seem larger. The top males and females received the most glances, while those who were lower in the hierarchy hung their shoulders and skulked around the periphery or skittered warily away.

Lucy took in all the smells as she passed down the hall on the way to class, the vast palette of chemicals that had been spread around for decades like poison, the dense smell of phthalates from plastics, the sharp odor of aluminum in the deodorants that everyone wore, the sickly sweet cologne, the perfume, and the thousand hair and eye and skin potions, wafting their volatiles past her as she swam through the chemical soup.

As she sat in the classroom, she found the range of communications taking place astonishing. Here at last were creatures who were at home in The Stream, while the adults seemed to have lost track of it. The students were all operating on several planes, as if each person were two or even three people at once. One of them was attending to the teacher and the subject. Or not. Another of them was fashioning a public persona, demonstrating to the crowd who he or she was. Yet another was sending messages all over the room. That's how it was done in the forest.

Dana—that was the name of a girl to Lucy's left and slightly in front of her—was telling Jonah, a boy with black hair, how much she loved him. Quinn was signaling the teacher that he hadn't done his homework. Jonah was trying to ignore Dana and was simultaneously sending snickering messages to his friend Dan about going out and doing some sort of sport. Eyes, body language, facial twitches, a million conversations going on at once, flickering across the room like heat lightning. And so much of the talk was about mating. Lucy couldn't keep track of it all, but she found it fun to try.

But after a few days, the novelty of it wore off. And as Lucy sat there, while the teacher droned on in the background, she realized that something was very wrong. All that communication was taking place, but she wasn't a part of it. As Lucy watched the people flashing their signals furiously across the room, she thought, Hey, what about me? She wanted to be in The Stream with them all. Yet it was as if she'd become invisible.

Lucy went home that afternoon feeling lost and dejected. When she entered the kitchen, Jenny said, "What's wrong? You look so sad."

"Everybody hates me."

"Don't be silly. You're completely adorable."

"Well, nobody talks to me."

Jenny took Lucy by the shoulders. "Look. You're a smart girl. And you grew up with bonobos. You know that you're the new kid. Didn't a new kid ever come to your family?"

"Yes, and they treated her horribly. If they treat me like that at school, I'm going to be miserable for the rest of my life."

"You'll make friends. You'll see."

"I'm going to go do my homework."

It went on like that for a week. Lucy went to school and sat in class feeling subhuman. She wondered, Do they know? Can they sense what I am? She made an effort to talk to people, but most of them responded in glum monosyllables and then walked away or turned with a lively air to more important conversations. Lucy avoided the cafeteria at lunch time, preferring to go to the library rather than feel the acute isolation that was imposed on her by the indifference of the crowd. She came home in the afternoons and stayed in her room, doing homework or reading. It seemed to Lucy that an overcast sky hung just above her shoulders the entire time. Jenny tried to draw Lucy out with games, movies, music, but she petulantly resisted the efforts. Lucy began to feel disgusted with herself. She thought, I'm turning into a brat.

Then one day, the sun came out. She found herself seated in history class, waiting for the teacher and trying to ignore all the messages zinging around the room in The Stream. Messages that weren't meant for her. The girl next to Lucy was rummaging in her backpack. She stopped and said, "Shit."

Lucy turned to look. "What's the matter?"

The girl bit her cuticles, frowning. "I forgot my frickin' pen."

Lucy handed her a pen.

"Thanks. I'll give it back after class, if that's okay."

"Accept it as my gift to you. I have another." Lucy admired her curling dark brown tresses and her athletic body. She had bright brown eyes and seemed warm.

Lucy expected her to turn away and ignore her, but instead, the girl said, "You're new, aren't you? Where're you from?"

Lucy hesitated. Jenny had rehearsed this with her, but here was Lucy's first real try at saying it to a stranger.

"Don't you know where you're from?"

Lucy laughed nervously to cover her embarrassment. "Yes, sorry. It's rather complicated. I'm British, but I grew up in the Democratic Republic of Congo." There, she'd said it.

"Oh, cool. My name's Amanda Mather." The girl put out her hand. Lucy wasn't sure what she wanted at first. Another pen? Then she realized what Amanda was doing and quickly took her hand. No one shook hands in Lucy's family. They groomed one another and slapped each other on the back and wrestled around on the ground by way of greeting.

"Lucy," she said. "Lucy . . . Lowe." She had to get used to saying that name. She had wanted to take Jenny's name to honor her, but also because it would be less confusing if their last names were the same.

"So you're British. What part?"

"London."

"Sweet. I've always wanted to go biking through Great Britain," Amanda was saying. "But I thought maybe like Ireland. Have you been?"

"Uh, no. Sorry." And she thought: I've never been anywhere.

"It's supposed to be so beautiful."

"Oh, cool," Lucy said, trying out Amanda's manner of speech. "Cool," she said again. She wanted to grasp the essence of its meaning. What an odd thing to say.

"You don't have much of an accent. A little."

"My father had a bad lisp as a child. He had a speech therapist who had no accent. So . . . I talk like him."

"So what are you doing in the United States?"

"Well, my parents died." There, it was out.

"God, I'm sorry." Amanda seemed genuinely concerned.

Lucy took a deep breath and pressed on, acutely aware of how little she had ever had to lie in her lifetime and how difficult it was. She tried to think of something to say that was simple and true. "My dad was a scientist and one of the other scientists is adopting me. She's from here, so . . . here I am."

"That's awful. How did it happen?"

"Civil war. Congolese militias killed them."

"Oh, my God, that's horrible. I am so, so sorry."

"Thanks." Lucy didn't know what else to say.

"Why don't you sit with me at lunch? I can introduce you to some people."

"That would be splendid." Amanda gave her an odd look. Lucy thought that she had probably said the wrong thing. She felt that she knew so little. How would she learn it all?

As the teacher began the class, Lucy sensed a change in the flow of The Stream. People had seen Lucy and Amanda in conversation, seen their expressions. Silent messages were flying around the room. Lucy could sense what had happened: By talking to her with true feeling, Amanda had conferred some of her status on Lucy.

As soon as they were seated in the cafeteria and Amanda had introduced Lucy to her friends, three girls and a boy, the conversation stopped and they all brought out sleek and colorful phones and began touching them. They weren't talking, just staring down at their phones and poking them. Lucy watched, fascinated. She leaned over to Amanda and whispered, "What are you doing?"

"Didn't you ever leave the jungle?"

"No. I was born and grew up there. Sorry."

"No, I'm sorry. That was rude. It's called texting. Take out your phone and I'll show you how."

Lucy froze. She didn't know what to say.

Amanda gave her a long suspicious look. "You don't have a phone?"

Lucy hung her head in shame.

"Hey, guys," Amanda announced. "Lucy doesn't have a phone. Is that cool, or what?"

"Word," said the boy named Matt.

"Sweet," said a blond girl named Melissa. "I wish I could get rid of mine. But how do you, like, *live*?"

Lucy felt her face flush hot.

"I don't even *remember* not having one," Melissa said.

"That's because your brain has been fried from doing too many bong hits," Matt said. Everyone giggled.

Lucy leaned over to Amanda and asked, "What are bong hits?" Amanda looked at Lucy with a blank expression. "Bonk Kits?" Lucy asked, and everyone laughed. Lucy felt her desolation expand to fill the universe.

"Oh, man. We are so going to teach you some stuff."

. . .

The school day was ending. Lucy was moving down the hall among the crowds of people when she heard a familiar sound coming from behind a set of double doors. The noises stopped her in her tracks. She cocked her head, listening intently with the hair on her arms standing up. She recognized the sound instantly, but it struck her as impossible: She was hearing bonobos screaming to one another in jubilant surprise at a sudden heated conflict. It reminded Lucy of the sound—at once thrilling and appalling—that everyone had made the day that old Lucretia had bitten the finger joints off of Zeus's hand. Only somehow this was different. The pitch was too low. She felt a rush of emotion, a quickening in her blood. Lucy could not ignore it. Someone was being hurt.

Without thinking, she slammed through the double doors and saw two boys entangled on the floor. One was wrenching the other's leg painfully behind him. The other was crying out in agony, even as the people sitting all around looked on and hooted and howled and screeched in horrible revelry. Lucy dropped her books and leapt to the rescue. She grabbed the attacker, raised him easily above her head, and simply flung him away. Then she extended her hand to help the wounded one to his feet. "Are you all right? Are you all right?" Odd, she thought, that he had no blood on him.

"Are you nuts?"

Lucy felt as if the wind had been knocked out of her. He had some sort of padded contraption on his head and wore a bright red skintight suit.

Only then did Lucy notice that the entire room had fallen silent. Lucy's senses began to return to normal speed. She heard a low moan coming from the boy she'd thrown. A stunned and shaken grown-up man with something shiny clenched in his teeth was moving purposefully toward her now. Lucy prepared to do combat with him. Then she heard the shrill whistle as his cheeks puffed out. He dropped the whistle and shouted, "What in the Sam Hill do you think you're doing, young lady, coming in here and busting up my wrestling meet?" Lucy was turning in a slow circle trying to determine what had gone wrong. It all seemed so clear one moment. But now this: What were these people doing here? Why were those boys fighting? Why had the people been cheering when one boy was obviously hurt? He said wrestling. Was this the Hellenic wrestling that she had read about? Then why weren't they naked?

The boy she had thrown was up now, dusting himself off. Her heart was hammering, as the man shouted at her and the crowd began to boo and grumble. Lucy realized that she had violated a grave taboo of this tribe. Unable to control her panic, she charged through the double doors and ran down the hall, knocking people out of her way. She reached the main doors and was outside, breathing hard, trying to think of where she could go. She saw strange sparkling lights coming up the street toward the school. She heard the wail of a siren. Lucy knew it meant that something bad was happening, and all at once she realized that it was happening to her. She fled through the neighborhood back yards, leaping fences as she went. She saw pale sunlight on wilted roses, squirrels on trash cans in alleys. She heard the syncopated, urgent rhythm of her breathing. As she loped across one yard, a large dog came flying at her, teeth bared, and she backhanded it out of the way and kept on going, hearing its pathetic squeal fade behind her.

JENNY SAT ON ONE SIDE of Lucy's chair. Her school counselor sat on the other, a thin and harried-looking man with thick glasses and a nearly bald head. The psychologist's office was cold and lit from above by fluorescent tubes that made an incessant hum and gave off a gray and gassy glow.

They all faced the psychologist, Dr. Ruth Mayer, who was in her fifties, soft and gray, with her hair pulled so tight that it seemed to stretch the skin of her face. She sat behind a large institutional desk tapping a pencil on a file folder. "Dr. Lowe, I understand that Lucy has gone through a traumatic experience recently. Given the nature of that experience, I wonder if she might be suffering from some sort of post-traumatic disorder."

"Yes, that's possible. I don't think it's the case, but it's possible." Jenny could tell that Dr. Mayer was a mischief maker of the worst sort.

"Has she had any counseling since the events?"

"No." Once Jenny had learned the truth about Lucy, sending her to a psychologist had seemed out of the question.

"Don't you think this might be an oversight on your part? After all, you're a doctor." Jenny could see where this was going. By assuming that someone could live without psychotherapy, Jenny had slighted the doctor's profession.

"I'm a PhD anthropologist, not a medical doctor. Lucy has shown no signs of distress. And I think that this whole incident was just a misunderstanding."

"Misunderstanding? She attacked one of the school's star athletes. I fail to see how that could be a misunderstanding."

"She'd never seen a wrestling match before. All she saw was one boy attacking another, and she went to the other's aid. Instinctively, if you will."

"Is that what happened, Lucy?"

"Yes, ma'am. That's what happened. I thought I was breaking up a fight."

"Every culture has sports, and most of them involve mock combat. What sort of community were you raised in?"

Jenny jumped in to cover for Lucy. "Her father was a primatologist. They lived in an extremely remote part of the Democratic Republic of Congo in the jungle."

This seemed to give Dr. Mayer pause. She eyed them suspiciously for a time. Then she turned to the counselor and said, "Mr. Wicks, what has your experience of Lucy been so far?"

"I haven't seen her that much," he said, clearing his throat and taking off his glasses to wipe them with a balled-up Kleenex, which he produced from the pocket of his tweed coat. "She tested out of many classes."

"All of her classes, actually," Jenny put in.

"Not disruptive?" Dr. Mayer asked.

"No, not so far as I know."

Dr. Mayer pored over the contents of the file folder for a moment. She adjusted her glasses and said, "Well, fortunately, the boy was not seriously hurt. And the police tell me that he does not want to press charges." Dr. Mayer pressed a finger to her lips and studied the file for another minute. "I'm willing to present this case to the disciplinary board as exceptional and ask that Lucy be allowed to continue as a student here. However, I will require that she receive psychological counseling to ensure that no other incident occurs and that any issues from her traumatic experience are resolved. Does that meet with everyone's approval. Dr. Lowe?"

"Yes, fine." Jenny knew that meant that Dr. Mayer wanted a chance to work Lucy over in private. But she didn't see any way out of it.

"Mr. Wicks?"

"Yes, that sounds appropriate."

"Lucy?"

"Whatever my mother says is fine with me."

Jenny felt herself choke up when Lucy referred to her as her mother. She wondered if Lucy was sly enough to do it for effect or if she really meant it. She felt the tension go out of her.

"Very well. Then if no further trouble occurs I'll consider the matter settled." As they stood up to leave, Dr. Mayer added, "Oh, and I will also require that Lucy undergo a complete examination by a qualified physician."

"Why would that be necessary? I had her examined by a qualified physician on her arrival in the United States. He's the one who signed Lucy's school health form."

"We'd prefer to have our own physician make sure that there isn't some occult condition that might have been overlooked. Violent behavior is not in the patient's normal repertoire of conduct." Jenny noticed that she had facilely transformed Lucy from a student into a patient. "She lived in a part of the world where exotic diseases thrive. Parasites. I'm sure that Lucy is just fine, but we'd be remiss if we didn't check. It is a matter of potential liability, don't you agree?"

Jenny could hardly disagree. Harry ran tests on patients all the time as insurance against a possible lawsuit. The school didn't want to be sued either.

As they drove home, Lucy asked, "Are they going to find out now? With their doctors?"

"I don't think so. There's no reason for them to do a genetic analysis, and that's the only way to tell. In the meantime try not to throw anybody else across the room."

Lucy laughed, and Jenny thought that she detected a bit of pride in what she'd done.

"Did you really want to call me your mother? Or did you just say that for the psychologist?"

"Oh, may I? May I call you Mother? No, Mom. That's more American, isn't it? May I please call you Mom?"

Jenny felt tears well up in her eyes. "Yes, of course. I'd love it if you did."

. . .

When Lucy returned to school the next day, she could tell immediately that two pieces of information had spread far and wide: The story of the murder of her parents, and the fact that she'd thrown that boy across the gym. She was really in The Stream with all those people now. As she passed down the hall, the crowd parted before her and a tide of secret messages began washing back and forth. She could feel her hair stand up. She tried to control herself as her heart fluttered in her chest. Breathe, she told herself. Breathe. Don't make a scene.

By third period, when she was about to have English class, Lucy was barely in control. She walked stiffly down the hall feeling the stares coming at her from every direction. In a bonobo family, only the leaders are looked at as much as those students were looking at her. When an individual received a certain critical mass of glances from others, he would scream and do something demonstrative like breaking off big branches and dragging them around. She could feel that welling up of emotion, a channel to a vast source of energy that she could not tame. Without realizing what she was about to do, she leapt into the air and landed in a squat atop the lockers that ran on either side of the corridor. She threw her hands in the air and chugged both fists at the ceiling. She let loose with a piercing scream of triumph that echoed off the halls. The crowds of students broke into cheers. Someone began chanting, "Lew-See! Lew-See! Lew-See!"

As more and more students took up the chant, Lucy leapt to the floor and continued on her way, now strutting down the hallway and swinging her hips. A chorus of voices followed her into the classroom, where she found that the students inside were chanting, too.

"Lew-See! Lew-See! Lew-See!"

She entered with a grin, her face flushed. Amanda caught Lucy's eye, smiling, and pointed her thumb at the ceiling. Lucy wasn't sure what that gesture meant, but it felt good to see Amanda's smile. As Lucy slumped into the desk beside her, Amanda said, "Well, screw 'em if they can't take a joke, is what I say."

"Yeah. Screw 'em." It was a phrase she'd never used before. It felt dangerous and powerful in her mouth.

"How'd you get so strong?"

"Growing up in the jungle. You know. All we did was climb trees."

"Tight." Amanda rummaged in her backpack. She came up with a plastic bag. "Here, I brought you some grapes."

"Thanks. How did you know I like grapes?"

"Everybody likes grapes."

"All right, class," Mr. Marx began in a droning voice. "I'm sure we'd all like to welcome Lucy to our school and give her a warm reception in America. But we do have a test next week. Turn to page two-oh-one in your text, please, George Orwell . . ."

II

JENNY HAD DROPPED LUCY OFF at school and was driving to the university campus. She had to put in at least a perfunctory appearance at her lab. Lucy was having her first session alone with the psychologist before school. She told herself that Lucy was a teenage girl and had all the rights of any teenage girl. But then that thought was immediately followed by another: Did Lucy really have any rights at all? And: If they found out, could they put her in a zoo? Could they take her away to study her in a lab? Could they . . . put her to sleep like they would a stray dog? Jenny had heard from Donna about what they do in the labs.

She tried to concentrate on the view. Lake Shore Drive flowed along the uninterrupted parkland that lined the shore. Sunlight glittered on the blue water beyond. Gulls flew low across the sand. People were jogging, walking dogs, riding bicycles, savoring the last warmth before winter clamped down. Jenny told herself that she ought to take Lucy biking along the lake. And then this thought intruded: We should get rid of Stone's notebooks.

Jenny's lab was tucked out of the way in an old university building. A lab bench of black stone, fitted with sinks and brass spigots corroded green with age, ran the length of the room under a high ceiling of beaten tin. Along the walls were dark wooden cases with glass fronts containing a profusion of specimens and chemicals and notebooks.

As she was unpacking, Charles Revere, her chairman, walked in. "Welcome back. I'm sorry about the circumstances. Spoke to David Meece at the embassy. We heard about Don Stone, of course." Staccato delivery.

"Hello, Charlie."

"Well, we're all glad you're safe."

"Thank you. It was pretty awful. I only wish I'd been able to bring his body out."

"I hear you barely got out yourself." Charlie was a tall, thin man with steel spectacles and bright eyes. His curly hair was reddish brown and flecked with gray. He wore a well-cropped cinnamon-colored beard. His constant training for marathons kept him sinewy. "David said you brought Stone's daughter back with you."

"Yes. She's lucky to be alive."

"Thanks to you, I guess. That's an extremely generous deed. You'd never met her before?"

"I did what anyone would have done."

"I wasn't aware that Stone was married." Charlie sat on a stool, making himself at home at Jenny's lab bench.

"He may not have been married. I never saw the mother."

"What did the girl say?"

"She was a bit delirious when I found her."

"Well, what's she said since then?"

"To tell you the truth she's been kind of fragile. I mean, her parents were murdered."

"If you didn't see the mother, how do you know she was murdered? Maybe she's alive and wondering where her daughter went."

"We're trying to track down some of her relatives in England. David's working on it."

Charlie let silence settle on them, then said, "Well, your teaching load is zero since you weren't expected back. Take your time and get back into the swing of things. We're very understanding."

"Thanks."

"I'll let you get back to your work."

He rose, pressing his hands to his knees, and went to the door. Then he paused, turned back. "Oh, by the way. How did you get the girl out?"

"David sent a helicopter."

"No, I meant into the United States. Meece said getting the girl a passport was hell on wheels. Then he clammed up."

Jenny could feel her stomach tightening as he bored in on the subject. He had a way of doing that. It had made him good at putting the screws to his academic competition. "I don't pretend to know how things work in diplomatic circles."

"I see. Well. Amazingly generous of you. Glad you're all in one piece." Jenny heaved a sigh of relief as he left.

On her way home Jenny stopped at the Hope Shelter. It was an industrial-looking brick building from the 1960s with a yard and a playground in the back. It stood across the street from a Lutheran church in an otherwise residential neighborhood of modest means. Jenny parked in back and crossed the lawn, where a number of preteen girls were playing on the equipment. She recognized none of them. She'd been away too long.

She went inside to find Nina, the administrator, behind a desk, looking overworked as usual. Nina looked up and began to ask, "May I help you?" Then she recognized Jenny. She beamed and came around the desk to embrace her. "Dear Jenny," she said. "Back on the front lines?"

"I'd like to be. I won't have vast amounts of time, but I'd like to keep my hand in."

"Yes, of course. Come along. Kathy's been using your desk."

Jenny followed her into the corridor. Nina was round and solid-looking with curly brown hair flecked with gray. She wore overalls and a work shirt and sneakers. "I'll just update your paperwork for you," she said.

As they entered the recreation room, Jenny smelled the familiar aroma of stale cafeteria food. A girl, perhaps seventeen years old, passed them going the other direction. Nina said, "Hi, Clarissa." The girl, who appeared to be eight or nine months pregnant, didn't respond. Nina gave Jenny a look.

They sat together at a cafeteria table while Nina filled out forms for Jenny to sign. Then Nina sat back and smiled. "Well. We heard that there was trouble in Congo."

"Yes, yes there was."

Neither of them said anything for a time. The sunlight fell

through dirty windows and made spandrels on the linoleum floor while a big institutional clock on the wall ticked out the seconds.

"Alice spoke to your mother," Nina said.

"How is Alice?"

"Fine. Just back from Greece." Nina hesitated. "She said something about a girl . . ."

"Lucy. A lovely girl with no parents."

Nina looked up at Jenny and smiled with understanding. "We know what that's like, eh?"

"I'm adopting her."

Again they were silent, and Jenny watched the shadows on the floor as the trees beyond the windows shuddered with the breeze.

Nina put her pen down across the papers that Jenny had just signed. "Do you think you ought to attend to that right now? It sounds as if you're going to have your plate full."

"Yes, yes, certainly." They looked at each other. "I do miss working here."

"Well, your paperwork is in order. You'll be back. It's all right. You take care of Lucy. Come by any time. We're always here."

Jenny stood, and they embraced again. Jenny whispered into Nina's ear, "I'm afraid, Nina. I'm really afraid this time."

"I know. Now you can't go home at five and be shut of it. But you're strong. And she's lucky to have you."

12

"TELL ME ABOUT your mother."

Lucy didn't like this woman. She didn't like her square jaw, which indicated that she could bite hard. She reminded Lucy of old Lucretia, the nasty bonobo who had bitten Zeus's fingers off. She could tell that Dr. Mayer was suspicious of her but the woman didn't know why. That made her even more suspicious. Dr. Mayer was used to figuring people out.

"I loved my mother very much," Lucy said. But that was all she could think of to say.

Dr. Mayer let the silence grow and grow. Lucy looked down at her hands in her lap. "Is that all? Surely you can tell me more than that. What color was her hair? Her eyes?"

"Black," Lucy said, thinking of Leda's body lying in the hut that last day, the hair on her chest matted with her own blood. "And brown."

"Did she tuck you in at night?"

"Yes." She recalled how Leda would make Lucy the nicest nests in the highest branches.

"Tell me about one of your fondest memories of your mother."

Lucy remembered the time well. Early one morning Leda had led Lucy deep into the forest through the high branches of the canopy. They had moved quietly, swiftly. About midday they arrived at a clearing where another family was living. Leda let Lucy watch them for a long time. They were downwind, and Lucy could smell their particular aromas. She liked their smell, their look. They all had healthy shiny fur and seemed gentle and playful. One big teenage male looked particularly attractive to Lucy. After a time she and Leda slipped back into the trees.

Lucy had known what that trip meant. Her father had said that she was coming of age. As a female she'd be expected to visit other families and mate with various males among them, eventually settling in with a neighboring tribe. It was then that her father said that they had to prepare to go to London now, before Lucy's relatives would drive her away.

"Well? Do you remember nothing of your mother?"

But what could Lucy tell her? How could she go on? She didn't know where to begin. Should she describe how she had clung to the hair on her mother's back as she went flying through the forest? Should she tell Dr. Mayer how she and her little cousins screeched and chattered around Leda as she copulated with Duke, or how they had delighted in watching Leda rub genitals with her best friend, Vicki, as they lay in the long summer grass? Perhaps Lucy could tell the good doctor how artistic Leda was. How much Lucy enjoyed lolling about on a sleepy afternoon watching Leda paint designs on the rocks with her own excrement.

Lucy began to weep softly. "It's hard. She's dead, and it's hard to remember."

Dr. Mayer began to write. When Lucy had composed herself, Dr. Mayer sat with her fingers tented, watching her. "Let's continue this at the next session, shall we?"

Lucy rose and hurried out the door without looking back.

The meetings with Charlie Revere and the school psychologist had Jenny wondering how long she and Lucy could keep their secret. In one sense it seemed so simple: Who would ever believe the truth? In another sense Jenny could tell that everything about Lucy's presence brought people's antennae up. She thought she knew why, too. It was what Lucy called The Stream, that flood of information that animals and even people exchange mostly without being aware of it. When a dog encounters another dog, they may sniff around each other or play or even fight. But there is one thing that they know for certain: They are both dogs. When a dog meets a fox, they instantly recognize by scent, sight, and myriad other signals that they are not the same species. They share many similarities. They even share a common ancestor. But they know that they are not the same.

And now the accumulation of clues had Jenny wondering if people were having that same moment of unconscious recognition that she'd had when she first encountered Lucy. Harry had noticed it, too. Everything from her smell to her strength to her exotic and charming looks poured out the message that she was not quite the same species. Of course, that thought would never rise to the level of consciousness, because, well, how could it? She looked like a teenage girl. She spoke, she smiled, she laughed. So people ignored what they knew. They pushed it away. Yet the residue of the revelation remained as a faint and nagging discomfort. Some deep and ancient part of them had learned the new information and would store it away for future reference. The clues would assemble themselves and blossom into knowledge at the slightest hint.

Not long after school started, Jenny's mother had come to dinner. She had become cautious in her old age and morbidly concerned about illness. She went about the house with a dispenser of disinfectant napkins, wiping off telephones and doorknobs. Lucy had invited Amanda, and Harry had volunteered to grill salmon. Jenny and Harry were in the kitchen doing the prep work with Amanda. Jenny's mother sat in the living room reading.

"Where's Lucy?" Harry asked.

"She's in the euphemism," Amanda said.

"What?" Jenny asked.

"She's taking a shower."

Amanda had just finished pulling bones with a pair of pliers. Harry grated ginger over the salmon fillet in a big Pyrex dish and then began cracking garlic on a cutting board.

"What else can I do?" Amanda asked.

"That's it, thanks," Harry said.

Amanda wandered out into the living room and turned on the television. Jenny heard her mother say, "Turn that thing off. I'm reading."

"Sorry, Mrs. Lowe."

"You should be reading, too."

Harry and Jenny exchanged a look. Jenny squeezed lemon over the salmon and then added a sprinkle of tamari.

"You never told me why you wanted her blood back."

Jenny felt her anxiety level rising.

"Well?"

"Not now, Harry."

Harry put down his knife, took her by the shoulders, and just stared into her eyes. Those piercing hazel eyes. Jenny turned away. "Harry, don't."

"You're hiding something about her, Jenny. I can't imagine what it is, though. Does she have AIDS? I didn't test for it."

"God, no. Nothing like that."

He began mincing the garlic with a surgeon's precision. At that moment she was grateful to see her mother come in, her thumb marking a page in *Pride and Prejudice*.

"Mother! Won't be a moment. The salmon is about to go on the grill."

"I don't know why you don't use that stove," her mother said. "I paid nearly a thousand dollars for it back when a dollar was worth something."

"You'll just love it grilled, Margaret. I promise. If you don't, I'll eat my hat."

"You mean your motorcycle helmet." Harry was the only one who could pull her stinger. "Best eat that motorcycle, too, while you're at it." She left the room muttering to herself, "Before it kills you."

Harry turned and winked at Jenny.

At dinner Lucy picked at her food and seemed withdrawn. Jenny knew that it was because of that psychologist. Mrs. Lowe dug into her salmon and said, "Mmm, Harry, you're right. This is good."

"That's a relief. The last motorcycle helmet I ate had bones in it. Unlike my salmon." He smiled at Amanda.

"This is delicious," Amanda said. "Thank you, Dr. Lowe. And Dr. Prendeville."

"Call me Jenny."

"You can call me Jenny, too," Harry said.

Jenny's mother chuckled but said, "Well, you can call me Mrs. Lowe."

They all laughed. It felt like family to Jenny, perhaps for the first time since her father died.

Harry spent most of the dinner charming Mrs. Lowe and deflecting her critical remarks with jokes. But when Jenny was driving her mother home, Mrs. Lowe said, "Jennifer, you must be out of your mind thinking about adopting that girl."

"I'm not thinking about it, Mother. I'm doing it."

"Well, there's something awfully peculiar about her."

"Like what?"

"I can't put my finger on it."

"She was raised in a foreign country."

"It's more than that. Mark my words, she'll bring you grief one day."

Jenny knew. She knew what her mother sensed and she feared that one day some meddlesome busybody would follow that subtle suspicion too far. She couldn't yet imagine how it would happen, but it left her with a queasy feeling.

On top of that, their circumstances were simply so unusual that they alone could set people wondering. Charlie had never met Lucy, yet he seemed to need more explanation than Jenny could give. Why would a woman in the middle of her career simply adopt a teenager from Africa? This had all started with the idea that Lucy would be reunited with her family in England. But no one would understand that there was no family, and anyway, Lucy had already stolen her heart.

About a week later Jenny and Harry met at one of those Greek diners that are everywhere in Chicago and that feature dozens of items on their long, laminated menus. When they'd first met, Harry had informed Jenny that—quiet as it's kept—there was a top-secret subterranean kitchen beneath the squash courts at the University of Chicago, which supplied all the Greek diners in the area through a system of pneumatic tubes.

They made small talk. Harry was generally too busy to concern himself with the random events in the rest of the world. But he could be a tenacious investigator when faced with a mystery. He began casually enough, asking how Lucy was adjusting. Jenny assured him that she was doing fine and had already found a true friend in Amanda.

Then he said, "Jennifer," staring at her evenly. Jennifer was the name he used when he wanted her to know that he wasn't joking anymore. "How long have we known each other?"

"A long time, Harry. We saw the Berlin Wall go down, remember?" She was trying to get him off on another track by reminiscing. Jenny would never forget the day that Harry had driven up from Chicago and rushed into her little cubicle at the Milwaukee Zoo. "Come on," he'd said, "we're going to Germany!"

"What for?"

He gave her those intense eyes and said, almost breathless, "The Wall is coming down." His Darth Vader voice.

He had driven her home and watched her throw a few things in a bag. Harry brought only one change of clothes. Within hours they were on a plane. The day the Wall came down, they were sitting on a curb in Berlin. Harry hadn't shaved for days and Jenny's jeans were filthy. Harry had taken off his Chicago Cubs baseball cap and was holding it in his hands. A man in an expensive-looking gray suit walked past, then paused and turned back. He reached into his pocket and dropped several bills into Harry's hat. They'd never laughed so hard.

Now, sitting in the little diner, he asked, "Don't you trust me?"

"Of course I trust you, Harry. You're my best friend. But I'm just asking you to be patient. I'm not ready to talk about it, okay? Respect that boundary, won't you?"

Harry didn't miss a beat. "Are you going to have time to volunteer at the shelter with Lucy in your life?"

As Jenny reflected on his gallantry, she thought, Maybe Mother is right. Maybe I should marry him.

But there was still that psychologist. She was a piece of work. A professional snoop. For a moment Jenny entertained the idea that she should school Lucy at home. But then how would she become socialized? Amanda had already begun to teach Lucy things that Jenny could never have taught her—how to talk, how to dress, how to behave, how to fit in. One afternoon Jenny had heard voices.

She peeked into Lucy's room to see who was there and found her standing in front of the full-length mirror striking poses. She was saying things like "Cool," and "Sweet," and "Wow." She struck a defiant pose and said, "No way." Then another: "Duh!"

Jenny crept away as quietly as she could, thinking, Oh, my God, she's turning into an American teenager before my eyes. Now she had to worry about the high school prom and even about sex. If Lucy were invited, she'd be the age of a freshman or sophomore at a dance with all those seniors. But what was the alternative? Should they become hermits?

Those were the kinds of thoughts that occupied her mind during Lucy's first months at school. And even as Jenny worked to protect her true identity, she thought that she had at last come up with a workable plan just in case the worst happened. She had to go up to Milwaukee to see Donna.

13

LUCY HAD LEFT the psychologist's office weeping. Jenny—Mom, as she was now calling her—had asked her about burning the notebooks as a precaution, but Lucy had hesitated. They were all she had left of her father. And they were the proof of who she was. If she destroyed them, she would forever wonder if the whole thing had been a crazy fantasy.

Lucy was dreading her first class, because it was gym, and she didn't want to run into the wrestling coach. Yet there he was, as if he had been waiting for her. Lucy tried to veer off, to avoid his gaze, but he homed in on her.

"I am so, so sorry," Lucy said, trying to imitate the way Amanda talked.

The man cut her off with a slash of his hand in the air. "Forget it. I had to do that for show. The kid you threw across the gym is an asshole. Excuse me. A jerk. He needed to be taught a lesson. He's probably on steroids, but the school won't let us test."

Lucy didn't have the faintest idea what he was talking about. "Thank you. I felt sad about what I did."

"Well, you can stop feeling bad. The truth is, our wrestling team sucks. Excuse me. I mean we're in last place. About fifteen years ago we made state and we have been sucking hind tit ever since. Excuse my French."

"You speak French?" Lucy and Amanda had been speaking French, and it was fun. Maybe this man could speak with them.

"Christ, no, I don't speak French. It's an expression. I'm sorry. I forget you're not from around here. Look. It's simple. I want you to try out for the team. Shows you how desperate I am. But I need some new blood."

"Blood?"

"Sorry. Another expression. Look. All the schools are getting girls on their wrestling teams nowadays. Title Nine crap, but some of 'em are actually pretty good. Would you like to be on the wrestling team, Lucy? That's what I mean to ask."

"Why would I want to do that?"

"To win."

"Win what?"

"Christ. For glory. For the school, you know. The old team spirit. You do well for the school. People will admire you."

"I see. Like gaining status in a tribe, you mean?"

"You could think of it that way, yeah. Yeah, I like that: Gaining status in the tribe. Maybe we can use that."

"I'll have to ask my mother."

Jenny objected at first. She didn't like the idea of something that would draw more attention to Lucy. But then she conceived of another plan to turn it to their advantage. They met with the coach, whose name was Tom Barneke. The students called him Coach Barnacle. Jenny told him that she would allow Lucy to join if he could convince Dr. Mayer to leave her alone.

"Get rid of the rag bag? Sure. With pleasure. She's always harassing my players. Telling 'em they must be queer if they like to wrestle other guys. My opinion, anybody who'd see a psychologist ought to have his head examined."

The next day after school, Lucy went to try out for the team. The practice room was at the far end of the gym, concealed off of a dark corridor. As she entered she was shocked that the entire room was blood red. The floor was springy beneath her feet. Then she realized that the room was padded—floor, walls, even the door she had just come through. It was intensely hot and steamy, almost like the jungle. Boys in pairs were down on the floor struggling. Coach Barnacle shouted, "Thirty seconds!" Each pair looked like a pure and singular muscle clenched upon itself, immobile with strain and roaring with metabolic heat.

"O'Brien, setup and takedown. You guys quit dancing. Set 'em up! Ten seconds! Push! Push!"

The hard-sprung bodies strained and streamed with sweat, and one or two jerked as if in response to a sudden pain. Then Lucy heard Coach Barnacle's whistle and all the couples collapsed, as if the heat had at last melted the metal armatures at their cores. Then the beautiful boys rose miraculously from the slurry, like creatures being born out of a blood-red swamp at the dawn of time. She felt a thrill at the thought that she might do such a dance with one of these fantastic animals.

To her surprise, her first opponent was the same boy she'd thrown across the room. As they squared off, he grinned at Lucy and said, "Let's see what you got, Tinker Bell." Lucy smiled at the remark and stiff-armed him. He went down on his back with a tremendous concussion that shook the building.

"Oh, I'm sorry, I'm so sorry." Lucy reached down to help him up. "It was just a tap."

The boy slapped her hand away and rose angrily to his feet. He grabbed at Lucy, but she easily evaded him. Growing more angry by the minute, the boy lunged at her. When he caught nothing but air, he lost his balance and went stumbling across the mat, tripping over his own feet. He jumped up, his face livid. He ripped off his helmet, threw it on the floor, and stomped out of the room.

Lucy was astonished that it was so easy. The boys had appeared so powerful a moment before. Coach Barnacle blew his whistle. "Out of bounds!" He came over to her looking grave.

"I'm sorry," Lucy said, "I've never done this before. Did I do it wrong?"

He cackled hoarsely and said, "Well, we do need to teach you a few rules."

"I'm sorry. Where would you like me to throw him?"

That elicited belly laughs from the other wrestlers and quite a few spectators who had gathered.

"Go, Luce!" Lucy looked up and saw Amanda. She waved and pointed her thumb at the ceiling. Lucy waved back and smiled. She showed Amanda her thumb, too, sensing that this was a good greeting for humans.

"Try'n keep'm inside this big circle, that's all," Coach Barnacle said. "You want to take 'em down and . . . Well, you're not supposed to throw anybody, but . . ." He seemed at a loss. Then he shouted, "Ayers! You're up next."

A towering bronze god descended from the bleachers and squared off with her on the red mat. Lucy could feel her heart going in her chest. She deliberately slowed her breathing. They locked arms circling each other, and then Ayers made his move. He seemed to have a firm hold on her. Then she was simply gone, standing several feet away, smiling at him.

Coach Barnacle stood over him and shouted, "Ayers, why the hell'd you let her go?"

"I didn't. I had hold of her."

"Well, something happened. Try it again."

Once more the boy approached Lucy. They circled each other, and Ayers had a hold on her once again. Then Lucy seemed to vanish into thin air and reappear behind him. She pushed him, and Ayers fell over.

The coach stood over Ayers, saying, "Well, you're looking pretty whopper-jawed, now, aren't you, Ayers?"

"She's cheating!"

"Yeah, whatever." Chewing on the stub of a pencil, the coach looked at Lucy and muttered to himself, "Raw talent. Brute strength." Then he hollered to the room in general, "Can any of you studs pin this little girl or what? Come on, gentlemen, is this a wrestling team or a ballet company? Are we on balls patrol or wimp patrol here?" Then he turned to Lucy and said, "Excuse my French."

One after another the boys came and squared off with her. Lucy felt bad. All she had to do was move out of their way. But it seemed to impress Coach Barnacle nevertheless. When the session was over, he took Lucy and a small boy named Weston Temple aside and said, "Wes, you gotta teach her finesse. You gotta teach her takedowns and good position. She's obviously got natural moves and strength up the gazops."

"Yeah, Coach, can do," Weston said. He looked very shy.

"Can you work with Wes, Lucy?"

"I suppose."

"Okay, and no shoving or throwing, Lucy. It's illegal."

"I'm sorry. I didn't know."

Coach Barnacle blew his whistle and shouted, "Ayers, Thompson, Mitchell. You guys go do your laps."

Lucy felt her blood pumping as she stood facing Wes. It was a good feeling, like when she used to play with the bonobo children. She wasn't sure what "pin" or "takedown" meant, but she felt that she would like for Wes to do it to her. She saw that to play this game she'd have to pretend to be weaker.

As Wes came at her now, Lucy let herself go limp. He turned her over and thrust her down onto the mat. She didn't resist. Then he was on her, his chin over her shoulder, his body pressed against hers. She felt a thrill, an exhilarating rush from her legs up through her stomach and chest and all the way, it seemed, into her brain. Coach Barnacle was down on his stomach beside them peering beneath Lucy's body. She let her shoulders touch the mat.

The coach blew his whistle. "There, that's a good pin. Good work, guys. You practice that, Lucy."

Wes popped to his feet as if he'd been spring-loaded. Lucy lay there on the mat looking up at him. She hadn't exerted herself, but she was breathing hard, confused at what she was feeling. Wes offered Lucy his hand. She took it and he pulled her up. They faced each other, eyes just inches apart. Lucy had a sudden impulse to grab him and wrestle him to the ground, but she held back.

"Thanks, Weston."

"Okay, now you try."

They continued to practice, with Lucy offering little resistance, until the mat was slick with sweat and Coach Barnacle blew his whistle and ordered them to run laps. As Lucy was going out the door, Amanda came across the room and put her arm around Lucy. "That was so totally bangin', Luce."

"Thanks."

Lucy followed her into the hall.

"Want to come over to my house?"

"After my laps." Lucy felt good. She felt powerful. Just then Dr.

Mayer came striding down the hall purposefully. She tried to pretend that she didn't notice the girls, but it was too late. They'd already seen her glance over. Lucy and Amanda grinned from ear to ear at her, and she hurried on beneath the harsh fluorescent lights. Then the girls burst out laughing.

THEY TOOK THE BUS from school, a roaring stinking ride that Lucy thought was all the more odd because the people on the bus ignored one another. It was one of those strange places where The Stream had gone eerily silent. She wondered why the people couldn't do something during the ride like wrestle or just talk. She wanted to know who all these people were and where they were going with such sound and fury. But they seemed to have lost all curiosity about others. She felt sorry for them. Losing curiosity was like losing the ability to love.

They stepped down from the bus and walked through a neighborhood of tired-looking homes. The eyes of their little windows seemed to droop as if they were weary. The trees seemed unhealthy. As they approached Amanda's house, Lucy heard the dog. It had recognized her. As they came up the steps, the dog began throwing itself at the door again and again.

"What the hell? Cody, quiet! What's wrong with that dog? He never barks. He is so the laziest dog in the world." As Amanda unlocked the door, Lucy could feel herself trembling with energy, prepared for the attack that she knew was coming. "It's okay. Cody is really, really friendly. I don't know what's got into him."

Lucy knew: She and Cody were in The Stream. They had bonded. They accepted it as natural that one of them would die on this spot. Lucy had backed away, prepared to make sure that it was Cody and not her.

"Could you . . . ? I'm really fearful about dogs. Could you perhaps put him somewhere?"

Amanda gave Lucy a strange look. "Sure. Just wait here."

She could barely make it through the door because Cody was trying to get at Lucy. But she managed to catch Cody's collar and slip inside. She returned after a few minutes, saying, "Jeez. He was going bonkers. Come on in. He's in the basement."

Amanda's house was different from Jenny's. The rooms were smaller and there was less light. The carpet and curtains were old. She caught strong smells—of stale smoke, dog, and alcohol like rotting fruit. Amanda hurried up the stairs. Lucy hesitated. She saw a big television like a great dead eye staring at a sagging chesterfield. Pizza boxes and wine bottles littered a coffee table.

"Come on," Amanda called down. Lucy hurried up the stairs. "Come on in." Amanda held open a door at the end of the hallway. "I'm sorry the house is such a mess." She closed the door behind Lucy.

"That's quite all right. Thank you for inviting me."

"This is my so-called room." Amanda swept her arm around. "Wreck that it is." The bed was unmade, and there were clothes and shoes strewn about. The walls were covered with posters from movies and music groups. Lucy wandered around the room touching things. There was a folding table with a computer on it and a secretary's chair with a torn seat. Lucy ran her fingers lightly over the keyboard and the computer screen leapt to life. It was covered with hearts and flowers and photographs of Amanda and her friends. "Oops, sorry. I didn't know it was on."

"It's always on, dude. I live on that thing. That and my phone. Are you on Facebook or YouTube yet?"

"Your what?" By the look on Amanda's face, Lucy knew that she'd committed another gaffe. "Your tube?" Amanda burst out laughing. "No, wait. You mean my tube?" Lucy felt her face flush hot. Amanda fell on the bed laughing. "What tube is it? I'm sorry. I'm going to shut up now."

"No, don't be sorry, it's okay. What we're going to do, my little Pop-Tart, is, like, give you this full-immersion course in American culture."

"I feel like such an idiot."

"No, no. It's okay. Hey. You didn't even have electricity. I so wish I could have the experiences you've had."

Lucy sat on the bed, feeling stupid. "So tell me some things I need to know." Then, almost to herself: "I must have a phone."

"Okay, so don't say, 'must have.' Say, 'I've got to get a phone.'"

"Got to get?" It sounded wrong.

"Yeah, that's American talk. Got this, get that. Gotta, gotta, gotta."

"Gotta get a phone?"

"You got it. See? Just put 'got' in a lot. Like I got home late. I've gotta go. You've got nice hair."

"It doesn't make sense."

"It doesn't gotta make sense. And, like, when Coach Barnacle asked you if you could work with Wes, you said, 'I suppose.' You don't say, 'I suppose.' You say, 'Yeah, I guess.'"

"Guess? Why do I have to guess?"

"It's just a manner of speaking, Luce. It's the way we talk."

"Okay. So what's, um . . . Your Tube?" Lucy knew that she still had it wrong.

"Come on. I'll show you." Amanda pulled another chair up to the computer. She typed and clicked the mouse and soon they were watching what looked like a small television set in the middle of the screen. It showed a pretty girl with curly blond hair.

"Here. This girl's named Nathalie. She lives in a small farming community in Illinois. Watch."

The video started with the girl smiling brightly, waving and saying, "Hello, YouTube. I'm making another video. Super! I didn't know what to talk about, but . . . I thought I'd give you guys a bunch of random facts about me." She paused to eat cereal out of the box, muttering to herself and chewing into the camera. "Random fact number one. I like to snowboard."

"What's does snowboard mean?"

Amanda stopped the video. "Have you ever seen snow?"

Lucy shook her head sadly. She felt as if there was an entire world out there that she knew nothing about. She'd been studying all her life—math, languages, music, history, science—and yet she knew nothing.

"Here, lemme show you." She clicked a few times and another

video appeared, showing tiny figures zigzagging down a big white mountain. Loud music played as some of the figures leapt and spun around in the air.

"Those are people?"

"Yeah, and they've got their feet strapped to a board, that's why they call it snowboarding. Snow. Board. Snowboarding."

"Wow. Can you do that?"

"Yeah, I can teach you, if you want. When winter comes."

"I would be ever so grateful."

"No! Just say, 'Sweet.'"

"Sweet?"

"Trust me: Sweet." Amanda held up her hand. "Slap my hand." Lucy slapped it. "Ouch. Not so hard."

"Sorry."

Amanda switched back to the video of Nathalie, who held up two fingers and said, "Random fact number two: I'm addicted to ChapStick."

"Do you know what ChapStick is, Lucy?"

"What do you think?"

"Your problem, Luce, is that you have a severe product deficit in your otherwise vast store of knowledge. You need a basic American primer. America is all about products. Buy, buy, buy, eat, eat, eat, consume, consume, consume." She took a breath. "Goods, matter, material, possessions—stuff."

"What for? That's what I don't understand. What's all the stuff for? We throw most of it away. So why get it to begin with?"

"I don't know. It's just junk. And here's the thing: There's always new stuff. Old stuff is no good. New stuff is always better."

"I always thought that old things were better than new things."

"Well, some old things are good, like if it's your grandmother's wedding ring or old music like Tom Petty and the Beatles. But when it comes to everyday stuff, they're always telling us that what we've got sucks. We need something new."

"Got to have it?"

"Yeah, gotta get it. Like your breakfast cereal. You know what breakfast cereal is, right?"

"Yeah, Fruity Cheerios."

"Okay, exactly my point. Once upon a time, when dinosaurs roamed the earth, there were, like, only classic Cheerios. Well, after a while someone came up with the idea of Fruity Cheerios and voilà! Something new was born."

"So what's ChapStick?"

"It's something that you put on your lips when they get all dry and cracked."

"Ohhh. Sure, we used the juice from an aloe plant for that."

"There you go: Aloe. Once upon a time there was just plain grease. Then someone put aloe in it. Bingo: Something new. So you like Fruity Cheerios? Well, get this: One day you'll go to the store and they won't be there anymore. Instead you'll find some kind of new and improved Cheerio, like hey, we've gotten rid of that nasty sweet fruity taste and you can now eat one hundred percent pure organic toasty Cheerios or whatever. And they'll probably be made out of ground-up clarinet reeds."

"They went back to plain old Cheerios, then."

"Right! And the assumption is that we're too stupid to notice. Which we are."

"I still don't understand. What's the point?"

Amanda leaned in close to Lucy's ear and whispered, "I think it's a conspiracy to make somebody rich."

Lucy found it all completely baffling. Why would someone want to be rich? But she thought that she already sounded stupid enough without asking. "Let's see some more people."

"On YouTube? Sure." Amanda played through a number of videos of teenagers talking about themselves and doing strange things. In one of them a girl held up a piece of notebook paper with the word "myself" scrawled on it in red marker. Then she made a face and picked up a pair of scissors. She held up the paper and cut it in half in front of the camera.

"What does it mean?"

"I don't know. I think maybe she cuts herself. There's a whole subculture on YouTube of girls who cut themselves."

"They cut themselves?"

"Yeah, I know. It's weird. I had a friend who was into it in eighth grade. She said it was like getting high. You know, like some kind of chemical is released when you're injured."

They shrugged and exchanged a look. Lucy felt comfortable with Amanda. They were communicating in The Stream.

Amanda typed on the keyboard again. One after another, the videos played, and teenagers said, I found out I was pregnant. I decided to commit suicide. I learned I was anorexic. I realized that my parents were proud of me. I questioned my religion. I got suspended for drinking. I got a reputation as a slut. Amanda explained that a large number of the people on YouTube were playing a game called tag. "If you get tagged, then you have to make a video telling five things about yourself and send it to five other people. Then they're tagged and they have to send it to five other people and so on."

"That means that if they do that only ten times they'll be reaching almost ten million people."

"Is that right? I mean, ten million? Or did you just pick that number at random?"

"No, it's five to the tenth power. Well, 9,765,625 to be exact. But if you do it just one more time, you'll be reaching almost fifty million people."

"How'd you do that math so fast?"

"It's just, you know . . . exponents."

"No, I don't know. Are you some kind of genius or something?"

Lucy laughed. "No, I just like math."

"Well, whatever. You're right. It's a lot of people. If you put something on YouTube that catches on, it happens really fast. Like you can be talking to millions of people in a few days. Here, let me show you something else." Amanda found another video. Lucy saw a girl writhing on the floor. She kept saying, "I don't drink," and laughing uncontrollably. She tried to stand but fell back to the floor. Then she began screaming and screeching unintelligibly, pouring out her sadness.

"Oh, poor thing," Lucy whispered. "What's wrong with her?"

"She's just drunk. Behind all the fun and games, there's a lot of messed-up teenagers out there."

Another video came on, showing three girls in a pool of bubbling, steaming water. Two of them began kissing, and it dawned on Lucy: They were turning into bonobos. That's what girl bonobos do, they kiss and fondle each other and laugh and act silly.

That's what alcohol does, she saw. It pushes people back in evolutionary time. Those girls think they're back in the forest.

Another video showed a number of girls in a big bathroom like the one at school with all the metal stalls, the too-bright lights. Everyone was talking at once, but the video focused on a girl who was stumbling around and slurring her words. She was laughing so hard, yet she was also screaming about how sad she was. It almost hurt Lucy to watch her and to hear her cries.

Without warning, the girl bolted toward one of the stalls, but she ran right into the edge of the open door and knocked herself out. As she lay on the floor, unconscious, several girls stood over her laughing. Lucy felt so bad for her. She saw that those people weren't merely going back in evolutionary time. They were falling down. Once you've spent ten million years learning to walk on two feet, then falling down can be so sad. Lucy covered her face and felt tears welling up in her eyes.

"Oh, my God, Lucy. What's wrong? What's wrong?"

"I just feel so bad for those people. I'm sorry."

"It's only a video," Amanda said. She put her arm around Lucy. "Hey. I'm sorry. I didn't mean to upset you."

"No, no, it's just . . ." Lucy didn't know what she was feeling. She was overwhelmed with sadness for those people. It wasn't only the drunk girls. She could see that everyone else was holding back from expressing anything deeply. Like the people on the bus who couldn't talk. But because these girls were drunk, they'd lost that inhibition and were sending the true message of . . . of . . . of this whole place. And Lucy wondered, What have I gotten myself into? Can I survive this place?

Lucy looked up and saw on the screen that the video of the drunk girl running into the bathroom stall door had been watched by almost a million people. "Why do they want to see other people so miserable?"

"I don't know," Amanda said. "You know. Then you don't feel so alone, I guess. It's messed up, I know." They sat in silence for a time. Then Amanda said, "My mom's a drunk."

Lucy didn't know what to say. She had seen people drunk only a few times, when Denis and his clan had had celebrations. "I'm sorry."

"She's okay. I mean, she has a job and all. But my dad left on account of her drinking. My dad's some kind of investment guy in New York City. He gives me money. But I pretty much fend for myself around here."

"You seem to be doing okay. You're in The Stream."

"The Stream? What's that?"

Lucy thought for a moment. "Well. It's kind of like YouTube, I suppose."

"I guess."

"Sorry. It's kind of like YouTube, I guess. Anyway, in the forest you have to fend for yourself. You have family, people who care about you. But it's so dangerous, you're really on your own. You have to be aware. So everyone communicates the way animals communicate. It's like a special channel called The Stream."

"The Stream," Amanda said. "I've never heard of it."

"You know how sometimes you'll meet someone and immediately like her? Or you meet someone who instantly makes you uncomfortable?"

"Sure, like you've either got chemistry or you don't."

"Yes. Or you hear about how animals might run away before an earthquake?"

"Sure, I've heard about that." Amanda thought it over, then she smiled and nodded. "Yeah. Yeah, I guess you're right. And speaking of The Stream, I've really gotta pee!"

They both started giggling, and then they couldn't stop. Rolling on the bed, Amanda said, "Stop! Oh, my God, stop! I'm gonna pee in my pants!" She leapt up and ran to the bathroom.

15

LUCY AND HER FATHER did not celebrate Thanksgiving or Christmas. She had read about Christmas in Dickens. When she asked her father about it, he said that it was a religious holiday and that religion was part of the problem and launched into a lengthy discourse about intolerance. But Lucy was just a child. She didn't care about all that. She wanted presents.

"We celebrate birthdays," her father said. "We give presents then." But Lucy knew how to manipulate him, and her father had a soft spot in his heart. So as a compromise they began celebrating the winter and summer solstices, exchanging small presents that they fashioned themselves. Not everyone seemed able to join in. But some of the family members would come with a twisted bit of grass, a bunch of flowers, an offering of fruit.

Seeing the holiday season in America for the first time was both thrilling and shocking to Lucy. It began with a crescendo of gluttony in the fall. Lucy and Amanda dressed up for Halloween and ran up and down the streets with the smaller children, gathering sweets in bags. At Amanda's suggestion, Lucy dressed as Dorothy from the *Wizard of Oz*. ("Because," she said, "you're not in Kansas anymore.") Amanda dressed as the Good Witch Glinda. Months later they would still have bags of candy.

Then Thanksgiving came. The Christmas decorations were

already in the stores. It was a system that seemed to be tripping over itself in its fervor. Lucy and Amanda helped to cook the meal, but the process seemed all out of proportion. Jenny's mother came. Lucy regarded the small busy woman with the nervous cough and asked if she should call her Grandma, since she called Jenny Mom.

"Don't you dare call me Grandma, young lady."

Lucy and Amanda were preparing sweet potatoes. Harry was slicing carrots. "Carrots!" he said in a theatrical voice. "Let's have a carrot joke." Then he intoned, "A zucchini and a carrot were walking down the highway when a truck sped past and hit the carrot. The carrot was rushed to the hospital. The zucchini paced nervously in the waiting room for hours. Then at last the doctor appeared. He said, 'Well, I've got good news and bad news. The good news is: Your friend is going to survive. The bad news is that he'll be a vegetable for the rest of his life.'"

Jenny said, "You tell that joke every time."

"Yeah, I crack myself up."

Lucy watched as his flashing hazel eyes met Jenny's and wondered if they'd ever mated. Most of the time they just seemed like old friends. But their feelings for each other were clear to Lucy in those fleeting glances.

Once everyone was seated before plates heaped high with food, Lucy asked, "Can we really eat this much?"

Mrs. Lowe said, "Eat up or you won't get big and strong. You're such a tiny thing."

"Oh. I don't think I'm going to grow much taller. And I'm already pretty strong."

"Smart mouth," Mrs. Lowe said, digging into her mashed potatoes.

"I only meant—"

"It's okay," Jenny said. "You're right. It is extravagant. Eat what you like, honey."

Harry looked up and said, "This is too delicious. I want no interruptions. Everyone, please switch your phones to 'stun.' That way we won't hear a thing when your phone rings. We'll just see you go rigid and slump to the floor." Mrs. Lowe giggled.

Amanda laughed and winked at Lucy, and then she knew that everything was all right. Because of her mother, Amanda had learned to be wary and to use all the communication channels that were available to her. When Lucy had invited her to come for dinner, she had added, "That is, if you don't have to be with your mother for Thanksgiving."

Amanda had laughed and said, "Oh, you don't want to be around my mom on holidays."

During dinner both Harry and Mrs. Lowe were stealing glances at Lucy as if searching for clues to something just out of reach. When everyone was cleaning up the dishes, Harry said to Jenny, "Her ears are set too high."

"You can have them surgically clipped," Mrs. Lowe said. "Aunt Josie did that for Becky when she had her nose job."

The following Saturday night Amanda took Lucy Christmas shopping in the Loop and Lucy saw snow for the first time.

Lucy felt the rush of adrenaline as the train dove from the elevated tracks into the dark tunnel, and the yellow firefly lights went swarming past. Amanda didn't seem to notice as she sat listening to music through her headphones.

When they emerged onto State Street, Lucy saw millions of glittering white lights all up and down the boulevard, caught up in the trees as if mysterious albino spiders had woven their secret webs in the night. The fat snowflakes glowed as they swirled around the high streetlamps, and she had the impression that she was floating in a fantasy world of those white spiders, all moving and pulsing around her, weaving her into a cocoon of fleece.

"Taste it, taste it," Amanda said. "It's good luck." And she tilted her head back and opened her mouth. As Lucy watched the white spiders fall into Amanda's mouth, she tilted her head back and let them fall onto her own tongue.

"It's snow."

"Duh, yeah, it's snow. Probably filled with yummy lead and mercury after falling through the air of Chicago."

"Sweet," Lucy said.

Amanda linked arms with Lucy and pulled her along, saying, "Come on, silly goose. Hey! Luce the Goose. That's what I'm going to call you."

They went along State Street, peering into the display windows at scenes from *A Christmas Carol* laid out in antique dioramas, with Scrooge and Tiny Tim and Marley's Ghost. Lucy ran up and down excitedly examining each display and reading the didactics aloud.

Inside the department store, Lucy felt as if they'd been shipwrecked on a stormy sea and were floating amid the scattered cargo of a vast and fallen empire.

"No way," Lucy said. "There's just no way that I can possibly choose from all this stuff." They came to a glass case full of beautiful sparkling stones, and Lucy said, "Ooh, how about one of these?"

"Nope. Inappropriate to buy your mother a wedding ring. And too expensive anyway."

"I have my allowance."

"Nope, nope, nope." Amanda took Lucy's arm and dragged her through the store. But Lucy had to stop and examine each dazzling new display that they encountered.

"Timepieces are good."

"Nope." Amanda dragged her along. "No watches."

"A carpet? They're pretty."

"Sorry, too big. Too expensive. Come on. I know just the thing. We're the shopping marines. We get in, complete our mission, and get out."

Amanda assured her that a sweater was the perfect gift for a daughter to give her mother. When they emerged from the store, the snow had grown much heavier and the wind was whistling in the wires. They ran for the train station, sliding on the sidewalk, and hurried down the stairs. On the ride home Lucy felt exhausted from all the excitement. The train climbed the grade from the tunnel and out onto the elevated tracks.

Amanda looked out the window. The snow was blowing sideways, impenetrable in the glare of the streetlights. "Wow, this is bad."

"Bad?" Lucy thought it was miraculous.

"It's a blizzard."

"Yes, but it's beautiful. It makes me think of Dr. Zhivago."

"Think again, my little rutabaga. It's Dr. Chicago."

Lucy wasn't sure what it meant to be in a blizzard until they set out on the walk home from the el station. The snow was already up to her calves, and walking was slow and wearying. She could feel herself getting colder and colder as they went. Her fingers hurt, and her toes had gone numb. It seemed that no matter which way they turned, the wind was directly in her face. The snowflakes were made of steel. About halfway home, Lucy stopped, and Amanda turned on her almost angrily.

"Don't stop."

"Where are we going? I can't remember."

"Come on!"

Lucy didn't understand why she was shouting. "I think I'm going to sit down for a while and rest."

Then Amanda began screaming and pulling on her, saying, "No! No, Lucy! Keep moving."

"Why?" She felt warm now and knew how good it would be to take a nap.

Amanda shook her shoulders and looked right into her face. "Because you'll never get up if you do that. Come on. It's only a few more blocks."

"I'm really okay. I'm warm now. I'm going to take off my coat."

Amanda grabbed her lapels and shook her. "No! No, you're not. Keep moving."

Lucy could no longer talk by the time they reached the house. Jenny was getting up to greet them as they opened the door. "Do you have a sleeping bag? Lucy's got hypothermia."

"Oh, my God," Jenny said. "I knew I should have driven you downtown."

As Lucy stared at them, a blank and puzzled expression on her face, her knees buckled. She sat heavily in the front hall without even taking off her coat. Jenny returned a moment later with a sleeping bag. Amanda was undressing, saying, "Get her clothes off. We have to warm her up."

Lucy felt like a rag doll as Jenny took off her coat and sweater and stripped her down to long underwear. Amanda stuffed her into the sleeping bag with Jenny's help. Then Amanda stripped and climbed in with Lucy, saying, "Zip it up. This is going to warm her up. Make something hot to drink."

Lucy was laughing.

"What's so bleeping funny?"

"Mom, I wanted to buy you a wedding ring."

Amanda held Lucy against her and said, "She did. She wanted to buy you a rug and a watch, too."

"God," Jenny said. "I'm so sorry."

"It's okay, Mom. I think I like blizzards."

"I'm an idiot," Amanda said. "I should never have taken her out there. Growing up in Africa, Jesus."

"Stop biting your cuticles," Lucy said.

Amanda laughed. "Come on, wrestling girl. Let's see you get out of this hold. You're in the zipperlock now."

An hour later they were sitting in front of the fire drinking hot chocolate. Lucy had a big down comforter wrapped around her and they were laughing about it.

"I knew I should have driven you girls," Jenny said again. "Thank you, Amanda. For knowing what to do."

"Oh, I've always been good at this rescue shit," Amanda said. "I practiced on my mother."

Jenny looked confused, but Lucy knew what Amanda was talking about.

16

LUCY MET WESTON TEMPLE every afternoon for practice. She liked the boy. The messages she received from him in The Stream were gentle. He didn't even realize that he was sending them, and she didn't want to embarrass him by mentioning it. She could tell that he was shy. Lucy had the impression that his father had put him up to wrestling as a way of making more of a man of him. What a silly concept. He was man enough.

Lucy thought that wrestling was such an odd pursuit: To take someone off his feet. It was all about status. For millions of years people had walked upright. It was one of their special gifts. To take a person down to the ground was so elemental. She understood why the crowds reacted as they did. At the wrestling meets everyone entered The Stream and received the powerful messages that the players sent by way of their actions on the mat. The triumph of one human over another. To turn a person into a beast. And she saw that sports provided a means for those lonely humans to communicate more deeply.

Wes had taught her how to take someone down, taught her the good positions for gaining points, and the pin. She had to be careful not to hurt him, and she had gradually learned how to conceal her strength. Then she learned to use those skills in the contests with other schools. She would take down a wrestler, and everyone would chant, "Lew-See! Lew-See!" Whenever Lucy received a big gold trophy, Coach Barnacle put it in a vitrine in the school hallway near the gym.

They traveled in buses and stayed in hotels. Lucy saw the countryside, which was mostly crops, then the yellow stubble of corn, the snow in the winter. Every time they passed through a stretch of forest, she felt a yearning to leap into it and fly through the crowns of the glorious trees.

By the end of the season, Lucy stood nearly undefeated. No one could explain how she could take down opponents so efficiently. She was interviewed in all the newspapers. When asked where she came by her uncommon agility and strength she attributed it to an active life growing up in the jungle. Someone had started a Jungle Girl blog to track her performance. And one Sunday, a headline in the *Chicago Tribune* read "Jungle Girl Goes to State." Jenny winced when she read that, thinking, If only they knew the truth.

Lucy had come to Jenny in tears after a big meet when she'd brought home the first of her trophies. As Jenny held her, Lucy had said, "It's not fair. I'm cheating. I had to lose to one of their wrestlers just to make it look like I wasn't some freak of nature."

She was right. But Jenny didn't know what to do about that. Her status as a star athlete served to hide Lucy in plain sight. Jenny told her that she could quit if she wanted. But Lucy said that she didn't want to disappoint her team and her coach and especially Wes. Moreover, Lucy's high-profile participation in sports had gotten Dr. Mayer off her back. No one argues with athletic success.

One night in winter, they built a fire in the fireplace and Lucy fed the first of the orange notebooks into it. They watched it curl and blacken and vanish into ash. But then Lucy said, "I can't do it."

"But what if someone finds them?"

"Mom, it's all I have left. That one photograph and these."

"Okay," Jenny could see how torn Lucy was. And anyway, who would ever know to look for them?

After the last big meet in Indiana, the wrestling team had checked in to a drab hotel of poured concrete, set at the intersection of two highways that roared and hissed like battling boa constrictors.

III

There had been a big banquet after the matches. Then the players had dispersed, and Wes and Lucy were standing out in the parking lot under a snowy moon. The air was chilled and the moon looked like a glowing boat in a fairy tale. Lucy could tell that Wes was nervous, trying to get something off his chest.

"What is it, Wes? What do you want to tell me?"

"I'm sorry, Lucy. I know I'm not supposed to think things like this about a teammate, but you're just so beautiful."

"Why, thank you, Weston. That's so sweet of you to say. You're not bad yourself."

"Thanks. Okay. I can do this." He took a deep breath. "Lucy, will you go to the prom with me?"

"Of course I will. You're really nice, Wes. Perhaps one day we'll mate."

She saw him flush crimson and recognized her blunder.

"Oops. My bad. I wasn't supposed to say that, was I?"

"It's okay. I know you meant it in a nice way."

On a weekend in April, they celebrated Lucy's fifteenth birthday with Amanda and a few friends from school. The temperature went up to almost 70 degrees and the wind picked up. The warm air, the saturated colors of the leaves, barely open, and a new kind of smell announced spring with great fanfare. Lucy and the other kids played on the front lawn in shorts.

Harry came over and made pizza from scratch, and Jenny tossed a salad. Harry and Jenny watched the children, now almost adults, as they laughed and talked with music blaring out the open front windows of the house. Amanda's boyfriend, Matt, threw a football to Lucy in the bright April air. With simian grace and improbably long arms, he'd launch the ball at the sky. But no matter where he put it, Lucy was there when it fell. Jenny looked at Harry and saw him smiling to himself in some private reverie.

He shook his head. "How does she do that?" he asked. Then he shouted, "Way to go, Luce the Goose!"

Lucy turned and beamed at him, then caught another one of Matt's passes.

Jenny watched Harry and saw the love for Lucy in his eyes. She thought, I really should tell him. Of all the people in all the world,

Harry would completely get it. He and Lucy had bonded. Lucy lit up when Harry turned those eyes on her. If anything, Harry would love Lucy even more once he knew the truth. And the secret would always be safe with him.

One warm and rainy day in May, Jenny made Lucy a cake with "Happy Mother's Day, Leda" stenciled on it in icing. It was waiting when Lucy came home from school. She had unexpectedly brought Amanda. Lucy wept and hugged Jenny when she saw the cake.

"What is it?" Amanda asked. "Who's Leda?"

"My mother."

"Oh, I'm sorry. I should let you guys be alone."

"No, don't go," Lucy said.

"Have dinner with us," Jenny said.

"No. I should probably go be with my mom." But Jenny and Lucy could tell how sad it had made her. And Jenny thought, I should tell Amanda, too. Or Lucy should. Here was this dear girl, Lucy's best friend, who didn't know the most basic thing about her. But then where would it all end? Where would they draw the line? And Jenny saw that their need to keep the secret was cutting them off from the people they loved the most. After Amanda went home, Lucy and Jenny had a quiet dinner and went to bed.

Yes, the secret had served them well so far. As the school year drew to an end, Jenny felt almost as if she and Lucy were home free. No one knew, and it seemed that there was no way for anyone to find out. Jenny began to feel that they had cast a protective web around themselves that could repel the busybodies and mischief makers of the world.

Lucy and Amanda had become inseparable. Amanda slept over almost every weekend. Jenny would make a big pot of vegetable soup or a casserole. Sometimes Harry would come over and grill fish and vegetables on the patio. They'd all eat together and then watch a movie or play Scrabble. Amanda was on the high school chess team and was teaching Lucy to play. Sometimes the girls stayed up late playing, and Jenny would go to bed to the sound of them whacking the clock and giggling as they practiced swearing in

French. She was feeling domestic for the first time in her life. And she couldn't imagine how Lucy would have managed without Amanda. Jenny recalled the first time that she found a box of Tampax in Lucy's bathroom and realized that she'd neglected one of her primary duties in Lucy's socialization. Thank heaven for Amanda, she thought.

At the end of the school year in a big auditorium, with mortarboards flying in the air, Jenny heaved a sigh of relief. The girls both graduated with honors. Lucy seemed the picture of normalcy. And that was all that Jenny wanted for her.

Amanda had helped Lucy study the college catalogs online. Their scores on the entrance exams were good, and by April they'd both been accepted to half a dozen schools. But Lucy wanted to live at home and go to Jenny's school. She said it so simply: "Mom, I can get the same education anywhere. I mean, look what I learned in the jungle. I want to be with you."

17

THE GIRLS WERE SO EXCITED that they couldn't settle down. They lay in bed together, talking for hours and enjoying the relief of having finished school. As they were nuzzling each other, trying to find sleep, Amanda buried her face in Lucy's shoulder and inhaled.

"You smell so different from other people. It's nice. Like the forest."

"That's cuz I'm the Jungle Girl."

"My friends at school think I've dumped them for you."

"I'm sorry. You should spend more time with them."

"No. I'm fine the way things are. They're just not as interesting anymore now that I know you. Matt asked me if you and I are lesbians."

Lucy felt a thrill go through her at Amanda's closeness, the way she used to feel playing with her brothers and sisters. But this was deeper, more urgent. She wasn't sure how to approach the subject with Amanda. "Go to sleep," Lucy said. And before she could think of what to do next, she had fallen asleep herself.

In the morning, the girls were yawning as Jenny pulled the car onto the highway. Amanda kept a continuous selection of CDs going into the car stereo, and the girls danced as best they could, rocking in their seats and waving their hands in the air. Even Jenny joined in, swaying from side to side. She yawned and said, "Lucy, we have to get you driving. We could take turns and then I could take a nap."

"I got my permit."

"Yeah, but I'm afraid to be in the car with you."

"And I'm afraid to drive on the highway."

"I'll drive," Amanda said.

"That would be great."

Amanda drove and let Jenny doze in the front seat while Lucy slept in back. They woke just south of Duluth. They spent the night in a little town called Superior. In the morning they stopped at the grocery store in Duluth to stock up for the week.

They drove up the north shore of Lake Superior, passing along the orange basalt lava flows and the gabbro on which the waves crashed and shot twenty feet into the air. An hour later they entered the old forest, and Amanda gazed out the window, saying, "Ooh, this looks like Hansel and Gretel country." It was Jenny's graduation present to the girls: A trip to the Boundary Waters. They had wanted Harry to come, but he was on call at the hospital.

In another hour, Jenny was in the kitchen unpacking groceries, as Lucy rushed through the cabin showing it off to Amanda. "Little house on the prairie," Amanda said.

"Mom, can we have this bedroom?"

"Take whichever one you like, girls."

Amanda and Lucy spent the first few days in lazy contentment, while Jenny chopped wood and paddled around the lake. Then in the long late yellow light, Jenny would lounge on the shore reading while Amanda and Lucy splashed in the water or explored the forest. The girls took the canoe out at night while Jenny built a bonfire on the beach. They paddled to the end of the lake beneath a chalky moon that was gathering light for its journey through the night. There in a small lagoon, they caught walleye. Lucy held one in the net and studied it. "I'm sorry, Wally. I'm sorry I have to eat you."

"You talk to animals?"

"Yeah. And they talk to me."

"What'd he say?"

"That if he'd been big enough he'd have eaten me, too. Fish'll eat anything."

The girls found their way back to the cabin by the squirming orange light of the fire. They drew the boat up onto the beach and fried the fish. They ate them with steamed rice and the vegetables that Jenny had roasted while they were out.

Early one morning Amanda and Lucy put on their backpacks, said goodbye to Jenny, and set out on a hike that would take them to the cliffs at Saganaga Lake five miles to the north. They made their way along the shore of Flour Lake, then turned north up the forest trail, skirting Hungry Jack. As they turned east, the sun was in their eyes, filtering through the dense woods. The scent of pine rose up, and Lucy inhaled it, feeling at one with the forest. She heard the ravens calling, and once, in a clearing, she and Amanda watched an eagle circle overhead.

They passed Bearskin and hiked up the northeast shore of Daniels Lake. In real wilderness now, amid the low and heavily forested hills of the Boundary Waters, Lucy stopped and put out her hand to Amanda. They stood still as Lucy sniffed the air.

"Wanna see a moose?" Lucy whispered.

"Sure."

They crept softly through the forest until they reached a rise above a swampy area. The cow was immense and dark, her ears decked with weeds. Her calf was cute as she dipped her head into the water and made lowing noises. Amanda took a camera from her pack and snapped a photo. Then the girls slipped away unnoticed and hiked back to the trail.

At lunchtime they ascended the low hills behind Rose Lake. Lucy could smell Amanda's sweet summer sweat. They found a flat rock and ate lunch on a high perch overlooking Canada. Lucy held up a finger and said, "Listen." A spring litter of wolf pups barked faintly in the distance.

They spent the afternoon exploring the forest floor below. Lucy showed Amanda the imprint of a deer's hoof, the burrow made by a vole, and unearthed the skull of a red fox. Then Lucy heard something and told Amanda, "Don't move." Lucy put her hand out on the earth, palm upward. Amanda watched and waited for what seemed a long time. But at last, a rabbit crept out of the underbrush and made its way cautiously toward them. It approached Lucy's outstretched hand, sniffed, and then crawled into her palm. Lucy lifted the small creature up to her face and began to stroke its fur.

"How the hell do you do that?"

"I just learned how to communicate with animals. You know, in the jungle."

"Can I touch him?"

"I don't know. You can try. It's a her."

Amanda reached out to pet the rabbit, but it bolted, arcing high in the air and vanishing into the brush. The rabbit's claws left a scratch on Lucy's arm.

"Oh, you're bleeding. I'm sorry."

"It's nothing. I heal fast."

Lucy caught walleye at dusk as the fish began to feed. They made a fire on a high rock and threw in some potatoes that they'd brought from the cabin. They roasted the fish on hot stone. The stars overhead made it taste that much sweeter. And when they were done, Amanda opened her backpack and brought out a plastic bag. She handed it to Lucy with a smirk.

"Sweet." Lucy opened the bag and held it out to Amanda, who popped a grape into her mouth and winked.

Late that night the girls lay on their backs in the grass watching the stars wheel across the sky. Lucy missed her home terribly then. Most humans, she knew, saw the jungle of Congo as a vast, humid trap of malarial mosquitoes. But to Lucy the forest was home. Her father had taught her how to read the waves of weather that promised a rich harvest of pink mushrooms and swarms of delicious termites, how to follow the itaba vine to its sweet roots. She learned the faint insect sounds that led to honey. All of that bounty came to them from the forest. And when the forest was done with them, it took them down and redistributed their materials to other creatures, no less deserving. That's what her father had told her.

But humans must have forgotten all of that long ago, he had said. The forest had come to seem hostile, impenetrable, perhaps evil. They had cut it and burned it and denounced it. They became a homeless people filled with longing and bedeviled by a subconscious craving to get back to the rich tenderness of the forest. And now Lucy wondered if she believed any of that at all. Those were her father's thoughts, not hers. But what did she believe?

"I gotta get some sleep," Amanda said.

Lucy rose from the forest floor. A big moon had come up to light their way. She took Amanda's hand and led her deeper into the forest, saying, "Now, since you've spent so much time teaching me the ways of your culture, I'm going to show you a jungle trick."

Lucy skittered up a tree so fast that Amanda said, "Dude, you really are so the Jungle Girl. How'd you do that?"

"Come on up."

"What on earth for?"

"We're sleeping up here."

"Are you crazy?"

But at length Lucy coaxed Amanda into the tree. With great difficulty she began to climb, muttering curses under her breath. "Crap, I'm gonna have to get my nails done again." Lucy directed her to sturdy branches. As Amanda came within reach, Lucy grabbed her wrist and pulled her up.

"O-M-G. Okay, this is really high. What now?"

"Now I make you a bed." Lucy began breaking branches and weaving them together.

"No way. How do you do that?"

"Just practice." Lucy built her own nest close enough to Amanda's so that they could talk.

"You slept like this in the jungle?"

"Yeah. I slept in a bed sometimes, too."

"What did your parents think?"

"Well, my mother slept with me."

"What? In the trees?"

"Yeah, she taught me."

"What was she, some kind of Congolese tribal person there?"

"Yeah, something like that."

"Wow."

And at that moment Lucy felt the same urge that she'd felt in bed with Amanda, and it made her want to blurt out the truth. Lucy felt cheated. Here they were at last with the vastness of this old forest embracing them, their shared solitude, the perfect moment of communion. Yet Amanda had no idea who Lucy really was. Lucy wanted to rebel against it, to claim and use what was rightfully hers. She desperately wanted Amanda to know her now.

"So what about your dad?" Amanda went on, seemingly unaware of the momentous transformation that was about to take place.

"He slept in our cabin." Lucy's voice was flat and dry now. What is there in life, she wondered, if not this moment, this friend, this time? It had to be now.

"So you and your mom would . . . what? Say, G'night, Pa, we're heading for the trees?"

"Yeah, more or less. He was used to it. See, my mom was an ape."

"Ha-ha. Very funny."

The truth hung between them, invisible to Amanda. And Lucy realized that there was nothing, really nothing, that she could add that would have convinced Amanda in that moment, no stigmata she could show that would settle the matter once and for all.

"Okay, climb in." Lucy felt empty and alone. For Amanda could not even entertain the possibility that what she'd heard was true. To her it was nothing more than an offhanded joke. Lucy understood: If she could find no place to live in Amanda's mind, how could she live in her heart? She lay her head down and closed her eyes.

"Hey, are you okay?"

"Yeah, I'm just tired."

"Okay. I think on the whole I prefer a nice hotel with cable TV and a shower, but what-ever."

In the morning they climbed down and hiked through moraines of granite and glacial debris. They climbed to the top of an esker and walked its ridge, looking down on balsam and spruce. They descended into a forest of thin aspens and saw pink and white lady's slipper growing in the understory. When they reached the shore, they heard a loon calling from afar. The day was warm, and they had both sweated through their shirts. At Daniels Lake, they set down their packs and took off their clothes to splash in the shallows, shrieking at the shock of cold water. After they'd washed off the sweat and dirt from the hike, they sat naked on a rock to dry their dripping hair in the sun. They nibbled on dried fruit and nuts and shooed away a whiskey jack that came begging.

They sat in silence for a time, breathing in the forest air, and watching a soft breeze make patterns on the water. After a while, Lucy stiffened and said, "Watch this." She pointed at the sky.

"What?"

"Just watch."

An osprey fell from the sky and hit the water like a stone shattering a ceramic dish. A moment later the bird was airborne with an improbably large fish in its talons.

"Wow," Amanda said, "that was really intolerably cool. How'd you know he was going to do that?"

"I don't know."

Amanda passed Lucy a plastic bag of nuts. "Lucy, can I ask you something?"

"Sure."

"What does it feel like when you wrestle guys?"

"Well, I get all excited, and it makes me quicker and stronger."

"It always seems like it would, you know, turn you on and you wouldn't be able to concentrate."

"I think when I first wrestled with Wes it was like that. I'm not sure. But the excitement I feel focuses me. When I'm in a match it's like the other guy is moving in slow motion. I can see what he's about to do and take my time to plan my next move. And it gets very quiet except for certain things that I can hear very clearly."

"Like what?"

"Like his breathing. I can smell him and know if he's afraid. And sometimes it's like I'm looking at him through a tunnel. It's really cool. The room goes away. I don't hear the crowd. All there is in the world is this lonely guy, placing himself in front of me like a king about to be checkmated."

"Damn."

They fell silent and watched the water. Then Lucy asked, "Amanda. Do you think I'm pretty?"

"Are you kidding? Everybody thinks you're beautiful. Haven't you noticed the trail of boys fainting in your wake?"

"Get out. You're making fun of me."

"A little. But you are beautiful. You don't look like anyone else I've ever seen."

"I think you're beautiful, too."

Amanda lifted her chin, exposing her neck, and said, "Aww . . ."

"No. I really mean it."

Again they fell into themselves, picking at the dried fruit. Lucy traced her finger along the patterns that were etched into the flat expanse of rock.

"Wanna go?" Amanda asked.

"Sure. Let's take a different way home."

"You know the way?"

"Yeah."

They dressed and shouldered their packs and hiked south along the western shore. After a mile, they entered the old forest, dark and strange. Lucy felt her heart quicken. She knew this place, northern jungle. As they penetrated into the interior, its darkness stole the sky and left them in a chaotic world churning with life and destruction. Where any light came, it dropped in great pillars and slim shafts, illuminating a mist that smelled of clove and myrrh mixed with the aroma of dying leaves.

"This is so beautiful."

Lucy led on through heavy old pine and fir, hung with ancient streamers of silver moss, towering out of a maddening tangle of deadfall, brush, and vines. They left the trail and entered an eternal twilight, where they saw a radiant darkness escape the forest and overspread the open land beyond. And only when the breeze came up to ripple the water did Amanda recognize that she was seeing a deep black lake, alive with fish. They made their way to the shore and stopped.

They heard the pebbles rattle as the waves withdrew. When a breeze came up, the aspen leaves clattered like coins. They heard a sneeze in the forest.

"Bear."

"Is it dangerous?"

"No."

"I'm a little scared here, Lucy. It's so spooky. Beautiful, but spooky."

Lucy felt Amanda's hand touch hers as they stood side by side looking out. Lucy put her arm around Amanda's waist, and Amanda leaned into her. They stood for another moment and Amanda turned toward Lucy. Lucy could smell the sun on her skin. Then they were kissing. Lucy tasted her and felt a warm energy rush through her. Amanda's lips were so soft, her tongue so sweet. And then just like that it was over. Trembling, they held each other for a moment longer.

"You're yummy," Amanda said, and then they laughed and broke the spell.

They hiked the rest of the way back to the cabin, lost in their private thoughts. Jenny greeted them with obvious relief. She had a tuna casserole in the oven. Candles made the pine walls of the cabin glow and the shadows squirm. Jenny listened to the tales of their adventure as they ate. Amanda showed her the photo of the moose on her digital camera.

"Were you aware, Dr. Lowe, that your daughter sleeps in trees?"

Lucy saw Jenny flinch at the question. Jenny stilled herself and smiled. "Yes. So I've heard."

After dinner Lucy felt very tired and excused herself to go to bed early. Jenny and Amanda made a fire and stayed up talking. Lucy could hear the murmur of their voices and their laughter as she began to feel the chills. The last thing she would later recall was Amanda slipping into bed next to her and then leaping out again as if she'd been burned.

18

IT WAS ALMOST TEN O'CLOCK when Amanda and Jenny said goodnight. Jenny stayed up to read a few more pages of her book before going to bed. But a moment later Amanda emerged from the bedroom looking concerned. "You'd better come and take a look at Lucy. I think she's sick." Jenny felt a wave of fear wash over her.

Rushing into the room, she found Lucy shivering with the covers pulled up to her neck. When Jenny touched her cheek, Lucy moaned.

"What is it?" Amanda asked.

"I don't know. Stay with her. I'll get a thermometer."

Lucy was running a fever of 103 degrees. Jenny was unable to coax her into swallowing an ibuprofen tablet. Lucy seemed only half conscious. "Get a wet washcloth. Quick."

Jenny heard the water running and a moment later Amanda returned with a bowl of water and a cloth. They spent the night ministering to Lucy, who occasionally jerked and cried out in her sleep. Amanda fell asleep in a chair at around four o'clock, and Jenny continued wetting the cloth and gently sponging Lucy off. Lucy's fever went up and down all night, spiking at 105. It broke at last at dawn and Jenny fell into her chair in the living room, exhausted. She woke in a sweat three hours later. The day was already hot. She went to check on the girls and found them sleeping.

Jenny put the coffee on and waited, looking out the window. The forest was alive with the racket of birds. Light fell in wheeling spokes through the forest canopy and lay in pools on the carpet of pine needles. Jenny thought over what she knew that might help. Bonobos were vulnerable to most of the same diseases that humans contract, in addition to a few more exotic ones that didn't affect people. If Lucy's fever continued, she'd need medical attention. They were a twelve-hour drive from the only doctor Jenny could trust. There was no mobile phone signal, so she couldn't even call Harry for advice.

As she took a sip of coffee, she heard a thrashing, choking sound and ran to the bedroom to find Lucy having convulsions. Amanda stood beside the bed, eyes wide, her hand over her mouth in shock. Jenny sat on the bed and held Lucy tight as she bucked beneath her. Think and be calm, Jenny told herself. Don't let fear overwhelm you.

"Go to the owner's house. Down the path. Run. Tell them we need an ambulance." Amanda seemed frozen to the spot, watching Lucy in horror. "Go!"

Jenny watched Amanda bolt out the door, then turned back to Lucy. She held her hand. "Hang on, honey. Hang on. I'm not going to let anything happen to you. Just stay with me." Then Jenny sponged her off and saw that her own hands were shaking. Half an hour later the Forest Service ambulance came crunching up the drive with its red lights searing across the cabin walls.

From the bedside, Jenny told Amanda, "Pack our things. Follow in the car."

The paramedic put in an IV line and gave Lucy oxygen. Jenny rode in the ambulance, holding Lucy's hand. It took an hour to reach the county medical center outside of Grand Marais. But the doctors there were unprepared for such a case, and a helicopter was called to take Lucy to Duluth. Jenny was waiting for it when Amanda arrived.

They sat in the emergency room on either side of Lucy. Curtains separated them from other beds. There was nothing to say. At one point Lucy opened her eyes and looked around.

"Lucy!" Amanda said. But she didn't respond.

When the helicopter arrived, Jenny told Amanda to bring the car to the hospital in Duluth and rode in the helicopter, holding headphones over Lucy's ears against the noise.

Skimming low over the forest, they reached the hospital in less than an hour. Much as Jenny didn't want anyone to have a drop of Lucy's blood, she knew that it would do no good to protect their secret if Lucy died as a result. She had no choice but to let them treat her. With a deep sense of dread, she signed the consent form. Lucy was in intensive care within half an hour. Amanda arrived about an hour later while the hospital lab was processing blood tests.

Amanda called her mother to let her know that she would be at least a couple of days late coming home. Jenny heard Amanda say, "I'm fine, Mother. I'm feeling just fine." And: "No, I want to stay with Lucy. Why? Because it's the right thing to do." Then with a disgusted look she handed Jenny the phone. "She wants to talk to you. She thinks I'm going to get sick."

Jenny assured the girl's mother that Amanda was not in the way, had in fact been a great help. She also pointed out that the two girls had been together continuously. If Amanda had been exposed to something contagious, sending her home now would do no good. And they were, after all, in a hospital. Jenny said, "As a mother, I know how you feel." She had never said anything like that before. But for the first time in her life, Jenny knew the truth about being a mother: That there was a fate worse than death.

"Okay," Amanda's mother said at last. "Okay, please take care of my baby."

Jenny and Amanda stayed with Lucy through the night. The only sign of life from her was an occasional muscle spasm accompanied by a haunting animal cry. The night nurse came and changed the IV bag. Jenny and Amanda tried to doze off in the chairs but found sleeping nearly impossible. Jenny rose and washed her face when the first light of day leaked in through the curtains.

When the doctor appeared at last, he said, simply, "Let's go to my office where we can talk." His nametag said Dr. P. Syropolous.

Amanda and Jenny followed him down the hall. He closed the door before beginning. Jenny knew that this was not a good sign.

She could feel fear descending into her gut as Dr. Syropolous began. "Well, basically I have bad news and good news. Lucy has a disease called encephalomyocarditis, or EMCV. It's a very serious illness, a virus that affects the brain and heart."

When he said the words, Jenny felt her heart leap with alarm. Now she knew what she had to do. She saw no point in beating around the bush. If he was going where she thought he was going with this, then all she could do was buy a little time. She might as well tackle things head-on.

"What? What is it?"

Jenny put her hand on Amanda's arm to still her. Then she turned to the doctor and said, "Yes, I know it. It's treatable with the poly-l-lysine complex, but it's not usually symptomatic."

He looked surprised. "Are you a doctor?"

"Not the kind you mean. I teach in the anthropology department at the University of Chicago."

"I see. Well, then you'll probably know that she should make a complete recovery. We've started her on PLL, which, as you point out, is the correct treatment. Fortunately, we've caught this within the first twenty-four hours of the illness, so you can congratulate yourself for having brought her in so quickly. And we at Mercy Hospital can congratulate ourselves for having a lot of good serological people, because frankly, I'm not sure I'd have caught on to what this was so quickly without them. In any event, we should see Lucy start to improve as early as tomorrow."

"She'll be okay?" Amanda asked.

"That's correct."

"That's good," Jenny said. "That's great news. When do you think she can go home?"

"Is it contagious? My mother wants to know. I never get sick."

"Well, that brings me to my next point about Lucy's condition. Yes, in fact, EMCV is contagious. She has a variant of the virus known as EMCV thirty slash eighty-seven. The trouble is . . ." He seemed reluctant to go on. He removed his glasses and looked around the room as if he'd lost his sight.

"What?" Amanda asked.

Jenny felt her stomach turn over. She already knew what he was going to say. For there was a catch. And Jenny was hoping that a doctor in Duluth, Minnesota, wouldn't be aware of it.

At last he spoke. "Humans can't contract thirty slash eighty-seven.But that leaves us with this puzzling question: What is Lucy doing with a disease that occurs only in pigs, mice, rats, rabbits, and nonhuman primates? It makes me wonder if the disease has jumped from animals to humans as diseases sometimes do. In which case it could present quite a threat to the public health. You see where I'm going with this . . . ?"

The silence seemed to go on and on as Jenny stood there trying to think clearly. Amanda bit her nails, looking from one to the other in anticipation. Jenny kept telling herself that Dr. Syropolous couldn't prove anything yet. He had only hunches, and so far they were the wrong hunches. He was looking for an abnormality in the virus, not in Lucy.

"Wait a minute. So are we supposed to worry or not supposed to worry?"

"That's the thing. I don't think this is a case of the disease jumping from one species to another. Because when a disease does that it has to make certain adjustments in its genetic makeup. We did some genetic workups overnight and . . ." Here Dr. Syropolous paused again, as if he had an extremely delicate matter to discuss. Jenny felt her heart sinking. It's over, she thought. All we can do now is delay.

"And what? Can I get it or not?"

"I think I can assure you that you will not get this disease, Amanda. It's the exact same form of the virus that animals get. It hasn't picked up the extra genetic material it would need to be contagious to humans."

"Wait, so how did Lucy get it then?"

"That's what I was asking myself."

"You know what? Lucy was scratched by a rabbit when we were in the woods."

"You didn't tell me that," Jenny said.

"It was just a little scratch. She said it was nothing." Amanda turned to Dr. Syropolous. "But even so, you said it could never infect a human."

"That's correct. But a rabbit carrying it could infect other animals."

"I'm confused. What does it mean?"

"I think it means that you won't get sick. Tell your mother not to worry." He turned to Jenny. "But that still doesn't explain how Lucy could have contracted it from a rabbit, if that's what happened. We're doing a complete genetic workup on Lucy right now, and that may shed some light on this rather mysterious development. You don't have any idea why—"

"No. None."

"Okay. Well, in the meantime, you and Amanda can stay with her if you like, or you can go and get some rest. The front desk can give you a list of nearby motels. Lucy's being well cared for, and I gave her something to help her sleep. She'll recover just fine. Any questions?"

Jenny could tell that the truth had not yet entered his mind. It probably wouldn't until he saw the actual genetic profile. It was simply too far-fetched. "No. Thank you, Doctor."

As she led Amanda out and down the hall, Jenny tried to imagine some way to stop them from doing a genetic workup on Lucy. But she knew that as a responsible physician, Dr. Syropolous would have to do it. In desperation, Jenny imagined snatching Lucy from the hospital and vanishing, but they already had her blood. And Lucy still needed treatment.

Jenny and Amanda returned to Lucy's room and sat on opposite sides of the bed to watch her breathe. The IV infusion pump made a whirring noise every minute or so as it pushed fluid into Lucy's vein. The hospital made all sorts of strange and urgent sounds. Jenny knew what Lucy would say: This is a place where it is impossible to tell when you're safe and when you're in danger.

Jenny told Amanda, "You should get some rest."

"No, I'll stay. I want to be here when she wakes up."

For a long time after that they said nothing. Jenny was thinking, Now they'll know. Genes don't lie. On the trail of an explanation for the EMCV infection in a human, Syropolous would have to take this all the way to the Centers for Disease Control in Atlanta. It was a matter of public health now. Within weeks, perhaps only days, the world was going to know the truth about Lucy. Jenny would have to rest and gather strength for what was coming. She had already gone to talk to Donna in Milwaukee. Donna had agreed to help if it ever became necessary. But that would be a last resort. What Jenny didn't know yet was how the world would greet Lucy in the meantime.

"Jenny."

"Yes, honey?"

"When we went camping?" Amanda began as if asking a question.

"Yes."

"Do you think I'll get sick, too?"

"No. Why?"

Amanda hesitated, her finger to her lips. Jenny looked at the girl, so beautiful, so innocent, so intelligent. "What is it, honey? You can tell me."

"I kissed her. In the woods."

Jenny felt her heart ache for them. She thought, The rest of the world will know soon enough. Amanda should be the first to know. Tell her, she thought. So that she knows why she won't get sick. But not here. Not now.

Jenny reached over and took Amanda's hand. She put her finger to her lips, looking around to make sure that no nurses were nearby. She knew that they could be overheard through the device that the patients used to call the nurse.

"We'll talk about this later," Jenny whispered. "But you won't get sick. Trust me. It's okay. I'll explain later."

"Okay." Amanda still looked worried. Then she said, "I'm so selfish. I should be thinking about Lucy."

"Shh. She's going to be fine. You, too. I promise."

19

LUCY HAD BEEN SHIVERING VIOLENTLY, she remembered that.
She had just wanted to sleep. Then Amanda was in bed with her.
Her body was warm, and Lucy wanted to reach for her, to hold her,
but then Amanda was gone. The next thing Lucy knew, she opened
her eyes and saw Jenny sleeping in a green reclining chair. Amanda
was curled up on the floor in her sleeping bag and sunlight was
coming in. Lucy felt hungry. Then she saw that she was in a strange
room with odd machines and unfamiliar noises. A tube ran into
her arm. Lucy began to shriek in fear. She saw Jenny vault across
the room, saying, "Honey, it's okay. I'm here. It's okay. Shhh . . .
You mustn't scream. You were sick. You're in the hospital. I'll be
taking you home soon."

A nurse was at the door with an annoyed look on her face.
"What's going on in here?"

"Sorry," Jenny said. "She was having a nightmare."

Amanda was sitting on the floor looking around. "What happened?" she asked.

"I screamed," Lucy said. "I'm sorry."

"I'll tell Dr. Syropolous she's awake," the nurse said, and left.

"What happened?" Lucy asked.

"You had convulsions and a high fever," Jenny began. "I had
no choice, I'm sorry. They've given you medicine, and you're getting better now."

Lucy sensed a disturbance in The Stream. But she was groggy and unsure of what she was perceiving. Jenny leaned in close to her. She pointed to a device on the bed with a cord running out of it. It said "Call Nurse" in red letters. Jenny put her finger to her lips. Then she picked up a pad of paper and wrote, "They can hear us." She wrote again, then held the page so that Lucy could read it. It said, "They have your DNA."

"Oh, no," Lucy said.

"What? What is it?" Amanda asked.

Jenny looked from one girl to the other and shook her head. "Be calm," she said. "Be very calm. Just wait until we're home."

Jenny sat on the bed in the smelly motel room with her head pounding, her mind racing through all the possibilities. She took ibuprofen and stood under the shower for half an hour until her headache went away. Then she put on clean clothes and returned to the hospital. She gave Amanda the key to the room and stayed with Lucy while Amanda went to shower. Jenny didn't want to risk leaving Lucy alone. While Lucy slept, Jenny thought about how their lives were about to change. She began to list in her mind all the passionate groups that were going to try to get in on the circus once it began. The true believers. She tried to imagine a happy ending, but she could not.

When Amanda returned, Jenny said, "Honey, I have to sleep. I have to think, and I can't think until I sleep."

"I'll take care of her. You go ahead. We'll be fine."

"Call me if you need to. I have my phone."

At the motel Jenny fell into profound sleep and woke at dawn. She couldn't remember what day it was. She dressed and hurried to the hospital. Amanda and Lucy were playing chess on a set that one of the nurses had bought them. They both smiled when she entered the room.

"I'm so sorry, Amanda. I slept all night. I didn't mean to. You must be exhausted."

"It's okay. I slept some."

Dr. Syropolous arrived at about seven o'clock. Just seeing him in the doorway made Jenny's heart jump. He asked if they could talk in his office, and Jenny left Amanda with Lucy.

Dr. Syropolous closed the door. "I have the results back from the lab, and I've been doing a bit of research." It was what Jenny had expected. She thought, He knows now. He just doesn't know exactly what he's dealing with yet. "Does Lucy have any health problems? Any abnormalities? Mental dysfunctions? Behavioral issues? Anything out of the ordinary that you can think of?"

"No. She's a normal teenager. Why do you ask?" Jenny knew perfectly well why he asked.

"Well, there's something very unusual in her genetic profile. Some congenital anomaly. I don't quite understand. It's out of my field."

"What congenital anomaly? There's nothing wrong with her." Jenny would continue to hold out for time even if it was only a few days. Let him wrestle with it.

"Let me just throw something out to you. It's going to sound crazy, I know. But bear with me."

She said nothing.

"Okay. I looked you up after our talk yesterday. And I learned that in addition to your teaching appointment you are a primatologist who studies bonobos in the Democratic Republic of Congo."

"Yes. That's correct. How is that relevant?"

"So you must know, Dr. Lowe, that bonobos are genetically more than ninety-eight percent identical to humans. I didn't even know what a bonobo was until I read up on it."

Jenny let him have the silence once more.

"But there are notable differences," Dr. Syropolous continued. "They have, for example, a completely different sequence for amino acid metabolism from the one that humans have. Bonobos probably can't digest meat very well because of it."

A pause. Syropolous seemed to want her assent, but she gave none.

"Also there are differences in the alpha-tectorin gene. The hair-keratin-associated protein is different, too."

"Yes, I know all of that," she said, as if impatient. "But why are you telling me?"

"Because Lucy has that genetic material. She has what appears to be a genetic sequence that is a combination of human and bonobo genes. Her hair and skin, for example, are not entirely human. Close, but not exactly the same. Her sequence for amino acid metabolism is quite a bit different. I saw it myself in the microarray sequencer or else I wouldn't have believed it."

"That sounds crazy."

"Yes, I know it does." And after another pause: "Does she eat meat?"

"Of course, she eats meat."

"Really? She refused the meat that the dietitian offered her. Lucy has some of the genes of a bonobo."

"That's impossible."

"I know, it would seem to be. I'm sorry. I'm just telling you what I saw. It's utterly baffling. I mean, my first thought was that it must be a contaminated blood sample. But you see, the trouble is that in order for us to have a sample of human blood contaminated with bonobo blood we'd have to have a bonobo. And the nearest ones—I checked on this—are in the county zoo in Milwaukee, which is about a ten-hour drive. Lucy's blood was taken when she first arrived here. I know the nurse who took it. So you see . . ." The silence hung in the air for a long moment. Then Dr. Syropolous said, "And then, the fact that you are a primatologist who works with bonobos in the jungle . . . It seems like a most remarkable coincidence, don't you think? But you say you know nothing about it."

"No, I'm afraid not."

"Because if hers is a natural mutation that allows her to be susceptible to a potentially fatal disease previously found only in animals—and by the way, bonobos are one of the animals that can contract encephalomyocarditis—then it's worth a paper in one of the scientific journals. And the CDC will certainly want some follow-up research done on Lucy. Then again, if it's not a natural mutation . . . Well, I don't know what to think."

Jenny remained silent.

"No thoughts at all on this?" Dr. Syropolous asked. "Nothing?"

"No. Sorry. None." She could see that he was a smart and curious man. He would wake at three in the morning thinking about Lucy. And even if he didn't do anything about it, the CDC would. Dr. Syropolous was bound by law to tell them.

"Dr. Lowe. I'm trying to help you. I respect patient confidentiality. But I think you're hiding something. And I do want to know. I mean, you're a scientist. Put yourself in my position. Wouldn't you want to know?" He paused. "Dr. Lowe, please. I'm not the police."

The mention of police sent chills up Jenny's spine. That would come soon enough. "When do you think she can go home?"

20

MEMORANDUM

FROM: M. George Glandon, PhD, Division of Viral Diseases, National Center for Immunization and Respiratory Diseases

TO: Distribution List, Centers for Disease Control and Prevention

CLASSIFICATION: Unclassified

ABSTRACT: A recent human infection with an enterovirus suggests that research is called for in human-to-animal contact with special emphasis on nonhuman primates. EMCV 30/87 is an enterovirus normally found only in pigs, mice, rats, rabbits, and nonhuman primates, such as apes. A case described by P. Syropolous, MD (Dir. Internal Medicine, Mercy Hospital, Duluth, MN), in a letter to the Division of Viral Diseases, National Center for Immunization and Respiratory Diseases, describes a fifteen-year-old female patient who presented with severe febrile illness and the potentially fatal condition of infection with encephalomyocarditis 30/87. She was treated with PLL and released in satisfactory condition. A genetic profile of the patient showed abnormalities indicating an increased susceptibility to the enterovirus, suggesting mutation not of the virus (to suit humans) but of the human genome (making the patient more susceptible to the virus). This confusing state of affairs deserves attention, but emphasis must be placed on determining whether Dr. Syropolous's methods were satisfactory and his conclusions correct. This may simply represent a misreading of the evidence or a contaminated sample.

RECOMMENDATION: CDC will take a clean sample of blood and produce a full genetic profile of both patient and virus to determine the appropriate course of action.

AUTHORITY: 42USC264.

21

JENNY SAT IN THE KITCHEN watching Lucy eat a banana with peanut butter. Lucy saw Jenny watching and gave her an embarrassed look. "I peel them at school," she said.

"That's a relief."

Jenny had considered stopping in Milwaukee on the way home from Duluth, but the fact that Lucy had been sick meant that she could be a danger to the bonobos there. Jenny called Donna, who agreed that the visit would have to wait.

Lucy sheepishly peeled her banana and spread peanut butter on it. She looked up at Jenny and took a bite. Jenny smiled and was about to say something, but the phone rang, and she jumped at the sound. She picked it up.

"Dr. Lowe, this is Dr. Syropolous. I trust you got home safely."

"Yes."

"Dr. George Glandon at the Centers for Disease Control asked that I contact you. They want to rule out the possibility that the virus has crossed over to the human species in some way that might pose a threat to the public health. They'd like to take a new sample of Lucy's blood for analysis on the off chance that our sample was somehow contaminated."

Jenny leaned on the counter. She already felt tired from what had not yet happened. They had decided at last how to respond.

And Jenny had her backup plan with Donna if the worst happened. But the question before the world would be: What is the appropriate response to Lucy's existence on this earth?

"Yes, yes," Jenny heard herself saying. "I think I'd like to delay this until Lucy is feeling a bit stronger."

"Well, I'm afraid that's not up to us. The CDC has certain powers under the law to prevent diseases from spreading. They can take Lucy's blood by force if need be. They're already a little concerned that she left the hospital. Even though she seems better, the virus is still in her system, and they need to sample it. They'll be sending someone over today, in fact, a well-trained phlebotomist from Northwestern University. It won't take five minutes."

"I see," Jenny said, thinking, We'd better get Amanda over here. It's time for the girls to get busy.

"They wanted me to be the one to call since I am, de facto, Lucy's physician at the moment."

"Yes, of course."

"The phlebotomist's name is Roberta Dyson, I'm told. So I wanted you to be expecting her."

Jenny hung up. She felt as if she were on speed, her mind racing through what the next weeks and months would bring.

"What?" Lucy asked. She had stopped eating and was staring at Jenny intently. "What is it, Mom? What happened?" But she knew. They had already discussed it all on the way home from the hospital.

The road they traveled from Duluth had stretched out ruler-straight for miles, cutting farm fields in half, as pastures fell away in gentle slopes toward island lakes. Dark clouds had gathered in the western sky as they entered the great expanses of forest in Wisconsin. Lucy caught the scent of deer and fox and even wolf in there. Somewhere around Washburn, Jenny said, "I think you should talk to Amanda now. The whole world is going to know soon enough."

Lucy was afraid, not knowing how Amanda would react. She felt as if Amanda should have known long ago. But even when she had tried to tell her in the forest, she saw that Amanda could not believe her. Not yet. Not then.

"The world is going to know what?" Amanda asked as they

plunged on through the darkening woods. A truck thundered past, going north, its headlights on. The sky had taken on an angry cast.

"That I'm half human. My mother was a bonobo."

"What's a bonobo?"

"It's a great ape," Jenny said. "Kind of like a chimpanzee. It used to be called the pygmy chimpanzee, but it's actually a separate species, very closely related to humans."

Amanda sat thinking for a while. "You two are putting me on, right?"

"No," Jenny said. "What she's telling you is true. That's why you won't get sick. I didn't want to tell you at the hospital. She caught the disease because she's genetically part bonobo. Her father was a primatologist studying bonobos in Congo. He decided to breed a female bonobo with a human male. Himself. Lucy was born from the female ape."

Amanda's hand came up to her mouth and she said, "Oh, my God. Oh, my God. This is so not funny. That's impossible, right? Tell me you guys are joking, okay?"

"I'm sorry, Amanda," Lucy said. A cold gust came down from the dark clouds, and drops of rain began to tick onto the windshield. The smell of wet dust and oil rose from the road.

Jenny said, "It's not a joke, Amanda. It's real and Lucy is here. And with a sample of her blood they're going to realize that she's genetically part bonobo. That doctor already knew before we left, and he's going to tell others. So we have to figure out what to do."

"Oh, my God. Stop the car."

Jenny pulled to the side of the road and Amanda leapt out before the car had come to a stop. She stood by the side of the road in the hissing rain, her chest heaving, her face pale with fear.

"Are you going to be sick?" Jenny asked through the open door.

"I don't know. I just need air. You guys're really scaring me. If you're joking, this is really mean."

But Lucy knew that Amanda didn't believe that anymore. Not the way Jenny had said it, so flat and factual. Now Amanda was going through all the clues that she had been unable to put together and that now made so much sense—Lucy's smell, her strength, her strangeness. The way Amanda's dog Cody had reacted.

Lucy waited, worried about what her response would be. She

was Lucy's best friend, her only real friend. And now she knew that Lucy had been living a lie.

The rain increased, and thunder murmured in the distance. Lucy stepped out of the car and crossed to stand beside Amanda. "Please don't hate me, Amanda. I tried to tell you the truth."

Amanda turned slowly around in a complete circle, looking at a world that had changed forever. As she came around to face Lucy, their eyes met. She stared at Lucy for a moment, then burst into tears. Lucy held her tight, saying, "I'm sorry. I am so, so sorry. I didn't know how to tell you." Amanda wept in her arms as the cars and trucks ripped past on the gleaming highway. A long V of Canada geese undulated across the purple sky behind them, their faint voices reaching them on the wind, as lightning stitched the clouds. Amanda straightened up, sniffing. Jenny had come from the car to stand beside the girls.

At last Amanda said, "Will they take you away?"

"Honey," Jenny said. "We don't know what will happen yet. But I'm not going to let them take Lucy away. Not ever."

Amanda stared at Lucy with tears in her eyes. "Didn't you think you could trust me?"

Then Lucy was weeping, too. "Yes, yes, of course, I trust you. I wanted to tell you so many times. I tried to tell you in the woods."

"I know. You did, didn't you?"

"You don't hate me?"

"No, I love you. I love you and I'm really scared for you. What are they going to do to you now?" Amanda gave Lucy a sharp look, as if she could stare right through her, all the way back to her conception. She saw clearly what Lucy represented now. "Why did he do this to you? Didn't he love you?"

And for the first time, Lucy began to see something that she had avoided all along. Amanda didn't even have to say who she was talking about. Lucy saw it clearly in her eyes. Amanda knew about these things. Most parents have children because they love them. Or they love children because they have them. But why, Lucy wondered, why did Papa have me? He saw his grand design, but did he really see the person he was creating? Amanda knew what it was like to have a parent who couldn't see her. And Lucy felt sick now. Sick for herself and sick for Amanda. They held each other tighter in the rain.

"Come on," Jenny said. "It's not safe here. You're getting soaked. Let's go home."

Amanda took a big shuddering breath and slipped from Lucy's arms. She returned to the car and Lucy followed, taking the backseat. Jenny quickly put the car in gear and joined the flow of traffic. Yellow headlights swept the streaming pavement beneath the troubled sky. They rode on with only the sound of the highway, the smell of the rain, the windshield wipers slapping back and forth.

"I love you, too, Amanda," Lucy said. "I'd never do anything to hurt you."

"I know that. I know that."

Amanda had played music constantly on the way up to the Boundary Waters. But there had been no music since they left the hospital. Lucy knew: It had been something in The Stream that Amanda could read, a feeling that something was coming. And now it had come.

Lucy watched her. Amanda was a survivor, annealed by adversity. Lucy could tell that she was thinking intently, finding another strategy in a life that had demanded many ad hoc strategies. Amanda bit her fingernails, frowning. Lightning flickered through the heavy clouds. A moment later they heard a concussion, a rumbling. Amanda took up her folder of disks and flipped through them in a leisurely way, as if waiting for one of them to speak to her. Lucy could feel her in The Stream. Amanda picked a Tom Petty disk and put it into the machine. She turned the volume up loud, and the guitars began in jangling sheets of sound. The drums hammered out an insistent rhythm. Then Tom Petty's voice: "Well, she was an American girl . . ." No one swayed or danced. Amanda sat nodding in agreement, it seemed, listening through the choruses until the guitars faded out at the end. Then there was only the ripping noise of tires, the sucking boom of big trucks passing. The rattling of the rain.

"I know what to do," Amanda said.

"What?" Jenny asked.

"Take control of the information. Don't let them set the agenda."

"What do you mean?" Lucy asked.

"That's how politicians do it. That's how corporations do it. Remember in African American history class? After centuries of oppression the black people took control of their own heritage. James Brown? I'm black and I'm proud? That's what you need to do. Don't let them be the ones to tell on you. Don't let them define you. You have to be the one to tell the world."

"God, she's right," Jenny said. "Why didn't I think of that?"

Now as Lucy sat in the kitchen licking peanut butter from her fingers, Jenny explained what was going to happen with the doctors and the CDC, the new blood sample. "Okay," Lucy said. "Then it's time."

"Yes, it's time." And they both understood what she meant: that it was time to tell the world.

Amanda had talked excitedly on the way home, mapping out how they would do it: The Internet. It was the new language of the culture. Everyone was on Twitter, Facebook, YouTube. It was The Stream of the global age. Amanda had been helping Lucy to prepare her own pages. Lucy had yet to put them up because, well, how do you tell people all about yourself when you're living a lie? Now she knew who she wanted to be: Herself. Her true self. It would all happen in a flash, at the speed of light. The moment their YouTube video was up and her Facebook page went live, the world would know. Amanda had assured Lucy of it: It would roll around the globe like lightning.

Lucy picked up her phone and sent a text message to Amanda. "Dude," it said. "Fasten your seat belt. It's going to be a bumpy ride."

Amanda came right back: "Is it time?"

"It's time."

"OMG. B right ovr."

Roberta Dyson, the phlebotomist, came in the afternoon. She was a polite young lady with her hair in a bob and a butterfly tattooed on her collarbone. She had trouble meeting the eyes of other people. She didn't know why she was taking the blood sample. She was just doing a job.

Amanda and Lucy had set up a video camera and were taping in the bedroom when Roberta Dyson arrived. Amanda, who was operating the camera, said, "Lucy, this is perfect. Proof that we're not playing some prank on the world." And she fell to blocking the scene and positioning the phlebotomist beside Lucy's chair. "Rolling," she said. "Go ahead, Miss Dyson. Lucy, say what's happening." Lucy stuck out her arm and made a fist, narrating, as the puzzled woman took two vials of blood. When she had left, Amanda and Lucy were laughing.

"That poor woman," Lucy said. "She didn't have a clue what was going on."

"She's about to have her fifteen minutes of fame."

Jenny felt a rush of love and hope as she watched the girls work excitedly on their project. She wanted to leave them alone, to let this be their event, but she found it difficult to sit still and kept poking her head into the bedroom to see what they were doing. Then she'd pace the house, puttering, straightening up. At midday she brought the girls sandwiches. In mid-afternoon, Lucy called from upstairs.

"Hey, Mom. Do you want to be on our YouTube video?"

"No."

"Okay. Well, will you get Papa's notebooks?"

Jenny climbed the stairs. "What do you want those for?"

Amanda and Lucy looked so excited, their eyes bright. Jenny hadn't seen them look that happy since prom night.

Amanda said, "We're going to show some of the passages in the notebooks to prove that this isn't a hoax." Then she caught herself and said, "I can't believe this is real."

"Yeah," Jenny said. "I know exactly how you feel, Amanda." She went to the cabinet where she kept the backpack and brought it to the girls. Lucy began sorting through the notebooks.

"Girls. I can't stand the suspense. I'm going out. Anyway, I have to tell Harry. I'd like to do it in person."

"Okay, Mom."

"Take your time," Amanda said. "We'll probably be up all night."

"Is there any way that I can help?"

"Yeah, Mom, could you pick up some Cool Blue Gatorade?" Lucy asked. "We're going to order pizza later, but Piero's doesn't have Gatorade."

· · ·

Jenny and Harry met at a Thai restaurant that had been their favorite place in the days when they'd had a favorite place. It had an outdoor deck on the second story that overlooked a quaint row of shops in the old part of town. The sun had gone down and the lights were on in the hippie shops. They sat under an awning as a soft summer rain fell. The pavement gleamed with streetlights and headlights, and people hurried along the sidewalk beneath umbrellas.

Jenny laid out the story as simply as she could. His calm in the face of amazing news didn't surprise her. It was one of the reasons that she had always been drawn to Harry. She could have told him that her throat had been slit and her hair was on fire and he would have said, Hmm . . . Let's have a closer look, then.

Once Harry had digested the information, he said, "I actually had a thought like that. Not that first night when I examined her. But you were so tight-lipped about why you wanted her blood back that I kept trying to think of possible explanations. And her strangeness had struck me from the first. I thought, Is this some kind of Joseph Conrad nightmare? Then I said, Naw. That couldn't happen. Just didn't allow myself to believe it."

"I always said you were one of the world's great diagnosticians."

"It's a sixth sense. Not something they can teach you in med school."

"Yeah. You're in The Stream."

"The Stream?"

"It's a subtle system of communication that Lucy uses. All animals use it."

"Yes, I've read about this," Harry said. "Nonverbal communication. Paul Ekman. Elaine Hatfield. Emotional contagion and micro-expressions. What's her name? That pheromone gal at your school?"

"Martha McClintock."

"Yeah. All the senses. Mostly people just ignore it."

"Lucy's taught me a lot. Amanda, too." They fell into silence for a time, staring at their drinks. "Anyway, I'm sorry I didn't tell you sooner."

"No, you're not," he said. "I'd have done the same thing. For Lucy's sake." He rubbed his five-o'clock shadow and shook his head. "What on earth was that man thinking?"

"That's exactly what I asked myself when I first found out."

"Was he just completely mad, you think?"

"I don't think so. He was young, passionate, and pretty god-damned unusual. Lucy was just a concept at first. But when she started walking and talking I think he realized what he'd done. It's in his notes. His guilt and remorse. His worry over what would become of her if he wasn't there to protect her. Or even if he was. He loved her. He really did. And he saw what a grave mistake he'd made."

"That poor girl. They're going to eat her alive."

"Not if I can help it. We're hoping that the bright light of publicity will serve to protect her. Anyway, there's no turning back now."

"Have you considered going to another country? One that's not such a police state as the U.S. has become?"

"She doesn't want to run."

"She's only fifteen. You're her mother. Stepmother. Whatever. Christ, Jenny, when you get into trouble, you don't go halfway, do you?" Then, after a pause, "So how can I help? Come to the house anytime. You know where the key is hidden. I have my place up in Wisconsin, too. You're welcome up there, of course."

"Thanks, we may take you up on that."

"I'll be on call. I always have my beeper. Just let me know."

"Thanks."

He shook his head again. "That poor girl. She's very lucky to have you."

"Yeah, well, I guess we'll see about that."

22

JENNY JERKED UPRIGHT out of a deep sleep, thinking that something was wrong. But when the girls came into focus, they were giddy with excitement. "Come on, Mom," Lucy said. "It's ready. You've got to see it."

Jenny looked at the clock. "It's two in the morning."

"Not in Japan," Amanda said. "Come on. The Internet never sleeps."

They led her downstairs and sat on the couch, one girl on either side of her. Lucy put the computer in Jenny's lap. Jenny yawned, and Lucy pressed the space bar. Tom Petty's "American Girl" began over a black screen. The image dissolved to a Google Earth zoom from outer space right down into the green jungle of Congo. Then the song faded out and Lucy appeared on the screen.

"Hi, everybody. My name is Lucy Lowe and I'm only half human. You may think this is some kind of YouTube joke but it's not, as you'll all find out soon enough. Today is Wednesday, June twenty-fifth, two thousand and seven, and the Centers for Disease Control just took a sample of my blood." The image flipped, and Roberta Dyson appeared, applying a tourniquet to Lucy's arm as she continued to narrate, voice-over.

"They're doing a genetic analysis and it's going to prove what I'm about to tell you: That my mother was a bonobo." Lucy's face returned to the screen. "I'm here to tell you my story because I'd prefer that you hear it from me rather than from some government agency. So that's why my friend Amanda and I are making this video. Say hello, Amanda."

Tears came to Jenny's eyes as she watched. Tears of all sorts, from joy and pride for the girls to fear of what was ahead. Right now they were as delighted as if they'd just played the biggest prank imaginable on the world. But not everyone would be amused. Amanda came into the frame and sat beside Lucy. "Hi, world. I'm Lucy's best friend, Amanda Mather. And Lucy is sooo telling you the truth. I'm going to let her tell you how it all happened."

Jenny watched with her heart in her throat as Lucy narrated her life story. She took her audience through it, from an explanation of what bonobos were to her father's dream. She showed pages from Stone's notebooks, and the girls took turns reading. "I know there's going to be a pretty big ick factor in this for some of you," Lucy said. "I'm just telling you what happened." She showed the photograph that Jenny had salvaged from the ruined camp and narrated their escape from the civil war and the trip upriver. She recounted her first day of school, her wild impressions, and how Amanda had helped her.

Then Amanda followed Lucy around with the camera so that people could see her room. "This is my so-called room," she said. She had made it her own in the year that she'd lived there. She had a love seat with flowered upholstery and a collection of stuffed animals. She had posters on the walls from movies and music groups and some photos of her and Amanda and the other kids at school. As Amanda swung the camera around to the bookshelves, Lucy grabbed one of her wrestling trophies. "Oh, and I almost forgot. Some of you will remember that I'm the Illinois state wrestling champion."

"Go, Lucy," Amanda called in the background. Then Amanda put her face in front of the camera. "And Lucy's awesome at speed-cubing, too. Show 'em, Luce." The camera turned and showed Lucy standing in the center of her room. Amanda's arm reached into the frame and handed her a scrambled Rubik's Cube puzzle. Lucy turned it this way and that so that she could see all the sides. Then in a flurry of clicking movements too rapid to follow, she unscrambled it so that all of the sides were solid colors once more.

"Awesome," Amanda said.

There was a cut, and then Amanda and Lucy appeared, seated

on the love seat among her stuffed animals. Lucy gazed into the camera and said, "So now you all know the truth about Lucy Lowe."

"AKA Jungle Girl," Amanda said.

"And I simply want to say this: I know some people are going to be totally freaked out by this. Some people may even hate me for being what I am. But like all of you, I didn't ask to be brought into this world. And if there's something wrong with what my father did there's nothing I could do about it then and there's nothing I can do about it now. I'll bet a lot of you can relate to that in your own way, too. Anyway, I'm here, and I am what I am. I don't want any special treatment. All I want is a chance to live a normal life, to go to school and contribute something to society. So, I don't know. I think I've turned out to be a pretty normal girl, given all that I've been through."

Amanda put her arm around Lucy. "She is. Totally."

"So with that," Lucy said, "I'll let you all judge for yourselves. Whatever my genetic material looks like, I'm just me."

"Oh, and don't forget to check out Lucy's Facebook and MySpace pages. They rock."

"Goodbye, everybody. Thanks for watching."

"Bye," Amanda said. And they both waved.

Jenny closed the laptop. She put her arms around the girls and drew them closer. She heaved a big sigh.

"What do you think, Mom?"

"You're the money, baby," Amanda said.

"I think we'd better get you some new clothes," Jenny said. "You're going to be on television."

At about five o'clock that morning the phone rang. A gentle rain was still falling. Lucy could hear it ticking on the maple leaves outside the window. She heard Jenny talking down the hall. Amanda slept while Lucy went to find Jenny propped up in bed.

"What? You want us to get on an airplane now?" Jenny said into the phone. "You'll send a car . . ." Then: "No, it's not that. It's just that it's five in the morning here. We need some sleep. Can you call back later?" She hung up.

"What's that, Mom?"

"*Good Morning America.* They wanted to fly us to New York to be on television. How did they find out so quickly?"

"Wow. You want to go?"

"No. There'll be plenty of time for that. Go back to sleep. You've been sick. Oh, and unplug that phone, will you?"

"Sure, Mom." Lucy unplugged the phone and returned to lie beside Amanda, who was snoring. They had done the math beforehand. She and Amanda began by telling everyone in their address books, mostly kids from school. Amanda sent out open-access Tweets and announced it on her MySpace and Facebook pages. They told everyone to watch the video and then tell all their friends. Lucy had calculated that if each person told only twenty others, in just seven steps more than a billion people would know. In addition, people would be putting it on their blogs and news organizations would take notice.

By the time they all woke up again, it was nearly ten o'clock. The rain had gone, and light was streaming in through the kitchen windows. A cardinal stood on the tip of the topmost branch of the maple tree and sang his wolf-whistle call over and over. Jenny paced around the kitchen with the phone to her ear, listening to all the requests and dictating the information to Amanda, who sat on a stool at the island taking down the names and phone numbers. Lucy was at the stove making a Velveeta omelet with salsa and heating tortillas. Amanda had declared Velveeta-and-salsa omelets to be "the most ultra-yum breakfast."

Amanda's phone rang. She had downloaded "American Girl" as her new ringtone. She looked at the screen.

"Uh-oh. It's my mother." She put the phone to her ear. "Hi, Mom."

"Have you seen the news?" She sounded angry. Amanda may not have realized that Lucy could hear her mother clearly. "Is this some sort of harebrained stunt? Because it's not funny."

"No, it's not a prank."

"Well, you come home this instant."

"She's my best friend, Mom. I have to stick by her."

"You can't have a monkey as your best friend," her mother shrieked. Lucy glanced over to see if Jenny could hear it, too. But Jenny was still on the phone. Lucy thought: Wow, she doesn't know the difference between a monkey and an ape. She wondered what it was going to be like out there in the world.

"Don't say that. That's awful. Are you drinking?"

"That's none of your business. You come home right now."

"No. She needs me. We have a million things to do."

"Young lady, you're not an adult yet, and I still make the rules around here."

"Mother, I turn eighteen in a week. And I'm staying here. I'll go live with Dad in New York, if you like."

A long silence. Then her mother said, "Well, if that girl is what she says she is, you are going to regret the day you ever met her."

"I'm sorry you feel that way." Amanda hung up without saying goodbye. She put her chin in her hand and bit her nails.

"That sounded rough," Lucy said.

"My mother can be so ignorant."

"Would you really move to New York?"

"Of course not."

Jenny was still listening to messages, now writing down the numbers on Amanda's notepad. She finished and set the phone on the island.

"What?" Jenny asked, looking at Amanda.

"My mother. She wants me to go home and have nothing more to do with Lucy. Which is so not going to happen."

The doorbell rang.

"What the—" Jenny said. "Who is that? Amanda, will you go upstairs and look out the window? See if you can see who it is. But don't let them see you."

"Okay."

As Amanda ran upstairs, Lucy asked, "Mom. What?"

"I don't know. There are a lot of nuts out there. And I have no idea what your legal status is. I don't know. I don't know. You're only fifteen and I am a little scared."

"Amanda's mother called me a monkey."

"You heard?" She caught herself. "Duh. Of course you heard. Well, you see? We don't know how people are going to react. We have to be careful from now on. People with guns shooting up college campuses. I mean, who knows what might happen?"

With all the excitement of making the video, Lucy had forgotten about the risks. Working all night together, she and Amanda had been swept along with the feeling of taking control of the situation and doing something bold and exciting. Now Jenny's words snapped Lucy back to reality.

Amanda came running down the stairs with her finger to her lips. "There's like a thousand reporters on the lawn and they've got satellite trucks and everything."

"How did they find us?" Lucy asked.

"I'm in the book," Jenny said.

"What book?" Amanda asked.

"The phone book. You've probably never seen one, right?"

Amanda looked puzzled. "No, I think my mother has one . . . somewhere."

"What're we going to do?" Lucy asked.

"I'm going to tell them to get the hell off my lawn," Jenny said, standing up and marching to the door.

Amanda and Lucy listened as Jenny chewed someone out, saying, "She'll do it when she's good and ready. Now I'm going to call the police if you don't get off of my lawn." She slammed the door. Lucy and Amanda were giggling behind their hands as Jenny came sweeping into the kitchen looking angry. Jenny stopped, glaring at them, and then she laughed, too.

"I guess you told them," Amanda said.

"Damned straight. Nobody tramples on my *Koeleria cristata* and lives to tell the tale."

The phone was ringing again. Jenny turned to Lucy and said, "Give me your phone." Lucy handed it to her and Jenny dialed. A moment later, she said, "Harry. I need you."

Lucy heard him say, "I'll just transplant a few more hearts and be right over."

"I'm not joking," Jenny said.

"I know. I figured things might get dodgy, so I got someone to cover for me today. There in a jiff, doll."

Jenny hung up and said, "Come on. Let's pack. We're not going to get any peace here."

Half an hour later, they were waiting in the garage when Harry phoned. Jenny opened the garage door and Harry's car rolled in. She quickly closed it again.

"This is totally bangin'," Amanda said. "I feel like I'm in a movie."

The girls laughed as they loaded the car and got in. Jenny opened the garage door and Harry pulled out. As he drove down the alley, a group of reporters came jogging up from the other end.

Lucy looked around at the crowd and felt a chill. Amanda turned around, too.

"People are chasing you," Amanda said.

"They're just reporters," Harry said.

"They're chasing you, too," Lucy told Amanda.

Then Amanda and Lucy exchanged a grim look.

As she watched the reporters, Amanda said, "Wow. This is pretty hairball."

Late that afternoon, Jenny sat in the kitchen and watched Harry work, while the girls explored the secret spaces of the old house like two puppies. Harry brought out a great steel wok for a stir-fry. Jenny began to cut lemons to make fresh lemonade.

"I suspect it'll be all fun and games for a while," he said.

"Yes. The latest public obsession."

"I assume you have a plan. For when things get ugly."

"Yes, I do."

"Don't tell me. I don't want to know. What about Amanda?"

"She and Lucy have been inseparable. She's deep in."

"But when things turn bad. What will happen to Amanda then?"

"She'll be with me. Until she wants to leave." Jenny knew where Harry was going with this, but she didn't have a better answer.

"I'm afraid for you, Jenny. I was always afraid for you in the jungle, but now I feel it even more."

"Well, why don't you come with us to New York and we'll get this show on the road?"

"New York, is it?"

"Good Morning America."

"I can't. I'm sorry. I have surgery."

"It's okay."

"Dinner in thirty minutes. Maybe you could find out where the girls have disappeared to."

Jenny shook her head, laughing. They sounded like an old married couple. She began wandering through the labyrinthine house, thinking about what might have been.

Harry's house offered a deeper insight into who he was. He bought it when he was a young doctor. Jenny had only just met him and teased him that it was probably haunted. The old woman who owned it before him had died in there. It was hung with heavy maroon drapery. Deeply stained threadbare Oriental rugs covered the battered hardwood floors. When Jenny made fun of them, Harry had said, "My dear child, this is a silk Tabriz."

"Yes, but the moths have chewed it to shreds."

"Picky-picky."

The fireplace in the living room had been designed to burn coal, and the gaslights still worked. But as young as he was, Harry had a long-range plan. Little by little over the years he had ripped down the drapes to let the light in and refinished the floors. When he began making serious money, he gradually added to the improvements until it was once again a grand old Victorian, with the Belgian crystal chandeliers all cleaned up and glittering. This was the palatial estate that he had once offered to Jenny if only she had been willing to give up the jungle. And as she looked around now, she felt a twinge of nostalgia for those simpler days when she thought that she knew what she wanted and could just say no without a backward glance.

For the first time, she truly appreciated the remarkable thing that Harry had done with the house. He had created a place of exceptional silence. The virgin pine beams that lay beneath the plaster, hard as iron with age, the colossal rooftrees somewhere above, the ancient stone pediments outside, and all the scrollwork and moldings and shingling enclosed her and muffled the world of noise out there so that she could hear the swish of her own jeans as she climbed the stairs to a beautiful suite of rooms furnished with period pieces, lush and moody, smelling of dust and tung oil. A watery sunlight fell through ancient imperfections in the window glass.

French doors led to a deck overlooking an English garden. It looked like the courtyard of a museum, the naked candelabra of pear trees espaliered against a high stone wall like Shiva. Meadow saffron, naked ladies, butcher's broom, led along narrow cobbled paths. In neat beds were bistort, foxglove, throatwort, lenten rose, and, in a far corner, live forever. Harry's dark sense of humor. All of those plants were poisonous.

The girls were sunning themselves in chaise longues on the second-floor porch. Jenny stood at the door watching them. They both wore bikinis, Lucy in yellow, Amanda in blue. They looked so beautiful. She felt her heart go out to them as if by force of emotion alone she could somehow protect them. Lucy was doing something strange with her hand. Jenny took a step closer to the screen doors to see. Amanda was giggling, saying, "No way."

"Yes, way," Lucy said. "Watch."

Then it came into focus. A cabbage white was fluttering around between the two chairs. Lucy put out her hand, saying, "Come on. Come on." The butterfly landed on her hand. "Okay, watch. Now fly," she said. The butterfly began flapping around between the chairs again. "Now land," she said. Jenny watched the butterfly alight on her hand again.

"Get out of here! I don't believe it. Do it again."

Again, Lucy made the butterfly take off and land. And Amanda said, "That is so money. I want to learn. Show me how to do it, Lucy."

"I can't show you how."

"Why not?"

"You're too human."

An ominous silence fell between them. An injured look crossed Amanda's face, and Lucy looked sorrowful.

"I'm sorry," Lucy said. "That was mean. I'm sorry I called you a human."

The two girls stared at each other for another moment. Jenny had never seen them at odds before and wondered how they'd resolve it. Amanda looked as if she were about to cry. Then a light of comprehension flowed into Amanda's eyes, her expression changed, and she broke up laughing. Lucy realized what they'd just done and began laughing, too. Amanda shouted, "I can't believe I was just offended when you called me human!" Then the girls couldn't stop themselves and fell into a fit, rolling out of their chairs and onto the deck, where they lay cackling, as the butterfly flitted away into the garden. When the laughter died down at last, they lay there groaning and holding their stomachs. "Dude," Amanda said, "you really know how to turn a bitch's world upside down."

23

AMANDA HAD TAKEN CHARGE of Lucy's wardrobe. "Let's go six-ties. What do you think?"

"What does sixties mean?"

"I mean the fashion of that time period. The 1960s."

"You're asking me about fashion?"

They'd had just enough time to make it to a vintage clothing store that Amanda knew in the East Village. Jenny let the girls go on their own, out into Manhattan. New York. Who could have dreamed up such a place? The throb of noise, the dazzling colors and the lights of Times Square, steam rising from the street in white columns as if the heart of the city smoldered with eternal fire—it all left Lucy breathless. She had to force herself to stop pay-ing such close attention.

At the vintage store, Amanda clawed through the racks and came up with one she liked. "There," she said, holding it up against Lucy's shoulders. "A nice A-line patterned dress with bell sleeves. That and a little pendant. I have just the thing."

Lucy had not known what Amanda was talking about, but she wore the clothes. And early the next morning, in a dark and cav-ernous space like a warehouse, she tottered uncertainly on heels as a woman led her through a clutter of equipment manned by shad-owy figures. Cables snaked underfoot everywhere across the floor.

"Watch your step," the woman said. The darkened forms of technicians hunched at their stations, peering at dim red and green lights.

They emerged into a cauterizing light, where a pretty, blond woman sat in what appeared to be a disembodied living room, torn free from its house and set inexplicably down here for no apparent reason. The woman sat in a beige easy chair, beaming as if she'd lost her mind. So this was the illusion, Lucy thought. All this mess led to that clean picture on the little screen.

The blond woman leapt up and embraced her. "Oh, my dear darling girl, I am so honored to meet you. Welcome. Welcome. I'm Diane." She sat once more, smirking and saying apologetically, "I can't go too far. My microphone."

"Thank you," Lucy said, as she sat in the other beige chair before a great television screen that said "Good Morning America" on it. A technician approached and attached Lucy's microphone.

A rumpled man wearing headphones, his jeans falling down, came forward and said, "And ten seconds, Diane." She smiled at Lucy and held up a finger, as if to say: Wait.

Lucy watched as the man counted silently with his fingers: five, four, three, two, one—and then pointed at the woman, who clasped her hands together and beamed at someone who wasn't there.

"We are so lucky today to have with us our incredibly special guest, Lucy Lowe. I'm sure you've all heard already, but just in case you haven't, Lucy is a hybrid human. Astounding as it might seem, her mother was a great anthropoid ape. Lucy, welcome."

"Thank you." Lucy saw several television screens before her, and was trying to figure out where to look. "Sorry, I've never been on this side of the television screen before."

The woman laughed. "That's quite all right. I understand. Now, let's jump right in. First of all, we have heard from the Centers for Disease Control that this is not a hoax."

"No, it's not."

"So tell us what it's like. What is it like to be a hybrid human?"

"Yes. Certainly." Lucy thought for a moment as her face flashed across continents. In homes, offices, restaurants, airport lounges, and even in hospitals, the image of Lucy hung before the world, as she contemplated what she was going to say. She looked down into her lap, then up at Diane. "I think that I'm really like a lot of teenagers. I think that what I feel is exactly what many of them feel. Something happened long ago that I had nothing to say about. No one asked me if I wanted to be here. Someone made me without my consent. Before I knew what was happening or why, there I was, walking around, talking, drawing with crayons, and having all the experiences that make up a life. By the time I was old enough to question it, well, it was too late. I'm glad I'm here. I'm glad I'm me. But I didn't make myself. Someone else did that. And I feel kind of like a stranger in a strange land. Don't you think all teenagers feel that way at some point, Diane?"

The woman clasped her hands in front of her, and a pained expression crossed her face. "That is so touching, Lucy. And I think you're exactly right."

The show lasted only a few more minutes. The woman seemed to be rushing to a place where she would never arrive, hurtling across space in her little biopsy of a living room. Lucy said goodbye and was led back to the greenroom, where Amanda and Jenny waited. Amanda threw her arms around Lucy. "You majorly rock, Luce. You were awesome."

They were led to the front door of the building and out to the street where the limousine waited. As they emerged, a crowd of people pushed in, shoving papers at Lucy, trying to ask questions. She stopped to sign autographs, but the limousine driver urged her into the car, and then they were off to the next show.

Sitting in the car between Amanda and Jenny, Lucy said, "I'm having a hard time getting my mind around this."

"You're a star. Get over it."

Jenny didn't look as elated. "I'm hoping it protects you."

As they quickly discovered, fame was a chronic condition for which they knew of no immediate cure. One moment, Lucy was an ordinary teenager, caught up in the trivialities of life in high school. The next, she was swept up in a whirlwind of publicity, television shows, and interviews.

Lucy lost track of time, but she did remember the sea. She had never seen it before. They checked into a hotel called Shutters, which was right on the beach in Santa Monica. The room that Amanda and Lucy shared had sliding glass doors that opened onto a patio overlooking the water, and that first day, Lucy and Amanda hastily dressed in their bikinis, Lucy in yellow, Amanda in blue, and went screaming into the surf, where they played like two slick dolphins for most of the afternoon. Then, in the slanting red light, they lay in bed. Lucy was reading to Amanda—"and the sea the sea crimson sometimes like fire and the glorious sunsets and the fig trees in the Alameda gardens yes"—when Jenny came in with the first offer in her hand.

Amanda, of course, made fun of it. "It's a cool idea, I have to admit," she said. "How about a self-help book called *Getting in Touch with Your Inner Ape*? Then you can follow up with a video called *The Jungle Girl Workout*."

But Lucy was remembering that even before she could read, she had loved books. She had carried them around and hoarded them. Then she remembered when her father was teaching her to write, holding the pencil and looking at the page and thinking about what a monumental thing it was to write. To write a book seemed so essentially human. To place a mark on a surface that could then move someone to laughter or tears. Only a human could do that. If she could write a book, a real book, then no one could ever say that she wasn't human enough.

Lucy crisscrossed the country with Amanda and Jenny and wound up back in New York for photo shoots with *Teen Vogue* and *Rolling Stone*. Then they were at the airport again, heading home at last. As they waited in line to pass through a security checkpoint, people gathered around and asked for autographs.

When they reached the magnetometer, the functionary of the Transportation Security Administration smiled and gave Lucy a thumbs-up. He was about to wave them through when an officer whose nametag said Stockton stepped in.

"I'll handle this, Gomez," he told the man, who stepped back from the magnetometer. Lucy could see that Stockton was obviously the higher-ranking male in the hierarchy.

Stockton stepped through the magnetometer toward Jenny and said, "I'm sorry, ma'am, we can't let her through." And he pointed at Lucy. The man he called Gomez was watching with a pained expression.

Lucy and Amanda looked at each other, then behind them to see if perhaps Stockton were pointing at someone else.

Jenny had been smiling and chatting with a fan before Stockton spoke. Now she stopped, a puzzled expression on her face. "What do you mean? Is something wrong?"

"Yes, ma'am, we can't let her through. All animals have to be caged and put in the luggage compartment."

Jenny laughed, thinking that it was a joke. But there was no humor in the man's face. "You're joking, right?"

"No, ma'am, we don't joke here. I can't let her through. You'll have to see your airline representative and make proper arrangements for transporting animals."

"Hey, boss, come on."

"At ease, Gomez. I'll handle this."

Gomez turned away. "I'm going on break."

Lucy and Amanda moved up beside Jenny as a crowd of people gathered around to see what would happen.

A woman in her forties in a business suit stepped forward, her face red, and addressed Stockton. "You moron," she said. "This girl is more human than you are. Let her through this minute."

Stockton lifted his hand and motioned to a police officer. "Remove this woman, please." Then he turned to Lucy and whispered, "You're an abomination before Christ. You should be put to sleep." He looked so unhappy. Lucy felt sorry for him.

The police officer stepped forward and positioned himself between the angry woman and Stockton.

"I'm a lawyer for the city. You touch me and you'll be cleaning toilets for the rest of your career."

"I'm sorry, ma'am, you'll have to leave now. You can't make a disturbance here."

"I'm getting on an airplane. I'm flying first class."

"No, I'm afraid you're not. Not now," the policeman said. "You cooperate, you might catch a later flight."

Lucy and Jenny and Amanda watched with wide eyes, scarcely able to believe what was happening. Now the crowd rose up and began shouting and booing Stockton. Several other guards rushed into the fray, and some of them began to radio for help. Jenny lifted her phone and took Stockton's picture, then turned to the girls and said, "Let's go."

As they retreated, the crush of people parted. They slipped away from the checkpoint and moved toward the outer doors of the terminal. Police and TSA guards were closing in on the chaotic scene from all directions.

"What are we going to do?" Lucy asked.

"I don't know. But we're not going to get arrested."

Jenny led them outside into the clouds of exhaust by the taxi stand.

"You okay?" Amanda asked.

"I guess. He called me an animal. And I guess I am."

"You're a person. And he was wrong."

"He was a religious nut," Jenny said. "But we don't want to fight that battle here."

"But how will we get home? I want a shower. And some grapes."

The dispatcher at the taxi stand hailed a cab, and Jenny told the driver to go to the other side of the airport where the private planes were. "We're going to do a little high-class hitchhiking. I did this once in Kinshasa." Sitting between the girls, she took their hands in hers. "Don't worry. It'll be fun."

Lucy could see the cab driver eyeing her in his oversized rearview mirror. "Hey," he said, "you're that, uh, monkey girl, aren't you?"

"Yeah. Ape, actually."

"Same difference, right?"

"Not really. Apes don't have tails."

"Yeah?"

"That's right. Do you have a tail?"

He laughed. "No."

"And neither do I. Also monkeys go along the tops of branches on all fours. Apes swing under the branches."

"Hey, I never knew that," the cabbie said. "Say, you sound pretty smart for being half ape."

"Yeah, I have all sorts of talents." Lucy began to cheer up, seeing that Jenny and Amanda were watching with growing pleasure as she toyed with the cabbie.

"Yeah, like what?"

"Well, I'll make you a bet. Is that your lunch there on the seat beside you?"

"Yeah, why?"

"Well, if I can tell you what's in the bag, we get our cab ride for free. How's that?"

"Deal. But you gotta gimme uh autograph."

"Deal." Lucy already knew what was in the bag, but she sniffed the air for effect. "Hmm," she said. "Let me see . . . Today you're having a ham and Swiss cheese sandwich on pumpernickel with mayo, yellow mustard, and onion. There's also a container of coleslaw in there. You have an apple. And something with chocolate—wait. I've got it: Reese's Peanut Butter Cups. I can't tell what the drink is because it's in an aluminum can."

The driver pounded the steering wheel and guffawed loudly. "Holy smokes, you're right!"

"See? It pays to get in touch with your inner ape."

As he pulled up to the general aviation facility on the other side of the airport, he turned around with his trip log in his hand. "Wow. So, how about that autograph? My wife's gonna get the biggest kick out of this. She saw you on the *Oprah*."

As they entered the general aviation lounge at LaGuardia, the pilots and passengers stared and then followed their progress across the room.

"I think you're being recognized," Jenny said. "That's good. Amanda, do you want to do the honors? You're nice and articulate."

"Do what? What are we doing?"

"Asking for a ride to Chicago. Someone who's going west must have a few empty seats."

Amanda glanced around the crowded room, biting her cuticles. Then she took Lucy's arm, cleared her throat, and spoke in a stage voice. Drama club paid off. "Ladies and gentlemen, do you recognize this girl?" Now all eyes were on them. "This is Lucy Lowe. You may have seen her on TV."

A few people said hi or waved. They all looked puzzled.

When Amanda explained what had happened, there were disapproving murmurs in the crowd.

"So we're here to find a kind soul who'd be willing to take us to Chicago. You'll not only get the rare opportunity to meet and talk to Lucy in person, but you'll have a heck of a story to tell."

Silence fell. No one moved. Lucy could feel their tension. They were all confused and fearful. The lounge was a bright, nondescript room with a terrazzo floor and an acoustic tile ceiling that held recessed fluorescent lights. A service counter stood at one end, attended by two women in uniforms. An elderly lady dressed in a purple suit stood with some effort and crossed to them with a magazine in her hand. "Excuse me," she said to Lucy, "but I was wondering if you would mind autographing this for me." She had bright green eyes and a beautiful smile. "For my granddaughter." A star sapphire winked at her neck.

"Not at all," Lucy said, taking the magazine from her. It was *Time*. Lucy's face was on the cover with the headline "What Does It Mean to Be Human?"

"What's your granddaughter's name?"

"Holly."

Lucy signed the magazine and handed it back. The woman smiled and squeezed Lucy's hand. Lucy looked down. The old woman had beautiful hands. They reminded Lucy of Leda's, the skin as delicate as paper.

"Can you give us a lift?" Amanda asked her.

"I would, dear, but I'm afraid I'm merely a guest on the airplane, and in any case, we're going straight to Rome."

"Thanks all the same," Amanda said, and the woman returned to her seat.

People came and went as the private jets taxied in and out, and gradually the lounge emptied. It seemed that the rush hour was over. Lucy and Amanda sat slumped and sullen in plastic chairs, listening to their music. Jenny returned from the restroom and sat between them, patting their hands. "Hey," she said brightly. "We can always go home on the train."

Lucy perked up, taking her ear buds out. "Oh, could we? I've always wanted to ride on a real train."

"We could."

A businessman with a briefcase entered from the street side accompanied by two pilots. They approached the service counter, and one of the pilots began filling out forms. Amanda rose to intercept them as a small white jet was just pulling up beyond the wall of windows. Lucy turned to look because the engines sounded different from those of the other jets, louder and with a whistling tone above the roar.

Jenny got up and joined Amanda at the counter. Lucy watched an elderly man and woman descend the stairs of the small jet that had just landed. A younger man, dressed in jeans, came down behind them. They entered the lounge and approached the counter. For no reason that she could explain, Lucy now joined Amanda and Jenny at the counter.

"I'd gladly take you to Chicago," the businessman was telling Amanda, "but my company doesn't allow it."

"I don't think our insurance would cover you," one of the waiting pilots said.

The elderly couple now stood at the counter waiting their turn, accompanied by the younger man. "I understand," Jenny said. She turned to the girls. "Well, maybe we will take the train."

The couple had moved up to the counter as the businessman and his pilots stepped away. The man was small and unremarkable in his appearance. He could have been the janitor reporting for duty. He wore the sort of gray cotton slacks and shirt that someone would put on for a Saturday afternoon of puttering in the garage. His gray hair was uncombed, but his gray eyes were clear and sharp. He and the younger man stood at the counter, engaging a young woman in a conversation about fuel.

The elderly woman was tall and thin with gray hair that hung straight to her jaw and tapered down toward her neck, which was cabled with tendons. She had dramatic lines around her mouth and a prominent mole on her left cheek. Her eyes were remarkably blue, and she looked around her with an air of alert curiosity. Lucy's attention was on the woman, and sensing it, the woman turned to her and smiled. Lucy smiled back. Jenny and Amanda had caught wind of it, and they now turned to watch.

The woman stepped forward and extended her hand. "I'm Ruth Randall. I recognize you."

Lucy shook her hand. "I'm Lucy."

"Yes, of course." She reached out and touched her husband's back. "Dear. This is the girl who was on the news."

"Just a moment, sweets."

"That was a terrible thing they did to you at the airport," said

Ruth Randall. "It's all over the news. It's sure to embarrass the agency."

"This is my mom, Jenny, and my friend Amanda. Mrs. Randall."

"Ruth, please." They shook hands.

"Pleased to meet you," Jenny said. "We're trying to get home to Chicago."

"Yes, of course." The men had completed their business and turned from the counter. "This is my husband, Luke, and our pilot, Roy."

Luke beamed at them with a jolly smile. "Don't let those TSA guys get you down," he said. "Airport security is BS. Just a jobs program. We live in New Mexico. Chicago's right on the way. We'll be happy to take you."

"That would be so generous of you," Jenny said.

"Sometimes it makes me ashamed to be an American these days. Come on, lemme show you the Saberliner."

"What's a Saberliner?" Amanda asked.

"It's that jet there," Luke said, pointing.

"I'll just use the ladies'," Ruth said, and walked, strong and erect, across the bright room, her white tennis shoes squeaking on the polished floor. A few minutes later, when Ruth had returned, Luke picked up two of the suitcases, the pilot picked up the third, and the group emerged into a bright and windy day and crossed toward the waiting airplane.

"Wow," Amanda said, "I've never been on the tarmac before."

"Don't say 'tarmac,'" Luke said. "There's no such thing as tarmac. It's called the ramp, dear."

"Sorry."

"Not your fault. Every time a reporter talks about airplanes, it's tarmac-this and tarmac-that. Buncha knuckleheads."

They ascended the stairs to find themselves in what appeared to be a small but comfortable sitting room. The décor was ivory colored with dark wood accents. The windows were large for an airplane, and the interior was bright. On either side of the aisle were two cream-colored captain's chairs facing each other across a table. There was a couch against the rear bulkhead.

"This is great," Lucy said.

"It's so kind of you," Jenny said.

"Yeah," Amanda said. "This most definitely does not suck."

"Sit wherever you like," Ruth said, indicating the chairs. "We'll have some refreshments once we take off."

Amanda and Lucy sat across from each other in the starboard chairs. Jenny and Ruth took the other two.

"What about Luke?" Lucy asked, watching Roy retract the stairs and secure the door.

"Oh, Luke flies the plane. Luke and Roy."

Indeed, the two men were already seated and preparing to go. A moment later, they heard the whistle of the engines powering up. It was much quieter inside than out. Ruth leaned across the aisle and patted Lucy's hand. Lucy looked over at her and smiled.

"Like my husband says, don't let those TSA guys get you down. We're Christians, dear, and I always believed that there was a God, and that he made people to be good caretakers of the earth and all its creatures. As I grew older, I wasn't quite as certain of all that. I mean, look at the world. And I also learned that if it walks like a duck and quacks like a duck, then it's probably a duck."

"Duck?" Lucy asked.

Ruth laughed. "It's an expression. It means that you seem like a perfectly lovely young lady, and that's good enough for me. I would no more go looking into your genes than you'd go looking into mine. I always believed that what people do in the privacy of their own jeans is their business." They all laughed and then sat listening to the whistling roar.

"Do you mind my asking what you and your husband do?" Amanda asked. "I hope you don't mind that I'm curious. I've never been in a private jet before. I thought you had to be, like, a movie star or something."

"I don't mind at all, dear. We have a chain of retail stores. I say 'we.' Luke founded it. I didn't do much. You've heard of them. You may have shopped in them. They're everywhere now. Denton's?"

"Oh, my God," Amanda said. "You guys own Denton's?"

Ruth smiled modestly and bit her lip. "Well, dear, it's a publicly traded company now, but yes, we do. Luke is a modest man and doesn't like to show off. Frugal to a fault. Or as my mother used to say, he can pinch a penny until it squeals."

They were taxiing now, moving away from the terminal buildings and along the side of the runway. Jenny watched Ruth as she spoke and sensed her strength. She wore a necklace of misshapen freshwater pearls and a thin gold chain that disappeared below the neckline of her pale blue shift. The way her head tilted and her shoulders moved gave an intimate and inviting impression. Her face was mobile and lively, and a half smile played upon her lips, even when the corners were turned down. Every now and then as she spoke, she would pause for a moment and bite her lower lip while thinking.

"Take this airplane, for example," Ruth continued. "Our accountant told Luke to buy one of those fifty-million-dollar Gulfstream jets. They have beds and bathrooms, can you imagine that? Luke wouldn't hear of it. He had to have some sort of transportation, because he visits all the stores in person every year. He's like that. He bought the cheapest, most practical thing he could find. This airplane is almost forty years old. Refurbished, of course."

"May I ask you a question, Ruth?" Lucy said.

"Certainly."

"If you don't want to spend a lot of money, what's the point in having it? I hope I'm not being rude."

"No, not at all. It's a legitimate question." Ruth looked off in the distance as if she could see the past somewhere out there. "We didn't really plan to get rich. Luke was simply, well, I guess you'd have to say that he was obsessed. Obsessed with the minutiae of retail operations. His father and grandfather were retailers. And Luke wanted to perfect all the operations, all the details, like one of these people who build great and intricate ships in bottles. The point wasn't the end, it was the process." She pursed her lips, and wrinkles caressed her mouth and eyes. "The money was a side effect of his obsession. I travel with him now, because otherwise I'd scarcely see him at all."

"So what do you do with the money?" Lucy asked.

Ruth laughed sadly. "I started a foundation. I give it away. That's our little joke. He makes the money, and I give it away."

"Why are your stores called Denton's?" Jenny asked.

"They're named after our son," Ruth said, and glanced down into her lap, where her hands were worrying each other.

"That's nice," Amanda said.

Ruth lifted a sad smile and played her watery eyes back and forth from Amanda to Lucy and back again. Then she seemed to remember something and busied herself fishing in a pouch attached to the wall beside her. "I almost forgot. When we have guests on the airplane, I'm supposed to give the safety briefing. I feel silly doing it, but it's a federal law." She withdrew a card of printed instructions in case of emergency. "There's not much to it, really. One door. And a small window in the cockpit that pops out. I doubt if I could get through it. Keep your seatbelts fastened, and all that. There are oxygen masks if the cabin loses pressure, which it won't do, because this airplane is built like a tank. Oh, and unlike the airliners, we provide smoke hoods in case of fire. They're under your seats. I think that's it."

The plane was accelerating down the runway. Less than a minute later, Lucy was being shoved back into her seat as the airplane angled away from the earth. As it climbed away from New York, Ruth smiled at her guests and said, "Do you like tuna salad?"

"Oh, yes," Lucy said. Amanda and Jenny smiled and nodded.

Ruth looked at her watch. "It's way past my lunchtime. I get low blood sugar. Makes me feel faint." She lifted a telephone from its cradle beside her. "Dear, it's me." A pause as she bit her lip. "Well, who else would it be?" Another pause. "Do you mind leveling off for a bit while I get some sandwiches? All right, will you and Roy have one?" She listened, smiling at Lucy. "Very well. Love you, too." She hung up the phone and smiled at Jenny. "It'll just be a minute. All the air traffic controllers know him. They delight in giving him special treatment. It doesn't hurt that Luke gives them a twenty percent discount at the stores."

After climbing for a few more minutes, the plane leveled off. Ruth flipped the catch on her seatbelt and rose to go aft, where she rummaged in a locker. She came back with sandwiches in plastic wrap, obviously homemade, and cans of apple and cranberry juice and bags of potato chips, all bearing the Denton's logo. She set them on the tables and went back for more. She brought lunch to the cockpit. When she was seated and had fastened her seatbelt again, she looked over the sandwiches. "I hope you like it. I made the tuna salad myself this moring. The other stuff is from the store." And the engines spooled up as the aircraft continued its climb.

"Papa said there'd be some good ones."

"Good whats?" Ruth asked.

"Good humans."

Ruth's eyes sparkled as she laughed and unwrapped her sandwich. Lucy liked her easy laugh and the way she would sometimes purse her lips and frown to get her words just right. She was not concealing anything. She was in The Stream.

The tuna salad was creamy with crunchy bits of celery in it and the sharp tang of lemon juice and mustard. As they ate, Lucy watched the world out the window, so oddly transformed by distance. In the jungle, there were no such vast distances. Everything was always close at hand.

An hour later, Ruth was sleeping, and the plane had begun its descent. Lucy kept her vigil at the window as the mysterious puzzle of the ground gradually solved itself. And when the wheels barked onto the pavement in Chicago, Ruth startled awake, saying, groggily, "Did I miss my stop?"

They could see the crowd behind the high chain-link fence as the plane taxied to the ramp: Throngs of television and press reporters, along with protesters carrying signs behind police barricades. A number of the signs said things like, "Welcome, Lucy!" or "Down with TSA" and "Smash the Police State." But many of them bore biblical references like "Ezekiel 16:50" and "Leviticus 18:23" and "Jude 1:7."

"This is crazy," Lucy said. "How did they find out?"

"The Internet," Amanda said. "You use it. It uses you."

Ruth asked, "What's your friend's name? Harry? Is that who's meeting you?"

"Yes, I see his car," Jenny said. "Oh, dear. We have to get through all that."

The plane was parked, and Luke came back from the cockpit. "What's going on out there? Who are those lunatics?"

He pulled a handle and the door opened. The stairs unfolded and rested on the ramp. The noise grew abruptly louder. Someone was speaking through a bullhorn, a man's voice: "Leviticus chapter twenty, verse sixteen: 'And if a woman approach unto any beast and lie down thereto, thou shalt kill the woman and the beast: they shall surely be put to death; their blood shall be upon them.' "

"Who are these creeps?" Amanda asked.

"I'm sorry," Ruth said. "It makes me ashamed to be a Christian sometimes, the way these people act."

As they looked out the windows toward the fence, they saw Harry gesturing and talking to a group of policemen, who turned and followed him to the gate. One of the officers unlocked the gate, and the group moved toward the plane.

Watching from the window, Jenny said, "Good work, Harry."

Luke had already descended the stairs to greet him. They were talking now. He poked his head back into the cabin and said, "It's all right. These officers will get you to your car."

Ruth was standing, pressing a business card into Jenny's hand. She gave one to Lucy and Amanda as well. "This is our office in Albuquerque. If you ever need anything, anything at all, don't hesitate to get in touch. I'm quite serious about this."

"Thank you so much," Lucy said. "You've been ever so kind."

"Goodbye, dear. Excuse me for not coming down. Be careful out there."

At the bottom of the stairs, Harry embraced Jenny, then Lucy and Amanda. Luke said goodbye, as the police urged them forward, surrounding them. As they hurried toward the gate, something in the crowd caught Lucy's eye. It was a lone protester. He was a young man with a buzz cut and a drooping handlebar moustache, dark tattoos on his arms, standing off to one side of the main group. He held a sign. Scrawled on a piece of poster board was the word "Euthanasia," followed by the number fourteen. That was all, but the word and his sinister appearance had an effect on Lucy. He was different from the other people in the crowd. He was creating a disturbance in The Stream. Lucy knew: He was really dangerous.

The reporters began shouting questions through the gate. The police pushed on through the crowd toward Harry's car.

"Lucy, what do you think of the new Senate bill?"

"We haven't heard about it," Jenny called out.

"Please just get in the car, ma'am," one of the officers said.

Just as Lucy was nearing the car, a woman broke from the

crowd and shouldered between two of the police officers. She leaned forward and spit in Lucy's face. As the police were wrestling her to the ground, she shouted at Jenny, "Shame on you! For shame!" She was trying to grab a crucifix that dangled at her neck, but the police had already snapped on handcuffs and were dragging her away. Lucy stared after her with a forlorn expression.

"Come on!" Amanda shouted as a police officer pushed Lucy into the car. Harry took a white handkerchief from his pocket and handed it to Lucy. She wiped the spit from her cheek.

As Harry sped away, quiet fell once more. Jenny asked, "What bill were they talking about, Harry?"

Harry sighed. "Steven Rhodes, the Republican from Utah, introduced a bill this morning defining a human being as having the genetic profile that was decoded from the human genome by the National Institutes of Health in 2003. It's Senate Bill 5251. They're calling it the Lucy Bill, because if it passes, she'll officially be a nonhuman animal and won't have human rights."

"Jesus wept," Jenny said.

Amanda and Lucy just looked at each other. Lucy felt tears well up in her eyes. She thought, Why do they hate me? She knew. She knew. The darkness of the jungle will always remain like sand and gravel beneath our feet. And the peril of cat and cobra will follow us even into this bright place that people have created. Lucy looked over at Jenny, then Amanda, who were both staring at her. She saw it in their eyes. The lost knowledge of what had been. The three stared at one another, their eyes flicking first to one, then the other, and they felt the love flowing back and forth in their shared understanding. Harry sensed it and turned around as they waited at a stoplight. Then four sets of eyes passed their silent messages back and forth. Lucy saw. They all saw: They had become a tribe.

24

"DEAR LUCY," the letter began. "My name is Jeremy Levin. I am a thirty-five-year-old attorney from Philadelphia. I am generous, caring, intelligent, and have a good sense of humor. I like walks on the beach, ethnic cuisine, fine wines, and opera. I am especially interested in the environment, world peace, and global warming. I also like snowboarding and have a condo in Snowmass. I hope that when you turn 18, you will take my offer of marriage seriously, as I think I could give you the best possible life in this world. I would like to have the honor of helping to create the new race of people that your father envisioned. Please consider my offer seriously and write to me soon. I'm enclosing a photograph of myself so you can see that I'm not too hard on the eyes and that I like to keep in shape."

It was signed, "Sincerely, Jeremy."

Lucy sighed and put it on the pile. Jenny sat across from her and Amanda at the dining-room table opening another stack of mail. Amanda had the laptop open and was going through the messages and comments on Facebook and MySpace.

"Yuck," she said. "Not that again."

Jenny stood and looked over her shoulder.

"Don't read it, Jenny."

"Dear Lucy," it began. "How RU? I wud rully luv 2 cam with U. Hit me up on Yahoo! 549Bigtoad. I have cam 2. Usually on Friday and Saturday nights & I have an honest 9 inches."

"Yuck, indeed," Jenny said.

They had stayed at Harry's off and on since the world had discovered Lucy. But after their whirlwind tour, Jenny had brought the girls home, hoping for some semblance of normalcy.

Lucy picked up another letter. Jenny watched her as she read it. She saw Lucy's face change and knew that it was one of the bad ones.

Jenny received her share of mail, too. Even Amanda was getting mail. "Dear Dr. Lowe," one of Jenny's fan letters began. "I'm a 59 year old widower in Toronto and believe that I could provide the missing ingredient in young Lucy's life: A father. A young girl needs to be taken firmly in hand . . ." And so on.

Jenny had also received a letter that began, "You Evil Whore. I don't believe there ever was a Dr. Stone. May you burn in hell for the sin of bestiality. You not only lay with a monkey, you allowed that demon child, spawn of Satan, to fester in your womb and then to enter our sacred nation when you could have left it to die in the jungle where you both belong."

They made a separate pile for those kinds of letters. Another category of letter that she received was from teenage boys asking if they could date Lucy. Some asked if they could come and live with them and be Lucy's brother.

"We have to stop reading all this mail," Jenny said. "It's not good for us." Lucy handed her the letter she'd been reading.

"Do you know the 14 words?" it began. "Robert Matthews died a hero and a martyr to our Race. God rest his soul. If we can rob an armored car of $3.8 million and bring down the Alfred P. Murrah, then we can certainly find you. When we do, we have a quick and simple solution to your problem: Euthanasia." It was signed, simply, "The Order."

"Do you remember that guy? When we arrived at the airport?"

"What guy?" Jenny asked.

"Yeah, I saw him," Amanda said. "Really spooky-looking guy. Tattoos and a moustache?"

"Yeah," Lucy said. "And he had that sign that said Euthanasia and the number fourteen."

"What does it mean?" Jenny asked.

"I don't know," Lucy said.

"I'll Google it." Amanda typed in the phrase. "Wikipedia says the Fourteen Words is a saying frequently used by White nationalists, Neo-nazis, and White Pride supporters. The slogan was coined by David Lane, an imprisoned member of The Order. The fourteen words are: 'We must secure the existence of our people and a future for White children.' The slogan was inspired by a statement in Volume 1, Chapter 8 of Adolf Hitler's *Mein Kampf*: 'What we must fight for is to safeguard the existence and reproduction of our race and our people, the sustenance of our children and the purity of our blood, the freedom and independence of the fatherland, so that our people may mature for the fulfillment of the mission allotted it by the creator of the universe.' Blah-blah-blah."

"Jesus, they're Nazis," Jenny said.

"Wow, listen to this. Sometimes the slogan is combined with 88, as in 1488 or 8814. The '88' stands for the eighth letter of the alphabet twice, or HH, which means Heil Hitler."

Jenny said, "This would be comic if it weren't so sick." She glanced at Lucy and caught a look in her eye that she'd seen a number of times. It was a very brief glimpse into the world of the jungle and the true powers of her lineage. In that brief flash, Jenny saw that in a real fight—if she thought that she or Jenny or Amanda were in danger—Lucy could and would kill.

"Is this real?" Lucy asked.

Jenny tossed the letter on the pile of hate mail. "I think it's possible. But I think it's fair warning that we have to be careful from now on."

Lucy passed her an invitation: Meet the provost at the university, where Lucy would be going in the fall. It appeared to be a chance for Lucy to meet some of her future faculty and classmates.

The phone rang, and Jenny reached for it. The caller ID displayed a number in New Mexico. Jenny pressed the button and said, "Hello?"

"Is this Jenny?"

"Yes."

"Jenny, it's Ruth. I hope I'm not disturbing you."

"No, not at all. Hi, Ruth."

"Fine then. That's good. I just wanted to ring you up and tell you how delightful it was to meet you and the girls. I really have been thinking about you ever since."

"Well, thank you, Ruth. The pleasure was all ours, I'm sure."

"I took the liberty—I hope you don't mind this—of having our lawyer put in a call to TSA. I think you'll be getting a letter of apology for what happened at LaGuardia."

"How did your lawyer do that?"

"Well, the man who refused to let you board wasn't acting on any official policy. Evidently they'd had trouble with him before. Profiling or something. I think they knew that the incident was already an embarrassment and could wind up being costly if you decided to sue."

"That's so kind of you. Thank you."

"I'm glad you don't mind that I did that. I was very angry with them, and I acted a bit impulsively, I'm afraid. But I think it's for the best. Anyway, I don't think you'll be having any more incidents now."

"You did the right thing."

"Good. Well, then. I got to thinking about that scene at the airport when we landed. And it occurred to me that you and the girls might like to get away someplace where you can be left alone. So I thought I'd invite you all out to the ranch."

"The ranch?"

"Yes. Luke and I have a ranch in New Mexico. It's very comfortable and there's lots of space. We have two old horses. I like to swim and hike. I think the girls would enjoy it. I can come out and pick you up in the plane if you like. Anytime. Just think it over."

"How generous of you."

"Well, frankly, I could use the company."

"I'll definitely talk to the girls about it."

"Good. Good. The ranch is a nice place to get away. You'll all be completely safe there, too."

"Thank you, Ruth. I'll let you know."

"Okay, then. Call me anytime."

"Goodbye, Ruth."

Jenny returned to the table, lost in thought. Maybe it wasn't such a bad idea to get away for a while. She was about to tell the girls when Lucy handed her a letter bearing the seal of the United States Senate. Jenny read it.

"What is it?" Amanda asked.

"They're having hearings," Lucy said. "They want me to come. Senator Martin Cochrain of Connecticut says he wants to protect my rights."

"Well, good," Jenny said. "Good for him."

"Wanna go, Mom?"

"Definitely."

Wherever they went people crowded around and pressed in, asking for autographs, snapping photographs with their phones. Lucy was able to read most of the people, who were simply curious, and clearly friendly. But there were outliers in the crowds, and Lucy could not help thinking about John Lennon, stepping out of his car in front of the Dakota on a normal evening, when a madman who thought he was Holden Caulfield shoved through the crowd and shot him in the back. Growing up in the forest, she knew what it meant to be careful and vigilant. But in the forest there were rules. Here it was wide open. There was no common language of intentions.

When Lucy first arrived in the United States, she thought she would never make it. When she met Amanda and settled in at school, she began to think that things would be all right. But she could no longer see into the future now. She couldn't imagine how she would go forward—into college and life. Would she marry and settle down? Where? There had been a moment at the senior prom with Weston Temple when she thought perhaps she might.

Lucy had had such fun preparing for prom with Jenny and Amanda. They went downtown to shop, and in Bloomingdale's Lucy fell in love with a sage green dress, which Amanda called her "gownless evening strap" because it showed so much back. Amanda was exquisite in red.

In the weeks before prom, Weston had taught Lucy how to dance. They practiced in the wrestling gym after everyone had left. Slick and sweaty from practice, wearing tights, they would hold each other. "Now, lady, just make your mind a blank and let your feet make that box. One, two, three, four . . ." She had a difficult time concentrating when he held her that way.

Then came the day of the dance. Amanda and Lucy slept in. After breakfast Jenny took them to have their hair and fingernails and even their toenails done. By evening they had showered and had done each other's makeup. They stood in their bras and panties before the full-length mirror, their things scattered everywhere.

"There it is, cupcake," Amanda said. "You are hot-hot-hot."

"I want hips," Lucy said, looking at her slim body. "My arms are too muscular. I want to be a woman."

"Sufficient unto the day is the evil thereof."

The dance was glorious. It took place in a great vaulted terrace, and a brilliant white light was spinning, flashing, randomly singling out faces, breasts, elbows, bare backs, buttocks, and torrents of blond hair. The room was air conditioned but the bodies all gleamed with sweat as they poured out their chemical messages. The hormonal aromas overwhelmed even the artificial perfumes as the couples twirled, clasped together in the dim light. On the stage the band leapt and sang. Lucy thought of those nights of the rain dance in the forest, when the elders would break branches and fling themselves about for all to watch, inciting them to join in.

With their small athletic bodies, Weston and Lucy fit precisely to each other, like two hands praying. Weston's pelvis was pressed against Lucy's, and she had no choice, it seemed. She pressed back as if she would simply tumble over backward if she didn't equalize the strain of that invisible force between them. Then, just as she thought that she might pass out or explode from the whirling forces and chemicals and lights, it was over. All too soon the room brightened. And then they were just a random group of boys and girls once more, staring around them, blinking in the light, attempting to assess what had just happened.

Late, going home in the limousine with Amanda and Matt, Lucy thought, I could learn to love this life. I could learn to love this boy. She tried to imagine what her father must have been thinking when he decided to create her. Didn't he think she might want all this? Lucy had blindly loved him because he was her father, her teacher. And now it made her sad and sometimes angry to think that perhaps all she had been to him was a piece of his great plan. But no, Lucy thought. She had fond memories of what a good father he had been, too. She knew in her heart that he loved her. It was in his notebooks, along with his deep and growing doubts about what he was doing. "What if I'm not there when she needs me?" he had once written. And on Lucy's tenth birthday:

"What a glorious child the forest has given us!" He loved her, of that she had no doubt. He celebrated her. It was so confusing. She wished that she could have crawled into his brain just once to know what it was like to be him.

The limousine dropped Weston off at his house, and on the steps they kissed. Weston pressed against Lucy, and she felt the same thrilling rush from her legs to her stomach that she had felt the first time they wrestled. It was all she could do not to throw him to the ground and jump on top of him, and that thought made Lucy laugh out loud right in the middle of their kiss. Then Lucy felt a tender sadness overtake her, because her laughter had clearly embarrassed him. He must have thought that she was laughing at his kiss. Lucy realized that she had completely destroyed the moment. "I'm sorry," she stammered. "I'm sorry, Wes. I wasn't laughing at you, I swear." But he quickly muttered goodnight and went inside.

When she returned to the limousine, Matt and Amanda were kissing. They jerked apart as Lucy opened the door.

"Don't let me harsh your mellow," Lucy said.

"Way to pick up on the lingo, Lucy," Amanda said.

"Nah, that's okay, Luce," Matt said. "You didn't assassinate my penguin. Just surprised us, that's all."

The car dropped Matt off, and the driver took the girls home in the early-morning hours. Amanda and Lucy lay in bed, exhausted but unable to sleep. The evening had given Lucy a vision. She saw a shining beam of light that could carry her into her own future. She saw how she had truly come out of the jungle and into this crazy culture. She could see herself growing up and getting married and living a regular life.

But that had been months ago. Now she couldn't imagine any of it. When word came out about who she was, Weston, poor boy, had phoned her. "Lady, I can't see you anymore. I want to, believe me. But my parents threatened not to send me to college. They'll take my car away. I'm sorry, lady."

Lucy's first thought was that Weston was shallow. But then she realized that he was a part of his own culture just as she was a part of hers. Their worlds were separated by an unbridgeable gulf that they had dared to cross. It was no good.

Amanda, too, had suffered. Her mother had all but disowned

her. Her father gave her money, but she had effectively come to live with Lucy and Jenny after her eighteenth birthday. Lucy was glad for that. But she also feared that if Amanda continued on with her, then Amanda, too, might be doomed.

On a Thursday night Jenny and Lucy drove to the University of Chicago. They were under the impression that they were going to some sort of event where there would be other students, but that turned out not to be the case. Charles Revere, the chairman of Jenny's department, met them at the entrance and ushered them into a grand office. Though he was smiling and polite, Lucy could sense that his intentions toward Jenny were bad. Green-shaded library lamps glowed dimly on either side of a broad leather-covered desk. A small man with a bald head and a red bow tie sat behind it like an icon in a shrine. He was as bland as a rock, giving off no messages at all, it seemed. Jenny and Lucy sat on a leather couch and Revere sat on a claw-footed chair. Once they were introduced and the niceties were out of the way, Jenny said, "Charlie, what is this? I thought this was some sort of orientation event. Clearly it's not."

The provost, whose name was Dr. Edmund Tanner, cleared his throat and began, "No, I'm afraid not, Dr. Lowe. I'm sorry if there was any confusion. You see, this whole business about Lucy's lineage has caused considerable consternation in the university."

"Is that so?" Jenny asked.

"Yes. Consternation of a sort that a university cannot abide, I'm afraid. There are deep questions that this raises. Deep philosophical questions and also practical issues. Even legal ones. And I'm afraid these questions are going to take some time to resolve."

"I don't quite—"

"One of our largest benefactors has threatened to withdraw all of his family's support, for example, if we allow Lucy to matriculate here."

"Why?"

"Precisely," said the provost. "We don't know all the whys and wherefores at the moment, but as the provost here, it's my duty to safeguard the institution."

"Isn't it your duty to safeguard the people in the institution, too?" Jenny asked.

"Yes, that, too. And in doing so, at least until some questions are answered as to Lucy's status, I'm afraid we're not going to be able to let her attend school here."

"I see," Jenny said.

Lucy was unable to speak. She felt hollow inside. What the man was saying didn't surprise her, but she felt as if something had been taken out of her, stolen from that deep place where she kept her secret hopes and dreams.

"Jenny," Revere interjected, "we're going to have to ask you to take a leave of absence while things are decided."

"What?" She couldn't conceal her surprise. "What does my work have to do with this?"

"Everything, I'm afraid," said the provost. "You see, there are ethical issues here about the provenance of this . . . well, about where exactly Lucy came from and who is responsible for the fact of her existence."

"Charlie, what on earth are you two talking about?"

Revere answered. "We're talking about the issue of whether you were involved in Lucy's creation, or whether you simply stumbled upon the work of your colleague, Dr. Stone, as you claim."

"Are you suggesting that I somehow bred Lucy?"

"I'm not suggesting it," Revere said. "There are people in the academic community, however, who find it difficult to believe that two primatologists, working on the same subject a few miles from each other for years, could fail to know about each other's work. Some find your altruism in adopting her suspicious in and of itself."

"We were two days' walk apart, and he pointedly avoided my efforts to get to know him."

The provost intervened. "Dr. Lowe, I'm sure what you say is true. But we have to conclusively resolve the issue. The creation of a human-animal hybrid is a serious breach of ethics and probably illegal as well. In truth, we have to determine—and forgive me for saying this, but the question has been raised—we have to determine whether or not you actually gave birth to Lucy."

"Jesus Christ." Jenny was on her feet now. "Any competent doctor could tell that I've never given birth."

"Then I'm sure you'll be vindicated on that point," the provost said. "But that still leaves many other issues unresolved."

Jenny stood up and grabbed Lucy's hand. "Come on, Lucy. Let's get out of here." When they reached the door, Jenny stopped and turned. Lucy had never seen her so angry. "Charlie, don't be an idiot." He angled his chin up at her, his steel spectacles picking up the green glow of the library lamp. "You didn't have to stage this farce. You know that we have Stone's notebooks and that they document everything in great detail."

"Yes. But there's still the business about how Lucy got into the United States. Meece gave some indication that it wasn't entirely legitimate."

"So you see, Dr. Lowe," said the provost. "We have to investigate all of these matters."

At home that night Jenny alternately ranted and went silent. Then she'd admonish herself, grumbling, "We knew this was coming. What did I expect?"

In the morning, the *Chicago Tribune* ran this headline on its front page: "Illinois High School Association Strips Jungle Girl of Title."

Lucy was squatting in a corner of her room. Her face was in her hands. Amanda's hand was on her shoulder. Lucy was trying not to cry. The world seemed to be spinning. "I hate this place. I want to die."

"No, you don't."

"I'm glad they took the title away." She sobbed as she spoke. "I cheated. Just being me is cheating."

Amanda sat on the floor beside Lucy and wrapped her arms around her. She buried her face in her hair. "Lucy. You just did what you had to do. We all do what we have to do sooner or later. I love you. I don't know what I'd do without you. We'll find you a school, and I'll go there, too. That's how much I care."

Lucy raised her head and looked at her with tears in her eyes. "You'd do that?" Amanda nodded.

25

MEMORANDUM

FROM: Louis Eisner, DVM, PhD
 The Alamogordo Primate Facility
 P.O. Box 956, Holloman AFB, NM 88330

TO: Captain Wilson Colvin, MD, MPH
 U.S. Navy Medical Corps
 Defense Advanced Research Projects Agency
 DARPA Defense Sciences Office
 3701 North Fairfax Drive
 Arlington, VA 22203-1714

SUBJECT: Research Proposal, human-animal hybrid specimen

1. Organization of Research
 The undersigned is cognizant of DARPA's interest in developing potential warfighting and other capabilities based on the study of the subject hybrid. It is the opinion of The Alamogordo Primate Facility (APF) that clarification of the neurological source of the hybrid's special abilities will greatly assist in shaping a strategy for this research.
 Chimpanzees, bonobos, and the other great apes enjoy their superior agility and strength by dint of the anatomy and

neurophysiology of their brains, not through any special characteristics of their muscles. Human and chimp/bonobo musculature are virtually identical. The difference lies in the restraining effect of the neocortex, especially the frontal cortex, in humans. Indeed, there are documented cases in which humans have demonstrated strength as great as that of chimps in extreme situations, many of them in battlefield settings.

Therefore, in order to maximize the value of the proposed research, it would be logical to first determine the anatomical configuration and physiological processes that take place in the hybrid brain under various conditions of extreme stress.

As you are no doubt aware, fMRI and PET scan technology, while extremely valuable, are limited in scope. The gold standard for this type of in-depth brain research is direct implantation of microelectronic sensors. APF is the premier facility of its kind for this type of research, having been engaged in it with higher primates for many decades.

A five-stage process for maximizing the research harvest is therefore proposed by this facility:

First, that the hybrid be brought here at the earliest opportunity.

Second, that a craniotomy be performed with extensive implantation of microelectronic sensors throughout the neocortex and motor-sensory areas of interest to DARPA.

Third, that thorough mapping and testing be done at APF to provide baseline data for the appropriate research arms of DARPA. This would include the most detailed anatomical and neurophysiological picture of the hybrid brain possible, along with response times, stress hormone responses, and brain mapping during extreme stress events, such as waterboarding.

Fourth, an implantable miniaturized monitoring device will be interfaced with the electronic sensors so that the hybrid's actions and reactions can be monitored wirelessly under simulated battlefield conditions.

AND

Fifth, at that point the hybrid will be delivered to a USNORTHCOM- or DARPA-designated facility fully equipped for field exercises in which all the military objectives for research can be realized in the most effective manner possible.

It is the considered opinion of this facility that this five-point plan will maximize this unique opportunity.

2. Legal Considerations

The legal counsel of APF, after consultation with the Department of Justice, the Federal Bureau of Investigation, and the Department of Homeland Security, makes the following recommendation:

The presence of the human-animal hybrid within the borders of the United States, along with the stated purpose of her presence here, can be viewed—at least technically—as an act of terrorism. Taking that view would effectively sweep away any presumed rights and associated difficulties for interested researchers. Inasmuch as the stated reason for the existence of this hybrid was to displace the human race, it would appear that there is prima facie evidence of intent to commit acts that are "dangerous to human life," as well as "intended to intimidate or coerce a civilian population," as defined in 18 U.S.C. § 2331(5).

Under provisions of the USA Patriot Act it is clear that the appropriate authorities have the right to seize and place subjects at their discretion without any obligation to report their whereabouts, health, or legal status.

However, should Senate Bill 5251, the so-called "Lucy Bill," pass, all legal considerations would be irrelevant, since the subject hybrid would be declared, de jure, an animal and not a human.

In that regard, it is noted for the record that the U.S. Department of Agriculture, which enforces the federal Animal Welfare Act (the only legislation that might influence this decision), has no jurisdiction over APF, as the Animal Welfare Act specifically exempts U.S. government research facilities, which are free to handle animal specimens as they see fit.

26

THE *TEEN VOGUE* COVER STORY was called "Behind the Scenes with Lucy Lowe." The photograph showed Lucy and Amanda wearing two different outfits from Betsey Johnson's "beat chick" collection, their hair all done up. Inside was a vapid interview in which the magazine had made the girls sound like banana-heads, making such remarks as, "I just like to chill with my friends."

"Harry, I swear, I did *not* say 'chill,'" Lucy said.

"She definitely did not say 'chill,'" Amanda said.

"Never do I say 'chill.'"

"It's true," Jenny told Harry. "She doesn't say 'chill.'"

It was August and they were on his deck overlooking the English garden. A tray on the table bore tomatoes, cheese, and olives from the farmer's market. Unfamiliar music was coming through the French doors from the dining room, and Lucy asked Harry what it was.

"Bobby Blue Bland. It's rhythm and blues."

"Since when do you listen to R&B?" Jenny asked. "Didn't you always play, like, Miles and Coltrane in the operating room?"

"Yeah, mostly jazz. Nothing too chaotic. You don't want to start rocking to the beat when you're trying to cut. But lately I've been playing slow rhythm and blues in the OR. I don't know why."

"You play music while you're doing surgery?" Amanda asked.

"Sure. Every surgeon I know plays music during an operation."

"You think the patients can hear it?" Lucy asked.

"We don't know. We don't really know what a patient can feel during surgery, mainly because we give them propofol and it causes amnesia. In fact, the anesthesiologists call it 'milk of amnesia' because it's white and makes you forget."

Jenny was rummaging through the clippings. "Look, Harry. Here's *Rolling Stone.*"

Harry picked it up and held it before him. "Well, look at that. My little girl made the cover of *Rolling Stone.* Not entirely sure I agree with their concept here."

It showed Lucy in torn jeans, her hair slightly spiked out, standing in a sort of rock-and-roll pose holding a banana and slouching with one arm raised to the branch of a fake tree as if she were about to climb. It had been shot in a studio.

"Wait'll you read it," Amanda said. "It's this, like, Orwellian grope through all the political and sociological and ethical issues that they could sweep out of the gutter."

Harry read, " 'When a scientific experiment goes wrong,'—this is from an evangelical preacher in Texas—'the scientist destroys his undesirable materials in the most humane way possible and moves on.' I'm telling you, Lucy, watch your six. This world is full of whackos."

"I have observed said whackos," Lucy said.

Steven Rhodes, who had introduced the Lucy Bill, was quoted as saying that while he did not favor putting Lucy in an actual zoo, he did think that a suitable facility could be found to house her in a way that would ensure both her safety and the safety of those around her. "There," said Rhodes, "she could be studied by the appropriate scientific experts and live out her life in comfort, while benefiting humankind in the most acceptable way." When asked about Lucy's education, the congressman said, "I believe that the training of animals is the business of the Ringling Brothers and not of the scientific community."

Harry also read a quote from an evolutionary biologist at Stanford who said, "Would I like to study Lucy? Of course I would. Do I think that ought to be allowed? No, I don't. In the most important ways, you see, Lucy is just like you and me. Would you want your teenage daughter to be studied by a bunch of scientists? So the issues here revolve around her father's decision to bring her into the world, which most of us would agree was a very bad decision from an ethical point of view. But we must keep that ethical issue separate from the very good outcome of that bad decision. Lucy is a remarkable person. Her father did something reprehensible, but that in no way detracts from her value as a human being. I think her biggest problem is not going to come from any legitimate scientist, though. It's going to be the religious crackpots and government zealots. If history is any guide, her worst nightmare is going to be some completely innocuous-seeming bureaucrat who can't think and always goes by the rule book."

Harry said, "He's right, you know. It was those kind of people who made the Third Reich possible."

27

IN THE BRIGHT HEARING ROOM of the Senate Office Building, Lucy sat in a witness chair, watching Senator Martin Cochrain prepare to speak. Jenny was in the audience. The dark oak benches were filled, and people stood around the room, which was paneled in the same wood and hung with heavy gold curtains.

"Good morning, everyone," Senator Cochrain said. "Thank you for coming. Thanks especially to Lucy Lowe and her mother, Dr. Jennifer Lowe, for making the effort to travel here for this session. Also testifying today will be John P. Alonzo, a judge with the Seventh Circuit Court of Appeals, who has ruled on many matters pertaining to civil rights; Eugene Miller, with the law firm of Abbot, White, McCardle, who is an expert in civil rights law and a professor of law at Harvard University; Professor William B. Conklin, who chairs the bioethics department at Stanford; and Dr. Judith Drosnin, who teaches and practices psychiatry at the UCLA Medical School. We welcome our witnesses and thank them for their service."

The senator cleared his throat and drank some water. Then he straightened the papers from which he'd been reading and put them aside to speak extemporaneously. "We are more than a quarter century into the biotech revolution, and yet it has taken the unsanctioned act of a solitary scientist working alone in the jungle to bring this matter before a legislative body. In addition, the U.S.

Patent Office has rejected attempts to patent a human-animal hybrid three times in five years, and that happens to be the first government agency to say anything at all on the subject. The reason for the rejection was clear: The Thirteenth Amendment of the United States Constitution prohibits slavery. A human being cannot be property and therefore cannot be patented. Thus the Patent Office clearly sides with the view that Lucy—or any human-animal hybrid—is to be considered a human being, with all the rights and obligations of a human being. But with all due respect for my colleagues at the Patent Office, that is probably not the best venue for deciding weighty ethical and scientific issues like these.

"Now, I can certainly understand how various people and groups are going to have strong feelings about the way in which Lucy came to be in our midst today. I don't think any of us here would sanction such an experiment if it were brought to us through normal channels. But the fact is that Lucy is here. She does exist. And as I will make amply clear today, she is fully endowed with human qualities and is a delightful, intelligent girl. That notwithstanding, we can expect this issue to confront us again and again in the coming years. This, of course, raises many extremely important—and, I daresay, deep—questions. But for our purposes here during these hearings, I believe, it is our role to accomplish one thing and one thing only: To do everything in our power to afford Lucy all the protections and opportunities of our society.

"To that end I would like to introduce our first witness, Lucy herself. I just want to make sure that everyone here sees firsthand what a remarkable young lady she is. Good morning, Lucy, and welcome."

"Good morning, Senator."

"Do you mind telling us a bit about how you spent your day so far before arriving here?"

"Not at all. I got up about six with my mother. We're staying at the Madison. A very cushy hotel, thank you."

The laughter in the room was general. The press was eating it up.

"And while Mom was showering, I checked my e-mail and logged on to Facebook to check my messages there."

"You have a page on Facebook?"

"Yes, of course. Doesn't everyone?" More laughter. "I switched over to MSN, but my IMs were capped."

"Beg pardon?"

"I got too many messages."

"Very good. Then what did you do?"

"When Mom was finished, I took my shower, and we got dressed and went down to the dining room for breakfast."

"What did you have?"

"I had the oatmeal. They make the best oatmeal at the Madison. But it got cold, because people kept coming up to me to ask for autographs or to have their picture taken with me."

"How do you like being famous?"

"Well, I don't much like it. I didn't ask for it."

"But you put a video on YouTube."

"We had to do that. The CDC was going to announce what they'd found anyway. I wanted the story told in my own words, not theirs."

"I see. Well, Lucy, it's my intention to submit a bill to Congress declaring that you are human and that you have all the rights of any normal human. Is there anything you'd like to say for the record in support of that idea?"

"Yes. I am human. As any legitimate scientist will tell you, a human is a type of ape. All people are closely related to the chimpanzee and pygmy chimpanzee—the bonobos, as they're now called. A few million years ago there was a hominid called *Australopithecus*. Then later there was *Paranthropus* and *Homo habilis* and *erectus* and *ergaster*. Those were all new types of humanoid apes or early people. I am born of *Homo sapiens* and *Pan paniscus,* two forms of ape. So I, too, am a new type of human. And so I say: Yes, I am human, and I am ape. You are, too, as is everyone in this room. Once, perhaps one hundred thousand or two hundred thousand years ago, your kind were new to this earth. I merely happen to be newer. I'm very proud of my heritage."

The applause was mixed with boos as the senator banged his gavel. Gradually the commotion died down, and then Senator Steven Rhodes stood up and said, "Senator, if I may have a moment with the witness, please."

"Recognize the esteemed senator from Utah."

Rhodes stood at his place. He was a tall, robust-looking man with a shock of silver hair and bushy eyebrows. On the table before him was a package of some sort wrapped as a present. It was about a foot and a half long and ten inches high. Jenny thought that it seemed oddly out of place.

"I'd like to begin," Senator Rhodes said, "by thanking the witness for coming here today. And Dr. Lowe. But I do want to clarify something concerning Lucy's testimony. I am not an ape. And my relatives are not chimpanzees." The applause was wild and deafening as people stomped their feet and cheered. Senator Cochrain hammered his gavel, but the people continued talking and grumbling among themselves.

"Now, Lucy, I want to ask you a personal question, and I don't want you to take offense at it. It has an important point."

"All right."

"Have you reached puberty?"

"Beg pardon?"

"Have you had your first period yet, Lucy?"

"Yes."

Jenny felt pained as she saw Lucy flush red.

"Thank you." The senator turned toward the audience. "I ask this rather indelicate question because, although none of my relatives are apes, they could be if this girl begins to breed as she evidently intends to do. I have a grandson about her age. Who knows? They could meet and fall in love. She's obviously very charming. But this is an extremely serious matter that I think should concern all of us."

Senator Rhodes now picked up the package and approached the witness table where Lucy sat before a microphone. Jenny watched in puzzlement, wondering what the senator had up his sleeve.

"Just one more thing, Lucy, and then we'll be through. Would you take that between your hands and crush it for me, please? Could you do that for me, dear?"

"Sure."

Jenny could not sort out what was happening quite yet. Why would he give her a present and ask her to crush it? Then all at once she had the answer. She was up on her feet, shouting, "Lucy, no!"

But Lucy had been too fast. The deed was done. Almost too quickly to see, Lucy had simply put one hand on either side of the package and pushed. Senator Rhodes now lifted the package and tore away the wrapping to reveal a steel toolbox as mangled as if it had been a Coke can. He held it up for all to see, turning this way and that in the lights with a satisfied smile. The television cameras caught it all.

"This is a standard Craftsman toolbox made of steel. I know that apes can do things like this. But do any of you humans think that you could wreak this kind of destruction?" Jenny saw Lucy glance at her apologetically, as she, too, realized how she'd been tricked. "Lucy may be very clever and charming," the senator went on. "There is a long history of clever and charming and indeed very talented trained animals. But they are not human. She is not human. As you may have noticed in the news a few days ago, she was stripped of her state wrestling title because of the superhuman strength she possesses specifically as a result of the fact that she is not human. And in making your decisions about the bill that my respected colleague proposes here today and the one that I have put forth, I just want to make sure that you all know what you're dealing with here. No further questions."

The room broke into spontaneous applause, punctuated by boos and hisses once more, and Senator Cochrain again banged his gavel for order. "Thank you, Senator, for that poignant demonstration. I think Lucy should have a chance to respond. Is there anything else you'd like to say to those who might argue that you do not deserve all the rights of a human but perhaps should be protected instead under the Animal Welfare Act or maybe even studied by scientists?"

Lucy answered without hesitation. "Yes, there is. I would say this:

> *The quality of mercy is not strain'd,*
> *It droppeth as the gentle rain from heaven*
> *Upon the place beneath: it is twice blest;*
> *It blesseth him that gives and him that takes:*
> *'Tis mightiest in the mightiest: it becomes*
> *The throned monarch better than his crown . . .*

Jenny held back tears as Lucy finished. "And if you put all of the bonobos in all the world into a room for all the ages of history. And if you gave them all the training you could give. They would still never quote Shakespeare to you. I can. I will. I do."

28

LUCY AND JENNY returned from Washington the next day, arriving from the airport in a hired car at midday. The first heavy drops of rain had begun to fall. As Lucy stepped from the car and smelled the air she felt her heart quicken. The air was full of electricity. A few reporters were waiting, but Jenny turned on them, teeth bared like old Lucretia, and barked, "No!" They looked at her quizzically for a moment. Then she shouted, "Bad dog!" And they retreated, glancing back at her as if she were mad.

"Nobody's afraid of tough anymore," Jenny told Lucy. "But everybody's afraid of crazy."

The driver wheeled the luggage up the sidewalk. Amanda opened the front door and hugged Lucy.

"I'm sorry. I screwed up."

"No, you didn't. That bastard tricked you, Luce. Anyway, you got the last word, and you were bitchin'. The guy's a pinhead. Harry called. He told me to tell you he watched you on TV and that you were—his words—'preposterously superb.' He said the *Merchant of Venice* was, quote, 'insanely great.'"

"It just came out."

Jenny put her arm around the girls and ushered them inside.

The windows were open and the electric air was billowing the curtains. Lucy looked outside and saw that the wind was lifting the skirts of the trees and whipping leaves into eddies and whirlpools. The big drops hit the window glass like stones. The northwestern sky lit up, and there came a deep rumbling that rolled over the neighborhood in successive waves.

Amanda had made a pasta salad for lunch, but Lucy felt unable to eat. Her heart was pounding, and she couldn't seem to sit still.

"What's the matter, Luce? You're not getting sick again, are you? Please don't be sick."

"I just feel weird. I think it's just the stress. You know. Cars and jets and hotels and people." But she felt as if she were coming unglued. And she didn't really want to say what she thought it was.

By nightfall the storms were general throughout the area, and Lucy was too agitated to concentrate on anything. She knew that she had to control this thing, especially now, with all the attention. She tried reading but kept going over the same passage again and again. As deep night folded over the house from the east, she was enclosed in a sense of dread at what was coming, dread and thrill, as she felt one part of her personality slipping away to be replaced by another. She found herself down in the garage with the big door open, nervously rocking from foot to foot, watching the torrential rain descend in great cascading sheets. Thunder and lightning exploded together right over her head. She could taste the copper in her mouth and smell the ozone. She heard Jenny and Amanda calling from upstairs but could not respond. At last she heard their footsteps hurrying down the stairs, and Lucy thought, Oh, maybe they can save me. Maybe they can stop this. If only Lucy could explain to them what was happening to her, then maybe they could tell her what to do.

Lucy turned to see them enter the garage, looks of concern on their faces. She tried to speak. But at that moment another crash of thunder and lightning exploded overhead, and when Lucy opened her mouth, only a furious panting and hooting noise came from deep within her chest.

Amanda screamed and clamped her hand over her mouth, her eyes wide.

"Lucy, what is it?" Jenny asked. "What's wrong?"

Lucy opened her mouth to explain, but only a shriek came out.

Amanda screamed again. "What is it? What's going on? Lucy, you're scaring me."

"Oh, my God, it's the rain." Jenny approached Lucy gingerly. "It's just the rain and thunder, honey. You're going to be okay." She put her hand on Lucy's shoulder.

"What?" Amanda asked. "What about the rain and thunder? What's happening? Why is she doing this? Lucy, stop."

Lucy could feel every muscle in her body vibrating as Jenny tried to comfort her. Lucy wanted to say something but was afraid of what would come out now. She could only stand there panting and making low noises in her throat. Then all at once another blast of thunder sent her howling out into the night. She couldn't stop herself. She began running all over the yard, swinging around tree trunks with one hand waving. She grabbed her clothes and ripped them into shreds of fabric. She ran naked up the tree as if she'd come unstuck from gravity. What had been a sense of dread had turned into a sense of joyous liberation. She was free. She was home in the forest once more. Lightning flared, and in its light she saw Amanda and Jenny running around in the rain below, their clothing soaked, shouting and trying to see Lucy in the branches where she swayed.

"Lucy, no!" Jenny called. "You have to come down." But hers was like a distant voice in the forest, and Lucy could only answer with another shriek. It was now raining and blowing so hard that the tree itself was rocking from side to side. Lucy tore off a stout branch and descended to the ground, dragging it along and screaming louder. A blast of thunder answered.

Lucy could see the neighbors peering out of their lighted windows to learn what the commotion was, but she could do nothing to stop herself, as Jenny and Amanda ran after her and tried to corral her.

"Lucy, please!" Amanda cried. "Oh, please, Lucy, stop."

Not even as the sirens began could Lucy answer. The glorious claps of thunder and the wild sheets of rain drove her on in her dance, and up the tree she went once more, rejoicing in her freedom. The police cars pulled into the alley in back of the house, their crazy lights sparkling as the thunderstorm cell passed away to the east. For the first time all afternoon, Lucy felt the agitation release her. The police piled out of the cars in groups, and spotlights set the dripping trees aflame. Lucy could hear the dark voices below and snatches of conversation.

"... psychiatric ..."

"... animal control ..."

"Is it a girl?"

"It's just my daughter," Jenny called out in a cheerful voice. "There's nothing wrong. We're okay."

"It was called in as a disturbance, ma'am."

"No, it was just us horsing around," Amanda said.

"Does she have clothes on?"

"She's in her bathing suit," Amanda said. "We just wanted to play in the rain."

"Where's your bathing suit?"

As Lucy's eyes adjusted to the light and her mind began to settle down, she could see that she was trapped.

"Can you get her down here so we can talk to her?"

"Yes, turn off your lights, and I'll get her down," Amanda said.

"We can't turn 'em off, miss, it's regulations."

"Then just aim them away a bit," Jenny said.

Someone whistled, and then the lights lowered. Lucy seized the moment and scampered across the branches and onto the roof of the house. She let herself down the side, punched through the dining-room-window screen, and swung inside. She hurried to her room, jerked on her bikini, and ran down the stairs to the garage. As she walked out onto the driveway, a burly policewoman with a battered face and short red hair shined her flashlight into Lucy's eyes.

"There she is now," Amanda said.

"Yes," Lucy said. "We were just fooling around, right Amanda?"

"That's what I was telling them. Sorry for the confusion."

"Hey," the policewoman said. "You're that monkey girl."

"If there won't be anything else, then, we'll be going inside," Jenny said, putting her hands on their shoulders.

"How'd you get into the house?" the policewoman demanded.

"Come, girls," Jenny said. "No more playing tonight."

The officer lowered her flashlight and noticed a soggy scrap of cloth on the ground. As Jenny steered the girls into the garage, the policewoman picked up a piece of Lucy's shirt. "Hey, what's this?" Then she turned to one of the other police officers, who were gaping in puzzlement, and said, "I think we should take 'em in for questioning."

"About what?" the other cop asked.

At that moment, television news vans pulled in from both directions to flank the police cars in the alley. Camera crews and reporters began emerging.

"Oh, shit, just what we frickin' need," the policewoman said.

"Lucy! Lucy!" one of the newsmen shouted. "Can we get a statement?"

Another called out, "Lucy, were you and Amanda drinking?"

"Taking drugs?"

"Let's get out of here," one of the police officers said. "You do not want to be on TV, trust me, I was there once."

As the police returned to their cars the policewoman shouted, "Get those vans out of our way!"

29

IT WAS A HOT DAY. They were waiting beside an exhibit of small penguins arrayed around a moat that reeked of feces. Presently, Donna came down a wooden walkway, tan and robust and smiling, her long black braid swinging behind her. Jenny had always liked her Native American look. At the bottom of the ramp, Donna hugged Jenny powerfully.

"Hey, Jen," Donna said. "Thank you for comin'. I'm honored to meet you, Lucy. You must be Amanda."

"Hi," Amanda said, shaking hands.

Lucy said nothing. Her eyes darted around excitedly, and her chin lifted as she sniffed the air. In The Stream, Jenny thought, hearing and smelling all the animals. She hoped that Lucy could stay calm.

"Listen," Lucy said. In the distance, elephants and big cats were calling out. "They know."

Donna watched her with a knowing look and nodded. "Yep. Everybody's talkin' 'bout you. Come on."

She led them up the wooden ramp and across a bridge through the forest. They arrived at the great ape exhibit to find the bonobos behind thick glass windows. Lucy stood back at first, reluctant, while Amanda went forward to look. The bonobos swung on ropes hung from the high ceiling and climbed on artificial trees. Others lay on the ground, resting, and a few were playing together or grooming.

"They're so beautiful," Amanda said. "They look so human." Then she thought for a moment and said, "Well, duh . . ."

Donna and Jenny watched Lucy. Jenny could see that she was vibrating in that intense way she did when she was communicating deeply. Gradually, the bonobos began to quit whatever they were doing and drift to the window where Amanda stood. Now all was quiet. Amanda moved back from the window as the bonobos crowded around it. Lucy hesitated about ten feet away. The bonobos closest to the window began placing their hands flat against the glass. One by one all the others pushed forward to place their hands on the glass, until it was completely covered with the beautiful black palms and delicate fingers. Then they leaned in close to peek through the spaces between their fingers.

At length, Lucy took a step forward. Then another step. Very slowly, she approached the glass. Then she lifted her hand and placed it flat against the glass, her pale skin startling against that dark and eerie tapestry of hands and eyes. All at once the bonobos broke from the window and began jumping up and down and screaming. Lucy stood for another moment, listening to the sound, and then sat cross-legged on the floor. She put her face in her hands. Amanda and Jenny rushed to her and held her.

Donna came forward and said, "I've never seen them do that. In more than twenty years of working here I've never seen anything like it. Come on, let me take you in back."

They helped Lucy up, and she said, "I'm sorry. It's so sad."

"It's okay," Amanda said.

Donna opened a door with the ID card that hung around her neck and led the way into a windowless concrete corridor. Down and down they went until they had reached an area of steel bars where the rest of the bonobos were kept. It smelled of damp concrete and rotting fruit. As they approached, the bonobos continued their shrieking cries.

"Do you mind if I talk to them?" Lucy asked Donna.

"No, I was hoping you might," Donna said.

Lucy let out a piercing shriek and a barking sound and the bonobos fell completely silent.

"Holy smokes," Donna said. "I wish I could do that. Come on, I'll take you to the back fence."

They followed Donna up a flight of concrete stairs and through a steel door that led outside to the forest, where the leaves were just beginning to take on a tinge of their autumn colors. There they could approach the very back of the bonobo area, which was enclosed by a high chain link fence. The bonobos rushed into the yard and came to the fence, now murmuring more softly at the nearness of Lucy. They began reaching out through the fence with their fingers. Lucy moved forward.

"Be careful. They can be dangerous," Donna said.

"They don't want to hurt me," Lucy said.

"She'll know if one of them is dangerous," Jenny said.

"They're fast," Donna warned.

"So is Lucy," Amanda said.

Lucy slowly approached the fence where all the fingers reached out through the chain links, palms held upward. Then she went along the fence, gently brushing all the palms, the bonobos murmuring softly in little squeaks and high keening notes. Lucy made soft noises in response, almost like singing, as Jenny and Donna and Amanda watched in wonder.

"Even I don't dare do that," Donna whispered to Jenny. "They'd tear my fingers off. I don't wear shoelaces cause I'm afraid they'll rip me off my feet. This is just amazing."

Lucy moved back and forth for half an hour, touching hands and murmuring with them. Then she turned from the fence and said, "I'd better go now. They don't understand why I can't come in with them. I'll say goodbye now." Lucy turned to them and began shrieking in a way that was painfully loud and sad. All the bonobos took up a chorus of shrieking, and it grew to such a deafening pitch that Amanda and Jenny had to cover their ears. Then, abruptly, the bonobos scattered back into the building.

Amanda, Jenny, and Lucy followed Donna through the building and back across the wooden bridge. At the front gate of the zoo they stood in pale sunshine and heard the distant trumpeting of the elephant, the thunder of lions. Amanda put her hand on Lucy's shoulder, and the two girls stared into each other's eyes.

Lucy turned to Donna. "Thank you for that. It's been a long time."

Donna nodded. "Now that you're in the spotlight of publicity, what will you do?"

"I don't know. I was going to go to college, but they won't let me now."

"That's terrible. Can you find some school that'll take you?"

"We will," Jenny said. "Don't worry, honey. We're going to find a place."

Donna thought for a moment. "Can you still go through the trees, Lucy? Are you fast?"

"Oh, yeah. It's easy. And fun."

"She gave us a pretty good demo of that last night, in fact," Amanda said.

"During the storms?" Donna asked.

"I'm sorry. I kind of cut loose."

"No, it's natural," Donna said. "Our guys got pretty wild last night, too." Then she went on: "Lucy, me and Jenny have been talkin' about what to do now if you need a safe place to go."

Lucy shrugged and said, "Sure. Go ahead."

"They will come after you. There is no doubt in my mind about that now. Bad people who want you dead or want to do experiments on you. When the time comes—and it will come—you'll need to have a plan. Jenny thought of it and got in touch with me. That's why you're here. Because I can help."

"Okay," Lucy said, looking at Jenny. "Mom?" she asked, uncertain now.

"It's all right, honey. You can trust Donna. Listen to the plan."

"Okay," Donna said. "First, you get into the trees. Like you did last night. You can maneuver across the canopies faster than they can move on the ground in their cars. The streets will slow them down. And second, you'll come here. I'll protect you. I have special places they can't get to."

"How will I get all the way here?"

"Through the trees," Jenny said. "Stay in the trees all the way."

"Can it be done?" Amanda asked.

"Yes," Jenny said. "It's trees all the way up. Donna and I already checked. When we get home I can show you the route on Google Earth."

"It's broken in places," Donna said. "Sometimes you'll have

to go through neighborhoods. But there's plenty of water along the way. You won't need to eat. It'll take you three days at the most."

"You guys have really thought this through, haven't you?" Amanda asked.

"Yes," Jenny said. "I knew we had to have a plan if worse came to worst."

"Don't talk about this on the phone or in e-mail," Donna continued. "No text messaging about it. When it happens, Jenny and I won't communicate with each other for a while. Amanda, they'll be watching you and Jenny to see if you'll lead them to Lucy. So you'll just have to wait. Jenny and I worked out a code to communicate through ads on Craigslist."

"This is pretty spooky stuff," Amanda said. "How'd you figure all this out?"

"She was working with primates in the military labs before she came here," Jenny explained.

"Yeah. It sucked. I couldn't stand the way they treated the animals. The experiments. I left when they started inoculating chimpanzees with *Yersinia pestis* for their biological warfare research."

Amanda asked, "What's *Yer*—what did you say?"

"It's plague," Lucy said. "Bubonic plague."

"Oh, that's horrible," Amanda said.

"Yeah. It was pretty awful. But I learned a lot." Donna paused as if making a difficult decision, then said to Amanda, "I still have contacts in the military. So let's just say that I am positive they're coming for Lucy."

"Then why doesn't Lucy stay here now?" Amanda asked. "As a precaution."

"Because we don't know when it'll happen," Donna said. "I can't even say who or how. And if Lucy just disappears from her regular life now, they'd come looking for her."

"Or it might not happen," Jenny said hopefully.

Donna gave Lucy a business card, her name printed on the front, Donna W. Feather.

Lucy studied the card. "Where will you take me? If I come."

"I'd better not tell you that now." Donna took a step forward and hugged Jenny. She shook hands with Lucy and Amanda.

"Goodbye, then. Be safe." Then she turned without ceremony and went past the penguins.

They watched her go back up the ramp and vanish into the forest.

"Mom, why did you bring me here now?"

"I don't know. I've just been having this feeling that we'd better get our signals straight."

"Yeah, me, too. You're getting it in The Stream."

Amanda asked, "Do you think she's right? Will they really come for Lucy?"

They looked at one another. Jenny thought about her question and reminded herself that the United States government was holding ten-year-old children in cages at Abu Ghraib prison in Iraq. And they'd done nothing but have the wrong father. Lucy was guilty of the same crime. Since the suspension of habeas corpus they could hold anyone they wanted anywhere they wanted. So Jenny feared that Donna had it just about right.

But all she said was, "Let's go home now, girls."

Jenny left the girls watching *When Harry Met Sally* and painting each other's toenails. When she went outside and saw that Harry had brought the motorcycle and an extra helmet, Jenny said, "I'm glad I didn't have my hair done and my heels on."

"Well, if we'd been going to Charlie Trotter's, I would have brought the car. But pizza at Amici calls for a Ducati."

The restaurant was in a shabby neighborhood that was coming back to life as people moved in and fixed up apartments. A dark wine bar and a bright hair salon had already opened. When they were seated in a corner with a carafe of wine and a candle between them, Harry lifted his glass. "Here's lookin' atcha." Their eyes met. Jenny still felt a jolt when she saw those eyes. But she couldn't shake her sense of dread. Something in The Stream, as Lucy had said.

"What? What is this, Harry? I've known you all these years. We go back to the eighties. And we've gone out on real dates—what? Five times maybe?"

"I'm not sure. Something's going on, and you're not telling me about it."

"You told me not to tell you."

"So it's that, is it? Things getting ugly?"

"Yes, I'm afraid they are. I don't even know exactly what it is yet."

"Then that's the reason we're here." The humor was gone from his face now. "I love you, Jenny. You know that."

She felt her heart jump. "Yes, of course, I do, Harry. I love you, too. We're old hands."

"But we just never seemed to be in the right place at the right time for . . ."

"For what?"

"For more."

Jenny sighed. "We tried."

"Not really. You were in the jungle. I was an ambitious surgeon."

"Yes, I know. No one's to blame."

"Well, we both had priorities. But what about now? You can't go back to Congo. You know, I've completely fallen in love with Lucy."

"She does have a way of stealing your heart, doesn't she?"

"And I know she likes me. I don't think she'd mind having me around."

"What are you suggesting? I mean, I am here, that's true. But if anything, my life is more complicated than it's ever been."

"Does that mean you'd be interested if it weren't so complicated?"

"Harry. Interested in what?" It had come so out of the blue that Jenny was having trouble even imagining what he was thinking. Then without warning, Jenny was weeping. She wasn't even sure why. "Damn you, Harry."

Harry reached across the table and covered her hand with his. She was reminded of how rough and strong his hands were. Carpentry was his hobby. He liked to work with things that were physical. "I'm sorry to be so abrupt. I'd like to be there for you when the time comes. You're going to try to do it all on your own."

She wiped her eyes with her napkin and looked at him.

"Listen, kiddo, forgive me for bringing all this up. But I watched my sister die of cancer. I learned what it means to love someone so much that you can hardly stand every day that passes as you watch that person go, by such small increments, and then pass on into . . ." He opened his hands as if releasing a bird. "Nothing. And I feel somehow that I'm losing you now. I don't know how or why. It's just a feeling."

As she listened, watching his kindly face, she began to understand what was happening: Harry was experiencing the same sense of dread that had driven Jenny to see Donna. And he didn't know why. They were both picking up the same signals, but Harry didn't know what they were. And his response was to try to pull Jenny closer. He interpreted his impulse to protect her as love, the only explanation that he could come up with to satisfy his logical mind.

Jenny no longer felt like weeping. She felt a sudden strength course through her. She looked up at Harry and saw the goodness of his heart. She wondered why he'd never found someone else. He was certainly a catch. "I love you, too, Harry. I do. And I'm so touched by your gesture. But I think it might just be too late for us." The way he looked at Jenny pierced her heart. Then he dropped his eyes, and it was her turn to reach across and place her hand over his. "You will always be my dearest friend." And it felt good. Good and true.

30

"ONE OF MY EARLIEST MEMORIES," Lucy wrote, "was riding on my mother's back, clinging to her fur as she flew across the forest. She would leap, almost as if she could fly, and at the top of her arc I could feel my stomach drop as she descended. Then she'd grab a branch and swing hard to gain momentum for her next move. I had to hold on tight or risk being thrown off. Sometimes on those trips, we were traveling for a specific purpose, such as getting to a tree where the fruit was ripe. Sometimes we were escaping from a big cat. But at other times, it seemed, we did it just for fun. Sometimes the whole family moved through the trees like that, screeching and laughing and just relishing the feeling of being alive in the beautiful jungle."

"Hey, you're fast." It was late at night, some weeks after they had visited the Milwaukee Zoo. Amanda was leaning over Lucy's shoulder watching the screen as she typed.

Lucy studied the paragraph. "What do you think?"

"Awesome. Just a few hundred more paragraphs like that and you're done."

"Shut up. Come on, help me."

"How can I help you? I don't know what happened."

"You said you'd help."

"Well, you write stuff down, and then I'll read it. I'll pretend to be your editor. You want me to leave you alone so you can concentrate?"

"No, you be my muse. Rub my neck."

"Sure. I give a mean massage."

Amanda's strong fingers dug into Lucy's shoulders, and Lucy let herself relax into a sort of trance. In that state, she let her fingers tell the stories, her eyes nearly closed. She wrote about nursing at her mother's breasts and how Leda would toss her into the air like a doll and gently catch her before she fell. She wrote about how she would wrestle and tickle and play with the other children for hours at a time on the aromatic forest floor. "When we were a little older," she wrote,

we'd all go screeching into the trees, up and down and around, chasing one another for the sheer physical joy of moving. There were dangers, to be sure, but the jungle really was a sort of paradise for us. We lived naked in the pleasure of our flesh and knew no shame or guilt. We simply lived, embracing both our pleasures and our pains with all the heart we had.

But at the same time, something was very different about me, and I knew it from the earliest age. I knew it in that intense way that children know things before words have come to circumscribe and define their knowing. For I was the child of man. I was hairless and walked upright and I spoke in words and I loved the man.

Soon the man put an instrument in my hand, and I began to draw. It was no more than scribbling at first, and some of my brothers and sisters did it, too. But then something happened. The man taught me letters, and the other children could never make letters, only scribbles. Then the letters became words, and it was clear that the other children would never ever be like me. I was no longer like them, either. I was alone, apart in some essential way. At last the words became thoughts, and a great gulf had opened between me and my siblings that could never be crossed again. My gift came with a terrible cost, for it closed me off from the ones I loved. Yet I had effected a magical transformation. I could put my thoughts into the man's brain by symbols alone, without speaking and without The Stream. Another cost: Language let humans forget The Stream. And even as a small child I was struck by both the magic and the sadness of that mysterious process. But the price of that gift was that I was cast out of Eden, out of the deep communion of my family.

I remember one day when I was sitting in the sun writing. Papa was nearby, working on the generator. I looked out across the clearing where our little hut was and saw several of the bonobos sunning and playing. And I looked over at Papa bent over the machine with a screwdriver in his hand. Then I looked down at my own hand with the pencil in it, the words on the page. And for the first time that I can remember I had this thought: I'm human.

Lucy stopped writing and let Amanda sit in the chair. Lucy stood and rubbed Amanda's neck as she read. After a time, Amanda turned with tears in her eyes. "Lucy, it's so beautiful. This is going to be a great book, I just know it is."

And seeing her tears, Lucy thought, To make a mark that can move someone to tears is to be human. Maybe I really am human. And she felt her own eyes fill with tears. Amanda stood, and then they were in each other's arms, a warmth against the world, a place where language fell away.

Amanda led Lucy to the bed, and they held each other in the dark. Lucy recalled how unhappy she had been in this very room when she first arrived. It was all so different now. Amanda's hair was in her face. She smelled like the sea.

"I love you, Lucy."

Lucy felt a thrill rush through her. "I know. I love you, too. You don't think I'm too weird?"

"You are the absolute weirdest, my little turnip."

"Shut up."

And Lucy fell fast asleep with her heart thumping in her neck. That night she dreamed of Figan and Melissa, Flo, all of her old family. But included in the group were the bonobos she'd met in Milwaukee. They had just discovered a stand of towering fig trees where the fruit had ripened perfectly, and they sat in the branches laughing and talking and eating. The sweet nectar dripped down their chins. A mist was rising. When they had had their fill, they all held hands in the trees, celebrating their good fortune. Then they scrambled down so gracefully and made a big circle on the ground. They all hugged one another in one great pile of fur, slapping backs and laughing. In the dream Lucy had fur, too, and she caressed it, reveling in its softness and warmth, while Miff and Olly groomed her. Gone was the human Lucy. She was pure bonobo now. She had returned to Eden and was happy at last.

Then somehow the dream changed and snow began to fall right there in the rain forest. All at once, Lucy was the only one with fur. The others had become inexplicably human, and they were naked. They talked among themselves, saying that they were going to freeze if they didn't have fur like Lucy's. They were talking calmly like any group of humans. Then one of them suggested that they could simply take Lucy's fur and wear it to keep warm. One of them had a knife. Lucy tried to tell them not to do it, but she found that she could no longer talk. She could only make shrieking and barking sounds. The others held her down as the one with the knife began slitting the skin right up her belly. Her dark fur was covered with blood. Lucy began screeching and shrieking and lashing out at them. She woke with Amanda shaking her shoulder saying, "Luce, Luce, wake up. You're having a nightmare."

Lucy sat up in bed, gasping for breath. Gradually her heart slowed and she and Amanda looked at each other. After a time, Lucy said, "Amanda, why have you stayed? You had all those friends in high school. Don't you miss them?"

Amanda thought for a long time and then said, "It was you. It was you, Lucy. The first time I met you I knew you were something special." The two girls stared into each other's eyes and felt a warm energy flow back and forth between them. "What did you dream?"

"I was in the forest playing with other bonobos. They turned into people and started attacking me."

"That fits. All our talk about having to be on the run."

"Sometimes I hate being me."

"It's tough being human."

Then they both fell into a fit of laughter, which they tried to stifle because it was three in the morning and they didn't want to wake Jenny. Their laughter gradually faded, and they sat for a moment with downcast eyes. They both looked up at the same time. Their eyes met once more.

"Listen," Lucy whispered.

"What is it?"

"The crickets stopped." Lucy listened through The Stream. Beneath the city sounds she could sense the signals. "Someone's here," she said.

They both listened for a time and then Lucy stood and began to dress.

"What are you doing," Amanda asked.

"I have to go."

"Is this for real?"

"Yes. Yes, it is. Amanda, listen to me. I want you to go back home to your mother or father. I want you to go to college and have a good life."

"What are you talking about? I'm having a good life. Growing up with my mother, I always dreamed of having a real family, and now I feel like I have one. Lucy, we can figure this out. Please."

"No, no, listen to me. I'm trouble, Amanda. I'm real serious trouble. I don't want to see you hurt."

"Luce, I'm not leaving you alone."

"You don't understand!" Lucy shouted. "I know things that you don't know. I have an animal mind. I know what's coming before it comes. And I see you getting hurt. I mean hurt that you don't walk away from. I see myself hurting people, too, Amanda. I see myself maybe even killing, and I was taught not to kill. I don't want you hurt, and I don't want you to see me that way."

"See you what way?"

"The way I'm going to have to be to get through this."

"Are you really going through the trees like Donna said?"

"Yes. I'm sorry. I'm going to have to move fast now. I'll be on the run." Lucy took Amanda in her arms. "Goodbye, Amanda. I love you. I'll always love you." Lucy could feel Amanda begin to sob.

"You're not really going. Tell me you're not really going. Lucy, this is so mean."

With her heart aching, Lucy let go of Amanda and went down the hall to Jenny's room. As Lucy entered, Jenny said, "I heard."

"They're out there. Maybe only watching, I don't know."

Jenny was up now, standing bleary-eyed before Lucy. She took Lucy's wrist and looked her in the eye. Jenny's face was so loving and fierce that it almost hurt Lucy to look at her. "Lucy. Some people care about us. Don't you think there might be another way?"

"No, Mom, no. You planned it. And anyway, you know now. You're in The Stream."

"Yes, I know." Jenny relaxed her grip on Lucy's wrist. "You're right. I just don't want to believe it."

"Mom, every day I stay in here I get weaker and they get stronger."

"I'm just not ready for this. I don't think I'll ever be ready."

Jenny's face was so sad. Lucy grabbed her, and they held each other for a long time. "Mom. Mom. I love you. I'm so grateful for all you've done for me. But you've got to trust The Stream."

Jenny let go and sat on the bed in silence. Lucy slipped across the room. She could sense that Amanda had come to the door but she didn't look back. She unlatched the window screen and leaned it against the wall. Then she reached out, took hold of a branch of the maple tree outside, and was gone.

Jenny sat on the bed in shock. Cool air with a hint of early autumn lifted the curtains as she listened to the rustling in the trees fade away. Jenny waited to see if she would wake once more and recognize that it was all just a nightmare. Amanda stood framed by the doorway with tears in her eyes. She crossed the room and sat beside Jenny. Then she collapsed against her, tears soaking into Jenny's T-shirt. Jenny said, "Shh, shh," and held her tight. "Come," Jenny said. "Come look with me."

She led Amanda down the hall. The window of Lucy's room faced the street. Jenny parted the curtain and looked down. A dented blue utility van sat at the curb. The streetlights were reflected in the windows. The words "Miles Electric" were painted in fading letters on the side. Jenny strained to see but couldn't tell if anyone was inside.

Amanda came up beside her. "What is it?"

"Just a van. But what's it doing here?"

"What do we do?"

"Wait."

"Will we ever see her again?"

"I don't know." Jenny caught herself. "Of course we will."

They waited an hour in silence. When they checked the street again, the van was gone. There was no way to know what it meant. All they had was Lucy's intuition. Jenny had sensed it, too, but maybe it was nothing. Maybe Lucy had panicked after the visit with Donna. Maybe she was running from nothing. It was a horrible thought.

Jenny and Amanda tried to sleep. At about eight in the morning the doorbell rang, sending a chill through Jenny. She threw on her robe and went to the girls' room. Amanda was peeking through the curtains.

"Who is it?" Jenny whispered.

"A car. I can't see anybody."

The doorbell rang again.

"This is ridiculous. I'm going down." Jenny ran down the stairs and jerked the door open.

Dr. Ruth Mayer said, "Good morning."

"Dr. Mayer. What are you doing here?"

"I knew I was right about that girl all along. I knew there was something wrong with her. I couldn't have imagined how serious it was. I have enlisted the Department of Children and Family Services to look into her case, and I felt I should warn you that I will be doing the evaluation and subsequent counseling. I have to work with the entire family, so I wanted to give you and her a fair chance to meet with me first, even though her ultimate placement may not be with you."

The woman herself, as well as what she said, struck Jenny as so preposterous that she couldn't help laughing.

"I assure you, Dr. Lowe, this is no laughing matter."

But Jenny couldn't stop herself now. "I'm sorry. I'm really sorry for you." She closed the door and leaned against it, laughing high and weak, covering her mouth with her hand, and then sobbing. Amanda came to the head of the stairs and looked down at her.

"Jenny? Are you all right?"

31

LUCY SWUNG EASILY through the night sky, her way lit by a moon torn ragged in the shadow of the earth. As she went, the woods grew more dense, and she saw how much like her old home this forest really was. Except for the biggest ones, almost all the old creatures were still there. They merely remained hidden most of the time. As she progressed from branch to branch, she settled into The Stream. She picked up signals of coyote and fox and even an old female cougar. Who knew that she still kept her vigil here? They know me, Lucy thought. These creatures know what I am, like the dogs who were never fooled.

She migrated west with the setting moon and she reached the edge of the Forest Preserve just before dawn. She reached a dense growth of oak over the old river. As the first light was coming up in the east, she made herself a nest and fell asleep to the sound of a cardinal standing high in a tree and telling his lover one of those tall tales that redbirds like to tell. They're such liars, Lucy thought. She laughed to think how proud of himself he was.

She slept through the day and descended at dusk to drink from the puddles. She didn't dare drink from the river, which smelled of chemicals and sewage. She sat on the ground and ate a few grubs. A rabbit came to inspect her.

"We're in the same boat now, aren't we, Rab?"

Rabbits, Lucy knew, weren't much for conversation. Some

creatures were just plain blabbermouths, like those crickets and that redbird. But rabbits will let you know what they think. Rab wrinkled his nose at Lucy, scratched at a flea, and said, "We're all prey here in the end."

"Yeah," Lucy said, "we're both sitting on the forest floor scratching for something to eat, watching out for the hawk." Rab stretched like a cat and then chewed on a low-hanging leaf. "Night's falling, Rab. I'd better make my way north."

"Mind how you go."

Then Lucy flowed up into the trees and was off again.

She went carefully in the dark until moonrise. Then she stopped to drink and continued at full speed. After a time she came to a swampy area where the trees grew farther apart. Many of them were topped by the sprawling nests of great blue herons. A few of the birds were standing down below in the water, talking in a throaty bark and speculating excitedly about Lucy. As she made great leaps from tree to tree to bridge the gaps, they took off in a running ascent and began circling out over the treetops and off to the east against the rising yellow moon.

Lucy heard the helicopter sometime before dawn. At first she didn't think that it concerned her as it flew past. But then it turned and came back. It passed over her once again, turned and slowed. Then its searchlight came blazing over the tops of the trees. Lucy dropped from branch to branch with her heart hammering. The bright beam shattered in the branches and filtered down across the forest litter as the engine's thunder shook the earth. Lucy thought, How did they find me? She had to calm herself and think. She reminded herself of what Jenny and Donna had said: Her advantage was that she could think. I'm human, she told herself. I have logic and reason. Think. Think.

She reasoned that the only way they could have found her was with infrared. Perhaps they had followed her all the way from the house. How? Satellite? It didn't matter. She knew that they must be detecting her body heat.

She moved quickly from tree to tree until the mud of the riverbank was sucking at her feet. It sucked her sneakers off, but she kept going. The water rose past her knees, and then she was submerged up to her neck. It was cold, but she could stand it for a while. She put her head under water and let the current pull her quickly along. Periodically, she lifted her nose for a breath. She wasn't sure how long she rode the river. She knew that she was going in the right direction and that was all that mattered. After a time, she passed under an old concrete bridge and emerged into the open in moonlight. She lifted her head to listen. The helicopter engine was far away now.

But for how long? Maybe she should be trying to blend in with a crowd instead of moving at night on her own. But her clothes were a mess now, torn and muddy and wet. She couldn't appear in public like that.

She maneuvered her way to the bank and crawled out through the mud and into the forest. She listened intently: No helicopter. The Forest Preserve was a narrow strip of dense woods less than a quarter mile wide in places. It ran through neighborhoods and farmland all the way to the Wisconsin line. Shivering and wet, Lucy navigated east by the moon. She came to a road. She listened for traffic, then hurried across the street and into a warren of closely packed suburban homes.

She crossed through backyards, quietly leaping fences and smelling the smells. Dog. Cat. Raccoon. Rabbit. People. The racket of air conditioners. House after house, she could smell the families sleeping. All the houses were dark except for a few with spotlights in the back. Staying out of the pools of light, she came upon a home at the end of a cul de sac a few lights shone inside. Three cars were parked in the driveway. Curtains closed. Air conditioner off. Lucy went to the back and smelled at the crack in the door. No one had been there for some time.

She crossed a patio to a pair of sliding glass doors. The metal clasp gave way easily. She slid the panel back and stepped through the curtains. She stood for a moment to confirm that she was alone. Somewhere a houseplant was dying. She went through the house quickly. Den, kitchen, living room, dining room. Upstairs she found the master bedroom with a portrait of Mom and Dad and three kids framed on the bureau. Teenage girl with hair dyed red.

Lucy went through the parents' closet, but the clothes weren't right. She crossed the hall to the teenager's room. Her clothes were too large. She took a pair of sunglasses and a hat. And then she had a thought: She opened the girl's bathroom door and rummaged through the cupboards. In the linen closet Lucy found tubes of temporary hair coloring in red and blue and green.

Down the hall, she found the younger girl's room. She held up a shirt that was about the right size. The sun was coming up as Lucy quickly stripped out of her clothes and went to the shower. She washed herself and shampooed her hair. As she let the water run over her, she felt a great sense of relief. She stepped out of the shower, and with her hair still wet, carefully began to color long strips of it, listening to the birds, detecting some sort of disturbance in The Stream. When she had finished with the dye, she had a multicolored head of red, green, and blue hair.

She returned to the younger daughter's bedroom and slipped into one of her thongs, her pink jeans. She wore her blue Crocs and a stretchy green halter top. She listened again. The birds had resumed their morning chatter. She took an iPod and put the ear buds in her ears. She put on the sunglasses and hat, then examined herself in the full-length mirror. She struck a pose and said, "Sweet." She cocked her hip and threw her shoulder back, saying, "No way." She felt certain that no one would recognize her now.

The sun was shining on the quiet neighborhood as Lucy went down the sidewalk to the street. She stood for a moment inhaling the morning air. The lawns were wet with dew. The newspapers were wrapped in plastic. She felt a rush of confidence. She felt like a real American girl.

At first she thought that she'd been stung by a bee. Then she looked down and saw the dart sticking out of her thigh. It had gone right through the pink jeans. She looked up and saw a blue van halfway down the block, a man in its open door pointing a rifle. He lifted his head from the telescopic sight to look at her. Lucy read the words "Miles Electric" and felt a buzzing dizzy sensation. She barely had time to be afraid. She was trying to put together the pieces of her world, which seemed to have broken apart. An electric van. A man. A rifle. What did it mean? Then her eyes wouldn't focus and she sat heavily on the sidewalk, feeling a dreamy warmth flow through her. She flopped backward, and her head landed in the soft wet grass. The last thing she saw was the blue sky and a happy little cloud floating past.

32

ONLY SIX MEN SAT in the large conference room, where ordinarily twenty or more might have attended the morning meeting. They sat in high-backed leather swivel chairs at a vast table. The large skylight cast reflections on its polished surface. Carafes of coffee and pitchers of water had been placed at intervals. The chair at the head of the table was empty. The men waited without talking, scribbling notes or busying themselves with handheld devices.

A broad white fireplace dominated the wall behind the head of the table. On its mantel, a Nobel Peace Prize medal was encased in Plexiglas, and a portrait of Theodore Roosevelt on horseback hung above it. Tall service flags hung from stands along one side of the conference table. A painting by Thomas Whittredge of the River Platte hung above a peach-colored couch and matching chairs. Lamps on end tables cast a yellow glow on the creamy walls.

At exactly eight a.m., the men heard the door across the hall open and close, and a moment later, a short man with salt-and-pepper hair entered briskly, nodded at the room, and motioned with his hand to indicate that no one need stand. He sat at the head of the table. His eyebrows ran together over the bridge of his nose. His eyes were set close together, and his thin lips were compressed into a concerned frown. He wore a dark suit, a pale blue tie, and a small pin on his left lapel depicting the American flag. He hastily flipped through several papers in the leather folder before him and then put his hands flat on the surface of the conference table and pushed himself to a standing position. Now the others rose to their feet.

"Gentlemen," he began, "if we might welcome the Very Reverend Gerald Pinkus from Plano, Texas. Welcome, Gerry. It's a blessing to have you here today. If you would do the honors, we can begin with a prayer. I think today is a good day to focus on the presence of evil in our midst."

The six men bowed their heads, and some folded their hands, interlacing their fingers. Pinkus began: "Dear Lord, we are humbled in your sight this morning as we sit contemplating this ominous sign that has appeared in our midst in these already troubled times. Dark clouds seem to be gathering at an accelerating pace, and we humbly beseech you for assistance in guiding us at this crucial time. And please, Lord, help to speed the noble work of our colleague, Senator Steven Rhodes, to free our hands for the actions that we will be required to take to dispel the evil that has come among us." He lifted his head and nodded at the senator. Rhodes nodded and pushed a Bible across the table toward Pinkus and then bowed his head once more. "I'd like to conclude with a reading from two books of the New Testament." He opened the book to a page marked by a red ribbon. " 'And if I by Beelzebub cast out devils, by whom do your children cast them out? Therefore they shall be your judges. But if I cast out devils by the Spirit of God, then the kingdom of God is come unto you.' Matthew twelve, twenty-seven and twenty-eight." He paused, found a second passage marked by another red ribbon, and read, " 'And I saw three unclean spirits like frogs come out of the mouth of the dragon, and out of the mouth of the beast, and out of the mouth of the false prophet. For they are the spirits of devils, working miracles, which go forth unto the kings of the earth and of the whole world, to gather them to the battle of that great day of God Almighty.' Revelation sixteen, thirteen and fourteen. Please join me in the Lord's Prayer. Our Father, who art in heaven . . ."

33

AFTER DR. MAYER HAD LEFT, Jenny made breakfast, but it was by force of habit only. Neither Jenny nor Amanda wanted to eat. The uncertainty was gnawing at them, not knowing where Lucy was or how she was getting along. Not knowing if her fears and Donna's warnings were real. Jenny and Amanda took turns crying and comforting each other, and sometimes the stress would seem to reach a climax, and they'd fall into a fit of paradoxical laughter.

At about noon the phone rang, and Jenny startled and leapt up. It was Harry. She was reluctant to say anything, fearing that she'd be overheard, so she pretended that everything was normal. He asked if there was anything he could do. Jenny told him no and rang off. And what happened next was the most maddening thing of all: Nothing. Nothing at all happened. The police didn't come. The Nazis didn't come. The world went on about its doggy business as if nothing were amiss. Jenny continued to receive requests to interview Lucy. She turned them down with the excuse that Lucy was working on her book.

The weather was pleasant, and Jenny spent the long hours sitting on a lounge chair in the garden, a copy of *Le Roi des aulnes* unread in her lap. She found herself going over in her mind what she was like at Lucy's age and what Lucy must be going through. At fifteen Jenny was a sophomore in high school. Her mother was vivacious and active, involved in every cause that caught her fancy. Her father had died shoveling snow in the middle of a blizzard, leaving his wife well off and leaving Jenny bookish and reclusive.

Jenny discovered boys that spring but had no idea what good they were. A boy named Dylan gave her a copy of *Cat's Cradle* by Kurt Vonnegut, and she devoured it in one sitting, feeling as if her mind had been blown open. Pattie Walinsky was her best friend. She was homely and the boys made fun of her, but Jenny loved her mind. Her father worked at the observatory, and one summer night she took Jenny there. She saw worlds being born and dying. Pattie went on to teach at Stanford. Jenny wondered, Would Lucy ever have the chance to develop her fine mind?

Jenny heard a noise and turned. The sun was in her eyes. She saw a beautiful girl in a yellow bikini in a halo of light. Her heart leapt. Then Amanda's shadow fell on her face, and she realized that it was not Lucy.

"You're wearing Lucy's bikini."

"Yeah. It smells like her." Amanda gave Jenny a weak smile and shrugged. "I know. Call me weird. I'm going to lay out."

"Lie out," Jenny corrected.

"Now you sound like Lucy."

Amanda lay in the sun and sent text messages. Days passed like that, in the garden or wandering the house when the weather was too cool. They went shopping for groceries and Jenny busied herself preparing elaborate meals that they barely touched. They saw a few movies. Amanda tried to teach Jenny how to play chess, but Jenny kept hanging her queen. Lucy's absence was like a death in the family. Every day, more than once, Jenny checked Craigslist, searching for the coded ad that Donna should have placed by then.

One day Amanda called Jenny into her room—Lucy's room—and showed her a video on YouTube. It was a preacher named Gerald Pinkus from Plano, Texas, and he was saying, "One of the most apocalyptic events in the history of the world is in the Bible and is scheduled to happen very soon. There is a war coming that is going to kill two billion human beings. Now why would I think such a thing? It is the appearance at this moment on earth of the demon seed in the form of a cross between a human and an ape, namely the one we've all seen by now on TV and on the Internet who calls herself Lucy Lowe."

"Turn it off, honey."

"He's saying that the only way to save humanity is to sacrifice Lucy."

"I know, honey. We already know there are crazies out there."

"But that's the same preacher who was invited to the White House last week. It was in the *Washington Post:* Like, what is the president doing inviting this whacko preacher to the White House? So it's not just the garden-variety crazies, Jenny—the people in charge believe this stuff."

"I know. But I don't know what to do about that."

"Lucy should have gotten to Milwaukee and be somewhere in hiding by now."

"I know."

"I think we should talk to Donna."

"She said we might accidentally lead people to where Lucy is."

"But she should have contacted us, don't you think?"

"Maybe."

"We'll go by back roads. We can make sure we're not followed that way."

"I'm going crazy here," Jenny admitted. The idea of getting out appealed to her. The idea of having something to do. "We could call that senator."

"Do you trust him?"

Jenny had to think about that. Senator Cochrain had defended Lucy in public. On the other hand, he might have simply wanted publicity. Jenny felt that anyone who had risen that high in American politics had already slept with the devil. No one would ever know his true motives again. "No. I guess I don't."

"We can't just hide in the house like criminals."

They packed a few things and set out early the next morning through the vast wasteland of malls to the north and west. They took the interstate to Rockford and drove the state roads across the border into Wisconsin. They switched to county roads and wound their way north through rolling hills dotted with dairy farms and churches. In a little town called Helenville they found a diner beside a lake and had lunch. The trees were turning colors. They were the only customers, and no one who passed on the street gave them a second look.

"How do you feel?" Jenny asked.

"Good. I think we're okay."

In the afternoon they traveled on deserted stretches of road for long periods. No one could be following them without their knowledge, Jenny thought. At last they turned the old Toyota wagon east and found their way into Milwaukee on city streets. They reached the edge of the heavily wooded compound and slipped into the zoo through a back gate. They made their way through the forest to the area behind the bonobo enclosure. There they waited for the better part of an hour until Donna appeared wearing blue rubber gloves, filthy rubber boots, and a canvas apron. When she saw them, Donna motioned for them to wait. She disappeared inside and a few minutes later emerged wearing jeans and a work shirt. She led them deeper into the woods.

"I think we can talk here. What's happened? Has something happened with Lucy?"

Jenny and Amanda looked at her in confusion.

"What do you mean?" Amanda asked. "She came to you."

"No," Donna said. "I haven't heard from her."

"You haven't seen her?" Jenny cried out, louder than she had intended.

Donna motioned for her to be quiet, then shook her head. "Haven't seen her. Nothing. Tell me what happened."

"She left, saying she was coming to you. Through the trees, just like we planned."

"No," Donna said. "When was that?"

"Weeks ago," Amanda said.

"It's been about ten days."

"Oh, crap," Donna said. "They must have caught her."

"But wouldn't we know?" Jenny asked. "Wouldn't there be some news of it? I mean, if a person is arrested, there's a record."

"This wouldn't work like that. It's too much of a legal gray area. Any one of a dozen agencies could have picked her up."

"And not tell someone?" Amanda asked.

Donna shook her head. "You don't know these people."

"Isn't there some way we can find out?" Jenny asked.

"I don't know. I can try my contacts in the military. I can try to find out. I don't know."

They stood there saying nothing, each wrapped in private thoughts. Jenny felt physically sick with worry at the thought that Lucy was a captive somewhere under conditions that were impossible to imagine.

"I'll do everything in my power," Donna said. "If they've captured her she could die from the stress alone. We have to find her."

"She said she might have to kill someone," Amanda said. "And then everybody who wants to kill her would have a reason."

They both stared at Amanda with blank looks.

LUCY WOKE WET and shivering on a concrete floor. She felt a deep pain in her thigh, and her head was throbbing. She smelled urine and feces. She heard the hum and hiss of electric lights high overhead but couldn't yet open her eyes. They were seamed with dried scum. Her tongue and throat were so dry that they hurt. At first she thought that she was paralyzed. Even though her mind was telling her to get up, she couldn't seem to make the first move. She curled her toes. She clenched her fists. Slowly her muscles began to remember. She felt sore from head to foot. She pushed herself onto one elbow and managed to open her eyes at last. Her heart jumped in her chest. There was blood everywhere. No, wait: It was blue and green as well as red. Then she remembered the hair dye. Some of it had washed off onto the concrete floor.

As the world around her began to resolve into recognizable images, she realized that her clothes were gone. She saw that there were bars in front of her. Black steel bars. She turned her head. There were bars all around. She looked up into the blinding light. More bars. She was in a cage.

"Oh, no."

Breathe, she told herself. Don't go off now, not now. Just breathe and think. Breathe and think. She felt tears well up in her eyes, and her throat closed. She desperately needed water. She managed to fight back the tears. Be strong, she told herself. Don't let your guard down. This is like the jungle now. Think, don't just react.

Lucy gripped the bars and pulled herself unsteadily to her feet, trying to remember what had happened. She had been going through the forest. She found a house. She dyed her hair. She stole some girl's clothes. Wet grass. A blue sky. A white puffy cloud. Then: Nothing.

Wait: A dart. She looked down. A livid purple bruise spread across her right thigh. She rubbed it to see if it was hair dye, but it wasn't. There was a nasty hole in its center, scabbed over with blood.

She hobbled along, clutching the cold bars and trying to look out. She was in a lab or an operating room of some sort. There was an operating table with lights above it, turned off. She saw equipment of all sorts, steel shelves of bottles, linens. Pale daylight filtered through skylights from high above. What kind of place was this? She'd never seen such a place.

"Hello," she called. Then louder: "Hello! Is anybody here?" She heard far-off noises muffled by the doors and walls but couldn't identify them. She looked all around the cage for some way out, but it was stoutly welded and the lock looked formidable. She paced back and forth. She was freezing, holding herself. Why was she wet? Why was she naked? Nothing made sense.

And then she remembered the security guard at the airport, deadpan, without feeling, saying, "All animals have to be caged and put in the luggage compartment."

I'm in a cage, Lucy thought, because I am officially an animal.

She sat down, shivering, and hugged her knees. She wondered, How could they do this? She knew how. Her father had explained it all. When Lucy was eleven years old, he had made her read *The Rise and Fall of the Third Reich*. As she read and gradually realized what was going on and what those people were going to do to other people, she had begged him not to make her go on reading. "Read," he'd commanded. "I want you to know what you're up against. Those people are not all Hitler, are they? One man you can dismiss. But almost eight thousand men and women oversaw Auschwitz. Can you dismiss all of them as being, by chance, criminal psychopaths? No. They're human beings. That's their trouble.

That's why you're here. To change that." Then with morbid fascination, with wonder and love and horror, Lucy had read Anne Frank's diary. How she had wept for Anne. An ordinary girl, she thought. And so modern. There she was, in the midst of her nightmare, falling in love with Peter and reading about Oedipus, Orpheus, and Hercules—all that knowledge, Anne's beautiful and tender mind, which would simply vanish as she languished in Auschwitz, fetched off in the flowering of her youth. And this was the girl who wrote, "I was born happy, I love people, I have a trusting nature, and I'd like everyone else to be happy too." Now Lucy told herself, Be strong like Anne. Keep that core inside you intact for whatever's coming. They can take your freedom, they can hurt you, they can even kill you. But there is a last bastion within the spirit that they never killed in Anne. She stayed in The Stream to the end. But even as Lucy told herself those things, she could feel the depth of her dread. Then she heard something. Voices. Muffled. Far off. She held her breath and listened.

"You vote for Yamaguchi?" a woman asked.

"Of course, I voted for Yamaguchi," said another. "Four times. I musta hit redial a million times."

"You check the ass on that girl?"

"I'd have an ass like that if I'd been ice skating since I was two."

Just random people talking in the hall. But where are we? Lucy wondered. What is this place for? She heard a key hit the lock and sprang to her feet. A middle-aged man with receding hair and a thick red nose came shuffling in, leering at her with an uneven smile. He wore the gray shirt and slacks of a janitor and a matching baseball cap cocked back on his head. A surgical mask hung around his neck, unused. He went to the wall, took down a coil of green hose from a hook, and moved toward the cage. He compressed his tongue between his lips, aimed the hose, and squeezed the spray nozzle. Lucy screamed as the icy blast of water hit her. She scrambled to the back wall as he played the jet of water across the floor and washed the urine and feces into a drain beyond the bars.

"What are you doing?" Lucy shouted. "Are you insane?"

"So you're that monkey girl, eh? You been out for a few days." He stared at Lucy in a way that made her long for clothes. "I'll tell you one thing, you sure look good to me, clean you up a bit."

"What happened to my clothes? Why am I in a cage? Who are you people?"

"You came in here like that. And you're in a cage because you're a monkey."

"You can't do this. I'll die in here. Do you not see a girl before you?"

"Like I said, you're a sight for sore eyes. They told me not to be confused just because you look human. They seen your genes. They seen 'em. They know what's what. They're scientists."

Lucy felt a trembling alarm at the idea of scientists. "Where are we?"

"They're gonna study you."

"Study me? Who? What kind of study? What are they going to do?"

"Beats me. I'm just the factotum."

"Where are we? What city?" He smiled in that crooked way. Lucy could see that she was talking to the wrong person. "Listen," she said. "Can you give me some water? And clothes? It's freezing in here."

"I just wash out the cages. The doctor'll be along soon." The man turned to leave.

"Wait," she called out. "What doctor?" He turned back and grinned. Lucy could see his brown teeth. She could feel his eyes going all over her, and it made her skin crawl. "Could I have some water? Some water from your hose? Please."

He shook his head with a chuckle. "Now, don't that beat all," he said, and went through the door.

Then Lucy couldn't help herself. She collapsed on the floor and began weeping. They were going to study her. She had been right all along. She was in a science lab, and somebody was going to study her. She had heard tales of what happened to apes in labs. And she was terrified. More terrified than she had ever been. She heard her own high keening voice echoing off the walls. She became aware that someone might be listening. She looked around for microphones but saw none. That didn't mean they weren't there. There could be cameras as well. She stifled her crying and clutched herself tighter. The concrete was cold and rough on her skin. Her mouth was so dry that she could hardly swallow.

35

JENNY AND AMANDA went straight to Harry's when they returned from Milwaukee. They were waiting for him in the kitchen when he returned from the hospital that evening.

"What a pleasant surprise," he said as he crossed to the refrigerator and opened the freezer. "I have some split pea soup. Loaf of bread. You hungry? You two look like your dog got run over. Where's Luce the Goose?"

As Harry began thawing the soup on the stove, Jenny explained everything to him. He took the news without any visible reaction. When she had finished, he said, "I'm sorry. I was wondering why you'd been avoiding me. I thought it was because of our date."

"No, I'm sorry. I should have told you sooner. I just thought in the end that I'd have better news. That she was safe somewhere. But she's not."

Harry handed Jenny a baguette. "Here, cut this, will you?" Harry was used to death and suffering. Jenny didn't have much of an appetite but she knew his approach to life: Bad things will always happen. Let's make ourselves strong so that we can deal with them.

"Can I help?" Amanda asked.

"Go down and get some wine, if you don't mind."

Amanda turned toward the basement stairs.

"Harry, are you angry?"

"No, I'm thinking." Harry continued to think for another moment as Jenny cut the bread. "Well, I have a very good lawyer if you want to try that route. Then there's that senator."

Amanda came up with a bottle and showed it to Harry, whose eyebrows went up. "Chambertin Clos de Bèze, eh? A girl of wealth and taste."

"Did I get the wrong one? I'm sorry. There were so many I didn't know what to pick."

"No. That's good. Really good. Might as well. You know, you don't want to get hit by a bus and be lying in the gutter thinking, Damn. I should have had the Chambertin Clos de Bèze."

Amanda laughed. "That's good, Harry. I haven't laughed in a while."

Jenny smiled, watching them.

"Yeah? You want another laugh? Well, try this: Chambertin Clos de Bèze 'offers several octaves of fruit, herbal, floral and mineral notes, leading to a reverberating finish.' Robert Parker said that. Or something close."

"But you're supposed to be solemn," Amanda said. "It's a sad occasion."

"No, my dear child. Laughter quiets the amygdala."

"What's the amygdala?"

"It's a little peanut in your brain that makes you freak out when bad things happen. Better, I think, to shut it up and get on with business."

"How did you get to be so calm?" Amanda asked.

"Well, I like to start slow and taper off. Let that breathe, will you?"

The following day they went to meet Harry's lawyer at an office on LaSalle Street in downtown Chicago. Sy Joseph was a small man of fifty or so. He kept an old leather book bag that he had used since law school beside his worn wooden desk. Papers were stacked on the hardwood floor. He was framed by floor-to-ceiling windows that hadn't been cleaned in years. They looked out onto the colorless buildings and the busy street below. Harry, Jenny, and Amanda sat in straight-backed chairs before him.

"I've done some research, and think I have an answer," Joseph said. "At least, a partial answer. If any local police agency had Lucy, we would know. State, county, and municipal police are still bound by habeas corpus. On the other hand, if the federal government has her, then essentially they can do anything they want."

"But they'd have to charge her with a crime and leave some record of her whereabouts, right?" Jenny asked.

"No, I'm afraid not. Under the provisions of the USA Patriot Act they really can hold someone indefinitely without charge and even without probable cause."

"What about due process?" Jenny asked.

"Well, as I say, that applies to local police forces. But under the Patriot Act, there is no more due process. And what I'm telling you applies to human beings in the traditional sense. When you take into account the fact that Lucy is an interspecific hybrid, then you enter terra incognita—there's no law to cover that. They can make it up as they please."

"What do we do?" Amanda said.

"I'm sorry," Joseph said. "I'm just telling you what I know."

"Any advice, Sy?" Harry asked.

"I'd report her to the local police as a missing person. The local police still have rules, and they still generally prefer to solve crimes rather than commit them."

36

LUCY WATCHED THE GLOW that filtered through the skylight as it changed by imperceptible increments. Then she heard a key in the lock again. In walked a thin gray man in a lab coat and a surgical mask. He had close-cropped silver hair and rimless spectacles. He was neat to a fault, his shoes bright against the wet concrete floor. His name tag said, "Dr. L. Eisner." He hurried in and studied Lucy with a disapproving look. She could hear his breath whistling faintly through his nostrils. She could not discern his intentions. He was giving off no signals in The Stream.

"Who are you? Why am I in this cage?"

"I'm sorry. Pure incompetence. The heavy hand of the military. I'm shocked. This was not my intention at all, I assure you."

"Okay," Lucy said, taking a deep breath to try to calm herself. "Okay. Good. Then you can help me. I'm cold, and I need water."

"Yes, yes, of course. Just a moment." He turned and left the room.

"Hey, wait! Where am I?"

But he was gone. Lucy slumped against the bars. She thought, Have I lost my mind? Is that it? I've gone psychotic from the stress and this is all in my imagination. She went through a check of her own sanity. What's your name? Lucy Lowe. Where do you live? Illinois. Who's your best friend? Amanda. What day is it? She didn't know. Who's your mother? Jenny. No, Leda. I don't know, she thought. I don't know anything.

She heard the key in the lock again and the man returned with a blanket, a hospital gown, and a plastic bottle of water. He put the items through a chamber in the side of the cage, a small door that she could open only after he had closed the outer door. Lucy drank half the bottle before taking a breath. Then she tied on the hospital gown and wrapped herself in the blanket.

"I'm very sorry about this. I gave strict orders that you were to be treated in a humane way. Unfortunately, I wasn't able to be there."

"Who are you? Why am I being held prisoner?"

"I'm Dr. Eisner. And I promise, much more comfortable accommodations are being arranged."

"But why am I here at all?"

"For your protection. I assure you that I have only benign intentions toward you."

"I was shot and left naked on the floor." Lucy could hear her voice rising. Stop, she told herself. Don't go off on him. Try to be calm.

"Yes, that was unfortunate. I should have known better. I promise that you'll be treated humanely throughout the procedures from now on."

Lucy thought, Perhaps it is he who is mad. Because he wore a surgical mask, she had seen only his eyes. But she had seen enough. She tried to speak in a normal tone of voice: "What, what, what—" She couldn't get the words out. "What procedures? Where are we? What are you going to do to me?" For a fleeting moment she had the thought that she could reach out and grab his arm. And before he knew what had happened, she could batter his skull against the bars like a box of strawberries. She concentrated on breathing. Don't show your strength, she told herself. Make him think you're weak.

Eisner studied her. "Remarkable. The moment I saw you on television I knew that what I'd long dreamed of was real. You are, as your father would say, more human than human."

Lucy felt a stab of alarm go through her. "How do you know what my father would say?"

"We took them, of course. Naturally, we had to have your father's notebooks." And seeing the look on Lucy's face, added,

"Don't worry. They were out at the time. No one wants complications. We made it look like an ordinary burglary."

She felt all hope drain from her as she stared at him in speechless horror. At the same time, she could feel a fury rising inside her. She could feel strength pouring through her. She deliberately held herself still. If she started to rant, she knew, she might show how dangerous she could be. Don't show yourself, she thought. Weep. Weep now and show him that you're a helpless child.

Lucy fell to the floor weeping into her hands.

"I'm sorry. This was really the only way. Higher powers want you destroyed. They have these irrational religious beliefs. There's no reasoning with the Christian right. They hate science. They fear knowledge. I crave it. I'm determined to protect you for as long as I can. Don't you see the scientific opportunities here? Together we can fulfill your father's dream."

"I don't want to fulfill my father's dream!" Lucy shouted through her tears. "I just want to go home."

"Yes, I understand. Of course you do. But I'm afraid that's impossible."

Lucy wept for a time as Eisner stood watching. "Soon," he said, "you and I will establish trust. That's something I've been able to do here only a very few times over the years. *Pan troglodytes* and the very few specimens of *Pan paniscus* that we've seen here are very intelligent, but they can also be very dangerous, especially after they've undergone some of the necessary procedures. You can't explain things to them and get them to cooperate just because it seems reasonable. With you I believe I'll be able to do that at last."

Lucy's tears had stopped as she had a revelation: Papa said that killing was wrong. Yet Lucy now saw that she might have to kill this man. And it dawned on her that she could do it if she was forced to. Papa was wrong.

"What are you going to do to me?"

"We'll start with some standard tests. This afternoon we'll perform a craniotomy. You'll be given a local anesthetic. The brain itself has no pain receptors, so you won't feel anything there at all. I'll explain as we go along. You'll be awake for most of it. I'll place electronic sensors in your brain. You won't feel them. They're extremely fine wires. They do no damage to the tissue. The surgical incisions will heal for a few days. Then we'll send tiny electrical signals down the wires and make a complete map of your brain. It's an unprecedented opportunity."

Lucy quailed. Her whole body was vibrating. She could no longer help herself. She could feel her guts churning as he spoke, and then the water that she'd drunk came exploding out of her mouth. She bent involuntarily and heaved a few more times before she was able to breathe again. Her vision was blurred with tears.

"I'm sorry. I didn't mean to upset you. I assure you that this operation is completely safe. I've performed it many times, and there are no lasting effects."

She tried to speak, to reason with him, but all she could say was, "Don't," her voice a hoarse croak. "Please don't."

"It's really going to be just fine. We will give you a sedative to relax you. I've done these operations for decades. I'm the leading expert. It's quite safe, I assure you. I know it's hard. But it's for science. For the good of humanity." He turned to leave, saying, "My staff will be in shortly to prepare you."

"Don't. Please don't cut me." Lucy clutched the bars as she watched him go. She couldn't stop herself now. She flailed against the bars. "Don't do this! Let me out! Please don't do this!"

He vanished through the door. She listened as it shut with a metallic clang. Then silence fell once more. She wept uncontrollably for a time. She didn't know how long. Her throat was raw from screaming. And through an act of will, she pulled herself out of the abyss and sat, clutching her knees. Be still, she told herself. Be still and don't let them know your strength.

Lucy paced the floor, wrapped in her blanket, her mind racing. She could feel the panic rising within her breast. It was all she could do to keep from screaming and throwing herself at the bars again. She had to get out. There had to be a way. But nothing came to mind. She seemed to be splitting in two, undergoing a kind of mitosis of the psyche. On one side she was a child, weak and weeping. But from the other side she heard a cold and rational voice. Think, the voice said to the child. You're smart and you're strong. Stop whimpering and think.

She looked all around. Now she saw that there were instruments on a tray near the operating table. Perhaps she could pick the lock with one of them. But she had nothing to reach with. The blanket. Maybe she could use the blanket to knock something off the tray and drag it to her. She unwrapped the blanket from herself, reached her arm through the bars, and whipped one end of it at the tray. She tried again and again, but the tray was too far away. The door opened again, and a group of people in green hospital scrubs entered. Lucy froze. There were two very large men and three women. They wore surgical masks and gloves and clear safety goggles.

One of the women unlocked a steel cabinet and brought out a rifle. She stepped forward. "If you fight us, we'll have to dart you. Tell me you understand."

Lucy couldn't think straight. Was it better to be darted than whatever they were going to do to her?

"Tell me you understand, or we'll have to dart you."

"I understand."

"Okay then. We're going to take you out and you're going to lie on that table, do you understand?"

"Yes." She was shaking so hard that she could barely speak. The woman aimed the rifle at Lucy while another unlocked the door of the cage. Lucy retreated to the far end as the two men entered.

"Come on," one of them said. "Nice and easy."

Lucy calculated the distance. She knew that she was fast enough and strong enough to take the two men. But the woman with the rifle was too far away. She'd shoot. Lucy saw that this was not her moment. She hung her head and shoulders. They would be unconsciously receiving the signal that she was harmless. She thought, I'll do as I did when wrestling. I'll lull them into complacency and show my strength only at the decisive moment.

The woman motioned with the rifle. Lucy stepped between the two large men. The concrete was wet and cold on her bare feet. The rifle followed her movement.

"Up on the table, please."

Lucy climbed onto the table. She felt the smooth white sheet. She smelled laundry detergent. She saw the skylight overhead.

"Lie down."

She lay down, and then straps shot out and immobilized her. She struggled briefly, then forced herself to relax. Not now, she told herself. Wait for the right time. Someone covered her with a sheet.

"Don't do this. Don't let him cut me. Please."

"He's not going to hurt you. Dr. Eisner has been doing this for years." The woman turned to the man and said, "Hold her arm."

"Please don't."

She tore open a white paper envelope and removed a long needle from it. She put a rubber tourniquet on Lucy's bicep. Lucy felt a pinch and looked down to see the needle going in. She felt tears streaming down the sides of her face and heard the blood singing in her ears.

"We're going to give you something to relax you. Just breathe normally."

"Don't. Please."

The woman held a syringe up to the light and tapped it. Her fingernail made a ticking noise that echoed in the vaulted room. Her goggles flashed as she bent down and injected a clear fluid into the fitting in the tubing.

"Don't. Oh . . ."

Lucy felt a dreamy lightness come over her. She gradually split in two, as if one part of her wanted to panic while another part didn't care what happened next. She was back in the forest. Leda and her father had been killed, and she was putting one foot in front of the other without caring whether she lived or died.

The other woman had put the rifle away. Now she approached and bent over Lucy. She smoothed the thick hair back from Lucy's forehead. It was a comforting touch. Lucy thought, She's grooming me. Maybe they understand at last. Maybe they realize that they, too, are bonobos and I'm human. We are all one now. Lucy felt the love of the woman's touch.

Then the woman brought her other hand up, and Lucy saw that in it was a set of electric clippers. The clippers began to buzz noisily. She lowered the shears to Lucy's head and began cutting off her hair. Lucy could feel the great heavy tresses fall away. She could feel the cold air against her bare scalp. Lucy thought, She's shaving my head. I'm going to be bald. But she couldn't seem to decide how to feel about that. The person who was terrified had grown very small, as if Lucy had a baby just beginning to form inside her. A tiny baby who could not speak yet. A child who was getting smaller, not larger.

37

JENNY KNEW IMMEDIATELY that something was wrong. She pulled the car into her garage, and nothing was out of place. But she sensed that something had changed.

"What is it?" Amanda asked.

"I don't know. I'm afraid."

"Should we leave? We could call the police."

"Yes, let's go." But Jenny didn't move. She searched the garage for a clue. She felt the maddening dilemma that Lucy had talked about, in which the demands of logic defeat what you know to be true. "What do I tell them? That I was picking up signals in The Stream? They'll think I'm nuts."

"Well, what are we going to do?"

"I'm going in. You wait here. If I'm not back in five minutes go to the police."

"Jenny, I'm scared."

"Scared is good. Just don't be too scared to move if I don't come back."

Jenny opened her door and stood in the garage looking for a weapon. She took up a claw hammer from the pegboard where tools were hung. As soon as she opened the door to the house, the smell hit her. It was man smell. Not Harry.

At the top of the stairs she gently pushed open the door. The hair stood up on her neck and arms.

"We've called the police," she shouted.

Nothing. No sound at all. She took two steps so that she could peer into the living room. The television, stereo, and DVD player were all gone, wires hanging out. She exhaled and dropped her shoulders, remarking to herself how odd it was that she could be grateful to be the victim of a simple burglary.

She hurried down the stairs to the garage. Amanda was sitting halfway out of the driver's-side door. Jenny said, "Somebody broke into the house. I don't think anyone's there."

Half an hour later, the alley and the street in front of the house were lined with police cars. Jenny and Amanda were touring the house, listing for the detective what was missing. His name was Danny Nelson, and he looked too young to order a beer. He conscientiously wrote down everything they told him.

"There's been a crew of kids working this part of town. They go for the things they can sell quickly. We already know who they are."

They were making their way to Jenny's study as he spoke. As they entered the room, Jenny stopped. "They got my computer."

"Approximate value?" Detective Nelson asked.

"New it was $1,600."

"Oh, no."

Jenny turned to see Amanda in the doorway. "What?" Then she saw the open cabinet. Jenny stepped across the room and knelt before it.

"What?" Nelson asked. "Something else missing?"

"Lucy's father's notebooks," Jenny said. "You know the story of who Lucy is?"

"Yes, of course."

"Her father's scientific notebooks were in there. They're gone."

"What do you think that means?" Detective Nelson asked.

"I think it means that someone faked a robbery to get them. This was not a group of kids."

"And where is Lucy now?"

"I don't know. I think we'd better file a missing person's report."

"Was she here?" he asked. "Do you think whoever took the notebooks kidnapped her?"

"No. Yes. I'm sorry. It's complicated. I'll explain."

38

LUCY HEARD MUSIC and wondered, Is that possible? Where are we? Relentless violins were chugging along like a railroad train. The mad unstoppable logic of oboes, French horns, violas, all marching in lockstep. Then she remembered: It was Bach. She recognized the Brandenburg Concertos. Yehudi Menuhin. She opened her eyes. Eisner's face floated above her, inverted.

"We used to shave the head entirely," he said as he worked. "But we discovered that shaving left microscopic cuts in the scalp that provided opportunities for infection. So now that we do only a buzz cut, we see fewer infections." Eisner turned to one of the nurses and said, "Let's get ready to clamp her, please."

It took two men to lift the complex metal contraption. It had pointed screws on the sides and top. They lowered it onto her head.

"Good. Right there."

A bright light flashed on her left side, but she couldn't turn her head to see what it was. Eisner said, "Can you see all right?"

"Yes, fine, just keep working," said another voice.

Lucy heard a whirring noise, then a complex click like the shutter of a camera. There was a flash, a whining sound, then another flash.

"Got it," the new voice said, and the low melancholy chords of the adagio began.

Eisner turned the screws, saying, "This may pinch a bit." Lucy could feel the points of the screws touch her scalp and then start to dig in as he turned them tighter. At first it felt as if someone were squeezing her head in a powerful grip, as the cruel insistent hammering of the allegro started up. Then she felt a searing pain on both sides of her head. She began to scream. "Give her a bit more fentanyl, please." Lucy screamed and screamed, and then all at once it stopped hurting and she fainted.

Lucy opened her eyes to the sound of a machine, a grinding noise that was inexplicably inside her head. She smelled smoke, burning flesh. The menuetto was playing. She saw Eisner, inverted, bearing down on her. His glasses were bright white disks before his eyeless head. He had something in his hand. He leaned in on Lucy and grunted with the effort. She heard the lunatic precision of the bassoon playing against the oboes in waltz time. Then she noticed that she could see Eisner clearly reflected in the big overhead light. He was drilling a hole in her head. He'd been right, she felt no pain. But she could feel the pressure, and the noise inside her head was terrifying. The camera clicked and flashed again—she realized now that she was being photographed.

Beneath her head, between Lucy and Eisner, was a blue plastic garbage bag. She could see the blood streaming from her head into it, bearing away fragments of cream-colored bone. The celebratory marching of the trumpet began.

"Turn the music up a bit, please."

"Yes, Doctor."

No, no, Lucy thought. Please, don't make it louder. It all seemed too insane to be real. It felt as if the machine and the orchestra were both inside her head, the harrying trumpet piercing her brain with each note. She struggled against the restraints.

"Relax her a bit more, please," he said, and continued drilling. "Just one more hole and then we can lift the piece out." Then all at once the noise stopped. Lucy could hear the insect machine noises of the operating room and Eisner's whistling breath, now heavy from his exertion. The strobe flashed once more.

"There we go. All done." Eisner lifted a section of Lucy's skull and dropped it into a steel pan held out by a nurse. Lucy thought, A part of me is gone. A melancholy movement began with Menuhin's violin crying against the wheezing lament of a recorder.

"Let's just make a small incision in the dura, then, and we'll be ready with the electrodes. Cautery knife, please." The device was placed in his hand. The bright tip of the knife sparked, and smoke rose from the hole in her head. The strobe popped, and the trumpet began again. Not the trumpet! It felt as if the trumpet were cutting her with their sharp electric sound.

She let her eyes close, weary now and filled with amazement. She wondered, Did I really come all that way to experience this? What would the rest of her life be like? And where were Jenny and Amanda? Would they ever know what happened to her? She could see the red of her own blood through closed eyelids, as the strobe went off and another lumbering freight-train allegro began.

She didn't remember blacking out, but she had the sense that some time had passed, an interval lost. They were taking her off the table. Armies of violins were charging at her in a final berserk attack. She was slung in a sheet. A dozen hands lifted her onto a gurney. She could hear Eisner saying, "Intensive care. But I want someone with her at all times. Keep her in restraints. She's too valuable to take chances with." She opened her eyes and looked up at the tableau of nurses arrayed around her, at herself in the center of this scene, the violins racing like insects scattered from a nest on fire. Then she looked at Eisner as he leaned in with an expression of satisfied zeal. He took a small flashlight from his pocket and shined it into her left eye, then her right, his thumb lifting the lids. "Hmm. Good. Excellent." He flicked off the flashlight and replaced it in his pocket, pursing his lips in thought beneath his mask. Lucy studied his face now, so sure, so eager, so energized with passion, and she recognized for the first time what had struck her before that she had not quite been able to put her finger on. She knew what she was seeing. She was looking at the bland, indifferent, earnest face of true evil.

39

"THE STORY OF LUCY LOWE, widely known as the Jungle Girl, has taken a new and bizarre turn this evening," the newscaster said. "Her adoptive mother, Dr. Jennifer Lowe, has reported her to the local police as a missing person." The newscaster stood on the lawn in front of the house as he and Jenny had agreed. A light breeze was rattling the leaves on the trees, which had begun to turn as autumn moved south.

"Dr. Lowe has agreed to talk with us, so stay tuned for an exclusive interview, right after these words."

The newscaster came inside during the commercial break and sat across from Jenny. When the commercials ended, Jenny walked the reporter through the story, explaining that Lucy had left to visit a friend and that no one had seen her since. After checking with other police departments, hospitals, and morgues, Detective Nelson had found that two witnesses in a suburb called Northbrook had reported seeing a girl in pink jeans being picked up from the sidewalk, where she'd apparently collapsed. Two men carried her into a blue van and drove away. After investigating, the police discovered that the girl was picked up in front of a house that had been burglarized while the family was away. But the only things taken were clothes, sunglasses, an iPod, and hair dye. The girl in the pink jeans had multicolored hair.

"And what do you think all this adds up to?" the reporter asked.

"I believe it was her. She was trying to disguise herself, because she feared for her own safety. And someone, whoever it was, caught her. That same van had been parked in front of our house the night she left. Our house was burglarized while we were away, too, and the scientific notes that Lucy's father kept were stolen. I can't believe that a common thief would do that. I believe that someone in our own government did it and that they have Lucy now. We want to know where she is, and we want her returned safely to her home."

"And how would you suggest going about that?"

"I'd suggest that Congress order all of its federal agencies to disclose if any one of them has her. And I would suggest that the FBI investigate the various radical groups from which we've received threatening letters, e-mails, and phone calls. She's a fifteen-year-old girl with a very delicate constitution, and she needs her mother."

"And what if Lucy just ran away? Kids do that all the time."

"Then I want to know who stole the notebooks and why. And I want to know who the girl in the pink jeans is."

"And that's the breaking news in the Lucy Lowe story. Michael Khoury, ABC News."

But Jenny's effort seemed to backfire in a way. Once the public knew that Lucy was missing, the sightings and conjecture began. Experts were interviewed, and speculated that such a creature might take to the forest and never be found again. Others pointed out that with her delicate constitution she might have perished somewhere and suggested that a search for her body be undertaken. The hotline that the police had set up was receiving several hundred calls a day. An organization that helped to find missing children published a photograph of Lucy on its Web site. She was spotted on the commuter train, on top of the Sears Tower, down by the lake, and at a popular nightspot.

40

OFF AND ON in the night Lucy woke to the strange sounds of hospital machines. At one point she fell asleep and dreamed that she was back in the jungle with her father and Leda and Toby and Viaje and little Faith. They were happy, all gathering the caterpillars that had begun to rain down from the branches above.

When she woke to morning at last, her head was swimming with the drugs they had given her. She had an excruciating headache and the Brandenburg Concertos were still pounding in her brain. She felt the stitches pulling where they'd sewn up her scalp. Her head was wrapped in a bandage, and bundles of fine wire hung beside her shoulder. A thin woman in her forties sat by her bed. Lucy tried to sit up, but she had been shackled.

"Can I have some water, please?" The woman lifted a plastic cup, and Lucy drank. "Where are we?"

"You're in the hospital, dear."

"No, I mean what state are we in? What city?"

"I'm sorry, dear. I'm a Christian. I'm sorry for you. But I don't think we should be talking."

Lucy lay in bed for days as an ever-changing cast of nurses and aides came to guard and feed her. They came in shifts of four hours each. Most of them watched the television, and the jerky mania of the broadcasts made it impossible for Lucy to think. She needed to plan.

Eisner came once a day to flip through Lucy's chart and to ask how she was. The first day, she had made the mistake of telling him that she was in pain, and he had ordered her to be drugged again. She didn't mention the pain after that.

Lucy attempted to appeal to each person who attended her to see if she could break through their defenses and somehow connect with one of them.

"Do you have a favorite soap opera?" she asked a matronly woman.

"Why, yes. We watch *All My Children*." Lucy tried to discuss the show with her, but she had seen it only once or twice. She didn't know any of the characters and couldn't follow the story. The woman quickly soured and fell silent.

Lucy asked a young muscular aide, "Do they get cable here?"

"I think so. Yeah."

"Do you think there's any sports on? You like NASCAR?"

"It's okay."

"What do you like?"

"Hey, you know what I like? I like you to shut the fuck up."

Lucy was attended on the next shift by a pregnant woman with gold earrings and pretty black hair. She was no more than a teenager. Lucy thought she might be Puerto Rican. She spoke to her in Spanish, and the woman's face brightened. Lucy drew her out. She had come from Mexico, as it turned out. Her husband was an electrician with the Air Force. But he had gone away, and she hadn't heard from him for two months. She was worried about how she would manage once the baby came. She didn't want to leave an infant in child care. "A baby needs his mother," she said.

"Yes. We all need our mothers. Even when we're not babies. You're close to your mother?"

"Claro que sí."

"Yo, también. Echo de menos a mi madre. Necesito regresar a ella."

The woman looked at Lucy with a hard countenance. She was soft but Lucy saw that she could be tough, too. She shook her head.

"No te puedo ayudar," she said. "Lo siento. Tengo que cuidar a mi bebé, y este trabajo es lo único que me queda."

"No, no," Lucy said. "I know that. I wouldn't want to get you in trouble." Lucy studied the young woman, who turned her face away. "What's your name?"

"Margarita. People call me Rita." She turned back to Lucy.

"Rita, I like that. Rita, please tell me where we are. That's all. Just what city we're in."

Rita held that hard look on Lucy like a cop holding a flashlight. Then she leaned over and whispered in her ear, "Alamogordo, New Mexico. We're on Holloman Air Force Base."

"An Air Force base? What am I doing on an Air Force base?"

"Alamogordo Primate Facility. Me and my husband live on base housing. But now that he's gone I think they're going to throw me out."

Of course, Lucy thought. A primate facility. It makes perfect sense. "Can I use a computer?" Lucy thought that if she could just see a map, she might have a better sense of the terrain.

Rita gave Lucy an odd look. "What, what? You're a ape. They tole me you're a ape. A ape doan use a computer."

"Do I look like an ape? Do I speak like an ape?"

"No."

"This is all a huge mistake. I'm a girl just like you. I'm helpless and afraid. Look at me. I'm tied down. Now help me out."

"Jew use a computer?"

"Rita, I have an iPod and a laptop at home. I'm just like you. I went to the senior prom and graduated from high school. An American high school. Please, Rita. They've hurt me. They're going to hurt me again. I'm just a girl. This is all just an awful mistake."

Rita's eyes grew big as she stared at Lucy. "*Puta madre.* That *pinche* doctor. I knew he was a bad man the minute I saw him." Then she stood up and left.

"Rita, wait," Lucy called. But she was gone.

The next day Lucy was attended by the burly young aide and the thin Christian woman again. But Rita returned that night with a furtive air. When she was sure that no one was in the hall, Rita said, "I can't help you escape. I have to protect my baby. But if you do get out of the building, here's where you are." She unfolded a piece that she'd torn from a road map. She'd marked the position in the center. "I can't give it to you. Memorize it." As Lucy studied the layout, Rita said, "I knew what you was when I saw you on *Oprah*. I said, That ain't no ape. I knew you was just a girl. You remine me of my little sister."

41

HARRY TOOK JENNY AND AMANDA back to see the lawyer, Sy Joseph, and to begin the process of filing the lawsuit. Jenny contacted Senator Martin Cochrain, and he agreed at once to squeeze her into his busy schedule. The trip to Washington was three days away. Harry had agreed to go. The time seemed to be taking forever to pass. But at least Jenny felt that she was doing something, taking directed action toward a goal. There was even a hopeful ray of light when Joseph called to say that a recent Supreme Court decision suggested that habeas corpus might eventually be reestablished in the United States.

"But don't get your hopes up just yet," he added. "They've written similar opinions in the past and the government has just ignored them."

Early one morning Jenny was in her study trying to get some work done. There had been an odd autumn storm in the night, and as the lightning and thunder shook the neighborhood, she had been filled with sadness as she remembered Lucy's rain dance, which had brought the police screaming up the alley. Now the clouds had peeled away to reveal blue sky. The air was clear. As the sun retreated to the south, the birch leaves had turned bright yellow, and Jenny recalled the quiet evenings that she'd spent with the girls when they were still in school. She recalled one night in particular when Lucy had recited one of her favorite passages from Edna St. Vincent Millay:

> *Not the feet of children pushing*
> *Yellow leaves along the gutters*
> *In the blue and bitter fall,*
> *Shall content my musing mind*
> *For the beauty of that sound*
> *That in no new way at all*
> *Ever will be heard again.*

"Because when you die, you go," Lucy had said. "But where does your voice go? Nothing else in the world can make those particular sounds. Just like when a thunderstorm goes, there will never be exactly the same thunderstorm again. Every day, things happen that have never happened before. And there are things that happen that will never happen again." She paused, then said, "Like me."

And Jenny wondered, What had happened to that beautiful mind, a mind that would never happen again? Where was Lucy's voice now, which had sung Italian arias in the garden?

As she sipped her coffee, she wondered what would have happened if she hadn't found Lucy or if she had decided to leave her in the jungle. Could she have lived among the bonobos without her father? She certainly knew their ways. Her mother was dead, but Lucy knew enough to understand that she'd have had to leave her family and go to mate with someone from another group. Would another family of bonobos have accepted her? Lucy had told Jenny about the time that Leda took her to see another family. So evidently Leda thought that Lucy would be accepted. She would have been expected to breed in the new family. Could she have become pregnant? She might be sterile. But if she had become pregnant, what sort of child would she have had there in the forest? Would a new race have arisen, one that her father had never even considered? Perhaps a race of talking bonobos instead of a race of people with bonobo-like qualities.

Jenny remembered from Stone's notes that Leda had bred with other bonobos after Lucy was born. They were out there now, teenage bonobos, who had some of Leda's human genetic material. What would their future be? Would they learn to talk? To make tools? Who would be living in that rain forest a thousand years from now? With a jolt of alarm at these thoughts, Jenny stood suddenly, knocking over her coffee cup.

"Shit."

She yanked a fistful of tissues from the box and mopped the desk, then knelt to clean the hardwood floor. The coffee had stained the Congolese rug that she'd brought home some years before. As she soaked up the coffee with the tissue, she saw something orange behind a small file cabinet that she kept beneath the desk. Crawling farther under the desk, she reached it. As she drew it out of the cobwebs, she realized that it was one of Donald Stone's notebooks. How did it get there? Could she have kicked it under there when his notebooks were strewn all over her study? It was certainly possible given her state of agitation that day. It could have simply been pushed off of her messy desk and fallen there. Or perhaps the burglars had dropped it in their haste. She stood, examining it more closely.

Amanda was at the door. "What's that? Is that one of his notebooks?"

"Yes, it was behind the file cabinet. I have no idea how it got there."

Amanda took it from Jenny and studied the cover. "Lucy should have that. One of the last ones."

"Yes. If only we could get it to her."

"Maybe send it to Donna. For safekeeping."

"Safer than here."

Jenny and Amanda stood reading it with their heads together. It was, in effect, a letter to Lucy, a final accounting.

"Did you see the news this morning?" Jenny asked.

"No, what?"

"Senator Rhodes, the guy with the toolbox at the hearing? His bill passed. Lucy is officially not a human."

"What does it mean?"

"Presumably, they can do anything to her that they could do to an animal."

Amanda put her hand over her mouth. Her face creased with anguish, but she made no sound. Jenny put her hand on her cheek, and Amanda fell against her.

42

LUCY WAS RETURNED to the cage, where she discovered that someone had installed a metal cot and welded it to the bars. She could smell the sharp odor of flux. The mattress was neatly made with white sheets, a single pillow, a thin blanket. A portable toilet had been placed in a corner of the cage with a roll of toilet paper on the floor beside it. Lucy sat on the edge of the cot in a blue hospital gown and hugged herself.

She had vowed to waste no more energy bemoaning her fate or feeling terrified. Her fear had turned to anger now, a seething, steady rage at what was being done to her. She saw now what her father had done to her. He'd been right. *Homo sapiens:* Watch your back. And seemingly with the best of intentions, he'd done just the sort of evil that he'd warned her people might do to her. He had made her live. She would not have chosen that. But she was in the world, and now she vowed to plan and think her way out. She was determined to act deliberately and boldly when the time came. She did not yet know what the weak link was in this web of iniquity, but she would find out.

Eisner came at midday. He still wore his surgical mask. "How are you feeling? I hope you find the new bed to your liking. They're still working on your other accommodations." She merely stared at him. "Is there anything special you'd like to eat? I understand that you like breakfast cereals. I can have anything you like brought to you." He paused, but Lucy said nothing. "I'm going to let you recover for another couple of days before we begin testing. We're going to do a standard Penfield map to start with. Do you know what a Penfield map is?"

Lucy was not going to volunteer anything. She would simply wait for an opportunity and act when it came. Eisner watched her for another moment.

"Well, I'm sure you'll perk up. I know you must be tired. I'll let you rest now. I've been called to Washington, so I won't be able to see you for a day or two. My aides and nurses will take care of you in my absence. The same ones you've already met. I want to build trust, and I don't want you to have to get used to new people. So I've given strict orders. No one but the ones you already know will be allowed in here until I return. There will be another veterinarian on call in case of emergency. But I'm sure that won't be necessary." Then he turned on his heel and left. It was the first time that it had occurred to Lucy that Eisner was not an MD. He was a vet. And the implication was clear: They could not have asked an MD to work on an animal.

She sat and watched the sunlight fall through the skylight and make its arc across the floor. The operating-room equipment had been removed and new equipment installed. A padded gray chair with a head brace and shackles. Many new electronic devices on wheels had been moved in around the chair. Lucy looked at the chair and saw herself in it, thinking, No, no. This is not me. This is not my end. I still have other plans.

Eisner had said, "Higher powers want you destroyed." And: "I'm determined to protect you for as long as I can." Lucy understood. A month, a year, ten years—who knew how long they could torture her? But eventually she would be destroyed. No trace of her would remain. She understood it all now. She had disappeared from the outside world of her own free will. She had run away and was lost in the forest. Drowned in the river. Jenny and Amanda and Harry would search, plan, scheme, grieve. And Lucy would be ash, circling the globe on the wind. No creature like her would ever exist again. Nor would there be any evidence that she had existed. She would have been a species of one.

All day long, Lucy thought as she watched the sun cross the floor. She recited poetry, plays, stories in her head to keep her mind active. "Wer, wenn ich schriee, hörte mich denn aus der Engel Ordnungen?" One of Eisner's aides came and slid a tray of food through the slot and left. Lucy ignored it. Food would be dead weight, undigested in the rush of adrenaline that she felt certain would seize her. In The Stream she could sense that something was coming, but she did not yet know what form it would take. She felt ready for anything.

Her mind descended into darker literature as the day went on.

> *Tu fermeras l'œil, pour ne point voir, par la glace,*
> *Grimacer les ombres de soirs,*
> *Ces monstruosités hargneuses, populace*
> *De démons noirs et de loups noirs.*

Then she rose once more with hope and confidence. "Now as I was young and easy under the apple boughs . . ."

She had settled into acceptance and was reciting Whitman as the light gradually faded to pink. "I have instant conductors all over me . . ." Darkness fell at last. The sodium vapor lights snapped on and buzzed menacingly high above her. In preparation for whatever she might have to do, Lucy drank the bottle of water that the aide had left with the dinner tray. She looked at the food, congealed in grease. An idea was forming in her head, but it was still unclear.

She heard the key hit the lock and held herself still, waiting. When the man entered, she knew at once that he meant her harm. He was giving off all the signals that precede an attack. The way he moved, the eyes, the bitter smell of his sweat—all that hit her like a slap. He was a big man, in his forties, dark brown hair cropped short, pale blue eyes. He had a strong square jaw, a broad nose, and a thick neck. She sat still, assessing him. He watched Lucy as he crossed the room at an angle to the cage. He wasn't coming directly toward her. What was he doing?

He opened a metal cabinet with a key. He brought out the rifle. She felt herself begin to tremble as she realized that he was going to dart her. Why? Where would he take her once she was sedated? Had Eisner asked him to do this? He would have mentioned it.

He'd been just as forthright as he was indifferently cruel. But as she watched the man, she realized that he was not going to shoot. He was doing something else. But what was it? She knew that he didn't belong there. He wore jeans and a plaid shirt. No scrubs, no lab coat, no surgical mask.

Carrying the rifle, the man returned to the door and left. Perhaps he was taking the rifle somewhere else to sedate an animal. Lucy's mind was racing, her heart pumping, as she deliberately slowed her breathing and tried to think. No, that was wrong. She knew that he meant her harm—her specifically, not someone else. But he had done nothing. He was preparing something. He would return. And then he would do something appalling. She was sure of it. Perhaps he was going to put more anesthetic in the gun. Or poison. The possibilities tumbled through her mind, but she knew that it would do no good to guess. What had Eisner said? No one but the aides would be allowed in. So who was this man? "Higher powers want you destroyed." Lucy knew that somehow she had to take away the advantage of the gun. Otherwise, she was certain to be killed. She had to make the man open the cage and come inside. She had to meet him one on one.

Think, she told herself. Think. Think. She remembered a conversation that she'd once had with her father about prayer. She had been reading about prayer and he told her that since they didn't believe in gods, they didn't pray. But Lucy had argued with him. She said that she prayed even without believing in gods. "To what? To whom?" he had asked.

"To the forest," she said. "I pray to the forest to arrange things in a beneficial way."

He had paused deep in thought and said, "I never thought of it that way. I never called it prayer, but I do that, too. The forest is the source of everything. Yes, I guess you're right," he said, and laughed at himself. "I guess we all pray even if there are no gods."

And Lucy thought, Maybe he was wrong. Maybe there is a god. So now Lucy prayed to her god or her long-lost forest. For enlightenment. For wisdom. What could she do before that man returned that would force him to open the door of the cage? She sat very still, listening to the beating of her pulse in her ears. As she was waiting on the universe for an answer, she heard voices in the hall.

"No," one voice said. "Don't clean up in there tonight. I've sent the aides home. I don't want anybody in the room with that hybrid."

"Sure, Doc. Sure thing, Doc." Lucy recognized the voice of the night cleanup man.

"Goodnight, then."

"Night, Doc."

Was it the on-call vet that Eisner had mentioned? He wasn't supposed to come unless there was an emergency. She knew: He wanted no witnesses. Lucy felt a deep lethargy come over her. She simply wanted to sleep. Then all at once the answer rose from the mist of her mind like the first rays of sunlight in the forest morning.

Lucy stood and crossed the cage. She took the tray of dinner from the compartment and flung the food onto the floor. Mashed potatoes spread in white blotches like fungus. She stepped on the food and smeared it around. She tore the sheets and mattress and scattered the shreds around the cell. She reached up and dragged the bandage off of her head. She ripped the wires out of her skull. She winced at the sharp pain as her scalp tore. She took off her hospital gown, soaked up the blood that was flowing from her head, then put it back on. Then she smeared blood over her face and neck and arms. She lay on the floor as far from the cage door as she could, arranging her body in an awkward way as if she'd fallen. She closed her eyes and concentrated on her breathing. She heard the muffled sounds of the building's ventilation system.

She felt her heart fill with a dread that spread through her stomach and thighs as the quiet grew. She thought back to the forest, to the time that the female leopard had come and snatched poor little Offie, the savagery of the bonobos' counterattack. Offie was dead, but they had massed and charged the cat anyway, throwing stones and screaming. At last Lucy found what she needed: Rage. Rage at the thought of what those people were going to do. All at once, she was wide awake, filled with strength and energy. But she kept still. She made her mind a blank. She could see herself as if she were looking down on the cage from high above: A dead girl, filthy and smeared with blood, lying on a concrete floor, her neck jerked back in an attitude of anguish.

She was not sure how long she lay like that before she heard the key slide into the lock again. She held her breath. She dared not look. This would either work or it would not. There was no middle ground. She heard footsteps, then a sharp intake of breath and the word "Shit." She heard footfalls. "What the hell—" She heard a clatter as the man set the rifle down. She heard a metallic jingling and then the sound of the big key turning the tumblers in the cage door.

She heard him say, "Goddamnit."

She could feel her heart hammering. She allowed herself to view him through barely slit eyelids. She saw the five-o'clock shadow on his jaw, a small mole on his neck, as he approached to look more closely at her. She felt an electrical crackling of energy surge through her belly and legs.

This is what she learned in the jungle. Some things are automatic. When a big cat is onto you, you have to pick the right moment. You have but one chance to act. Even more than her strength, that was what had made her a good wrestler. You don't really decide. You simply act from a place that is below the level of consciousness. An impulse rises within you that is irresistible because it is right, and if it's not right, you simply don't contribute any more to the gene pool. That's what Lucy felt at that moment. It was the same feeling that she'd had the first time she went to Amanda's house and the dog Cody had wanted to kill her. She knew that one of them would die on that spot. And that was fine. The one right thing that she had to do rose within her. There was no other choice. Now she felt the same. What she did was absolute and irrefutable. The forest had arranged it this way.

As the man leaned over her, Lucy rolled back, pulling her knees to her chest, and kicked him in the head with both feet. His head snapped back sharply. She heard it crack as he went flying across the cage and hit the bars. His head made the whole cage clang and vibrate as he went down with a heavy sigh, his neck askew. Lucy was on her feet and out of the cage. She grabbed the nearest heavy object she could find, a cinderblock. Everything was going in slow motion, sharp and clear. She turned and stepped back into the cage. She stood over him, the concrete block above her head, ready to smash his skull. She waited for him to move, but his neck was broken. He stopped breathing. The scent of his blood was sharp and metallic. She watched it flow into the drain where the janitor had washed the feces and urine.

Panting, glowing with sweat, Lucy dropped the cinderblock to the floor. She took off her hospital gown and rinsed it quickly with the hose. Then she tied it tight around her and picked up the cinderblock again. She flew across the bars of the cage, over the top, and up the steel beams that gripped the walls. She reached the skylight at the top and threw the cinderblock through the glass. She watched the glittering pieces fall and crash in slow motion onto the cage below. They broke into smaller fragments and settled around the body. She drew herself up onto the roof and ran to the edge. She took a quick look at the distance and then jumped rather than climbing down. She landed and rolled, then popped to her feet and was gone in the night.

AMANDA WAS GOING to interview for a job and then to have lunch with her mother. She wanted to try to mend some fences. School had started. She had decided not to go to college yet. She wanted to keep her options open until they learned what had happened to Lucy. She and Jenny had agreed that it wasn't good for her to sit around the house worrying. Amanda had to get out and live her life. She had to be with people her own age and reenter society. Jenny needed something to distract her as well, so she had returned to volunteer at the shelter. Nina, the administrator, had welcomed her back with the comment, "Now I know you're ready. I think I have just the thing to take your mind off of your own troubles." And she had introduced Jenny to a sixteen-year-old girl whose father had kept her locked in a basement for two years.

Jenny had just made coffee. She could hear Amanda upstairs in the girls' room, dressing for her job interview. Jenny went outside to bring in the newspaper. It was the sort of autumn day that made her glad that she lived in an area that had actual seasons. High thin clouds hurried across the sky toward the lake. The sun made colors jump out of the background, and the wind bumped her with sudden gusts that made her widen her gait.

In the kitchen she glanced through the headlines. How much more did she want to know about the Mideast? How much violence could she stomach this morning? She wondered why she even subscribed to a newspaper. She knew: Because her mother had done so all her life.

Amanda came down looking smart in a gray pantsuit and a black cashmere sweater.

"Breakfast?" Jenny asked. "I'll cook."

"I'll just grab some cereal."

"Fruity Cheerios?"

"Yum."

They exchanged a look, then Jenny turned to the national news page, where she found short summaries of incidents from various states. Double murder at a Taco Bell in Texas. A chemical plant explosion in New Jersey. A man fell from a construction site in midtown Manhattan and landed on a car, killing himself and the driver. A veterinarian had been killed by a chimpanzee at a primate facility in New Mexico. The story struck Jenny as odd the moment she saw it. But newspaper stories were often odd, raising more questions than they answered, so she paid no attention to it at first.

She and Amanda ate cereal with bananas. "What time is your interview?"

"Eleven."

"What is it?"

"Internal marketing. I thought I'd do a little shopping since I'll be downtown. Want to get some retail therapy?"

"Thanks. I have to go to the shelter. They took in a new girl. Terrible story. You don't want to know."

"No, I don't."

As they were cleaning up the breakfast dishes, something that had been nagging at the back of Jenny's mind rose to the level of consciousness. She dried her hands and crossed to the table. She turned the pages of the newspaper and found the story. Amanda was loading the dishwasher as Jenny reread it. A veterinarian. A chimpanzee. The story said that a thirty-nine-year-old chimpanzee named Buddy had escaped from its cage when a member of the staff happened to enter the area. Robert Walton, 41, was found dead of a broken neck when the morning shift arrived, according to the county coroner. To herself, Jenny said, "What?"

"More nonsense about Lucy?"

There had been more huffing and puffing from Congress after Lucy went missing. But then Senate Bill 5251 had passed, and it seemed to cast a pall over those who might have wanted to protect Lucy. Ruth Randall had offered a reward for Lucy's safe return. The lawsuit that Sy Joseph had filed was grinding its way through an endless maze.

"Come here and look at this," Jenny said.

Amanda dried her hands and read the short item. "Yeah, that's too bad. Gives apes a bad name. You think the guy screwed up?"

"Well, it doesn't say much. You have to be awfully cautious with a middle-aged male chimpanzee. But what's even stranger is this cause of death: His neck was snapped."

"Yeah, well, chimps are really strong, so . . ."

"Yes, they're plenty strong enough. But they don't fight that way. They have very characteristic ways of killing. They draw their victim near and bite ferociously. They always go for the scrotum and the butt. They'll bite off the fingers and then attack the face with those huge incisors. When a chimp kills another chimp—or a man—there are really dramatic wounds. Lots of blood and gore. Horrible. But no broken neck."

"Have chimps killed people before?"

"Definitely. There was one in 2006 at a chimp sanctuary in Sierra Leone. A chimp named Bruno, who was twenty years old, led a mass escape. These guys are really smart. A driver had brought some people in to see the chimps, and Bruno smashed the windshield and dragged the driver out. He bit off the guy's fingers and killed him with a horrific bite to the face. Then there was that lady in Connecticut. Same kind of wounds. Her face was gone, but she lived. Anyway, after millions of years of killing in this one particular way, a chimp isn't just going to stop and dream up a new strategy. Bonobos, though. They're different. They've been known to bite fingers off, but they fight with their feet when they mean to kill. They kick. A kick in the head from a powerful bonobo can snap your neck."

"What does it mean?"

"It means this guy wasn't killed by a chimp."

"What do you think?"

"I don't know." Jenny stared at the story as if she might somehow drag more information out if it. "I know this place. Alamogordo. It's a primate research lab at Holloman Air Force Base. Jane Goodall tried to get the chimpanzees released from there. It's been going for decades, and no one's ever been killed. There's just a lot more to this story. And this guy wasn't killed by a chimp."

"So if it's on this air base and all, why did they even release a story?"

"Well, someone was killed on the job. He was a doctor, a vet. Presumably he had a family at home wondering what happened. They had to say something. They couldn't say what really happened, so they blamed it on some obstreperous old chimp they wanted to get rid of."

"Oh, my God, Lucy said she might have to kill somebody. What should we do?"

"I don't know. But if Lucy was there and if this is how she escaped, then we'd better find her before they do."

"How are we going to do that?"

"I don't know."

THE TERRAIN AROUND the primate facility was rocky and exposed. To the west Lucy could see an airfield blasted in the glare of floodlights, so she fled in the opposite direction, stumbling over rocks and dodging low piñon trees. She reached a small pond and lay panting under a moonless sky. Now at least she had water. That was always primary: Get to water and you'll be all right. That's what her father had said. Papa, Papa, Lucy thought. Do I love you or hate you? Lucy could see now that he had prepared her for this. He had known what might come. But why, why? And then she asked herself, Would I rather not exist? No, she knew it more completely than ever before: She wanted to live. Cruel as it was, this world was just too sweet to give up.

She felt the blood trickling down her neck. She touched the wound on top of her skull. The piece of bone had seated itself. But she would need her head covered. All she had to wear was the hospital gown. She had to find clothes. She had to blend in. She had to get to Donna, and she no longer had the luxury of time.

She washed the blood off of her head with the brackish pond water. Then she sat and smelled the air. The wind was light and variable. The air was warm. Here on the thirty-something parallel, autumn wouldn't come for a while. The breeze shifted, and then Lucy caught the aroma of pine sap. She leapt to her feet and headed into the faint draft that carried the scent. Going as fast as she could over the rocky ground, she found an arroyo about thirty minutes later. She descended into the trees and down to a small stream. She drank again and moved on, following the watercourse. She knew that they'd be out with the helicopters and infrared as soon as they found the body.

She stopped to listen. Coyotes were yipping in the distance. She followed them, and they led her to a place where they had dug a small tunnel beneath the perimeter fence. Lucy squeezed through and continued on.

When the cover of trees petered out in a dry wash, she climbed a butte to see where she was. Another stretch of woods continued toward the east. She made her way to it and then navigated through scrub forest. Stars were hived in branches overhead.

She walked on, picking her way by starlight. The image of that man lying dead on the floor kept leaping into her head. After a time, she saw a break in the woods and moved cautiously toward it. At the edge of the forest a tennis court lay in darkness. She moved closer. It was part of an estate. A large adobe house in the distance lay in a wash of security lights. Lucy stepped onto the cold concrete surface and made her way across. A tall judge's chair stood beside the court. She saw a small building in the trees. She moved toward it.

It was made of adobe and had high louvered windows. She found the door unlocked and went inside. She could smell chlorine. It was a shower room. She felt her way along the wall in the darkness. She touched lockers, cupboards, hooks on the tile walls. She began opening the lockers one by one, and halfway down the row she found a pair of jeans. She dropped her gown and put them on. They were large but would have to do. She cinched the leather belt tight. Searching through the rest of the lockers, she found a T-shirt and then tennis shoes. They were too big but she wore them anyway. Her feet had grown soft during her time away from the jungle, and she could feel her blood sticking to the shoes.

Moving back toward the door, she ran her hand along the hooks until she found a baseball cap. She adjusted the strap and put it on. She picked up the gown and slipped across the tennis court and back into the trees.

She went as deep into the woods as she could go. Adrenaline had kept her going, but now she had to sleep. She checked the canopy overhead. The trees were not sturdy enough to support a nest. As she lay down on the forest floor, she felt the adrenaline begin to subside at last. Things had been moving so fast that she hadn't had time to think clearly. And now, as she tried to let her muscles relax, this thought came into her mind: I killed a man. I killed a human being.

All her life she had been taught not to kill, and now she'd done it. The worst thing in the world. She felt revulsion spread through her as the image of the dead man came to her once again. His blood. His pleading eyes. She thought of her father and felt grief and anger. All his preaching and effort had come to this. She wanted to scream, Why did you do this to me? But she also thought, Who, if I cried out, would hear me? She hated what she had become. She couldn't even remember who she'd been before they sank their hooks into her. The hawk. The hawk had gotten her. But she'd managed to escape. She desperately wanted to find a way back now. But back to where? She wondered if she would ever reach a place of safety where she might begin to heal.

Lucy buried the hospital gown and fell asleep. When she woke, she sat quietly and waited for sunrise. She knew it was coming when the birds began. She went into The Stream and waited. She could tell by what the birds and animals said that no one was near. She found a piñon tree and ate some of the nuts. Then the whole forest lit up with a beauty that was almost painful after her time in captivity. The trunks of the trees stood, twisted and dark, and the glittering green leaves seemed to hold the light and vibrate with an electric aura. Aromas rose around her.

But she had no time to enjoy it: They would be finding the body now, sending out the alarm. She wished that she could see what she looked like before going out, to know what sort of impression she would make. She had to pass for an American teenager. At least the ghastly wound in her head was covered.

She could hear a road in the distance. She forged her way through the woods toward it. A scattering of cars and trucks passed on a divided four-lane highway. She began to walk along the shoulder, where a crow picked at some roadkill. As Lucy approached, he cocked a dark and gleaming eye at her and shouted, "I know you! I know you! I know you!"

"Go away!" The crow lifted off and cackled back at her, his heavy black wings cutting the air.

Lucy stuck her thumb out. She had read about it in *The Grapes of Wrath* and *On the Road,* and now she wondered if hitchhiking still worked. She walked on with the sun at her back, casting a long shadow across the land like a great spider.

45

AMANDA WAS DIPPING FRITOS into a small container of bean dip and drinking a Diet Coke as the old Toyota crossed through the great irrigated fields of wheat and cotton on a deserted road in Oklahoma. Staying clear of the interstate, they had driven all day and all night, taking turns sleeping.

Jenny had called Ruth Randall, the only person she knew in New Mexico. She had gone to Harry's to make the call. She told Ruth only that they were accepting her invitation to the ranch.

"Do you want Luke to send the plane?" Ruth had asked. "It's no bother."

"No, we're driving."

"I always liked the open road. I can't get Luke to do it anymore, though. He's in too much of a hurry."

"We should reach your place tomorrow."

"I'll be waiting." Jenny thought she detected by a change in her voice that Ruth understood the subtext of their conversation. "It will be nice to see you."

Jenny had hung up and turned to look at Amanda, who had been standing beside her in Harry's kitchen.

"We're going to find her," Amanda said.

"I hope you're right."

"We're going to find her."

Harry had packed sandwiches for the trip. Jenny had not told him where they were going, only that she'd call when she could. Harry, as always, understood.

Now, after a long night on the road, Amanda slid a disk into the CD player. "American Girl" began. Celestial choruses of voices soared over wild guitar riffs. She smiled at Jenny. She held out a Frito with bean dip on it. Jenny opened her mouth and Amanda put it in. Jenny closed her eyes for a moment as she chewed.

"Why is that so good? It's junk food."

"The American sacrament," Amanda said.

"When you have children, you want to give them everything. I've never had children of my own, but now I think I understand that. You want to give them just everything. But you have to keep on living, too. And then you somehow feel guilty when you're enjoying what they can't have. It's a terrible thing."

"We're going to find her," Amanda said. It had become her mantra.

Tom Petty sang, "After all, it was a great big world with lots of places to run to . . ."

46

LUCY WALKED ALONG the highway with her thumb out as the cars and trucks tore past. More than an hour went by before anyone even slowed down. Lucy had begun to think that hitchhiking had gone out of style. But presently, a battered old Ford pickup truck, formerly black, pulled over and Lucy ran ahead to meet it. Through the open window she saw the smiling face of an old Native American man in a greasy cowboy hat and overalls. He leaned over and opened the door.

"Where you headin', sonny?"

She climbed in and said, "Albuquerque." Why, she wondered, was he calling her sonny?

"Today's your lucky day, then. Shut that door, son."

Lucy slammed the door, remembering that her head was shaved. As the truck rattled into the flow of traffic, she sighed with relief. This is perfect, she thought. Nobody will be looking for a boy.

"What puts you out on this highway so early in the morning?"

"I'm going to visit my grandmother."

"You don't see people hitchhikin' much anymore. It's a lost art. Before the war, why, I hitched all over this country. People are scared now." He turned on the radio and twirled the dial, but only static came from the single naked speaker, which was bolted to the dashboard. He lifted his foot from the accelerator, and the truck lurched and slowed. He raised his foot and kicked the radio, then resumed driving. Lucinda Williams came on, singing "Big Red Sun Blues."

"I gotta get that thing fixed one of these days."

After they had driven for about twenty minutes, the old man pointed out the window and said, "The spirits live out there. Have you seen the petroglyphs?"

"No."

"Drawings on the rocks of all the spirits. All this used to be rich farmland. Rivers runnin' through it. Wild grain growin' for miles. Plenty of fish and game. Then the spirits came and sucked out all the water. The human beings had to move on. Now it's all dry." Traffic slowed to a crawl and he asked, "What the hell is this?" He answered his own question: "Prolly a wreck."

But as they crept closer, he craned his neck out the window. "Some kind of police roadblock. They're inspecting the cars."

"What for?" Lucy asked in alarm.

"Beats me."

As they inched closer, Lucy could see that the police were questioning each driver and the passengers. She said, "Please, don't tell them you picked me up hitchhiking."

"Why not? You in some kind of trouble?"

"No. Please. Just tell them—tell them that I'm your grandson."

He looked at Lucy steadily. "What'd you do? You rob somebody?"

"No, no, nothing like that. I ran away from the orphanage. I lied to you. I don't have a grandmother in Albuquerque. I'm an orphan. But I couldn't stand the place. Please, don't let them take me back there."

He stared at her for a long time. They were next in line.

"Why should I believe you?"

"It was a Catholic orphanage. There was a priest there. He was molesting all the boys. I had to get away."

He looked up at the police cars and the officers in their sunglasses. Then he looked back at Lucy. "Shoot. I guess you could pass."

"Pass?"

"Say you're from the Mescalero Apache rez down around Las

Cruces. Your name is William Little Bear. My name's Ronald Little Bear. You got no ID because you're too young. You got that?"

"Thank you. Thank you so much."

As they pulled forward, two officers stepped up on either side of the truck. A tall one with a moustache leaned on the old man's window and asked for identification. The old man handed over his driver's license. The policeman on Lucy's side was short and Mexican-looking. He said, "Let's see some ID." He had a slight accent.

She felt a trickle of blood begin to seep from the wound beneath her hat.

"He ain't got no ID. He's just a kid."

Lucy said nothing. The trickle of blood was inching down her scalp. The Mexican officer asked, "What's your name, son?"

"William Little Bear."

"You two related, then?" the other policeman asked.

"He's my grandson."

"Seen anybody hitchhiking?" the Mexican cop asked.

"Nope."

Lucy could tell that the policemen were picking up all sorts of signals from her and the old man. But they could think of no logical reason to detain them. They had only a gut feeling. Lucy knew: In order to use The Stream you had to accept it. She could feel the trickle of blood reach the headband of her hat. She pushed her head against the headrest to try to stop it there. As she leaned back, she caught a glimpse of herself in the truck's side mirror and felt her heart sink. She saw the forlorn face of a boy with hollow cheeks and sunken eyes. It seemed as if her skull was trying to escape through her bloodless skin, the mouth drawn like a seam across the face. She almost reached up to touch her own face, as if to make sure that she was really there. But she stopped herself.

She knew that they could smell the blood. Any animal could. But they had become so used to ignoring their senses that they didn't even realize that they were smelling it. They were fighting with themselves, attempting to figure out why they wanted to keep them. But in their linear way of thinking they could find no reason.

The old man stared straight ahead. After what seemed like an eternity, the officer gave him back his license and waved him on. As the truck pulled away, Lucy let out the breath that she'd been holding.

The old man looked over at her. "What happened to your head? You're bleeding?"

"I fell. On the rocks. It's just a scratch."

"What're you going to do in Albuquerque if you don't got no folks?"

"I have a friend. He said I could stay with him."

"How old are you anyway?"

"Seventeen."

"You are not."

"Fifteen."

"Christ, I could go back to jail. I must be outta my mind."

47

A MIDDLE-AGED WOMAN sat behind a reception desk in the airy atrium at the Denton's headquarters. Jenny and Amanda announced themselves and signed in at 1:42 in the afternoon. A few minutes later, Ruth Randall emerged from a chrome elevator and walked smartly toward them, her white sneakers squeaking on the terrazzo floor. She hugged them both and said, "I'm so sorry it's come to this. Come in. You've had a long trip."

"Thanks," Jenny said. "We're exhausted."

"I have my foundation offices here."

They followed her to the elevator and rode up to an office with an open plan, laid out with a maze of chest-high cubicles. Ruth led them to a conference room, and they sat at a long table.

"My little cubicle is too cluttered. We can talk here. Let me get you something to drink or eat."

"Just water," Jenny said.

"Yes, water," Amanda said.

A young man had come to the door and stood waiting. Ruth said, "Ian, could you bring some water, please?"

"Certainly," he said, and left.

Ruth stood and closed the door and then sat with them. "You can talk here," she said. "It's safe."

When the man had brought their water, Jenny and Amanda

took turns bringing Ruth up to date. Ruth listened intently, biting her lower lip, the lines compressing around her eyes and mouth. Her blue eyes glittered with moisture, as if she could feel their pain.

"How dreadful," Ruth said.

"If I'm right and she escaped," Jenny said, "then she may try to get to you. Because you're the only person she knows in New Mexico."

"She'll be safe if she does. Lucy's smart. Smart enough to find us here. In the meantime, you need rest. Why don't I take you to the ranch?"

"Yes," Jenny said. "I do need to get some sleep in a real bed."

"There's nothing more you can do until Lucy makes contact. You can leave your car here. I'll drive you out."

Ruth drove them out of town in a white Chevrolet Suburban with the Denton's logo on the door. They entered into the wild yellow land between great reefs of red and brown stone under a cloudless sky.

Amanda asked Ruth, "Did you and your husband start the Denton's business together?"

"No, I married into it. When I met Luke in 1954, he was a retailer. His grandfather, Denton Randall, founded a general store in Lawton, Oklahoma. And Luke's father, Edward Randall, opened a five-and-dime in Tulsa. They were successful enough. Luke had come through New Mexico once, and he liked it. He also saw opportunity. There weren't many stores. So he opened up in Albuquerque."

"How did it get so big?" Jenny asked.

Ruth pursed her lips, and the lines tightened around her mouth. She glanced at Jenny and tilted her head with a tight sad smile. Then she began. "Well, Luke was always interested in ways of improving the business. He was ambitious and saw that by negotiating better discounts with his suppliers, he could pass those savings on to his customers and increase sales volume. He was passionate about the customer being satisfied. So the one store he had, Randall's, was a success."

"It was called Randall's?" Amanda asked.

"Yes, Randall's, in downtown Albuquerque. And it supported

us nicely. We were just going to settle down, raise a family, and live in the community. We had no great ambitions then."

A silence fell as Ruth turned off the highway and entered a rough and narrow road that led into the mountains.

"What changed?" Amanda asked.

"Well," Ruth began, and sighed. "Luke and I were married in 1956. We moved into a nice house on Mulberry. Our son Denton was born in 1958. Named after Luke's grandfather. Denton was the light of our lives, you see. Luke was always a very practical, hard-working man, but Denton just brought out the joy in him. I'd never really seen Luke play before that. At any rate, the store improved, and we were doing well. Denton had just started kinder-garten. I remember the day. Luke had taken off from work to go horseback riding with him. Denton was just learning on this gentle old pony named Leo. They came home, and I was fixing supper. It was their favorite, my meatloaf with mashed potatoes. Green beans. But Denton couldn't eat. He went and lay down on the couch after supper. I took his temperature and thought it was just the flu. Children in school, always passing germs around. But when I took his temperature an hour later, it was 106, and I was alarmed. I knew that wasn't right. By the time Luke and I got him to the hospital, he was having seizures."

As Ruth talked, Amanda and Jenny exchanged a look.

"Oh, no," Jenny said under her breath.

"He was dead within a day and a half."

"What was it?" Amanda blurted out, her voice cracking.

"Strep," Ruth said. And with a wild laugh, she said it again: "Strep! Who would have believed it? I mean, you have a sore throat, you take a pill, and then you're better. Isn't that the way it's supposed to be? But this one went into his organs, no one knew why. Before they could control it, the damage was done."

Jenny turned and put her hand on Amanda's knee, and their eyes met.

"I'm sorry," Ruth said. "What's got into me? I shouldn't be telling you this."

"No," Amanda said. "It's terrible. But I want to know. I want to know."

Ruth took a deep breath and looked over at Jenny, who nodded at her. "Denton was gone, and that was all. Luke was crazy with grief. He threw himself into his work. I tried to be there for him, but work was the only thing that could distract him. And I was a fair mess myself. Luke became a man obsessed with the minutiae of retailing, down to the kind of paper clips they used. He fought with his suppliers as a way of venting his feelings, and as a result, he offered the lowest prices and walked away with everyone's business. He could never rest. He was running from Denton's ghost, opening store after store, running faster and faster. We changed the name from Randall's to Denton's and had fifteen stores by 1966. He took the company public and kept right on going. He created an empire out of grief. A parent never recovers from a blow like that. There's nothing worse. Nothing. And I know that if he has anything to say about it, Luke won't let anything happen to Lucy. Luke would go to the ends of the earth to save a child. That's what the foundation is all about. If Lucy needs him, he'll use all his money and power to protect her."

They rode in silence the rest of the way, winding through the mountains until they reached a wrought iron gate set into a high stone wall. The gate swung open, and they drove for another ten minutes on a red dirt road. The main house looked like an old western saloon, with a wooden porch wrapped around it and high brick chimneys. Several smaller frame houses of natural redwood appeared, and as they drew closer, a swimming pool came into view. Ruth pulled the car up to one of the smaller houses, saying, "I'll get you settled, and then I'm going to take my swim and have a nap."

The house was paneled in natural wood and had a red tile floor with animal skins for rugs. Large windows and glass doors opened onto views of the mountains and valleys on all sides. Ruth showed them around and then said, "I'll be up at the big house if you need anything. There are soft drinks in the refrigerator. Just come up to the house if you care for anything to eat."

"Thanks," Amanda said.

"This is so generous of you," Jenny said.

"Oh, it's nothing." Ruth bit her lower lip and smiled. Her blue eyes settled on them, and then she turned and walked, tall and regal, across the tiles and out the door. Jenny watched Ruth leave, her sneakers squeaking on the tiles and then crunching in the red volcanic gravel on the drive. Jenny marveled at the woman's strength. To take something so horrible and make something useful of it. That was the secret. Jenny wondered if she had the strength to do it.

"I have to close my eyes, honey. I'm just going to lie down for a bit."

"Me, too. Don't worry. It does no good. Worry is a waste."

"Easy for you to say."

Amanda took Jenny's hands and looked into her eyes. "I grew up with my mother," she said. "I know what it means to worry about someone you love and depend on. I know what it means to worry until you're grinding your teeth in your sleep. And I gradually learned to let it go. I was just a little kid. You can figure it out, too." Amanda smiled at Jenny. "Which bedroom do you want?"

Jenny laughed. "I don't care. You choose." She watched Amanda cross the tiles to one of the bedrooms, thinking, What a marvelous creature she is. How did she get so wise so early? She knew the answer: She'd been given the gift of adversity.

Jenny kicked off her shoes and collapsed on top of the bedspread. But despite what Amanda had said, each time she pictured Lucy it was like a sharp stab in her chest. She fell asleep with images of horror swirling around her.

Jenny was in the midst of a dream. She was back in Congo at her little hut, watching a family of bonobos play in the clearing. One of them was Lucy, only she was two years old. She was happily wrestling with another small bonobo and making cheerful noises. Inexplicably, there was a telephone beside Lucy, and it was ringing. It rang and rang until at last Lucy picked it up, and said, "Hello?" Clear as a bell.

Jenny sat up in bed and saw Amanda through the open door holding the phone and saying, "Oh, my God! Oh, my God!" Then she screamed and said, "O-my-God, o-my-God!" She rushed into Jenny's room, her eyes wide, her face happy. "Luke's got her. Luke's got her. Ruth just called. They're coming here."

"Oh, thank God." Jenny put her hand to her chest to stop her heart from hammering. She closed her eyes and felt tears welling up. "How is she?"

Amanda jumped up and down and spun around, "He's got her, he's got her, he's got her!" she screamed, dancing across the room.

"When will they be here?"

"She said they were leaving now. What did it take us to get here? An hour?"

"Did I sleep?"

"Yeah, about three hours. I'm going to take a shower!" Amanda screamed, beside herself with excitement. "I'm going to take a show-errrr!"

"Me, too."

"Hurry, hurry, hurry. Oh, God, I'm so happy!"

Jenny laughed to see her so thrilled. She felt as if the entire world had been lifted from her shoulders. But as she undressed and then stood in the shower, steam rising around her, she thought, It's not over. They're not going to give up searching. And what if Lucy really did kill a man? There would be a nationwide hunt for her. It was probably under way now.

Jenny shivered at those thoughts. She stepped from the shower to dry off and dress, wondering if that had occurred to Amanda yet. As she was putting on her clothes, Amanda came dancing into the room, already dressed, her hair wet. "Let's get them to take us out to the gate so we can be there for Lucy. I wonder if Ruth has any grapes?"

"Grapes?"

"For Lucy."

"Sure. Let's go over to the house."

Ruth drove them out toward the gate in the Suburban. Amanda was quiet, sitting in the back with a plastic bag of grapes in her lap. She seemed subdued now.

"What are we going to do?" Amanda asked.

"Yes, I was having the same thought," Jenny said. "It's not over."

"But she's home, that's the most important thing," Ruth said.

"Yes," Amanda said, "we have her back." She looked at Jenny, searching her eyes.

"Yes," Jenny said, trying to smile. "Let's enjoy her while we can." She felt that her words hadn't come out right. "She'll have to go to Donna."

"Yes," Amanda said. "Donna." And Amanda's yearning eyes fixed on Jenny. "And then we'll see her again." She paused, bit her cuticle. "We'll be okay, won't we?"

"Yes," Jenny said. "We'll be okay. Of course we will."

48

RUTH STAYED IN THE CAR as Jenny and Amanda stepped down onto the desert floor. The sun was low, the whole land lit with a pink and yellow light. The clouds seemed to be on fire. The sky went on forever. Amanda kicked stones and Jenny examined wild flowers and cactus. They saw a lizard. A long-tailed magpie came to inspect them. Jenny scanned the low hills overlooking their position. Dry and beige with patches of green. Rocky defiles and sharp outcroppings.

Amanda picked up three stones and tried to juggle them, unsuccessfully. She laughed, musing on something.

"What?"

"Remember that time," she began, still juggling. "Remember that time at Harry's that Lucy called me human and I got all offended? And then the two of us got into this uncontrollable laughing fit?"

"Yeah . . ."

"And remember when she gave you that sweater for Christmas and we didn't know you were allergic to wool, but you didn't want to hurt her feelings, so you wore it all through dinner anyway?"

"Yeah, I had a rash for a week. And Harry mixed Oil of Olay with steroid cream for me and called it 'Oil of José.'"

"Then he went off on that rant about why didn't Mexico manufacture cars?" Amanda managed to get three rocks going and then lost the rhythm. The stones fell, and she picked them up and started over.

"Yeah, the Aztec car cracked me up."

"The Toyotl. Made out of stone. Two gallons to the mile. Harry's crazy. I mean that in a good way."

Jenny looked out over the land again. The sun had tinted the low hills with an eerie pink like the color of watermelon. Then she turned back toward the road and saw a cloud rise in the distance. Amanda let the stones fall to the ground, then stood with Jenny watching the dust cloud grow.

"It's her," Amanda said.

The car was still some distance off as the cloud of dust drifted away on the breeze. They stood and watched for what seemed the longest time. Then at last another white Suburban heaved into view. The gate opened, and the dusty vehicle pulled up to park nearby, tilting over the rocky ground. The red sky was reflected in the windows. Ruth had opened her door to watch. Luke stepped out of the driver's side and crossed to them. He gave Amanda a nod and then approached Jenny. He leaned in and whispered, "She's a little self-conscious about her appearance. She's been through a lot." Jenny was looking past him as Amanda approached the dark interior of the car. She hesitated a few feet from the door. Nothing moved for a moment.

"Lucy?" Amanda asked.

The passenger door opened. She saw a movement inside the car. A leg in blue jeans emerged, an oversized tennis shoe on the foot. Another foot, another leg. A teenage boy in a baseball cap stepped squinting into the late desert light.

"Where's Lucy?" Amanda asked, turning toward Luke, then looking back at the boy.

"What—" Jenny began. "Where's Lu—" She stopped herself, then asked, "Lucy?"

"Lucy?" Amanda asked.

The boy's mouth pursed, as if attempting to solve a difficult problem. He brought his hands to his face. Then Jenny and Amanda heard Lucy's voice say, "I'm sorry."

"Lucy!" Amanda said, and rushed to her. She wrapped Lucy in

her arms. "Lucy, oh, my God, Lucy, what did they do to you?" The two girls held each other and wept.

"Oh, Lucy," Jenny went to them and took them both in her arms, fighting back tears. "Oh, no. Oh, Lucy, Lucy."

Luke had come over to them and said, "Let's get away from this exposed area."

"Yes, come on," Ruth said. "Let's bring her to the house. She needs rest and food and—"

"Amanda, help me get her in the car," Jenny said.

"The girls will come with me, dear," Ruth told Luke.

With Jenny and Amanda embracing her from either side, Lucy made a tentative move toward the open door of Ruth's car. As they advanced slowly, Lucy said, "I did the best I could."

"You're with us again," Amanda said. "That's all that matters."

"We're going to take care of you now," Jenny added.

"We have grapes," Amanda said. "A big bag of grapes."

Lucy gave her a weak smile and said, "Yum."

"I love you, Lucy," Amanda said.

"I love you, too."

At first Jenny thought that Amanda had slipped on a stone. It was as if her feet simply went out from under her the way they do on ice. Then she was down. A faint pop reached them from far off, and they all turned toward the sound. But the watermelon light was gone, and the mountains were vanishing into a colorless dusk. Then Lucy's shriek split the silence. Jenny turned back to see her step away from Amanda, her hands over her mouth, her eyes wide in horror. They were both covered with blood.

"Down! Get down!" Luke was shouting. He grabbed Jenny and shoved her into the car. She stuck her head back out to see Lucy fall on Amanda, who was lying on the ground making a strange gurgling noise in her throat and kicking one leg. Lucy was screaming in that high keening sound that Jenny had last heard in the jungle, the essence of grief. Luke ran to pick Amanda up and then shoved her onto the seat beside Jenny. Ruth pushed Lucy into the car and got in after her, shouting, "Luke, drive!"

Luke jumped in the driver's seat and slammed the door, and then they were speeding off across the desert.

As they bounced over the rough terrain Lucy screamed, "Amanda! No! Amanda!"

Ruth looked on, her face a mask of horror, as Luke said, "Oh, Lord, oh, Lord."

Jenny looked down at Amanda, unable to think. A red stain was spreading across the center of her shirt. Jenny placed her hand on it and pressed, feeling the hot blood. "Amanda," she said. "Oh, no, Amanda."

Amanda's eyes focused first on Lucy, then on Jenny, flicking rapidly back and forth. She coughed once. "I tripped," she said. Then she stopped breathing.

"Oh, Lord," Luke said as the car leapt forward over rocks.

Lucy's cry filled the small space, as Jenny began compressing Amanda's chest with the heel of her hand, saying, "Come on, Amanda, don't do this. Amanda! Amanda!"

She put her mouth on Amanda's and tasted her blood. She blew air into her lungs and heard it bubble out of her chest beneath her shirt. By the time they arrived at the house, Lucy was curled up in a ball on the far side of the car hugging her knees. Amanda was not moving, her eyes rolled back in her head. Jenny and Ruth stared in disbelief.

The door opened, and Luke dragged Jenny and Lucy out and into the big house. Ruth didn't move for a time. Luke went back and led her inside. Then he carried Amanda into one of the back bedrooms.

Jenny sat holding Lucy on the couch. Lucy was shivering, her teeth chattering. She looked almost catatonic. They were both covered with dirt and blood.

"Okay, okay, okay," Jenny said. "Just breathe." But then in the middle of her attempt to take control, she burst into tears, too. Lucy and Jenny sat there unable to control their grief. Ruth stood, erect and grave, her face flushed, her blue eyes wide. She knelt before Jenny and Lucy and wrapped both of them in her arms, and they stayed like that. It was full dark outside.

49

LUCY'S FATHER USED TO SAY that there was a natural beauty in the world and that salvation lay in finding it, embracing it. Don't let it go, he would say. Because when the bad things come—and they always do—it's all there is to sustain you. Without it, you'll be sucked down into a darkness from which there is no escape.

"Death comes," he would say. "Death always comes. It's coming now. It's on its way. There's nothing you can do but see the beauty."

Maybe her father really was mad, Lucy thought. He certainly did a mad, mad thing when he brought her into this world. It was hard for her to think about him now. He was gentle to her, tender and smart and funny. As serious as he could be, he could be silly, too. One night Leda and Lucy were sleeping in the high branches, dreaming peacefully, when he appeared between them, hanging in a sling attached to a rope. Leda began screaming in alarm. Lucy startled and sat up in the nest. "Papa! What are you doing up here?" Leda jumped angrily up and down on the branches and went skittering off into the forest.

Her father sat in his sling grinning at his daughter. He produced a banana from inside his shirt as if by magic and held it out to her. She took it. "You see?" he said. "This is what it means to be human. It's a deep mystery. We're so bad. We're so good." He winked at her as she ate the banana. "Come for a ride?" he asked. Lucy climbed into the apparatus with him and he lowered it to the ground. "You see, by our clever inventions we lose the trees. So much fun. But so sad. Everything has its cost."

Oh, how Lucy grieved for Amanda. Her most human friend. Her most friendly human. Dear sweet Amanda. Amanda and Jenny. Poor Jenny.

Lucy knew death. She knew it from the forest. It was a natural part of life, but that didn't make it any easier when it came. The cat, the jackal, the hawk—they were always out there watching, waiting, hungry. Lucy knew death. Death was no mystery. It came for everyone. The mystery was life. She knew death well. What she didn't know was why she was alive.

Lucy grieved hard for Amanda that night. They all did, frantic and confused, unable to make sense of anything, as they waited for the police to come. Lucy lay with Amanda where Luke had placed her in one of the bedrooms. Lucy held her and smelled her smell one last time, her hair with the wind in it, the sun on her skin, the sharp reek of her blood. She kissed her on the lips and said, "I love you." Then she went out into the living room and sat with Jenny. They held each other and wept and in between, Lucy told Jenny what had been done to her, and they wept again. But Lucy knew that it was time to go.

"Mom, Mom," Lucy said when she had at last taken herself in hand. She stood and stepped away from her. "Mom, I love you. I love your selfless nature. You brought me out of the forest and showed me a new world. Thank you."

Jenny collapsed in Lucy's arms again, and Lucy held her until her sobbing subsided.

"Mom. I have to go. I can't stay here. I killed a man." Lucy heard Jenny's sharp intake of breath as she brought her hand to her mouth. "And now it's come to this."

Ruth and Luke sat holding each other on a couch across the room. Luke stood and crossed to Lucy. He reached into his pocket and handed her a wad of bills. "Here. It's only a couple thousand, but it should help."

"Thanks."

Jenny composed herself. She straightened and said, "Come here. I have to check you."

"Check what?"

"They found you. I think I know how. They would have been fools not to do it." Jenny began running her hands up and down Lucy's legs, feeling with her fingertips.

"What?"

"Just a second." She let her hands move gently over Lucy's arms and then around her shoulders and up her neck. She stopped, feeling a small bump on the back of her neck. "There. I think I've got it. I'm going to need something very sharp, like a razor blade."

"I'll get the first aid kit," Ruth said.

"Sit down," Jenny told Lucy. "It's a device they use for tracking animals. They inject it under the skin."

Ruth came back with the kit, and Jenny selected a scalpel, cotton balls, and alcohol. She wiped the spot on Lucy's neck with alcohol. "This is going to hurt."

Lucy made no sound when she cut her. Then Jenny put her open hand before Lucy. In her bloody palm was a silver device less than an inch long and no thicker than a pencil lead. Lucy stared at it. Jenny wiped the cut on Lucy's neck with alcohol and put a bandage on it.

Luke studied the device, grunted, and spun on his heel. He left the room and returned with a claw hammer. He put the device on the floor and smashed it with so much force that one of the floor tiles cracked. Everyone watched him as he left the room with the hammer.

Jenny looked at the shattered device on the red tile for a moment. Then she lifted her head and said, "Lucy, I love you. Please be careful."

Lucy backed away and Jenny said, "Don't try to call or write . . . Not for a while. A long while, I guess . . ."

"Yes, I understand." Lucy turned to Ruth. "Look after Mom, will you?"

"Yes. Of course we will."

Lucy kissed the top of Jenny's bowed head. She hugged Ruth and kissed Luke's cheek. Then she slipped out the back door and into the desert night. She had gone overland for no more than twenty minutes when she heard the helicopter. She thought, They've caught me in the open. But the helicopter flew right past, its green and red lights blinking, and thundered on into the night.

For a long time after Lucy left, Jenny and Ruth and Luke stood in the living room staring into space. No one knew what to say. Everyone was simply in shock, waiting for the world to spontaneously rearrange itself so that it made sense once more. Jenny could feel her whole body vibrating with a terrible energy that she feared might tear her apart. All she could do was breathe in and breathe out. She became aware of the smell of mesquite smoke on the breeze that was coming from the open front door. She became aware of Ruth, who had controlled herself until Lucy left and was now softly weeping. Jenny thought she heard Amanda's laugh from the next room, and the hair on the back of her neck stood up. Then she realized that it was a night bird calling from outside.

It wasn't long before they saw the lights of the Bernalillo County Sheriff's cars coming from the gate. A coroner's van followed the police cars. They went outside to greet the sheriff, whom Luke and Ruth called Bill. He was a handsome young man with his light brown hair neatly parted and a deferential manner. Luke repeated what he had told the dispatcher who had answered his 911 call. Jenny and Ruth had little to add. The sheriff said, "Well, we're figuring that the shot had to come from those hills to the south. We have deputies out there now, along with the state police. I'm real sorry about this. It's a terrible thing."

The coroner's assistants wheeled a gurney out of the house and up to the back of the unmarked van. They opened the doors and collapsed the gurney's legs to slide it in. Jenny crossed to them and said, "Wait." She stood beside the gurney and pulled the sheet back. Amanda looked as if she were asleep, her hair in disarray. Jenny touched her hair, so luxurious and soft. Tears welled up in her eyes. She kissed Amanda's forehead. "Goodbye, honey," she said.

Then they pulled the sheet over her face and Jenny went inside and dialed the phone.

"Harry," she said. "It's over."

50

LUCY FLED ACROSS the powdery waste among the stunted piñon trees. It was still dark when she caught a ride on the feeder ramp to Interstate 25 going north. It was a big eighteen-wheel rig carrying disposable diapers. The trucker's name was Ned. He said he was from Kentucky. They shared a laugh about the diapers. He bought Lucy breakfast in Colorado at daybreak. She had eggs and hash browns. One of the things that Lucy liked best about America was ketchup. Ketchup and Tabasco sauce. He let Lucy out north of Denver, and she picked up a ride on I-80 from a periodontist who kept putting his hand on her thigh and telling Lucy how much he admired young male athletes. He drove her to a rest area, where he tried to take her pants off. She bit two of his fingers off and left him writhing in pain in the grass beside the parking lot, the taste of his blood sharp in her mouth.

The leaves had already fallen in Iowa. The wind was blowing on the highway, and the weather had turned cold. A van full of Christian women picked Lucy up and drove her all the way to Milwaukee. One of the dominant females took Lucy by her hands and said, "Son, please consider accepting Jesus as your personal savior. Just consider it."

Once she reached Milwaukee, Lucy took a city bus to the zoo. She waited for sundown and slipped in the back way through the forest. The leaves were all down. She heard the bonobos begin to cry out as she drew close. The screaming grew to a crescendo, and after a time, Donna appeared by the back fence. Shivering with the cold, Lucy waved to her. Donna recognized Lucy immediately. She rushed into the forest and held her.

"Oh, dear, oh, dear," she said. "Is that really you, Lucy?" She looked at her and said again, "Oh, dear . . . What did they do to you? Who got you?"

"I'm sorry. They cut me. They cut my hair off. They cut the whole top of my head off." Lucy began to weep.

"Oh, no, poor thing." Donna began leading her toward the building. "At least you made it. How are—" She hesitated. "Is Jenny okay?"

"Mom was okay when I left. They killed Amanda."

"Oh, God. Oh, no," Donna said, and stopped. "I'm so sorry. I knew they'd come. What happened?"

"They found me. When they operated on me, they put a tracking device under my skin. I didn't know about it. They were looking for me, not Amanda. I'm sure it was meant for me. Amanda had long hair like me. And I look like a boy now. They must have thought it was me. I don't know. They shot her. We never even saw them."

"Oh, how horrible. I'm so sorry. I have to get you inside. Come on. Come quick. I'm ready for you. Come on. I've been waitin'."

Donna led Lucy to the building and into her cluttered office and shut the door. "I want you to wash up. I have fresh clothes for you. Do I need to examine you? Are you injured?"

"No, I'm not injured."

"What about the tracking device?"

"Mom took it out."

Donna opened a door and said, "The shower's in there. Wash up, I'll get your clothes."

Lucy showered quickly, gingerly washing her scalp. She dried off and Donna returned with a fresh pair of jeans, a work shirt, and sneakers. She gave Lucy a Milwaukee Brewers hat to cover her wound. When Lucy had dressed, Donna took a critical look at her.

"Good. Very good," she said, taking a jacket from a hook and giving it to her. "Wear that. It's cold outside."

"Can I say goodbye?"

"What?"

"To the bonobos?"

"Yes, sure."

They went to the back of the cages and the bonobos came quietly to the fence, putting their delicate fingers through the wire. Lucy walked along the fence touching each hand in turn. When she was finished she cried out and they cried out with her. She knew what it was like to be in there now.

"Come on, now. We have only one chance."

"Where are we going?"

"You're goin' to cross the parking lot and go out to the street. There's a bus stop there. Take the bus. It's the number 151. Get off at the end of the line. I'll meet you there. They can't track you now. I'll make sure no one is followin' me just in case. You'll be okay. Do you have any money?"

"Yes."

"Okay, I'll see you in about an hour." She kissed Lucy on the forehead. "I am so sorry about Amanda. I know you're grievin' now." Then she hurried out.

Lucy crossed the wooden walkway and went down past the penguins. She crossed the parking lot and went out to the street. Half an hour later she was on the bus.

51

JENNY AND HARRY took the back roads, eating at little diners and taking their time about getting home. Neither one of them was sure what life would be like once they got there. They were both afraid to face it. So they dawdled at local museums in obscure towns. They wandered in the Cimarron National Grassland and saw the bones of the woolly mammoths that had once roamed there in herds.

As they looked at the mounds of bones, Harry said, "People killed them all."

They drove through the Mark Twain National Forest and took a canoe trip at the Bass River Resort. They caught fish and fried them on the riverbank for dinner. That night in their room—for somehow it had seemed natural to economize and share a room—Jenny wept, thinking about the Boundary Waters. Harry held her until she had spent her tears.

She had showered and scrubbed but could not get Amanda's blood out from under her fingernails. As Harry and Jenny embraced and wept together, all she could see through a sheet of tears was her hand, the darkness beneath her nails.

At Dubuque they rode the funicular railway and ate dinner at a quaint old restaurant with red leather booths and chandeliers. Back in their room, Jenny took a long hot shower. She came out wrapped in her chenille robe to find Harry standing there as if waiting for her. He pierced her with his eyes, and Jenny said, "What?" Harry just kept looking, and Jenny didn't look away. Then he took her in his arms and held her for a long time.

"I miss the girls," he said. "I really, really miss the girls."

"I know."

They had avoided the news because of all the stories of candlelight vigils being held for Amanda and Lucy. But that night Ruth called and told Jenny to turn on CNN. Jenny and Harry watched in the motel room. Police officers from the Bernalillo County Sheriff's Department and the New Mexico State Police had located a suspect in the killing of Amanda Mather. When the suspect opened fire on them in a remote wilderness area, the police had shot him dead. His identity was being withheld pending notification of next of kin.

The next morning, as if a demon had been chasing them, they raced across Illinois, through Freeport and Rockford, stopping only for gas. It was mid-afternoon when they reached Jenny's house. Harry stepped down from the car and pulled her suitcase from the back. But Jenny just sat there looking at the ivy-covered house. Harry came around and opened her door.

"Harry, I've been living there alone with Amanda."

Harry didn't say a word. He didn't need to. He closed the door. He put her suitcase back in the car. Then he got in and drove Jenny home with him. There was nothing to discuss. With typical composure, Harry went to the refrigerator when they arrived, as if it were just another normal day. He took a container of vegetarian chili out of the freezer. Then they sat down and ate their dinner and began the process of trying to go about their lives.

Amanda had been buried by her mother while Harry and Jenny were on the road. Jenny didn't think that it would be good to try to attend. She had the sense that Amanda's mother would blame her almost as much as Jenny blamed herself. She didn't think that she could look her in the eye.

Within a week of their return, the Bernalillo County Sheriff's Department and the New Mexico State Police jointly released the identity of the slain suspect in Amanda's murder. When the suspect's face came on the television, Jenny realized that she had, in fact, seen him at the airport and in the crowds of protesters on more than one occasion. He was a sinister-looking young man with short hair and a drooping moustache. His arms were covered with tattoos. He was the one that the girls had seen holding a sign with the word "Euthanasia" and the number fourteen on it. As they sat watching the news, Harry said, "Bullshit."

"What?"

"How would this loser know that you guys were at the Randalls' ranch? I didn't even know that."

"Because either he didn't really shoot Amanda or someone told him where we were?"

Harry said nothing.

In the coming weeks Jenny refused all requests for interviews and avoided the news. The suspect was dead. The rifle found by his body matched the bullet that killed Amanda. The case was closed. The government firmly maintained that it had no idea where the hybrid person known as Lucy Lowe had gone. The press had a difficult time finding new angles on the story, so it drifted farther and farther back in the news and then vanished altogether. And then people did what they always do. They began to forget.

52

IT WAS ABOUT TEN in the morning on a cold bright day when Jenny stood in her kitchen and saw the sunlight illuminating the expensive stainless steel appliances that her mother had bought. Jenny thought, This is so not me. And instantly another thought came to her: That's Amanda talking. I have Amanda's voice inside me now. Amanda and Lucy. She knew from her scientific reading that when you repeat in your head the words that someone else has said, your vocal cords move just as that person's moved when she said those words, a movement as unique as a fingerprint. Thus do those you love hold the strings as if you were a puppet. Even from beyond the grave.

As she moved from the kitchen to the front hall, Jenny could hear the girls. From the front door, she could see up the stairs and into their room. She heard them giggling now, talking in that way of theirs. Lucy teaching Amanda Spanish slang one cold winter night.

"'Flipado,'" Lucy said.

"'Flipado,'" Amanda repeated.

"Yeah, like flipped out. And 'tranquilo.'"

"'Tranquilo.' What's that? Tranquil?"

"Yeah, 'chill.'"

"We don't say 'chill.'"

"Never do we say 'chill.'" And they cracked up.

Jenny could hear their laughter. The girls inhabited the house like spirits now. Lucy had asked where your voice goes when you die, and Jenny thought she knew now: It goes into The Stream. Into the vocal cords and brains of those you love.

She looked into the living room and saw the couch where they'd sat to watch the video that changed everything. The African weaving above the fireplace. Two hyenas menacing the innocent deer. Could she live here now? Could she live with their spirits?

Jenny went upstairs and stood in the door to their room. The closet was open and from the doorway she could see Lucy's sage-green prom dress. Thongs and bras and tube tops were scattered on the closet floor. Shoes of all sorts. The girls had teased Jenny, saying that she had a genetic defect. She didn't have the shoe gene. Jenny put her face into Amanda's bright red dress and smelled it, and it brought into her mind the ebb and flow of her own joy and tears. Who said that? Other voices, stilled long ago. Matthew Arnold. The turbid ebb and flow of human misery.

She turned and saw Amanda's brush reflected in the dressing table mirror. She crossed the room and picked it up. It still had Amanda's hair in it. Jenny pulled a long strand free from the bristles, careful not to break it. She held it in the light. It was dark and curly, and it shone reddish brown in the sunlight. Oh, Amanda. Dear Amanda.

She placed the hair back on the brush so as not to lose it. And as she did so, she felt how odd that was. What was she going to do with her hair, the brush, all of these things? She didn't want to turn her life into a museum. Memory was museum enough.

She went down to her office to collect some things to take to Harry's. She saw the wicker basket beside her desk. It was full of all the photos they had taken. She bent, picked up a folder of prints, and sat. Amanda and Lucy splashing in Flour Lake at the Boundary Waters. She picked up another. The three of them in the green-room at some TV studio. Another set of prints showed Amanda and Matt and Lucy and Wes standing in front of the limousine on prom night. Then she saw herself with Harry, Lucy, and Amanda, toasting the new year with her mother. Their only New Year's Eve together. Lucy wore a silver party hat and was laughing uproariously at the bad jokes that Harry was telling. "How can you tell the trombone player's children on the playground?" he had asked her.

"I don't know," Lucy said. "How?"

"Because they don't know how to use the slide and they can't swing."

"Oh, Harry," Jenny had said. "That is so lame." But Lucy laughed and laughed.

"Don't encourage him," Amanda said.

Jenny's tears fell on the print in her hand. She put the folders back. She wasn't ready for this. She thought of Luke Randall, endlessly fleeing his grief. If life is a museum of memories, then how do you live when you can no longer stand to visit the museum? She realized that she would never let go of the girls. Her girls. Her daughters. They inhabited her flesh. She could no longer live in this house.

The phone rang, and she looked at the caller ID. It was the hospital. She could picture Harry in his lab coat, sitting at a computer terminal at the nurses' station, his hair messed up, pockets overflowing. She picked it up.

"Hello, Harry. I don't think I can do this."

"Well, you tried. That's all you can do. Go back to the house, okay? I have surgery, but I'll be back for dinner."

"But what about all this stuff?" It wasn't the stuff, she knew. It was the ghosts.

"I'll help you. We'll do it together. Don't torture yourself. Just go back to the house now. Go back there and think about lemon-crusted Dover sole with an amusing little pinot. Robert Parker said that a light essence of smoke and rosemary rounds out the finish of succulent fruit." For the first time that day, Jenny laughed.

During the winter months Harry and Jenny cleaned out the house. They moved her things to Harry's. They threw a lot away. On a cold snowy night with the work almost done, they burned the last of her firewood and sat on the floor eating spinach lasagna from Piero's. When the first warm weather arrived they had a house sale with folding tables set out in the front yard. The remaining furniture, appliances, lamps, went quickly. The clothing and CDs were picked over. Late in the afternoon, with yellow light angling down through the maple tree, a shy-looking girl with tattoos asked Jenny if she still had any of Lucy's clothes. Jenny was jolted by hearing Lucy's name. She pointed to a box and a rack. The girl browsed the clothing for a while and then came back holding jeans, some undergarments, and a pair of Italian sandals.

"Were these Lucy's?" she asked.

"Yes, they were."

She paid and stuffed the clothes in her bag and turned to go. Then she turned back and looked at Jenny. "I know she's out there. She's out there, and she's coming back."

"I hope you're right." Jenny watched the girl go. She could feel her sorrow and wondered what she'd been through. She reminded Jenny of the girls at the shelter.

The next week Jenny and Harry took everything that was left and gave it to charity. The house sold a month later. When it closed, Jenny tried to give her mother half the money but she refused, saying, "What am I going to do? Save it for my old age? Take Harry and go to Hawaii. Did you know that you were conceived in Hawaii?" Jenny hadn't known. She was stunned that her mother would reveal such an intimate bit of information. Her first thought was: Alzheimer's? Then she wondered if her mother still hoped for grandchildren.

Jenny and Harry didn't discuss the fact that they were living together. Her house was gone, and that was that. He had told her to choose any room she liked for her study, and she chose the room that overlooked the upper deck through the French doors. She often sat there in the afternoon, watching the light change and remembering Lucy and Amanda in their bikinis, laughing so hard that they fell out of their chairs.

She still checked the ads on Craigslist. Since she had heard nothing from Donna, she had to assume that Lucy had made it safely to the zoo. That first year when she received no seasonal greeting card from Donna, she suspected that it was because she wanted no contact as a precaution.

On the anniversary of Amanda's death, Jenny and Harry were in eastern Chad, treating children who'd been injured by unexploded bombs and grenades. It was one of the most intense experiences she'd ever had, working in the trauma unit as children came in with arms or legs blown off, then working on reconstruction, and later fitting their prosthetic limbs. The kids were unfailingly bright and cheerful, even in the face of ghastly injuries. Experiences like that kept Jenny sane.

She returned to working long hours with the girls at the shelter. Nights, at home, she would try to write about the amazing experience that she'd had, but she couldn't. It was too raw. And she feared that she simply didn't have the chops, as Amanda would have said. She wrote a small scientific paper about the eating habits of bonobos, but no one would accept it.

On a bright spring day at the Hope Shelter, a new girl arrived. Even from a distance, Jenny recognized her deep inner core of power. She was a beautiful girl, very tall and thin with brown hair held loosely in a ponytail that tumbled past her shoulders. Even though the weather was warm, she wore a woolen ski cap. Red woolen leggings descended into combat boots beneath her roughly cut-off blue jeans. One of her ears was pierced a dozen times.

Some benefactor of the shelter had rented an inflatable waterslide for the day to celebrate the first of the warm weather, and the younger kids had mobbed it, screaming and running around and gleefully climbing and sliding over and over.

The new girl stood off to the side wrapped in her thoughts. Watching. The staff was supposed to be briefed on each new resident but no one had told Jenny about this girl. Sometimes people came on such short notice that there wasn't time for the paperwork to catch up. Their situations were too desperate. All Jenny knew was that she was sixteen years old.

Jenny observed her for a while as the girl stared intently at the smaller children and a few early teens, slick as seals and joyful in the sun. The girl didn't move, didn't smile. She stared. After a time she dug into her bag and came up with a cigarette. She lit it with a Bic lighter and continued watching. Smoking was against the rules, of course. But so was most of what had been done to these girls. Nina knew: Tell one of these girls not to smoke, and they'd say, "Sure." And then they'd disappear.

Jenny wandered over to her. "Hey. I'm Jenny."

"Hey, Jenny." She had an open smile and easily met Jenny's eyes. "I'm Elise. Want a cigarette?"

"No, thanks." Elise continued watching the children. Had she been beaten? Raped? Why was she there? Jenny couldn't see any evidence of bruises, though under all those clothes she might find some.

"You can go on the waterslide with the kids if you like. There's a couple of older girls there, too."

"I might do that later."

"If you want I can show you where you'll be staying."

"Word."

"Did you bring any stuff? Clothes or anything you want to put away?"

"No stuff," Elise said.

"Come on, I'll show you your room."

Elise dropped the cigarette on the ground. She followed Jenny into the building and up to the second floor. The rooms were simple, almost monastic. As they entered, Elise glanced around at the single bed, small desk and chair, a framed print of a country scene, and a cross on the wall. She moved past Jenny and took the cross from the wall. "I won't be needing this," she said.

"Okay. No problem."

Elise sat heavily on the bed and simply hung there as if she were tired.

"Do you want to talk at all? About why you're here?"

"Sure, I guess. It was on the news." Jenny sat beside her and waited. Elise sighed. Then she began, "Well, my mom, she got us up real early yesterday morning, me and my little brother Dave and the twins, Jill and Jolene. Mom said we were going to take a trip. And then she put us in the car and took us down to Hinckley and drove out onto the pier. It wasn't quite light yet. Then she just kept on going right into the lake. I had Dave's hand. I don't know what happened. I lost him. I was the only one who got out."

Jenny had heard all kinds of stories but this one left her completely speechless. She imagined that Elise had been watching those kids on the waterslide, thinking about her brother and sisters down at the bottom of the lake.

From her own experience, as well as that of the Randalls, Jenny had some ideas about how you might come back from something like that. She took Elise under her wing and over the next few months she began to come around. Elise befriended some of the younger girls. It turned out that she was an artist. Her father had been a commercial artist and taught her from an early age but he had left the family. As Elise came out of her shell, her talent became clear. She would sit at the cafeteria table and draw beautifully realistic portraits of the children—upside down so that the kids could see them take shape. Or she'd carve perfect bas relief faces using modeling clay and a butter knife from the lunch room. Jenny needed someone like Elise in her life. Elise had lost everyone in her family. Jenny could never feel self-pity when she was around her.

That's why she returned to Chad to work with Harry in the hospital for another two months. She could not think of her own sorrow when she was face-to-face with an eight-year-old whose hands had been blown off.

53

A WEEK AFTER THEY RETURNED from Africa, Harry took Jenny to dinner at the little Italian place in Rogers Park where they had gone on their last date more than two years before. She knew that he was up to something. She felt it. Waiting for their carafe of wine, Harry nervously rearranged the shakers of salt and pepper and Parmesan cheese.

"What is it, Harry? Are you practicing your interior decorating skills?"

Harry laughed and the waiter brought the wine. Harry poured. Then he reached in his jacket pocket and brought out a gray folder about the size of a greeting card and set it on the table. He lifted his glass to Jenny and said, "I found this while I was dumpster diving and thought you might want to have it."

She laughed. "What on earth . . . ?"

"Chin-chin."

They clicked glasses. When she picked up the folder, she realized that it was made out of duct tape wrapped around cardboard. Inside, framed in duct tape, was a snapshot of the two of them that someone had taken in Chad. Dressed in hospital scrubs, they looked exhausted, disheveled, and happy. Something lumpy was taped to the opposite side of the card. She rubbed her thumb over the lump.

"Pull off the tape."

Jenny pulled back the duct tape to reveal a diamond ring.

"Every girl should have diamonds and duct tape."

"Harry, you need adult supervision, do you know that?"

"Well, that aside, what do you say?"

"You're so romantic. How could I resist?"

Neither of them wanted a showy wedding. Born out of shared experience, their friendship, their love, simply wasn't like that. It had become clear that they were going to stay together, and so they made it official.

Jenny could do nothing to speed the passage of time. No one could bring Amanda back. Harry and Jenny had to try to live their lives, just as Ruth and Luke had. And between Harry's work and the shelter and Africa and the household, they found that they did have a life once more. And they learned that time, which they once believed had stopped forever, did indeed pass.

Great mountains of snow turned to gutters rushing with black water, and the temperature shot up into the seventies. A midnight thunderstorm lured lightning out of dark clouds, and Jenny lay in bed thinking of the girls and holding herself tight against Harry.

Ruth and Luke arrived the next day. They had come to visit half a dozen times already. Harry grilled tuna steaks and vegetables. They ate outside, and as the light fled, Harry and Luke talked and laughed on the lower deck overlooking the poisonous garden.

Ruth and Jenny were loading the dishwasher.

"I want to thank you and Harry."

"Oh, it was nothing. Harry loves to cook."

"I don't mean for that. I mean for coming into our lives. All the good. All the bad. I think the experience shocked Luke out of his—his whatever. After . . ." And here Ruth paused, sensitive to the raw and tender wound she was about to touch. "After Lucy left . . ." To mention Amanda would have been too harsh. "After that, Luke began to slow down. And over the last couple of years, he has really come back to me. Something like this? Just flying off to visit friends for a barbecue? Two years ago he'd have never done this— never. And going to Costa Rica like we did last year? I was in heaven."

Jenny dried her hands and hugged Ruth. "I'm happy for you," she said.

When Ruth and Luke had left, Jenny sat with Lucy's laptop at the kitchen table and browsed the ads on Craigslist. Harry was reading the newspaper and muttering about what a miracle God had wrought when he put so many idiots on one planet all at the same time.

The small ad was listed under For Sale—Books. It read, "Signed First Edition of Jane Goodall's *In the Shadow of Man*— $1,015." Jenny leapt up and shouted. Harry startled and grabbed her arm, thinking she was having a heart attack. He was about to administer first aid when she found her voice and told him.

The price was the time of day when they would meet in one week. Again, it felt as if time had stopped. Harry made her sleep in the guest room because she was grinding her teeth in her sleep.

When the day arrived, Jenny drove to Lake Geneva, Wisconsin. She sat at a wrought iron table at Chuck's Lakeshore Inn. The day was cool and windy. A front was coming down from Canada, but it was nice in the sun. She watched one lone sail jerking bravely across the lake. An elderly couple walked hand in hand. A waitress brought her a menu, and Jenny told her that there would be a party of two.

A few minutes later, she saw Donna coming from a block away, wearing sunglasses, her long braid swinging. She came on and on, growing larger with each step. When at last Donna stood before Jenny, she smiled and sat down. Donna pushed an envelope across the table toward Jenny's hand.

"She's good," Donna said. "She's doin' real good."

54

I SIT IN THE lodge, motionless, sweat pouring off of me as Bev Ann White Feather braids my hair. It's just about long enough now. My skin is brown from the sun and I gained back the weight that I lost and then some. I call Bev Ann Grandmother White Feather, old and wrinkled as a raisin, her long gray hair braided past her waist and decorated with beads. She brought me back to health, feeding me squab and squash and corn soup. For the first few months, she made me sleep where the moonlight could touch my skin, until my cycles came back into synchronization. I immediately knew that we could communicate deeply. The winters are so cold up here, though. I thought I'd die. At first I worried: What if I get sick? I may die. We all die. I don't worry anymore. And two and a half years of acclimatization have helped.

When I've sweated through my heavy woolen blanket, I stand and Grandmother White Feather stands with me, touching up my hair from behind. We walk out of the lodge and down the incline through the forest to the river. She takes the blanket and I step naked into the rushing water. The current is swift but the river is shallow, the bottom covered with smooth stones. I wash myself off in the icy water, and when I return to the bank, Grandmother White Feather is holding a big towel. I wrap myself in it. I make a little noise of surprise and put my hand on my belly. She pats my belly, asking, "Is he kickin' again?"

I smile at her as she carries the blanket, and we head back up the incline to the cabin.

I was asleep in Donna's car when we crossed the Dakota line. More than two years ago, now, it's hard to believe. I remember it as if it were yesterday. We came out of Iowa past Aberdeen and down the edge of the Cheyenne River Reservation toward Rapid City. Haunting spires of stone decked with quartz crystals had flanked our way as we passed through the Black Hills and descended across the hot springs toward Pine Ridge.

"These are my people," Donna had explained to me. "I come from here. This is our land, our sovereign nation. No one can get at you here. I have told my people who you are. I talked to them over many months. They'll welcome you. My grandmother loves me, and I told her that you are a sister to me now. She'll look after you."

"Will you stay with me?"

"No. My guys need me. And anyway it would be too weird if I just up and left my bonobos. I need them, too."

When we arrived on the reservation, we drove along the main road, and then there was a police car behind us with its lights on. Its siren sounded briefly and I nearly had a heart attack.

"It's all right," Donna said. "I know him."

The tribal policeman pulled up alongside of us, grinning through the open window. "Well, if it isn't Donna White Feather. I haven't seen you in an age."

"Hey, Peter. Meet Lucy. Honey, this is Peter Stands Alone. He's chief of police here."

"Hi, Lucy. And welcome."

"She's been sick. Had to have surgery," Donna said, tapping the top of her head. "I want her to rest here for a while with Grandma."

"Sure. There's plenty of good medicine here. Welcome back."

Donna drove us up into the woods to Grandmother White Feather's cabin and placed me in the old woman's care. She told me, "This is my grandmother. She will know what to do. Always do what Grandmother White Feather says and you'll get well."

"Welcome, child," Grandmother White Feather said. She crossed to me and put her hands on my cheeks. Her hands were as smooth as paper and cool to the touch. She looked deep into my eyes for a few moments and then chuckled to herself. She said, "My great-grandfather was one-quarter wolf." Then she let go of my face and took Donna's arm, still laughing deep in her throat. "We haven't seen one like this here in many generations."

Grandmother White Feather cooked freshly caught trout with wild rice. Donna stayed the night. For the first time in what seemed like ages I slept peacefully, with the moonlight on me and the night air coming through the window.

The next morning Donna and I said goodbye. We did not weep, for we knew that this was a time of new beginnings. I watched with Grandmother White Feather as Donna drove away. We could see the dust for a long time. Then she took me to bathe and rest. She made me a medicine bag from crow feathers, deerskin, horsehair, and beads. I wore it around my neck. Grandmother White Feather let me sleep in her cabin and waved at the smoke with a smudge fan of hawk feathers while she sang low in her throat. I slept under four full moons, and she said that it was a good sign that the sky had been clear during all of them. Moonlight heals.

Through the autumn she taught me her ways. She delighted in the way that I was able to talk to the animals. She talked to them, too. And when she saw how I could call the birds down from the trees or bring a rabbit to my hand, she told me that I ought to meet Stan Brings Plenty, who could talk a deer into coming right to him.

I liked Stan Brings Plenty right away. Without any effort at all, we began communicating deeply and spending time together. Not everyone was pleased that I was there. A young man named Tom One Horn told Stan Brings Plenty that he should stay away from me, that I'd bring a curse. But then Tom One Horn tried to sneak into my room at night. Grandmother White Feather caught him and beat him with a stick. I worried that he might get mad and tell the authorities where I was. She assured me that no one would betray me. "We settle our own quarrels here," she said.

The summer after I arrived, Stan helped me to build my own cabin. That fall he began to come to visit me at night in my cabin. I did a lot of soul searching then. In my nights of desperation I had asked my dead father many times what on earth he was thinking. So, too, I asked myself: What are you thinking? What is the right thing to do? I knew what had been done to me. I knew that there had to be some way to go forward. And I felt in my heart that it was right. Amanda would have wanted me to do it. Something had to change. And in the winter, at last, it happened. Grandmother White Feather gave us her blessing. We're building another room onto the cabin now.

I'd finally gotten back to writing my book. I had scribbled only the few pages that Amanda and I worked on. Now I was determined to write the story. I wanted to pay tribute to Amanda. And I wanted to be like Anne Frank and make this work my diary. I don't know if I'll ever be as wise as she was, but I always take inspiration from her. I loved her for embracing her suffering and turning it into a thing of beauty that could endure beyond her brief lifetime. And Anne gave me permission to forgive my father. Yes, he had done this to me. He had been a brilliant scientist, an idealist, and anyway, he'd been right about people. Look what they did to Amanda. Beautiful Amanda. His decision to create me may have been wrong but he had inadvertently given me a gift. The gift of struggle. And the gift of being able to chart a course for the future.

I had never seen the notebook that Mom sent. Donna brought it to me. It was one of the last ones he wrote before he died.

"My dearest, darling Lucy," he wrote. "I don't know if or when you'll ever read this, but I write to you with all my heart nonetheless. When I set out on this course, I was young and idealistic and perhaps even a bit angry at the world. I had had no children, so how could I know what a child really was? I saw you in the abstract as an idealized person, a strategy for saving the beautiful bonobos and for somehow redeeming mankind all at one go. A wild, ambitious, and even a crazy idea, I now see. Then in the process of raising you and coming to know you, I learned so many things that I was too callow to know when I began. I learned what a beautiful, brilliant, astonishing person you are. I named you Lucy not, as some might think, because of the australopithicine of the same name, but because the name means 'light.' And you became the light of my world. I fell in love with you. Yes, even parents have to fall in love with their children, who are strangers at first. And almost from your first contact with me—a glance, a happy cry, your tiny hand gripping my finger—the reality of what I'd done began to descend on me, and I was filled with dread and doubt. I was filled with such love for you, but that love was always tinged with worry, for at last I comprehended what I'd done. And the more beautiful and fully formed you grew, the greater my fear that there would be no escaping the pain that you would have to endure. For that I beg your forgiveness. And I beg you to accept my love if I cannot be there for you when you pass through your trials. Be steadfast, my beloved daughter. Be steady and strong. Embrace the struggle. And never give up. I love you—Papa."

I cried when I read it. I cried and forgave him and loved him once more. I think he understood the human saga: That we all bequeath some terrible gift to future generations, just as some mad protohuman long ago gave us the gift of fire, the gift of stone, the gift of iron. Papa, Papa, *requiescat in pace*. I'm not sure if my book will ever be published but I shall celebrate you in it, too. Now I have to let go of the outcome and just trust the process. I put the words on the page one letter at a time. There is no other way to do it.

Little news from the outside world reaches me now. I like it that way. Some of our people here live in modern houses and watch television, but I prefer the woods. I think of Mom and Amanda and Harry all the time. All these months and years I've had such love and pain in my heart for them. It seems so long ago, yet they all seem so alive. I think of them every day and nothing has diminished. They are in me. They inhabit me. Dear Amanda. You kissed me in the woods. Sometimes at night the breeze comes in through the window, and I catch your scent and I ache for you.

Donna had said that she would bring me news of Mom when the time was right. I waited and waited. Then a few weeks ago it happened. Donna was in the habit of coming to visit us a few times a year. And she came with the news that she was going to see Mom at last. She had made discreet inquiries among her old military contacts and she thought it would be safe to go now. I asked her if she could take a letter to Mom.

"Dear Mom," I wrote. "Donna tells me that the government isn't interested in us anymore. I guess they had no idea what to do with me and are just as glad now that I've disappeared. She said that they might suspect where I am, but they couldn't come onto the reservation without making a huge political mess. So as long as I stay out of sight, they're just going to pretend that I never existed. Anyway, there's a new president at last, and the word is that he would welcome us if he didn't think it would be political suicide to do so. Donna described it as a kind of truce. As she put it, 'Some things never happened even if they are true.' Anyway, the reporters have gone on to other stories by now and the public has the memory span of a housefly. It really is like I never existed. That's okay with me.

"I guess you're probably reading this with Donna watching you and so you most likely know all this already. She says it's okay for you guys to come now. I hope you will. I would like you to be here for the birth. And I wouldn't mind having Harry as my on-call doctor just in case. How is he? I'm dying to hear how you two have been doing and what you've been up to. Please give him my love and 'a big wet smoocher,' as he would say.

"Everyone wants me to have a boy but I hope it's a girl so that I can name her Amanda. Naturally I want to know what the future will bring. But with Grandmother White Feather's help I've learned to be grateful for the sun and the stars, the water and wind, and to take each day as it comes. Please do come. I want a hug and I want you to hold the baby.

"Your loving daughter,

"Lucy"